OUR

DARKEST

PATH

OUR DARKEST SERIES
BOOK TWO

SARAH BAILEY

Our Darkest Path Copyright © 2020 by Sarah Bailey

Please note the spelling throughout is British English.

Cover Art by Sarah Bailey

Published by Twisted Tree Publications
www.twistedtreepublications.com
info@twistedtreepublications.com

Paperback ISBN: 978-1-913217-19-8

To Rory and Ash,
Your son is precious in so many ways.
I'm so happy I got to give him a voice and a story.

PROLOGUE

Cole

Meredith Veronica Pope. That name was like a fucking taunt every time I heard it. Every time I saw her, knives dug into my skin, making me feel things I never wanted to feel for another person. Those damning green eyes and strawberry blonde hair curling around her shoulders. Every teenage boy's wet dream, except this one made me lose my fucking mind.

I couldn't have Meredith Pope.

Couldn't touch her.

Taste her.

Tease her.

Meredith Pope was out of bounds. Not least because she wouldn't look my way. Why would she? I was sixteen. She was two years my senior and in sixth form. Didn't stop me looking. Didn't stop me wondering. Didn't stop me planning to take her and make her fucking well mine. I might not have been with a girl before, but as far as I knew Meredith hadn't been touched either. Keeping an eye on her activities had become a game to me. Listening to rumours and gossip. Anything to do with Meredith and I was on high fucking alert.

Why I even liked her was a question I'd love answering. Meredith was rude, brash and overbearing. Apparently, I didn't care about her tendency to bulldoze over everyone and everything. It only made me want her all the more. I'd teach that girl a lesson. I'd teach her how to submit. Nothing would stand in my goddamn fucking way.

I didn't care if Meredith was out of my league.

I didn't care if she was older than me.

I'd make sure she could never forget me.

I'd be buried so deep inside her fucking soul, she'd never be able to dig me out.

Meredith Veronica Pope better fucking watch herself.

Because I, Cole Carter, am coming for her.

PART I

persevere

verb, per·se·vered, per·se·ver·ing.

to persist in anything undertaken; maintain a purpose in spite of difficulty, obstacles, or discouragement; continue steadfastly.

CHAPTER ONE

Meredith

ou know when you're relatively sure someone is watching you, but whenever you look around, no one is there? That's how I felt every time I sat in the library to study. Eyes were on me. Who they belonged to had me curious as hell. It started a few weeks ago at the beginning of term and it bugged the hell out of me. Always during lesson four right after lunch when I had study time on Tuesdays and Thursdays.

My eyes roamed across the room, hunting down the source. But no one seemed to be looking my way.

Who the fuck is watching me?

It was like an itch against my skin I needed to scratch. The gaze burnt into me and made me uncomfortable. There were several other students in here. A couple from sixth form who were doing the same A-Levels as me. Kyle and Lucinda were inseparable, usually glued to each other's faces. Some younger kids I didn't know the names of. And in the corner sat that kid two years below me, Cole Carter, who had five parents. Five. A mother and four fathers.

His brother, Raphael Nelson, was in sixth form with me and his other two older siblings had already left school. They all had the same mother and different fathers. It wasn't like their mother had gone through four different men. Oh no, their parents were in some kind of polyamorous relationship. Probably why they got teased relentlessly until Duke Scott, Raphi's older brother had beat a kid up for calling his mother a whore, then no one messed with them. At least, not as often as they had before.

I liked Raphi. He was smart, funny and respectful, most of the time. Cole Carter, however, was a law unto himself. I swear the boy had issues. It wasn't helped by the fact he was devastatingly attractive in a bad boy sort of way.

So yeah, I've noticed him. He's hard not to look at.

Dirty blonde hair and these hazel eyes, which whenever he turned them on anyone could captivate you. Didn't mean I had any interest in him. He was trouble. I didn't do trouble. If anyone tried to give me shit, I'd give it right back.

Probably why you have never been kissed. Boys don't like girls who're rude to them.

I shoved the thought away. Pretty much everyone I knew had lost their virginity. Not me.

Poor Meredith Pope. An eighteen-year-old virgin.

Thankfully, no one knew about that. It was fucking embarrassing. You were definitely judged for holding out on guys or being a prude. And gossip in this school was rife. If anyone got wind of it, I'd have people talking behind my back for the rest of the year like Wendy the year below me who fucked two boys in one night at a party. She'd been branded the school slut. Now all the boys leered at her and thought she was an easy lay. Teenage boys could be such dicks.

I did not want to join the ranks of those who had horrible rumours spread about them. Keeping my secret was paramount.

I hadn't ever talked to Cole Carter. He hung out with a couple of older kids who didn't seem to care about school. Cole, despite being trouble, did. At least according to his brother, who'd just sat down next to me

"Do those two really have to do that? Surprised Mrs Morris isn't down here telling them off," Raphi said, keeping his voice low and indicating Kyle and Lucinda sucking face two chairs down from us.

The school librarian didn't usually tolerate stuff like this, but she seemed to be busy today.

"Apparently so."

My eyes were still on Cole, who wasn't looking this way.

"Gross."

"Prude."

"Why are you staring at my brother?"

I immediately snapped my gaze away and looked at Raphi instead, taking in his chestnut hair and green eyes as he pushed his glasses further up his nose.

"Why aren't you sitting with him?"

"Cole doesn't like me cramping his style at school."

I scoffed.

"So what, your younger brother is cooler than you?"

Raphi shrugged.

"You have seen Cole, right?"

I shook my head and looked back down at my textbook, feeling my skin prickle with awareness. Everyone had seen Cole Carter. It was looking away from him which was the issue.

"You're just as smart and attractive as your brother, so I don't know what you're talking about."

"So you *were* staring at him."

I shoved his arm.

"I was looking out the window and Cole just happens to be in the way of it."

Liar, liar, pants on fire.

I glanced at Raphi, who had a smirk on his face.

"I'm not judging."

"Gross, Raphi, he's two years younger than us. Also, he's your brother and I'm so not interested."

I couldn't help looking over Cole's way again. This time I found his gaze directly on me and Raphi. The scowl etched on his features made me flinch. But it also made me very aware of the way my skin prickled with the knowledge he was staring at me.

Has it been Cole this whole time?

That was ridiculous. Why would he look at me? Boys didn't do that. All they saw was Meredith the girl who told boys to fuck off and die if they said anything inappropriate like 'nice tits' or asking me if my curtains matched the drapes. Boys could be right disgusting pricks.

8

"I'm joking, Mer. I'd advise against getting involved with anyone in my family. Trust me, having five parents is no walk in the park. Plus, my sister would actually straight-up murder you if you broke Cole's heart."

Fat fucking chance of that happening. More like the other way around given Cole's reputation.

"Really?"

"Rora's temper is genuinely terrifying."

I grinned. Aurora Knox had a reputation for being uncompromising.

"Aww, you scared of your big sister?"

"No! Just fed up with her and Duke arguing all the time. Why they won't move out, I have no idea. Mum likes having her babies under one roof even if we're not babies anymore."

"I'm sure she babies Cole more than you."

Raphi snorted and rolled his eyes.

"You have no idea. If you ever come around my house, you'll see exactly what kind of bullshit I put up with on a daily basis."

I raised an eyebrow.

"Is that an invitation?"

He eyed me for a long moment.

"You'd actually want to meet my whole family?"

I shrugged. I considered Raphi a friend. We'd known each other for years and not once had he invited me over until now. Though I'd kind of invited myself.

"Sure, maybe I'll get to see if they're really as crazy as you say they are."

He bit his lip and glanced over at his brother, who was still giving us evils.

"Okay. Dinner on Friday, that's when everyone is home. You can experience us all at the same time. Trust me, Mer, you'll never want to come back."

I stared at Cole too, wondering why he looked so pissed off at me and Raphi. What would he think about his brother inviting me to their house?

Why the fuck do you care?

"I'll be the judge of that."

"Don't say I didn't warn you." He picked up his phone. "I'll let my dad know since he'll be cooking."

Maybe it would be fun. Getting an insight into how their parents' relationship worked could be interesting. Either way, it would be an unforgettable evening in more ways than one. And if it pissed Cole Carter off, so fucking what?

CHAPTER TWO

Meredith

I rarely got nervous but waiting outside the school building with Raphi to get picked up by his dad had my stomach in knots. And by his dad I meant his actual biological father, not one of the others. The other reason I was feeling all sorts of shit was because his brother had joined us. Cole's eyes narrowed to slits the moment he saw me.

What the hell is your problem with me, Cole? I've done literally nothing to deserve it.

Who knew why he kept glaring. It's like he couldn't stand the sight of me. It bothered me. Why that would be the case, I couldn't quite put my finger on. I didn't care if Cole Carter liked me or not. I didn't know the boy. Just because I was friends with his brother, didn't mean I had to have anything to do with him.

"You actually getting a lift home with Dad today?" Raphi enquired.

"Mum said I had to be home for dinner," Cole ground out through gritted teeth.

His voice made my spine straighten. There was a deep note to it which made me feel... odd.

"You're such a mummy's boy."

"Fuck off."

Raphi nudged Cole with his shoulder, who gave him daggers. I looked between them. You could tell they were related as they had the same nose and jawline, but otherwise, they couldn't be more different. Raphi had a slimmer build. Cole's shoulders were broader, and his build more muscular. They both towered over my five-foot-five frame.

Stop eyeballing them. Raphi is your friend and Cole is... well... Cole.

"You know Meredith, right?"

Cole's eyes landed on me. I had a distinct feeling he was not happy to see me, nor that I was coming home with them.

"We've never officially met."

I could've stuck my hand out to him, but he was giving off don't come near me vibes. Too bad for him, I didn't care. If he was going to be rude, then I'd call him out on it.

"I'm sorry, do you have a problem with me?" I asked, my voice dripping with disdain.

Cole's eyebrow rose steadily and his eyes darkened as if I'd made him want to strangle me with that simple question.

Why does it make him look so... hot? I need to get a fucking grip. Cole Carter is not hot and I'm not interested in him and his attitude.

"Why would I?"

"The glare you're sending my way speaks volumes."

Raphi looked between us with amusement written all over his features.

"Cole glares at everyone."

"Shut up, Raphi," Cole muttered.

A car pulled up in front of us. Cole immediately went to the front passenger side and jumped in. Raphi rolled his eyes and walked to the back, opening the door for me.

"Don't mind grumpy, he's clearly in a mood… ladies first."

I stepped forward.

"At least one of you was raised to be a gentleman."

"You can thank my dad for that."

I raised an eyebrow. I was about to meet the man in question. Climbing into the car, I scooted across the seats to let Raphi in. He shut the door and grinned.

"Dad, this is Meredith. Mer, my dad, Eric."

I looked at the man in the driver's seat. Raphi was almost a carbon copy of him. The same green eyes stared back at me as Eric turned and smiled. His chestnut hair had streaks of grey in it and he was pretty hot for an older guy.

Why are you thinking that about Raphi's dad? Just stop already! You'll be perving over his entire family if you don't get your act together.

"Hello, Meredith, it's nice to meet you. Didn't think I'd see the day my son brought a girl home."

"Dad! I told you we're friends. Jesus, don't be embarrassing."

Eric winked at his son, smiled at me and turned to the front seat, giving Cole a sidelong look.

13

"Don't tell your mother."

"Why? Did she tell you and the others to behave?"

Eric pulled the car away from the curb.

"Something like that."

Raphi rolled his eyes and sat back. My eyes drifted to Cole, watching his profile as the soft tinkle of music playing on the radio filled the car.

"How was school?"

Cole looked over to Eric.

"Fine."

"Just fine?"

"It was school, what else do you want me to say?"

Cole's eyes flicked to mine. His gaze burnt into me, radiating irritation and something else I couldn't put my finger on. If he was going to look at me like that, I'd just stare right back.

"Cole…"

"Sorry, E," he muttered. "Just tired."

Eric reached out and patted his arm, which Cole seemed to accept. His eyes turned away from me and went to his… I didn't know how to describe his relationship with Eric. He didn't call him Dad, and yet Raphi had said they were all father figures to them.

"So, Meredith, Raphi says you draw," Eric said, looking at me through the rearview mirror.

I glanced at Raphi, who sent his dad daggers. Didn't bother me if he'd mentioned what I was into.

"Yeah, not people… landscapes, mostly. I'm applying to do production design for stage and screen at uni."

I'd always loved the theatre. My dad took me to the West End a lot when I was younger before he died. It'd been four years and it still left a gaping hole in my heart where he used to be. Losing him so suddenly to a heart attack had wrecked my entire world. Probably why I was guarded and, on occasion, terribly bitchy to other people. They didn't understand the pain of losing a parent who'd been my everything.

"Oh, really? That's interesting. Raphi's adamant he won't follow us into the family business."

I had no idea what they actually did. Raphi had never mentioned it.

"Yes, because working at a casino fills me with so much enthusiasm… not," Raphi muttered.

"A casino?"

Raphi glanced at me.

"Yeah, they own the Syndicate. All high-end with exclusive clients."

I'd never heard of it. Then again, I didn't pay much attention to anything outside my little slice of the world.

Eric eyed Raphi in the rearview mirror with a frown.

"We do other things, but yes, the Syndicate is our main business. And what he isn't saying is we've never forced any of them to be a part of it. I'm proud of him for wanting to do environmental sciences at university, even if it takes him away from home. It's your mother who doesn't want you leaving."

"Mum needs to chill out."

"Raphi…"

"What? She does. The thought of us flying the nest makes her go into full-on overprotective mode. It's exhausting. Probably why Rora and Duke won't move out, even though they're always trying to murder each other every five minutes."

I tried not to laugh. Raphi looked like he'd rather die than deal with that shit off his mum.

"More like Quinn won't let Rora do anything without his watchful eye over her," Cole put in. "Can you imagine what he'd be like if she told him she wanted to get her own place?"

Eric stifled a snort whilst Raphi grinned, his green eyes sparkling.

"When Rora brought a guy friend home, Quinn was up in his face asking what his intentions towards his daughter were. Rory had to drag him away and tell him to calm down." Raphi glanced at me. "That's Cole's dad."

I wondered at Cole's dad. Was he anything like Cole? If Raphi's looks were anything to go by, I could imagine Cole would take after Rory.

"Okay, so let me get this straight. Obviously, Eric is your dad, Rory is Cole's, Quinn is your sister's dad. Who's Duke's?" I asked, curiosity getting the better of me.

"Xavier. You'll meet them all soon enough. Trust me, it's super obvious."

Raphi knew I didn't judge them for their strange family dynamics. Not like I had any problem with it. They were clearly close and it must work for them.

The rest of the journey to their house was silent. Cole didn't look my way again, and for that, I could only be glad. His death stares were making me uncomfortable.

We all piled out of the car when Eric pulled up outside a big townhouse. I had wondered where they all lived since there were nine of them. Eric led us up the steps and unlocked the front door. Cole pushed past him into the house, not even bothering to give us a backwards glance. Raphi looked at me and smiled.

"Welcome to the madhouse."

I swallowed, unsure of what I'd let myself in for as I followed him in. Guess I was about to find out.

CHAPTER THREE

Cole

Why the fuck did Raphi have to invite her over for dinner? Did he like her? The thought of it made me crazy. Especially since Raphi was almost eighteen. Meredith was more likely to look at him favourably rather than me since he was her age and I wasn't.

She's mine. Meredith Pope is damn well mine.

She wasn't, but in my head she was. I'd staked a claim on her years ago, but I was far too young for her to look my way so I'd kept my interest to myself. Now I was sixteen and nothing would fucking well stand in my way. Not even my brother.

The way she'd spoken to me earlier had made my blood boil, and not in a good way. I wanted to teach that girl a lesson for it. Whatever Meredith's damage was, I had no fucking idea, but she needed to be put in her place.

"Cole."

I stopped in my tracks on my way to my bedroom at the voice behind me.

"Yes, Quinn?"

"Come here."

I turned and found him staring at me with a neutral expression on his face. You never knew what mood Quinn would be in at any one time. Sometimes he was reasonable and sometimes it was better to avoid him at all costs.

He walked back into his office and I knew then I was in trouble. Quinn had always been the disciplinarian in our household. Didn't matter if he wasn't my biological father. I might not call him dad, but he was that for me. They all were. It might sound odd to those who'd never been in our situation, but our family just worked that way.

I trudged after him, hanging my head and hoping I wouldn't get shouted at for the incident in my chemistry lesson earlier. Mum would be extremely disappointed in me and who knew what my dad would think. He wasn't the most talkative of people, but I was the closest to him out of our dads. He got me without me having to explain myself.

Quinn sat behind his desk when I reached his office. He put a hand out, indicating I should take a seat. I didn't bother shutting the door as I walked over and threw myself down in the chair, chucking my bag on the floor.

"I had a call from the school."

"Yeah, okay, I know, I shouldn't have poured my chemistry experiment all over Penelope's work, but she said something horrible about Mum."

Quinn raised an eyebrow. I hadn't told the headteacher about it. Didn't care if I got in trouble. Besides, Penelope got what she fucking well deserved. That girl was a stuck-up bitch through and through. I wished I'd pushed her face in it, but then she might have got injured from the chemicals and I wasn't about that. Better to scare her into keeping her trap shut than cause her actual bodily harm.

"What did she say?"

"That Mum's a greedy whore and she's clearly conned you all into being her own personal sex servants. And she said something about cuckolding, but honestly, by that point, I was too busy destroying her work to listen any further."

Quinn's lip twitched. Honestly, I was sick of people giving us shit over my parents' relationship. There was nothing wrong with it. If they saw the real love and support shared between them, then they wouldn't make idiotic comments about it.

"And you didn't tell this to Mr Hanover?"

"Why would I want to repeat that shit to anyone?"

"You told me."

I almost snorted. I knew better than to keep anything from Quinn.

"Yes, but you'd ground me or something worse if I lied to you."

"Well, I am going to ground you for a week even though I understand why you did it. You need to stop getting into trouble at school, Cole. It makes your mother anxious."

I didn't object to my punishment, knowing it would only get me in further trouble if I did.

"Have you told her and Dad?"

"Not yet. They're at the Syndicate."

Whenever my dad found out anyone had talked shit about my mum, he'd get this wild look in his eyes. Honestly, my dad could be intense as shit. Not to mention how he was with my mum. I could only be glad our bedrooms were downstairs. None of us wanted to hear our parents going at it. I shuddered at the thought.

"She's going to be upset."

"Can you blame her? Duke wasn't as much trouble as you and I've told you what Xav was like at school."

I smiled at that. Duke was a force to be reckoned with and his dad even more so. Xav might be in his fifties and liked to make fun of everything and everyone, but the guy was still ripped to shit. He could probably bench press Mum if he wanted to.

"No, I guess I can't."

"I don't want to have another conversation like this with you, Cole. Head down and concentrate on your exams, yes?"

I nodded. It wasn't like I didn't try at school. I was smart and all that shit, but people just pissed me off. Maybe I'd got that from my dad. My aversion to being around idiots. Mum said he used to be worse when she first met him, but my dad had gotten better over the years at being out of the house and around people. We were all well aware of our parent's pasts. They hadn't hidden that from us.

"Good. Now, you can go, but don't forget your presence is expected at dinner as we have a guest."

I got up from the chair.

"Yeah, don't I fucking know it," I muttered.

Quinn didn't tell me off for my language. Considering the way all of my parents, including him, swore like sailors, he didn't have a leg to stand on.

I trudged out, picking up my bag on the way. Walking towards my bedroom, I couldn't help fixating on Meredith Pope again.

Where did Raphi take her?

I fucking hoped the two of them were not hauled up in his room or something. That would have me on edge. As if I wasn't already. The damn girl had me worked up.

I passed by it, stopping to peer inside because apparently, I couldn't help myself. It was empty.

You live another day, brother.

I walked into my bedroom a minute later and threw my bag down before changing out of my school uniform. Raphi and Meredith didn't have to wear any since they were in sixth form. I would be fucking glad when this year was over. I wanted to do something with my hands as opposed to being studious like Raphi. My parents got annoyed with me for constantly tinkering with their cars, but it never stopped my innate desire to learn more about the inside workings. Might not be the most high-flying job, but if I wanted to be a mechanic, then so fucking what? Dad said he'd let me get my motorbike licence, much to Mum's dismay. She didn't have the heart to tell me no.

As much as I hated Raphi for saying it in front of Meredith, he was right about me being a mummy's boy. She let me get away with far more than the others as I was her baby. Probably why she left all the disciplining to Quinn.

I sat down at my desk and took out my homework. Might as well get it done. Then I could watch Meredith later without my parents harassing me over schoolwork. For now, I was safe in the knowledge Raphi had likely taken Meredith into the living room and they were not hanging out alone. If they were, I'd have a few fucking choice words to say to my brother.

Firstly, Meredith was mine.

Secondly, I would hurt him if he touched her.

And third, he better be telling the truth when he said they were just friends.

I would not stand for anything else. If that made me crazy, then so be it. I wanted what I wanted. That was Meredith Pope. And soon, I'd make sure she fucking well knew it too.

CHAPTER FOUR

Meredith

Raphi and I were watching TV when the rest of his family arrived home and the noise level in the house went from zero to one hundred in an instant. Raphi's dad was in the kitchen making dinner. Who knew where Cole was. Raphi told me Quinn would be ensconced in his office, so he didn't want to bother him.

I was a little overwhelmed when five people arrived in the living room. My eyes darted to each of them in turn. I knew Duke and Aurora, having been at school with them. The short blonde haired lady must be their mum, Ash. Next to her was a man with dirty blonde hair and hazel eyes. Lastly, there was an auburn-haired man with grey streaks running through it and striking blue eyes. He looked exactly like Duke apart from their hair colour. Duke used to have blonde hair, but it had changed to a lighter auburn colour similar to mine as he grew up. The man had to be his dad, Xavier, and he was the first one to open his mouth.

"Well, hello, is this the girlfriend you've been telling us all about, monkey?"

Raphi immediately scowled.

"Not funny. I told you she's just my friend. Repeatedly." He turned to me. "Please feel free to ignore him."

Xavier winked and came over, putting out his hand to me.

"You must be Meredith. I'm Xav, Duke's dad."

I shook his hand over the back of the sofa. It amused me how adamant Raphi was to his family about me being his friend. The feeling was entirely mutual. We got along well. Besides, if I was attracted to anyone it would be… *DO NOT SAY IT!*

I shoved aside all of those dangerous thoughts and concentrated on Raphi's parents. Ash and Rory had arrived by the sofa.

"It's very nice to meet you, Meredith. I'm Ash and this is Rory, Cole's father."

Ash put her hand out to me and I shook it. Rory didn't put his hand out for me, but to be honest, I found him a little intimidating. Especially the vibrancy of his hazel eyes which matched his son's. It's like he could see right through me and knew I'd thought about his son inappropriately.

Stop it. No one knows you think Cole is hot, okay? No one. Not even Raphi. And even if he suspects it, you just have to keep denying it. That's it.

"It's lovely to meet you all too," I replied.

"Has Quinn come out yet?" Ash asked, turning to her son.

"No," Raphi shrugged.

"And where's Cole?"

"How should I know? Probably in his room sulking."

Ash raised an eyebrow.

"Why would your brother be sulking?"

"This is Cole we're talking about. He's always grumpy about something. He spent the entire way home staring daggers at us for no reason."

Ash looked at Rory with some concern.

"Do you want to go or should I?"

"We should speak to Quinn first. He did text to say the school called again."

I raised an eyebrow and glanced at Raphi, who was rolling his eyes. What on earth had Cole done at school?

"Okay, well, we'll be back in a few as I'm sure E has dinner ready."

Ash and Rory left the room, seemingly having a silent conversation with each other over their son.

"All right, Meredith?" Duke said, throwing himself down on the sofa next to Raphi and nicking the remote.

"Yeah, you?"

"All good." He nudged Raphi's side. "You two really aren't dating?"

"Would you shut up? You're as bad as our dads," Raphi retorted, scowling.

Xav, who was still standing behind us, ruffled Raphi's hair.

"We're only playing, Raphi. We know you don't have a girlfriend. Hell might freeze over before that happens."

Before Raphi could say a word in response, he walked out of the room. That's when I noticed Aurora staring at me with interest.

"I could get a girlfriend if I wanted one," Raphi muttered.

"Doesn't that girl in chess club like you… what's her face, Mimi?" I said whilst still keeping my attention on Aurora, who'd circled the sofa and planted herself in one of the armchairs.

Raphi looked alarmed, pushing his glasses up his nose and glanced around as if Mimi was actually in the room.

"What? Jesus, no way in hell am I going there. She's a full-on stalker."

I grinned. He'd complained about it on many occasions.

"Mimi Lintott?" Aurora asked.

"She keeps asking Cole if I'll go out with her, even his death stares won't keep her away."

Mimi was in the same year as Cole.

Aurora gave Raphi a sly smile. Mimi Lintott's older sister was her friend, Colleen. Those two had been top dogs when they'd been at school. No one gave Aurora Knox shit or they'd have their head bitten off.

"Oh, I'm sorry, should I not have been encouraging her when she asks me about you?"

Raphi looked like he wanted to put his sister in the ground. Lucky for Aurora, his dad walked in and told us dinner was ready or I think Raphi would've had a go at her.

"My sister is a fucking pain in the arse," he muttered to me as we got up and walked through into their dining room.

"For once, she isn't giving me shit," Duke said as he shoved Raphi in the arm.

Raphi had me sit down next to him on one side of the large dining table whilst his brother and sister sat on the other side. His parents duly filed into the room. I guessed the one I hadn't met with greying black hair and little crinkles around his eyes was Quinn. He sat at the head of the table, his gaze landing directly on me.

"Is this our guest, Raphi?"

"Quinn, this is Meredith, my friend from school."

He gave me a quick nod in acknowledgement before turning his attention to his daughter, who was sat to his left.

"I have yet to see evidence of your family being anything other than normal except the whole four dads thing," I whispered to Raphi.

"Just you wait… dinner usually has someone getting into an argument, Xav making inappropriate comments, Quinn telling him to shut up and Mum trying to keep the peace."

I braced myself for the show as Eric and Xav came in carrying dishes and set them in the middle of the table.

"Did you tell Cole dinner's ready?" Eric asked, looking around the table.

"Yes," Ash replied with a frown. "He should be here."

The boy himself sloped into the room, glancing around the table before his eyes landed on me and the only free chair to my left. I watched his eyes narrow as he made his way towards me and sat down. The anger radiating off him scorched my skin. Why did I have to get stuck next to Cole? I didn't think Raphi had planned this, so I wasn't going to comment on it.

"Dig in," Eric said as he sat down at the other end of the table.

It was a free-for-all the next moment as people served themselves and passed dishes down to each other. There were three different pasta dishes, garlic bread and salad. It seemed Eric had catered for different tastes considering both Raphi and Cole only chose one type of pasta.

I barely had time to stick a fork full of food in my mouth when various conversations started up at different ends of the table. It was like watching ping pong as one person would talk across the table at another. I leant over to Raphi, who was busy eating and ignoring what was going on around the table.

"Is this how it is every day?" I murmured.

"No, usually it's only a few of us. Mum implemented Friday night dinners so we'd all spend time together as a family, and one Sunday a month we have our grandparents over for lunch. Everyone is expected to attend."

"Or what?"

Raphi grinned.

"Or they get guilt-tripped by Mum."

"No, they get an earful from Quinn," Cole muttered from next to me.

I glanced over at him, not realising he'd been listening to me and Raphi.

"That too," Raphi agreed.

I went back to my food, but it did not escape my notice that Cole kept staring at me with unnerving intensity. Goosebumps prickled all over my skin, making me hyper-aware of how close his body was to mine. Why the hell was I having this weird reaction to him? I wished he would quit giving me weird looks like he couldn't work out whether he wanted to strangle me fast or slow.

Seriously, what the hell did I ever do to him?

"So, Meredith, what A-Levels are you taking? Raphi didn't mention it."

I looked up at Ash, who was sat across from me.

"Art and Design, Drama and English… I'd like to be a set designer one day. My dad used to take me to the theatre all the time."

My heart tightened when I realised I'd mentioned him. Some days it would be normal to talk about him, but others, it would upset me. I tried not to think too hard about it.

"So the complete opposite of my son who likes all things science."

I smiled.

"Yeah, guess so. They do say opposites attract."

I had meant that innocently, but movement to my left caught my attention. Cole gripped his fork harder in his hand and almost slammed a glass down on the table.

Why would that bother him?

"What Mer meant is we get along just fine despite being different," Raphi interjected, "in a strictly platonic way."

"And here I was wondering why you can't get a girlfriend," Duke said, waving his fork at his brother. "Now I know. You're too pussy to make a move on a girl."

"Shut up."

"Dukey, don't wind your brother up," Ash said, frowning at her son.

Duke scowled.

"Don't call me that. I'm a grown man."

"If you're a grown man, then why do I still have to pick up all your dirty clothes off your bedroom floor, hmm?"

"Mum!"

Duke waved a hand at me like her embarrassing him was not on, even though he'd been intent on trying to wind his brother up.

"Serves him right," Raphi muttered.

I stifled a smile. No matter what Raphi said, his family was perfectly normal as far as I was concerned. There were a lot of them and they were loud, but I liked that. It was better than the silence at my house with me, Mum and Grandma. After Jonah moved out to go to university in Durham, things had become increasingly strained at home. Mum and Grandma were always arguing or ganging up on me with their snide remarks. It was a blessing to be away from the tense atmosphere for an evening.

The rest of dinner passed much the same. I engaged in conversation when I was asked questions by Raphi's parents. The only person who remained silent was Cole. I could see his dad glancing at him every so often with concern as if this wasn't usual behaviour for his son. I had a feeling it had everything to do with me being there.

When we were all finished and the dishes were being cleared, I asked Raphi where the bathroom was. He pointed out it was down the end of the corridor after all their bedrooms. I made my way out of the room and found the bathroom. There was a huge Victorian-style claw-footed bath and it was decorated in pale blues and greens.

After I'd gone to the loo, I walked out along the hallway to go in search of Raphi when a hand grabbed me and yanked me into a room. I barely had time to blink when the door was shut behind me and I was pressed up against it. There, towering above me, stood Cole with his arm resting above my head and his intense hazel eyes burning into my skull.

What the fuck?

CHAPTER FIVE

Cole

I t was safe to say I was done beating around the bush when it came to Meredith. Sitting next to her the whole way through dinner had been absolute torture. The way she'd quite happily interacted with my family without a fucking care in the world pissed me off. Mostly because she wasn't being the Meredith I knew. The one who spoke her own mind and didn't care if she offended people. But no, she was on her best behaviour just as my family had been.

Having her pinned up against my bedroom door probably wasn't my smartest idea, but no one could call me the nice boy you took home to your parents. Not like my brother.

"What are you doing?" she hissed when she'd got over the shock of me pulling her in here.

It amused me to see her surprised features. Meredith always had the upper hand in every situation she was in. Right now, I had it and I wasn't about to let it go.

"What am I doing? What are you doing?"

"Going to find Raphi."

My fingers itched to touch her. To tangle in her strawberry blonde hair and tug her head back, exposing that delectable neck. I watched her swallow and it only made me want to run my tongue along her skin.

"I don't think so, Meredith."

"What do you mean? I wasn't aware I had to ask for your fucking permission."

There you are my fiery little queen.

"Perhaps you didn't get the memo."

The blazing inferno in her green eyes made me smile.

"Look, *Cole*, I don't know what your game is, but I'm not interested in playing. Now move and let me out."

I leant closer, watching her breath hitch.

"No."

Her hands fisted at her sides as if she was contemplating shoving me away. She could try. Pity for Meredith I wouldn't let her move me.

"What do you want?"

So many things, Meredith, but most of all, I want you.

Reaching up, I curled a lock of her hair around my finger. Meredith's eyes fell on what I was doing, confusion painting her features.

"What do I want?"

"Yes."

My eyes met hers. I could think of many ways to take advantage of this situation right now. I wouldn't since Raphi would come looking for her sooner rather than later. Plus, I wanted to make her want me back. I wanted Meredith to beg for a piece of me. To crave me and everything I'd give her.

"Do you like my brother?"

She blinked, then scowled.

"Not that it's any of your business, but no. We're just friends. That's it."

My fingers were close to her chest and her ample cleavage. Meredith had a curvaceous body. Visions of it filled my fantasies when I was alone at night. I wanted to touch her. To brush my fingers over her skin and see if it was as soft as I imagined.

"Good."

"Good? Why do you care?"

I ran my tongue along my bottom lip, watching her eyes trace its path.

That's right, Meredith, look at me. If you wanted, I'd quite happily lick your lip too. Fuck, if I don't want to. I want to devour you. So. Fucking. Much.

"Raphi wouldn't give you what you need."

Those green eyes flashed with annoyance.

"Oh, and how the fuck would you know that? You don't know a single thing about me and I don't know you, so why don't you let me go and we can forget this ever happened."

I'd never forget Meredith, nor this moment. This encounter. The first time I'd had an actual conversation with her. Even if she probably wanted to punch my lights out right now. She'd change her tune soon enough.

"I know a lot about you. People like to talk and I like to listen."

"Whatever. There aren't any rumours about me."

I smiled.

"No? So, it's not true you've never been kissed then?"

"What? Where the hell did you hear that?"

The fear in her eyes told me it was true. Told me exactly what I'd wanted to know. Meredith was a virgin like me. The thought of taking her and making her mine completely made my dick swell. It's not like I thought our first time would be some momentous occasion, but after that... I'd learn exactly how to tease her curvaceous body until she was screaming my name.

"Not from anyone who would spread it around the school if that's what you're worried about."

"You know what, Cole, fuck you. It's not your business, now let me go."

Her hands came up and landed on my chest. A shudder went through her at the direct contact. Instead of pushing me away, she stared at where her hands were. I placed my own hands on hers and forced her to drag them down my chest and lower to my stomach. Meredith's eyes were like saucers and her chest heaved with each breath she took. I stopped when we'd reached the tops of my jeans. Her touch electrified me and made me want so much fucking more. I wanted everything.

"It's okay, Meredith," I murmured. "I know you want to touch me."

"Wh… what?"

I stepped closer until we were inches apart, keeping her hands pinned to my body.

"You want this. You want to know what it's like, don't you? To touch and be touched in return."

"I…"

"Don't worry, your secret is safe with me."

She shook herself and glared up at me as if coming out of a trance.

"What the fuck, Cole? I don't want to touch you and I certainly don't want you to touch me."

She shoved me then. I let go of her hands. Before she had a chance to disappear from my space, I leant down, my mouth brushing along the shell of her ear, making sure that was the only place my body touched hers.

"Liar."

"Excuse me?"

"I called you a liar. You can fool the whole fucking world, but not me. I see right through you. You think I know nothing about you, but I know a whole lot more than you'll ever realise. Mark my words, Meredith, you'll be back for more of what you think you don't want sooner rather than later."

I took several steps back, watching her try to regain her composure after what I'd said.

"You think you're so fucking smart, huh? Let me make one thing very clear, Cole Carter, I will never want anything from you so take your delusional bullshit elsewhere."

And with that, she ripped open my door and stormed out of my room. I rocked back on my heels and smiled. No doubt she'd been stewing over every word I said when she was alone, wondering what the hell I meant. Then she'd be back to find out.

And I'd be waiting.

CHAPTER SIX

Meredith

I swear to god that boy was the devil sent to drag me down into the depths of hell. The moment I escaped from his room with my heart pounding and my body trembling with feelings I didn't understand nor want to, I ran headlong into Cole's dad. He steadied me with two hands on my shoulders. When I looked up at Rory, I almost flinched. Given what just happened with his son, seeing those damning hazel eyes had me pressing a hand to my chest.

"Running somewhere?"

"Away from Cole," I blurted out without thinking.

Mouth, shut the fuck up!

Rory's eyes grew concerned as he dropped his hands.

"What did he do?"

"N… nothing."

In reality, Cole hadn't done anything other than taunt me. I'd been the one to touch him. Something I severely regretted.

But do you? Didn't you like the way he felt against your palms?

"Nothing? That doesn't sound like Cole."

I shook my head. As if I wanted to admit to his dad, Cole had flooded my veins with violent arousal just by talking to me. Something I didn't understand in the slightest.

And yet you just admitted it to yourself. That's why you're flustered.

"It was a misunderstanding. Nothing serious... I... uh... should find Raphi."

Rory eyed me for a long moment. He didn't believe a word coming out of my mouth. He knew his son had done something to me. I wasn't about to enlighten him, considering this was the first time I'd met the man. Also, I still felt pretty intimidated by him. He radiated this air of danger.

"He's in the living room."

"Um, thank you."

I ducked by him and hurried away, not wanting to prolong the encounter. Didn't stop me glancing back to find Rory watching me. Then he turned and knocked on Cole's door. I hoped his son would not say a word about what just happened between us.

I pressed my hands to my burning cheeks, wanting to be away from this house and Cole Carter. That fucking boy. I had no idea what he thought he was playing at. I'd never met a cockier and more arrogant sixteen-year-old in my life. He acted like I should just accept everything he said without question.

Fuck you, Cole. I don't want you.

My body had other ideas. My fingers tingled as if they were still planted on his solid chest. My skin thrummed in anticipation of his hands all over it. And the less said about what was going on between my thighs, the better.

How the hell did he know I was a virgin? Who had found that out and told him? He told me my secret was safe but I didn't believe a word coming out of that boy's mouth. How could I trust someone who'd dragged me into his bedroom and pinned me against his door like I was a ragdoll or a toy for his amusement?

And why did it turn me on?

Shoving all of those thoughts well away from my brain so I didn't have to think about the whys and hows of my body's reaction to Cole, I made it to the living room and found Raphi alone in there with the TV on.

"Hey," I said, trying to keep my voice level and even.

He looked back at me over the top of the sofa. His brow furrowed when he took in my appearance.

"Everything okay?"

"Yes… what are we doing now?"

"Well, we can watch TV or I can show you our games room."

I raised an eyebrow.

"Games room?"

"Uhuh, used to be our playroom when we were kids. Duke's probably in there and he might let you play co-op with him or something."

I had wanted to go home but maybe I needed the distraction. Home would only be filled with silence.

"What about you?"

Raphi grinned.

"We could persuade him to play Mario Kart."

"Oh, you are so on."

Raphi got up and led me through the house towards the back. We entered a big room with a huge flatscreen TV, a couple of old school arcade games resting along the wall and Duke sat on the large sofa with a controller in his hand.

"What do you two want?" he asked when he spied us lingering in the doorway.

"Want to play us at Mario Kart?"

Duke eyed us for all of two more seconds before he lugged himself off the sofa.

"Oh, go on then, I bet I'll kick both your arses."

Raphi and I took our seats and Duke got everything set up. For the next hour, the three of us were completely fixated on trying to outmatch each other. I almost didn't notice when Cole arrived. Except for the fact, my skin prickled at his mere presence. And I was not expecting him to plant himself between me and Raphi on the sofa.

Why are you here? I don't want you near me after what you did earlier.

"You here to ruin our fun?" Duke asked.

"No," Cole muttered and grabbed the last controller off the coffee table.

"You better not throw that at the screen like the last time you lost."

Cole glared at his brother.

"I won't."

Cole looked at me, his eyes burning into my flesh like he could see right through me. The smirk gracing his lips made me want to smack it off his face. I refrained and looked away, hoping neither Raphi nor Duke noticed their brother's interest in me. Whatever the hell that interest was.

You have a good idea of what he wants, Meredith. Don't lie to yourself.

Duke set up a new game and for the first race, nothing untoward happened. Before we started the second one, Cole shifted closer to me until our thighs met. I could've sworn my face was on fire, but I attempted to ignore him. Duke and Raphi had both leant forward in their seats, their eyes intent on the screen. When Cole leant over to me, his breath disturbing my hair, I shivered and tried not to react any further.

"You're still here," he whispered.

As much as Cole had rattled me, going home didn't appeal to me either. When I'd told Mum, I was going to a friend's house, she'd barely batted an eyelid. I wasn't sure when she stopped caring about what I did in life, but it had been some time over the past four years after my dad died. It's like she no longer saw me as her daughter. I was an inconvenience to her life and she'd rather I left like Jonah had.

"Not because of you," I hissed back. "Don't distract me."

"What did you say to my dad?"

I glanced at him, finding his gaze on the TV but his head was angled close to mine.

"Nothing."

"Nothing doesn't explain why he asked me what I did to you."

"It's not my fault I ran into him after you pushed me up against your fucking door, okay? Did you expect me not to be flustered?"

What the fuck? Don't tell him that! Jesus, Meredith, you're not helping your case here.

The smile on Cole's lips was so arrogant, I almost called him out for it. Clearly pleased with himself for having an effect on me.

Prick.

"Flustered? I don't think that's the right word for what I made you."

"Oh, and what would be the right word?"

I shouldn't have asked that question. I knew it the moment the words left my mouth. Cole moved his hands until his knuckles brushed against my thigh, all the while still holding the controller and keeping his attention on the race. My breath hitched at the motion and my body betrayed me entirely.

"Wet."

That one word made me hot and cold all at the same time. I nearly jumped away from him. Except then it'd be obvious to his brothers Cole was making me uncomfortable. I didn't back down from a fight nor did I let boys walk all over me.

"Don't make me fucking laugh," I hissed. "You can wipe that arrogant look off your face and go fuck yourself with it. I will never be attracted to you."

You both know that's a lie.

46

It was a question of whether he'd call me out on it. Yes, I thought Cole was hot. What girl wouldn't? The glaring issues with finding him remotely attractive reared their ugly head. Cole was two years younger than me. He was my friend's little brother. And I wasn't interested in playing games with him.

"If you say so, Meredith."

His fingers kept brushing against my thigh. It had the exact reaction I knew he was looking for. My body heated and flames licked over my skin, making me want him to keep going. It's not as if I didn't understand the mechanics of sex. I had explored my own body, wanting to know what the big deal was. I'd never had another person touch me in a distinctly sexual way or even look at me the way Cole had been doing when he dragged my hands down his stomach earlier. My body was confused by the new sensations and hadn't caught up with my brain yet. The logical thing to do would be to push him away and tell him to fuck off.

I wasn't being logical right then.

"I do."

"Tell me to stop then."

My words caught in my throat as his stroking grew bolder, his thigh pressing more firmly against mine.

"For fuck's sake," Duke grunted, chucking the controller next to him as he lost the race.

How Cole and I had kept playing and gained second and third place was beyond me at this point. Raphi had come in first and the smile on his face could light up the whole room.

Cole moved his head away from me but his hands remained where they were. I didn't know what to do or say, only that I needed to get away from him. He'd well and truly messed with my head this evening.

"Hey, Raphi, do you think one of your parents might drive me home after this one? I could get the bus if not."

I could feel Cole's eyes on me but I refused to look at him.

"I'm sure Dad won't mind," Raphi replied with an easy grin, completely oblivious to the way his brother was pressed up against me.

The sooner I could get away from Cole, the better. Then I might be able to sort through my messy emotions regarding the boy next to me. For someone I'd never interacted with on a personal level before, he'd sure left a fucking impression on me.

A bad one.

I was damn sure this boy was bad for me in every single way.

Why the fuck did my body not get the memo when I told it Cole Carter was off-limits and I was not going there. Ever.

Traitor.

CHAPTER SEVEN

Cole

Meredith knew my eyes were on her. The way her body kept angling away from me and her refusal to turn her head my way made it obvious. I'd bothered her. She didn't like her reaction to me on Friday. In fact, I think she hated it. But the way she'd spit fire at me when I taunted her only made my need for her worse. The need to force her to her knees and have her beg.

Perhaps I was fucked up for wanting shit like that from a girl I barely knew. Especially when I'd never been with anyone before. And yet I couldn't help it. My fascination with her bordered on the insane. I couldn't get Meredith out of my head. It'd been this way for years and now, I needed to *have* her. I wouldn't hold back.

The library was particularly quiet this afternoon. Somehow I'd ended up with the same free study periods as her. I only came in here to watch Meredith. The way her strawberry blonde hair curled over her shoulders. Hair I wanted to fist in my hand.

I noticed her stand up, leaving her books where they were as she walked towards the shelves. Rising to my feet, I followed her at a distance. She stopped down an aisle of books, her eyes scanning the titles. No one else was around. I stuck my hands in my pockets and leant up against the shelves a few feet away, just watching her.

"What do you want?" she asked in a quiet voice.

"Nothing."

"I don't believe you."

A smile graced my lips.

"You don't have to."

Her gaze fell on me, her green eyes a mixture of curiosity and irritation. She was holding back as we were at school and in the library. Meredith would probably lose it if we were alone. Just as she had done on Friday when I'd had her in my room.

"Seriously, Cole, what do you want? Here to taunt me some more? If you're going to continue, I will walk away and tell you where to go."

I shifted closer, watching her take a breath.

"I want you," I said, in a voice barely above a whisper.

She blinked as if not expecting me to give her a straight answer.

"You want me? What the fuck? Are you insane? You don't even know me."

I took a step towards her expecting her to back away but Meredith stood her ground. She turned to me fully, an expression of disgust written all over her face.

My fiery little queen. You really are magnificent.

"I know plenty. We already established that much."

The way her body tensed and her eyes flashed told me she hated anyone knowing her secret. She had nothing to be ashamed of. Not everyone liked to put it around and I respected her for that. Besides, I wanted to be the one between her legs. The only one. I'd take her virginity and give her mine in return. Then I'd make sure she never wanted to go anywhere else. I'd make Meredith mine.

"How do you know?"

"So you're admitting it?"

"I'm admitting nothing. Who told you?"

Her fist clenched at her sides.

"You really want to know?"

She nodded, biting down on her lip as if wanting to stop herself from flying off the handle at me.

"Girls like to gossip. When you make enemies of the people you thought were your friends they might have an axe to grind."

Her eyes widened and her entire body went still.

"Celia?"

Celia Tompkins and Meredith had been best friends right up until the summer. Then everything fell apart. The girl wouldn't reveal what happened between them but she was perfectly happy to spill the beans on Meredith's biggest secret.

You've never even been kissed, my little queen.

Extracting that had been easy. All it took was a promise to secure her a date with Duke who she'd had a crush on for years. That part was simple. Duke had taken her out, fucked her and chucked her as he often did. I hadn't told her about his reputation. And I'd made sure I got what I wanted before upholding my end of the bargain. When she'd had a go at me for Duke's behaviour, I merely shrugged and told her if she spread around any rumours about Meredith, I would come after her. I could be a scary motherfucker when I wanted to be. Celia would learn the hard way if she stepped out of line.

"That fucking bitch," she muttered when she saw the truth of it in my eyes.

"If you're worried about her telling anyone else, don't. I took care of it."

Meredith searched my face for a long moment.

"Why would you do that?"

"I already told you. I want you."

"That's not a fucking explanation, Cole."

The way she said my name breathed life into my dick. The mixture of disgust and agitation did something to me.

You really have a fucked up, twisted attraction to this girl.

"It is when it's the truth."

"You are impossible."

"I've been told."

By my mother, repeatedly, whenever I got into trouble. I might be her baby but she wasn't blind to my behaviour. Perhaps she should've expected it. Aurora and Duke had constantly accused her of spoiling me when we were younger. She let me get away with everything. Whilst Quinn instilled discipline, Mum always undermined him in small ways. Like giving me treats when I wasn't meant to have them or taking me out when I was grounded. And my dad did nothing to stop her. If you saw the way he doted on her, you'd understand. Rory Carter would do anything for Ash Bykov, including allowing her indulgence of their son. I was her baby and that hadn't changed because I'd grown up.

"There are several things wrong with you *wanting* me."

I raised an eyebrow as I reached out and ran a finger along her collarbone. Meredith's eyes tracked my movement.

"Care to elaborate on what those things are?"

"Well, for starters you're Raphi's younger brother."

"And?"

She raised her eyes to me, glaring. It was all for show considering she'd not stopped me from touching her.

"He's my friend."

"And?"

"You're two years younger than me. What the fuck do you think people would say about that? I'm not a cradle robber, thank you very much."

I grinned.

"I don't care what anyone else thinks. And I'm perfectly legal so it's not like you'd be doing anything wrong."

She let out a huff of air and stepped closer to me. Her head craned up to stare into my eyes. Being six-foot-one, I towered over Meredith's frame. My finger was still on her chest. Daring to test her limits, I flattened my palm against her, watching as her breath caught in her throat. She swallowed before opening her mouth.

"That's the difference between us. I care. And besides, I don't want you."

I leant closer. Yet again, Meredith didn't back down, standing her ground in front of me.

"Such pretty little lies falling out of your mouth. It's obvious you do or you wouldn't let me near you. I don't see you allowing anyone else to take such liberties."

Her eyes fell on my palm resting on her chest right above her breast. If I dragged my pinkie finger lower, I could brush it across her nipple.

"I don't want you to touch me."

"Tell me to take my hand off you then."

She hadn't told me to stop touching her in the games room on Friday and I knew she wouldn't now.

"I don't want you."

"Yes, you do… you just don't want to admit it."

"Do you not understand the word no, Cole?"

"You haven't told me no… yet."

Her chest rose and fell. I could feel her heart hammering erratically in her chest against my skin.

"Is this some kind of game to you? I'm not a toy, nor will I let you treat me like one."

"I'm not playing a game, Meredith. I. Want. You."

"Why?"

I leant even closer until I could see the varying shades of green in her wide eyes.

"Aside from the obvious fact, you're beautiful?"

Her cheeks flushed.

"No one thinks that about me."

"Then they're fucking stupid." I moved my hand from her chest upwards to cup the back of her neck. "You are beautiful."

My other hand curled around her back, drawing her closer to me. Fuck did I want to kiss those parted lips and devour her whole.

"As flattering as that is, you're missing the point. You are too young for me."

Her words didn't match her body's actions. Those dainty little hands of hers had curled themselves around my waist.

"Perhaps I was three weeks ago, but not now."

"You still haven't answered my question. Why do you want me?" Her eyes darkened as she stared up at me. "Is this some kind of trophy for you? Get Meredith into bed and take her v-plates? Has one of your friends put you up to this? Because it's not fucking funny either way."

I raised an eyebrow. She'd not realised what she'd finally admitted. And I wasn't that much of a cunt. As if I'd spread it around the school or tell my friends. I'd gone out of my way to make sure rumours about her didn't surface.

I couldn't understand why she couldn't accept my assertion at face value. Was she so jaded about boys she thought no one could like her for her? I guess she'd spent years keeping them all at arm's length. The fact she let me get close to her spoke volumes.

You like me, Meredith, you just think you're not allowed to because I'm younger than you. It's okay. I'll prove you wrong. I'll show you I can give you what you need.

"No, you're not a trophy and no one put me up to it."

She looked down at her hands and then back up at me as if noticing how close we were standing. It took a second for her eyes to grow from confused to annoyed. Then she stepped back away from me, forcing me to drop my hands from her body.

"You know what, I don't even know why I'm asking. You don't seem to like giving straight answers and quite frankly, I don't care. You're not getting anything from me. I've already told you I'm not interested."

"I can wait until you stop lying about what you want if that's what you need."

She glared at me again.

"I'm not lying. I have no reason to."

I shook my head, smiling at her.

"Yes, you are. When you're ready, you'll come looking for me and I'll be waiting."

Before she had a chance to retort, I backed away from her, shoving my hands back in my pockets before I turned and walked away. The indignant huff I heard from behind me only made me smile wider. She'd got the message. She knew what I wanted. And knowing Meredith, she wouldn't be able to contain her curiosity. She'd come to me next time. And like I'd told her, I'd be waiting to give her exactly what she didn't know she needed.

Me.

CHAPTER EIGHT

Meredith

W ho the hell did Cole think he was? I'd like to damn
well know. That boy had made it his mission to
mess with me. This business about wanting me
had to be utter bullshit. Not to mention he'd found out I was
a virgin from Celia. The thought of her made my blood boil
more than when Cole had been around me. And he'd heated
it for a very different reason.

My best friend since I was four-years-old had turned out
to be the biggest backstabbing bitch I'd ever met in my life.
Honestly, I never thought she would turn against me, but she
had over the summer holidays six months ago. The thought
of it made me angry and upset. So yeah, maybe Cole bringing
it up had put me on edge and I'd been extra bitchy to him. I
could admit to that much.

Does he really like me?

I stared down at myself, trying to understand what caught his interest. He'd called me beautiful. All I'd got growing up had been boys calling me carrot top, ginger nut and fire crotch. The leering had started when I grew breasts but I figured horny teenage boys would go after anything with a pair of tits.

Cole had said none of that. He hadn't leered either. The way he'd looked at me differed from other boys. Now I had time to calm down and think about it properly, Cole's interest felt… genuine. Even if he was a cocky little shit. There'd be no denying that part. And I liked that about him. I shouldn't like anything about Cole Carter. Not the way his dirty blonde hair often fell in his eyes where he'd let it grow long on top. Nor how his body had felt under my hands.

Stop it. He's too young for you. You can't think of him like that.

Cole had a point. He was sixteen and over the age of consent, but that didn't make it any better. I couldn't imagine what people would say about it if I got involved with Cole. Nothing good. Picturing Celia's judgemental stare made me want to smack the cow around the face. I couldn't believe she'd told him I was a virgin. She knew how embarrassed I was about it. Not that I had anything to be ashamed of. Keeping your legs closed wasn't a bad thing. It had more to do with boys not finding me attractive. No one had even wanted to kiss me.

I tried not to think about the incident involving spin the bottle when I was sixteen. Kyle had thrown a house party when his parents were away. It flashed through my head, making my cheeks burn all over again. When the bottle landed on me and Owen Blackburn. How he'd taken me in the cupboard and told me he'd rather get with Amanda Phelps, the nerdy girl with braces and terrible acne, than kiss me. If I told anyone we hadn't snogged, he'd spread it around I didn't put out. I'd kept my composure when we came out and had whoops and cheers from the others, carrying on with the game and being thankful when the bottle didn't land on me again. Later, when I'd gone back to Celia's for the night, I'd broken down in tears and told her the whole sorry story. She'd told me Owen was an arsehole and didn't deserve to be my first kiss anyway. I didn't want to share it with someone who didn't give a shit about me.

In a fucked up way, Cole gives a shit about you. He told you he took care of Celia and protected you from the rumour mill. Doesn't that show he likes you?

"You look like you're about to tear your hair out," came a voice from beside me.

After school, I hadn't wanted to go home, instead I'd made my way to the park near my house and sat under an oak tree. The fresh air helped clear my head somewhat even if my thoughts had been consumed by Cole and my ex-best friend, Celia.

I looked up, finding my brother staring down at me.

"What are you doing here? Shouldn't you be at uni?"

Jonah grinned and shrugged.

"Yes, but my sister sent me an SOS at the weekend. I don't have lectures until tomorrow afternoon."

I'd forgotten about that. Mum and Grandma's arguing had been getting to me no matter how much I tried to ignore them. And Jonah hadn't responded so I'd figured he was busy.

"I didn't want you to make a six-hour round trip for me. A phone call would've sufficed."

He sat down next to me and nudged my shoulder with his. He'd likely gone home first and found I wasn't there then came here to our spot.

"Don't you know I'd do anything for my little sister?"

Jonah would as well. He'd always been there for me, particularly after Dad had died.

My brother and I had opposite personalities. Whilst I was loud and out there, Jonah was quieter and more introspective. He always knew the right thing to say. We looked alike except he had blonde hair as opposed to my coppery red. The same jawline, nose and green eyes. Something we'd inherited from our dad.

"Are you sure that's the *only* reason?"

"Yes, don't bring that shit up today. It's not why I'm here."

I leant my head on his shoulder and sighed. Jonah had a good reason for wanting to get away from London other than because Mum and Grandma drove him crazy. And I knew how much it hurt him so I shouldn't have even insinuated it was the reason he was here other than to see me.

"What's wrong, Mer?"

"Everything."

"I see you've not grown any less dramatic in the past couple of months."

"Shut up."

He reached over and took my hand, stroking his thumb down the back of it. The soothing motion calmed me. My brother was the only person in the world who understood everything I'd been through. We were super close but him going away to uni had made things that much harder on me.

"I miss you," I whispered.

Jonah kissed my forehead.

"I'm right here."

"Right now, maybe, but on a normal day, you're hundreds of miles away, J. I feel like I'm drowning and I can't come up for air."

"Then why don't you call more often?"

I didn't want to bother him with my petty bullshit. Like how a boy was messing with my head. It didn't seem worth Jonah's time even though I'd been there for him when he was going through his own bullshit with boys. I say boys... it was really just one boy.

"You don't need me to unload my shit on you."

"That's what I'm here for."

"Yes, but you can't help me with this."

No one could. Not when I had a sixteen-year-old pursuing me. Even that sounded ridiculous to my ears.

"Meredith."

"It's embarrassing, J."

"Meredith."

"Okay, fine... it's a boy."

My brother squeezed my hand. He knew all about the Owen incident and how much it screwed with my head. When it came to boys, he got why I freaked out over anything to do with them.

"Do I know this boy?"

"Yes."

"You're not going to tell me who it is."

"Nope."

If I could see him, I knew Jonah would be rolling his eyes right then.

"Okay, and what exactly is going on between you and this boy?"

I was going to have to tell him why I couldn't get involved with Cole or he would tell me to stop being an idiot and let it happen.

"Well, nothing since he's sixteen."

I raised my head off my brother's shoulder to look at him. His brow furrowed and his eyes grew concerned.

"Sixteen? Meredith, who is it?"

I shook my head. There was a multitude of reasons why I couldn't tell him. Bringing that family up to Jonah would only cause problems.

"I can't, J. All you need to know is, he's no good for me, I can't date a sixteen-year-old."

Jonah's mouth split into a grin.

"You like him."

"I do not."

He pointed at me with his free hand.

"You so do. Your ears are going red. Did you forget I know all your tells?"

"I don't even know him, how can I like someone I barely know?"

Jonah scoffed.

"Easy, it's called attraction and chemistry, Mer, you might have heard of it."

I shoved his arm.

"Be serious."

"I am and there's nothing wrong with you dating someone younger than you, at least he's legal."

I gave him a sympathetic look. Jonah had a shit time of it a couple of years ago in his last year of school.

"There is when it's…" I faltered.

"It's who?" Jonah frowned and then his eyes went wide. "Oh for fuck's sake, Meredith, you are not serious."

I hung my head and nodded.

"Look, I realise I can't stop you being friends with him, but really, his little brother? What the fuck?"

I turned my head away and stared out over the park.

"I didn't ask for this, J. Cole told me today in the library he likes me and he knows about the whole virginity thing because Celia told him. I've never had anyone say they like me or call me beautiful before. I told him I wasn't interested, but that's not true and he knows it."

It's not like I'd done anything wrong. It was Cole who was coming after me not the other way around.

"You do not need any trouble in your life and this will only end in tears. I guarantee it."

"I knew I shouldn't have told you. This is why I wanted to talk to you on the phone."

Jonah had a way of getting everything out of me. If I'd spoken to him over the phone, I wouldn't have breathed a word about this shit. I would've only told him about how much Mum and Grandma were arguing and he'd have sympathised. But no, he had to come all the way here and force me into a confession I didn't want to give.

"Promise me you won't go there. I don't care if he likes you. I take back what I said earlier. You cannot date a sixteen-year-old, especially not him."

I'd known that but hearing my brother say it made it feel ten times worse.

"Okay, I promise."

You know promising your brother something like that is only going to get you in trouble.

I told my brain where to go. Jonah was only trying to keep me safe even if he was slightly irrational about this subject. It was for good reason.

Are you really going to let your brother's fears ruin your chance of a relationship with someone who might actually genuinely like and care about you?

Apparently, I was.

"Good… now, how about I take you to dinner as a treat? Then we don't have to go home."

I nodded, knowing the subject of Cole Carter and him liking me was at an end. Spilling the beans to my brother hadn't made me feel any better. It only made me all the more conflicted and confused.

"Sure."

I found my heart wasn't really in spending time with my brother any longer. I loved Jonah to bits but him projecting his own issues on me didn't sit well. And now I'd fucked myself over by making a promise to him I knew for a fact I was going to break.

I think I might actually be attracted to Cole. I want the chance to explore it.

Admitting it to myself just made my heart ache like a bitch.

Fuck.

CHAPTER NINE

Cole

I t took a week for her to come looking for me. An entire week of me wondering if I'd pushed her too hard, or if she really wasn't interested in me. I was beginning to think I'd have to go to her myself. Giving her time hadn't been me throwing in the towel. It was to see if she'd come to me or if I had to give her more incentive.

I sat on the benches outside with some older kids who were, admittedly, troublemakers. Half of them vaped, all of them drank and I won't even go there with the drug use. I didn't do any of that and yet they saw me as one of their own. Probably because of the number of times I'd caused problems for other kids at school.

My attention was on my phone and not on my surroundings or listening to the chatter. It's only when everyone fell silent I looked up. Standing there with her strawberry blonde hair braided down one side of her head and her green eyes cautious was Meredith.

"Can we help you?" Davey, who was sitting to my left, asked, his eyes narrowing on the girl in front of us.

"You can't," Meredith retorted.

I stifled a smile. The girl didn't take any prisoners. She'd certainly put Davey in his place if he started on her. It's me she failed to do so with. I didn't back down. Pushing her buttons gave me some kind of sick thrill.

Meredith's eyes fell on me and her expression grew darker. "Can I talk to you?"

I rose from my seat on the benches slowly, watching her crane her head up to keep eye contact. I could tell the guys were staring at me like 'why the fuck does Meredith Pope want to talk to you', but I didn't have to answer to them.

"Do you want to go somewhere more… private?"

"Yes."

I indicated across the playground towards where the sixth form block was.

"Let's go then."

Feeling the stares at my back, I set off with Meredith next to me. She held her head up although her eyes darted around as if checking if anyone was looking at us. I could've told her no one would care, but I doubted she'd listen. She steered me away from the main part of the sixth form building and instead, making a beeline for a quieter area near the trees. When we were out of sight, she turned to me, her face void of any emotion. It made me wonder what she wanted. She fidgeted for a long moment as if trying to gather her thoughts.

"You wanted to talk to me?" I said when she didn't volunteer anything.

"Yes."

"About what?"

Her gaze flicked away from me, fixating on the tree behind me.

"I need to know if you meant it."

"Meant what?"

I had a feeling I knew what she was getting at. Didn't mean I would let her get away with not spelling it out for me.

"About wanting me."

"Meredith."

"Yes?"

"Look at me."

This shy and timid girl in front of me was not what I'd expected. In fact, this entire situation was not how I expected any of this to go down. Where was the passionate girl who spit fire at me and everyone else she came into contact with?

She met my eyes and I could see vulnerability in those green depths. Something about it made my heart thump. I took a step forward, reaching out and placing a finger under her chin before I tipped her face up.

"I was entirely serious then and I still am now."

She rubbed her arm with her hand.

"And this isn't just about getting me into bed or anything like that?"

"No."

It never had been. I wouldn't deny I wanted to be between her legs. Hell, the thought of it made me fucking hard. But I'd never pursue a girl for that reason alone. No, my need for Meredith ran so much deeper than that. I wanted in her head. To understand her. And I wanted to make her submit to me.

"So you actually… like me?"

"I thought I made that clear."

"No, you said you wanted me. That's not the same thing."

I cocked my head to the side, trying to understand the motivations of this girl in front of me. Understand why she needed me to state the obvious.

"I like you, Meredith."

She let out a breath. Her hand clutched her arm as if she wanted to reach for me but held herself back.

"You know my secret… I've never been with anyone before."

"That changes nothing for me."

Her eyes searched my face.

"No, I suppose it wouldn't. Better for you if I have nothing to compare it to."

I almost laughed. As much as I relished the thought of being her first, ultimately, I didn't give a shit either way. I'd have made sure the only person in her mind and her body was me. I'd have erased the memory of anyone else. This way, I didn't have to go through that bullshit. I could make her mine and that would be fucking that.

"Are you saying you want me to…?"

Her eyes widened.

"What? No! Jesus, I'm not going to let you have sex with me, Cole."

I smiled, knowing she hadn't meant to insinuate she would in the first place.

"Why are you here asking me if I like you then?"

"I needed to know."

"Why?"

Her eyes flashed. Those damning eyes I couldn't get enough of.

My little queen. So beautiful. So strong-willed.

"I just do, okay?"

"Now who's not giving straight answers?"

Meredith's eyes scanned the area before she let out a huff.

"I should not be doing this."

"Doing what exactly?"

She waved a hand between us.

"Standing here talking to you like this."

"I didn't realise talking to me was such a crime."

The way her face contorted with irritation amused me.

"Why did I even think this would be a good idea? You're obviously not going to take me seriously and if that's the case, this is so not worth the fucking fallout it will inevitably bring down on me."

I reached out, snagged her arm and pulled her closer. She blinked and tried to back away. My voice pitched low and my grip on her tightened, "You haven't even told me what this is about, Meredith. So don't you start flying off the handle with me."

She glared at me, but it didn't stop me holding onto her to make sure she didn't run away. This girl was going to tell me why she brought me over here in the first place whether or not she liked it.

"I came to tell you I'd let you prove to me why I should give you a chance but now, I'm not sure you deserve it."

Oh no, you are not getting away with that shit, Meredith.

"No, I do deserve one and I will show you why."

I backed her up against the tree behind her. My hand curled around her braid and held fast, tugging her head to the side. Leaning down as I pinned her in place, my lips met her earlobe.

"You don't allow boys near you, let alone to touch you in any way shape or form but here I am, right up against you and you're not pushing me away. You want this but you're too fucking chicken shit to admit it."

Her hands came up and clutched my arms.

"Stop. Fucking. Lying. To. Me."

A pant escaped her lips, the sound fucking tormenting me.

"I want you to look me in the eyes and tell me you don't feel this. That you don't want me to touch you, taste you and tease you until you're a panting, writhing mess beneath me. Because that's where you fucking belong. Under me."

The more I ran my mouth, the more I could feel her arching closer as if she wanted it all.

"I'm not a nice boy, Meredith. I think dark, deviant and downright depraved things about you but I will treat you right. The way you *need*."

"You make it sound like all you want to do is *fuck* me."

Grazing my teeth along the shell of her ear, I pressed closer, feeling her soft, small body mould to my larger one.

"I want inside your head. This isn't some kind of joke or game to me. I want everything about you. I crave it. Let me have you. Let me show you why you need me too."

Another pant left her lips. Those beautiful lips.

"I'll take care of you. If you were mine, you'd be my queen and I'd treat you so fucking well."

The harsh sounds of our breathing filled the silence descending on us as I finished my last words. Meredith's nails dug into my forearms. I didn't tell her to stop. No, I fucking liked it. The sharp points of pain made me ache for her.

"You're actually crazy," she whispered.

"Perhaps."

I pulled back to stare down at her flushed face. Even the tips of her ears were red and it spread across her chest, dipping below her t-shirt. I couldn't help smiling. This wasn't anger. I recognised that in her all too well. No, Meredith found this arousing. The glazed-over look in her eyes painted the picture for me.

"Tell me you don't want me and I'll leave you alone."

"I…"

"You can't do it."

Her tongue snaked out, running across her lip.

"You can't tell anyone. Not a single soul, Cole. No one can know. If you promise me that, then I'll give you a chance. One chance so don't waste it."

I was about to open my mouth when she cut me off.

"And just so we're clear, this is not an invitation into my bed or even to kiss me. You want those things? You earn them."

My eyebrow raised. If that's how she wanted to play this, then fine, I'd earn the right to kiss her.

"If you expect me to promise not to tell anyone, I want something in return."

"What?"

My lip curved up at the side.

"Firstly, you are going to tell me why this can't be out in the open. Secondly, no more fucking lying to me. And lastly, this means I have the right to call you mine."

Meredith's eyes narrowed.

"I don't recall signing up for possessive arsehole bullshit."

"Not possessive, just making sure you know who you belong with."

"You're lucky you said belong with and not belong to. I'm not a possession."

I let go of her braid and stroked a finger down her cheek.

"Trust me, I'm aware."

My little queen, I'll only make you kneel and beg when you're ready to submit to me. And I'm going to make you beg so fucking hard.

She chewed on her bottom lip for a long moment.

"I don't like people knowing my private life nor do I want gossip or rumours. So this thing... it's between you and me only."

I was relatively sure that wasn't the whole truth, but something about Meredith's expression told me not to push her too hard. That she was even giving me a chance without putting up a huge fight was a fucking miracle.

"This thing is called a relationship, Meredith."

74

"It remains to be seen whether or not this will be a relationship."

Her fucking smart mouth. I wanted to teach her a lesson, but that wouldn't serve my purposes right now.

"I promise not to tell anyone about us."

She let out a breath.

"I won't lie to you."

"And?"

"I'm not going to see or be with anyone else, you know that."

"Say it, Meredith."

Her eyes darkened and her mouth set in a firm line.

"You're pushing your luck here."

"Say. It."

She loosened her hold on my arms and dropped her hands to curl around my waist, dragging me right up against her.

"If you earn the right to kiss me, Cole Carter, then I'll say it."

The fact she'd initiated contact with me had my body tightening in response. I didn't want her bolting when she realised the effect she had on me. Couldn't help it. She was so beautiful and made me ache with need.

"I'm going to hold you to that."

Her lips curled up into a slow smile.

"I know."

"You going to enlighten me as to how I earn your lips?"

Her green eyes sparkled.

"You're a smart boy, work it out."

This girl's mouth really did something to me. And by fucking god did I want to kiss her.

"Fine, be ready on Friday after school."

"For what?"

"For me to show you exactly why you won't regret giving me a chance."

You're mine, little queen. All. Mine.

CHAPTER TEN

Meredith

I had to ask myself repeatedly what the hell I'd been doing when I'd made the promise to my brother not to get involved with Cole. It'd been a stupid thing to do. I knew going out with Cole behind my brother's back would only lead to trouble. And my justification for breaking my promise? Jonah didn't get to run my life nor tell me who I could and could not spend time with. At eighteen, I was an adult and could make my own decisions. And if those decisions had led me into the arms of a sixteen-year-old, I'd have to deal with the consequences of my actions. Besides, I was merely giving Cole a chance to prove he was actually serious about me.

I had asked Cole why Friday considering I knew his family had mandatory dinners then. He told me not to worry. And when I had Raphi telling me his parents would love it if I attended again, I had a feeling that boy had played a hand in securing me an invite. Cole knew how to get his way, but I wouldn't be letting him run circles around me. He had to show me he was worth my time and energy.

The three of us had been picked up by Ash this time. She made small talk all the way back to their house whilst I sat watching Cole sitting up beside her. His smirk drove me insane. He knew I was staring at him. It's like the moment I stopped lying about my attraction to him, I couldn't stop seeking him out with my eyes. In the library yesterday, he'd sat on the same table as me a few seats down. My ability to concentrate on my work got completely shot to pieces. It was lucky Raphi didn't have the same free lesson as me on Thursdays or he'd have commented on me staring at his brother the whole time. He could not find out I'd got involved with Cole.

The minute we got in the house, their mother disappeared, leaving the three of us standing in the hallway.

"You mind if I steal Meredith to help me with my English homework?" Cole said to Raphi who stared at his brother like he'd grown an extra head.

"I don't get you and your insistence on doing homework on Fridays, it's basically the weekend."

Cole shrugged.

"Exams are coming up soon, so, you know, don't want Quinn on my case for getting bad results."

Raphi snorted and waved at us.

"Ask Mer, not me. I'd rather not get stuck helping you anyway."

Cole turned and winked at me.

"You want to be a Good Samaritan?"

I wanted to roll my eyes and shake my head, but I refrained.

"Fine, I guess I don't mind if you're *that* desperate."

"Just don't piss her off," Raphi said. "I'll be in the games room if you get bored with helping grumpy here."

He gave me a warm smile before ambling off away down the hall towards the back of the house. Cole had a sly smile on his face when I turned to him.

"This is your master plan? Doing homework?" I asked when Raphi was out of earshot.

"As if we're actually going to do homework."

He took me by the hand and pulled me down the other hallway. I stared up at him as we walked. His beautiful profile and the way his hair fell in his eyes but he didn't push it out of his face. Okay, I had it real bad for Cole Carter, however, he didn't need to know that.

He shut the door when we got in his room. I glanced around as I hadn't looked when he'd dragged me in here last time. It was full of posters of cars and motorbikes. He had shelves full of random car parts and models, a desk and his bed sat on the opposite wall to the big bay windows facing out onto their garden.

"Are you even allowed girls in your room with the door closed?"

He raised an eyebrow as he dropped my hand.

"I'm not a child, Meredith."

"Could've fooled me."

He was on me the next moment, backing me up against the wall as his very solid body pressed up against mine. His hand was on my side, fingers stroking just above where my t-shirt met my knee-length pale green skirt. I almost choked out a breath when his fingertips curled underneath and brushed across my bare skin. Cole's eyes darkened when they met mine. He stared down at me with no small amount of smug satisfaction written all across his features. This boy knew exactly what he did to me and I couldn't lie about it either. He'd made me promise not to.

"You were saying?"

"You're definitely not a child."

"No?"

I shook my head. Cole reached up and ran the pad of his thumb over my bottom lip. I wanted to lick his skin but I refrained. He leant closer, making my breath hitch. There was no way in hell I'd let him kiss me right now. He knew he had to work for it.

"Cole."

He paused in his descent, waiting for me to elaborate.

"No."

His eyes searched mine for a long moment. Then he dropped his hands from me and straightened. I clenched my fist to stop my body bowing towards his as it sought his body heat.

He stopped. Fuck. This only makes me want him all the more.

Despite never having been touched intimately before, my body knew exactly what it craved. And it was Cole Carter's hands and lips on every inch.

"You look beautiful today," he murmured as he took my hand and pulled it up to his mouth, placing a soft kiss to my knuckles.

"Thank you."

He smiled and pulled me away from the wall. My eyes roamed around his room again, wondering if I should ask him about all the car stuff. I did want to get to know him. Then again, there was something else bugging me about how he'd set this up.

"You know, you can't keep getting me invited around for dinner. Raphi will get suspicious not to mention the rest of your family will keep winding him up about it."

"Who said I had anything to do with it?"

I raised an eyebrow.

"Hmm, and I'm supposed to believe your parents just spontaneously decided Raphi should invite me over again?"

The twinkle in his eye told me he had everything to do with it.

"Perhaps."

"Cole, you promised no one would find out about this."

"And no one has."

I let go of his hand and wandered over to his shelves, brushing my fingers over one of the models of what I thought was a Ferrari sitting there.

"We can't stay here until dinner since I'm supposed to be helping you with homework. That doesn't take hours."

"Are you going to spend the whole time worrying about my brother getting suspicious?"

It did concern me. Keeping this from Raphi honestly made me feel worse than I did about hiding it from Jonah. At least my brother was hundreds of miles away. Raphi was right here. That made it all too real to me.

"Can you blame me?"

"Yes, Meredith, I can. I made sure we could spend time together today the best way I could and instead of focusing on that, you're thinking about Raphi."

I flinched. Getting called out by him made me want to turn around and give it back. Except if I did that, we'd end up fighting and that would be pointless when I was meant to be giving Cole a chance.

"You going to tell me about this stuff then?"

A minute later I felt him at my back. Leaning over my shoulder, he reached out and picked up the model I'd been looking at.

"I like cars."

"This seems like more than just liking them."

He let out a breath.

"Yeah… my parents hate me tinkering with their cars. Quinn banned me from touching his midlife crisis."

I looked back at him. The smile he had on his face and the softness of his eyes made him look so young. It made me very aware of our age difference. Even if it was only two years, Cole wasn't even a legal adult yet. I swallowed, realising I didn't care. Something about this boy got under my skin.

"Midlife crisis?"

"His Lamborghini. Mum and my dads bought it for his fiftieth birthday. He won't let anyone else drive it and I'm certainly not allowed under the bonnet."

Cole placed the Ferrari model back on the shelf.

"Is that what you want to do? Work with cars?"

"It's what I plan to do at college or maybe I'll go for an apprenticeship. Haven't exactly decided yet."

I touched my hand to one of the parts on his shelf, finding the metal cold.

"I can see it… you with oil-stained fingers, all sweaty from working with cars all day."

"I'd rather be sweaty for a different reason."

My face felt hot. He totally meant that in a dirty way judging by the seductive note to his voice.

"I'll bet."

He brushed a hand down my side before leaning his chin on top of my head. The way he casually touched me as if it was no big deal had my stomach tightening. I'd never let anyone outside of my family be so familiar with me. Not even Raphi.

"Can I ask you something?"

His hand curled around my waist.

"Yes, that's what we're doing here, Meredith, getting to know each other… isn't it?"

"It is."

"Then ask away."

I leant back into him. Being close to Cole made me feel good.

"Why do all of you only call your biological fathers, Dad, when it seems like they're all father figures to you?"

He was quiet for a long moment. I wondered if asking about his family was off-limits before he let out a sigh.

"Our family is complicated and yet, it's also very simple."

He reached for my hand before stepping away and tugging me over to his bed, making me sit down on the end. Cole walked over to his desk a few feet away and took a seat, turning around to face me. He ran a hand through his hair, spreading his legs as his other hand hung between them. The stance was so casual and yet so... Cole.

"Mum has always been very clear about who our fathers are and how their relationship came into existence. I have a relationship with all four of them, but Rory is my father. He raised me for the most part and it's the same with the others and their dads. We're still one big family, but we're not quite like anyone else's. Does that make sense?"

I nodded. My curiosity about the inner workings of their family was mostly to do with wanting to know more about Cole. There was also the reasoning why Jonah had told me not to get myself too deeply involved. He never explained the whole story to me, but he did mention they were dangerous. So far, I'd seen no evidence to suggest they were anything other than normal. I wanted to give them the benefit of the doubt since Raphi was my friend and Cole was... well... I don't know what we were yet.

"Raphi didn't explain this to you?"

"No," I shrugged. "I guess I never asked him either. After all the shit the four of you have had over it all, it didn't seem appropriate. Didn't want him to think I was judging or anything. I'm not. When I was here last time, it just felt like you were a normal family, you know."

Cole's lips turned up at the corners.

"Normal is the last word I'd use to describe my family. We get shit for it because no one wants to understand how my mum could be with four different men at the same time, not to mention two of them are also in a relationship with each other. They've been together for a long time. There's a love between them you can't manufacture."

I shifted on the bed, realising what he'd admitted.

"Wait, what did you just say? Two of your dads are also together?"

He rolled his eyes, reaching his hands behind his head and lacing his fingers together.

"I suppose that's not public knowledge at school."

"Sorry, I didn't mean to sound like I wasn't taking the rest of what you said seriously. I can see how much they care about each other. I just didn't know about…"

"Eric and Xav? It's not like they hide it or anything, they're just not overt about it. It's why Raphi and Duke are close, or didn't you notice?"

I had, but I'd never thought to ask Raphi why he seemed to gravitate to his older brother more than his other two siblings. It didn't seem like a big deal when I was the same way with Jonah.

"No, Raphi spends more time going on about how you don't like him cramping your style at school than Duke."

Cole threw his head back and laughed. I couldn't help smiling as I watched his throat work and his body shake.

Well, shit. Cole is actually walking sex on legs. How is any girl able to resist him?

Then again, I'd never seen Cole pay attention to a girl or hang out with one. It made me wonder if I was the only one who'd never been with anyone before. And if so, he was awfully confident about himself when it came to me.

"I don't know where he got that idea," Cole said when he finally settled down.

"You've got that whole aloof bad boy thing down to an art."

He leant forward, placing his forearms on his knees and eying me with a raised eyebrow.

"Do I? You got a thing for bad boys, Meredith?"

I leant my hands back on his bed and smiled.

"No, just a thing for you. And you can call me, Mer, you know."

The smirk gracing his lips had me biting mine.

"You admitting it now?"

I shrugged.

"Admitting what?"

"You like me."

I watched Cole stare at my tongue running along my bottom lip with rapt interest.

"If I admit to that, I might get suffocated by your ego expanding to fill the entire room."

I swear his smile got wider. He rolled closer on the wheels of the desk chair until my knees were between his legs.

"That smart mouth of yours is going to get you in so much trouble," he murmured, stroking his fingers along the tops of my knees. "You have no idea what it does to me."

"Oh? Should I be worried?"

His hands flattened against my skirt and he pushed them upwards, making the fabric move with it. My breath hitched and my mind went into overdrive. Cole liked to push the boundaries.

"Very."

"What are you doing?"

My skirt rode halfway up my thighs with his movement. He didn't reply, merely dropped his hand to where he'd exposed the skin and stroked his fingers along the inside of my knee. I swear to god this boy was the most brazen sixteen-year-old I'd ever met in my life. Taking exactly what he wanted and right now, that seemed to be me.

"Cole."

His eyes darkened as they met mine, drawing me into their hazel depths and making me want to keep my mouth shut. Hell, did I want Cole to take control, push me down on his bed and have his wicked way with me. Except I would not let him strip me down and touch me like he wanted to. This wasn't a casual thing to me. I couldn't let my walls down and allow him in without trusting he wouldn't hurt me. Those walls I'd built so high around every part of me after all the shit life had handed to me.

"You really have no idea of your own allure," he all but whispered. "You make me crazy... I want you so fucking bad."

I froze, the memory of Owen telling me how he'd never want me hitting me all at once. The thought of his words made my skin crawl. How could this devastatingly attractive boy in front of me want me? It made no sense. Shouldn't he want a girl his own age? Shouldn't he want a girl who wasn't an eighteen-year-old virgin who people took the piss out of for being ginger?

What is wrong with you? Cole isn't lying to you about wanting you. Stop it.

Before I knew what I was doing, I shoved Cole's hands from me and scrambled back on his bed so I was out of reach. The confusion marring his features made me want to run away and cry. I didn't want him to think I wasn't into what he was doing because I was, but my stupid brain had conjured up one of my worst memories.

No wonder boys are never into you. All you do is ruin things with all your stupid insecurities. Why on earth would Cole want your damage?

CHAPTER ELEVEN

Cole

Meredith looked like she'd seen a fucking ghost. Her face was void of colour and her green eyes were wide like saucers. I had no idea what I'd done wrong or why she'd suddenly pushed me away. Did I take things too far? I wasn't going to touch her any further than I had. I knew better after she'd told me no when I'd wanted to kiss her earlier.

"Meredith?"

She shook her head, curling her arms around herself.

"I can't do this," she whispered.

Those four words made my stomach sink to the floor and my heart lurch.

"Do what?"

"This. With you. I can't… it's too messed up. I'm too fucked up."

Next thing I knew, she'd jumped off my bed and was striding towards the door. I was up and out of my chair, my long legs eating up the space between me, Meredith and the door. I stood in front of it before she got there, preventing her from going anywhere. She couldn't say that and run away.

She froze in front of me, unable to meet my eyes.

"Cole, please let me go."

"No. If you go running off to Raphi now, he'll ask questions and neither of us wants that." I wanted to reach for her, but I wouldn't touch her. What if me doing that had triggered this? "What happened? Did I do something wrong?"

Meredith gripped the bottom of her t-shirt. Tears welled in her eyes. I'd never seen her look so vulnerable before.

Shit. You've really fucked this right up.

"It's not you, it's me. I'm the problem."

Then she burst into tears, burying her face in her hands as her shoulders shook. I stepped forward, helplessness driving through me. The need to comfort her had me lifting my arms, but being unsure she'd accept it, I hovered there in front of her instead.

"I'm sorry, Cole. I'm so sorry."

Why the fuck would she need to apologise to me? She'd done nothing wrong. That decided it for me. I closed the distance and wrapped my arms around her, pulling her into my chest.

"Shh, don't be sorry. It's okay."

I needed to protect this girl from the world. Seeing her this upset brought out all of my instincts to care for the person I thought of as mine. Resting my cheek against the top of her head, I stroked her back, trying my hardest to soothe away the pain she was experiencing.

"I don't know why you're being nice to me," she sobbed, "or... or why you even like me?"

I didn't want to admit this to her whilst she was upset. Tell her how from the very first time I saw her face, it'd been like a shot to the fucking heart. My first day of secondary school at eleven-years-old, I'd noticed Meredith with Raphi and his other friends at break time. And that was that. I had to know who this beautiful girl with strawberry blonde hair and green eyes was. Pestering my brother to tell me only made Raphi suspicious, but he'd relented. After that, I realised she was way out of my league and too old for me. I'd waited patiently for five fucking years until I was sixteen to make my move on this girl. To show her I was worthy of her. I'd make her my queen. Give her everything I had so I could be near her.

Here she was now, in my room, crying her eyes out on my chest like she wasn't worth my time. She was worth every single moment.

"How can I not like you? You're funny and smart, you don't take shit off anyone and you're not afraid to be who you are."

She dropped her hands from her face and clutched my t-shirt instead.

"That's not real. It's an act. I'm afraid of so many things, especially this."

I pulled her face away from my chest and cupped her cheek, wiping away the tears streaking down it. The misery in her eyes made my chest cave in. I wanted to help her, desperately. It's not so much I'd been a heartless piece of shit all my life, but there were only a very few people I gave a crap about. My family, who didn't always understand me but were there for me through thick and thin. And this girl.

"Why?"

"I'm scared if you see what's really inside my head, you'll think I'm too damaged to be with."

Her shoulders deflated as if it was the most honest she'd ever been with anyone in her life.

"You're not the only one with damage. Why would I ever judge you for that?"

"I don't know."

I leant down until we were eye level and forced her to look at me.

"I have absolutely no reason to lie to you and I will never judge you, regardless of what you tell me about yourself."

Her mouth opened and closed, telling me she didn't know what to say.

"This is new for me too, okay? You're not the only one who has no experience."

She blinked, then a smile appeared across her lips. The relief I felt at seeing it was palpable.

"You're awfully confident for someone who hasn't been with a girl before."

I shrugged. You didn't get anywhere in life if you didn't go after what you wanted. My dad told me I shouldn't let anything hold me back. He'd spent years not going after what he really wanted because of his past. Perhaps it made me overconfident, but I took that shit seriously. Life was about risks and taking chances. And I wouldn't let anything get in the way of me being with this girl in front of me.

"I think you like that about me."

"Maybe I do."

I dropped my hand.

"You going to tell me what upset you so much? I don't want to do anything wrong here, so I'd rather know if I caused it."

Her eyes darted away.

"It's not your fault. It's hard for me to accept you want me. People have bullied me over my appearance my whole life. It's made me feel small and it's why I put up such a front around everyone. Stuff happened and it has everything to do with why I don't speak to Celia any longer."

She sighed and rubbed her cheek, clearly uncomfortable talking about this with me.

"I'm really screwed up because of family shit as well. It's hard for me to talk about. I'm not trying to be difficult, but you have to understand, I don't let anyone in for good reason. All people have ever done is hurt me when I have."

I reached out and took her hand, stroking my thumb down the back of hers.

"I can't promise to never hurt you, but I can promise I'm not going anywhere. I genuinely like you."

She nodded and gave me a half-smile. I'd take that.

"Now, let's get you some tissues, then we'll go sit with Raphi until dinner. Maybe he'll let you win Mario Kart this time."

As much as I wanted Meredith to myself, I didn't want to make her uncomfortable or push her too hard. Seeing her vulnerability today told me I had to be careful with how I handled her if I wanted this to work between us. It didn't put me off her at all. It made me want to know Meredith even more.

For now, I'd go slow and prove she could trust me with her truths. Then, when she let me in, I'd make sure she knew she was mine for keeps.

CHAPTER TWELVE

Meredith

I spent the entire way home trying to work out where the hell sensitive and caring Cole had come from. For a boy so overconfident and cocky, he sure had more to him than met the eye. He'd held me whilst I cried and made me feel like I was important to him. Never in my life had I been treated with such kindness from someone who didn't owe me anything.

I'd ended up having a really nice time with his family. After dinner, they'd all gathered together for a family movie night in front of the big screen TV usually reserved for gaming. I'd been in between Cole and Raphi on one sofa, whilst Aurora and Duke sat on the armchairs. Their parents had taken the other sofa with Ash sitting in Quinn's lap, laying her legs across Rory whilst Eric rested his head on Xav's shoulder. I saw what Cole meant by the love between them.

Cole had tugged a blanket over me and held my hand under it the entire time. I'd been worried the others would notice, but no one had. Being included like this made me feel like I wasn't an outsider. I asked Cole if they suspected anything was between us before saying goodbye and he shook his head. I wasn't so sure, but I guess I would have to trust him.

As if you find it easy to trust anyone.

Cole hadn't given me a reason not to. If I was ever to move forward, I couldn't let my past dealings get in the way of this.

I thanked Eric for driving me home before slipping from the car and making my way to my front door. Unlocking it, I walked inside and was met by the sound of the TV blaring in the living room. I stopped in the open doorway, finding Grandma and Mum sitting at opposite ends of the ugly bright pink sofa my mum had insisted on buying. It was garish and didn't fit with anything else in the room, plus it being super uncomfortable to sit on made it ten times worse. Jonah called it the pink monstrosity.

"Hi, Mum, Grandma."

Mum didn't bother acknowledging me, but my grandmother looked up. The frown on her face said it all.

"Is that what you wore to school, Meredith?"

"Um, yes."

I knew what was coming, but it didn't make it hurt any less.

"That skirt is far too short. Diane, you shouldn't be letting your daughter go outside looking like she'll open her legs to any man who says hello."

Mum looked over at me, her pale blue eyes assessing me for mere seconds before they landed back on the TV.

"Meredith, throw that skirt away, it's unbecoming."

I bit the inside of my cheek on a retort. They could never say a nice fucking word about me. No wonder I stayed in my room where their barbs couldn't hurt me.

"Yes, Mum."

I only said it to appease them. The two of them didn't get a say in what I wore. Besides, I liked the way I felt in this skirt. It was flattering to my figure.

Grandma gave me one last scathing look before she turned back to the TV.

I trudged away, going upstairs and shutting myself in my bedroom. Dumping my bag on the floor, I slumped on my bed face first and groaned. They really knew how to ruin my evening.

I heard my phone buzz, so picked myself up and found it in my bag.

Cole: Thinking of you x

I squirmed and lay back against the covers again. One of the hottest boys I'd ever laid eyes on liked me. I tried not to focus too hard on him being only sixteen, even though it made me feel like I was doing something wrong. Especially given the promise I'd made to my brother.

Just don't think about it. Jonah is being unreasonable anyway. He doesn't even know Cole.

At least Cole could distract me from my mum and grandmother's scathing remarks on my dress sense. That had been relatively tame. Yesterday, they told me I looked fat. I had a little cry down the phone to Jonah, who told me in no uncertain terms to ignore them. I wasn't overweight by any means, but it didn't make their comments hurt any less.

Meredith: Does anyone else know you're actually a sweetheart behind closed doors?

I could picture his raised eyebrow and the dark look in his eyes.

Cole: Only for you, so don't go spreading that shit around or I'll have to teach you a lesson.

I dropped my phone on the bed and set about getting ready to slip between the sheets myself. As I brushed my teeth, I tried to think of an appropriate response. What kind of lesson did he have in mind and how would he teach it? The thought of Cole punishing me shouldn't excite me, but somehow it did.

Um, what is wrong with you? That's not exactly normal, is it?

I climbed into bed and picked up my phone, staring down at his message again. He'd be waiting for me to come back with a smart remark no doubt.

Meredith: I take that back. You're not sweet at all.

Cole: Can't be too sweet to you considering you're into bad boys.

Meredith: No, I'm only into you. That you happen to be bad doesn't factor into it.

As soon as I hit send, I regretted it instantly. Now I'd get him gloating over me finally admitting I liked him. He had irrefutable proof.

Cole: You have no idea how much I want to kiss you right now.

My lip got caught between my teeth. We were definitely flirting and I never did that with anyone. What was it about Cole? Why was he so different from everyone else? Maybe since he made me feel beautiful when I was with him. Made me feel… desired.

Meredith: Oh yeah? Just kissing? Sounds rather PG. I thought you had all kinds of dark intentions towards me.

Are you trying to push his buttons?
Was I?
Would he even respond well to that?
I almost hid my face in my hands.

Cole: Trust me, I have every intention of doing very bad things to you.
Meredith: I never said I'd let you.

Cole: You're going to beg for it... for me... maybe I'll give it to you, maybe I won't.

This felt like dangerous territory to be wading into with him. And yet I couldn't stop. Playing with fire when it came to Cole gave me a thrill unlike anything else I'd experienced before.

Meredith: Give what to me?

Cole: You need me to spell it out for you?

Meredith: Maybe...

Cole: It starts with the letter C.

I shook my head. My body felt hot at the thought of Cole giving me his... full attention.

Meredith: Please tell me you haven't named it.

Cole: No, unless you want me to refer to it as Little Cole, but I assure you there's nothing little about it.

Now there was no doubt in my mind. He was talking about his dick and images of us naked, limbs tangled whilst he took my virginity flashed through my head. I squirmed, growing steadily more aroused by our conversation.

Meredith: That's what they all say.

Cole: If you're good, I'll show you I'm telling the truth next time.

Meredith: Hard pass.

Liar, you want to see and touch him.

My phone rang in my hand, making me jump. I looked at the caller ID before answering. The last person I wanted to talk to right now given the conversation I was having with Cole.

"Hey."

"You okay?" my brother asked.

"Other than the witches downstairs telling me I dress like a whore, I'm fine."

"They what?"

"Grandma thinks my knee-length skirt is too short, inviting men to think I want them to sleep with them. I swear she was born in the wrong fucking era."

Jonah snorted.

"And let me guess, Mum told you to get rid of it?"

"Bingo."

I wasn't the only one who got shit from Grandma. Jonah had to put up with her judgemental attitude over his sexuality. She professed not to care, but she made snide remarks about it every time Jonah was home.

"They need to learn to keep their mouths shut."

"Yeah, never going to happen. It's like Grandma raised a clone."

"Are you really okay, Mer?"

I sighed, dragging my hand through my hair as my phone buzzed, signalling I had a text. It would have to wait until I got off the phone with my brother.

"Yeah, just tired. Long day."

Not to mention I ended up crying on the boy I promised you I wouldn't get involved with.

Guilt flooded me. Jonah would be angry and disappointed in me. Not to mention breaking a promise to him would be a betrayal. I was a shit sister. Then again, he shouldn't have made me promise in the first place. Just because he had issues with their family, didn't mean he could stop me from seeing Cole. Not really.

You're trying to justify the fact you're lying to your brother right now.

I told my brain to shove it.

"I worry about you."

"I know. I'm an adult now, J, you don't have to take care of me."

"You're my baby sister, taking care of you is kind of my thing."

The fact Jonah was so sweet made this whole situation that much harder on me. I wish he hadn't used my love for him against me. I wanted to make my brother happy, but it being at the expense of my own? That wasn't fair on either of us.

"Shouldn't you be out partying right now?"

"I can't think of anything worse."

"J, you need to live a little. I get you're still messed up over everything, but you can't spend the rest of your life pining over a straight boy."

The silence on the other end of the phone told me he didn't appreciate my bluntness. He had to suck it up. If he kept up with this shit, he'd never find the right guy.

"I hate that you have a point," he muttered.

"Well, I do talk sense sometimes. But seriously, J, it's been too long. Go out and meet a nice guy, yeah? You deserve to be happy."

"Thanks for the lecture."

"Tough love is the only way."

His chuckle made me smile.

"Fine, my flatmate did invite me out tomorrow night. Maybe I'll go."

"Wait, the player or the straitlaced one?"

Jonah had told me their names but I never used them. Robin and Damien were complete opposites and it caused no end of arguments between them. Jonah had met the boys in first year and only agreed to share a flat with them to save on expenses. I think he regretted the decision now, given how often he heard Robin fucking someone through the thin walls.

"The player."

"Ew, don't go out with him… or maybe do. He could help you loosen up if you know what I mean."

Robin swung both ways according to Jonah.

"Hanging up now!"

"Love you."

"Love you too."

I pulled the phone away from my ear, almost forgetting Cole had replied whilst I'd been talking to Jonah. And when I read it, I was glad I hadn't looked before. All that guilt I felt at lying to my brother came flooding back.

Suck it up. You decided to go behind Jonah's back so you have to deal with the consequences.

Cole: You say that now, but I know you want to see how hard you get me.

I swallowed. This boy had no shame. Also, he was right. I did. Knowing he desired me only made me feel giddy. Cole Carter and his cocky attitude were the perfect recipe to melt me.

Meredith: You have...

Cole: Yes?

Meredith: A dirty mouth.

Cole: You think this is dirty? You have no idea.

Meredith: Oh yeah?

Cole: I'm not sure you're ready for the full extent of my dirty mouth.

To be honest, I wasn't sure either. I could talk a big game, but when it came down to it, I was still a virgin. Sex talk wasn't really my forte.

Meredith: Maybe. Maybe not.

Cole: Trust me, when you are, I'll have you squirming whilst I whisper all the depraved shit I want to do to you in your ear. And when you're begging, I'll give you what you're craving. What you need.

I didn't have a clue how to respond to that. Brazen didn't even cut it. Audacious. Shameless. All the fucking words I could think of for the boldest boy I'd ever met in my life. And I had to admit… I kind of loved everything about it.

Meredith: Goodnight Cole.

Cole: Let me take you out tomorrow.

Meredith: I'll think about it.

Cole: Playing hard to get doesn't suit you. We both know you're going to say yes.

Meredith: Goodnight Cole.

Cole: Sweet dreams, my queen.

I stared at what he'd called me.

His queen?

He'd mentioned treating me like a queen, but I hadn't paid it any mind given everything else he'd said to me. I wasn't his anyway… yet.

I set my phone on its charging stand and curled up under the covers. Every time I attempted to drop off, my mind would conjure up vivid images of Cole and me together. Instead of denying myself, my hand drifted down my body. Cole would never know I'd touched myself whilst thinking about him.

If he knew how much he'd gotten under my skin, I would have no hope.

That boy would dig his way inside me in ways I never imagined possible.

And I'd let him.

CHAPTER THIRTEEN

Cole

I met Meredith in the city centre bright and early so she wouldn't spend the entire time worrying we might run into someone we knew. There'd be less chance of that lost in the millions as opposed to remaining close to Kensington where we both lived. Making sure she didn't bolt and keeping my promise this would remain between the two of us had become my top priorities.

Meredith looked cute today, tucked up in her coat and scarf. The breeze made her cheeks pink as we strolled along the South Bank hand in hand. She'd not appreciated me calling her early to get her up for this date, but I knew once she found out what we were doing, she'd be happy. Meredith wanted to give us a chance despite all of her insecurities and whatever else went on inside her head.

"So, what's on the agenda for today?"

I looked down, finding her head tipped up to me.

"You wanted me to plan something other than hanging out?"

Her eyebrow arched upwards.

"Hanging out? Is that what we're doing? Huh, and here I thought you were trying to date me."

I leant closer.

"I hate to break it to you, but we are dating whether or not you want to label it that."

Her mouth closed and she looked forward again, her cheeks flushing. At least she recognised the fact.

"You're not my boyfriend yet, Cole," she muttered.

I smiled. She'd agree to be my girlfriend, eventually.

"Do you hold hands with every boy who isn't your boyfriend?"

"No, I think you'd get jealous if I did that."

"You're right. I don't want anyone else holding your hand but me."

I watched her bite her lip and her hand tighten in mine.

"And before you get all worked up, I do have plans for us today. I didn't turf you out of bed for no reason."

She looked up at me.

"Yeah?"

I nodded. She looked so damn adorable staring at me with awe written all over her face. It made me want to take her in my arms and kiss that smart mouth of hers.

"I might not be able to take you out for a drink, but I can try to make our dates fun."

It'd be two years before I could take Meredith out to a bar or anything like that. The disparity in our ages was made clear by the fact she could legally drink and I couldn't. She was an adult and I was still considered a child. Wouldn't stop me from being with her as long as she didn't run because of it.

We arrived outside the National Theatre and Meredith stared up at it with a smile. She turned to me with confusion.

"Why are we stopping?"

"We're going on a backstage tour."

Her eyes went wide.

"What?"

"Come on."

I dragged her towards the entrance.

"No, but seriously, Cole, what did you just say?"

"We're going on a backstage tour, so you can see behind the scenes and all that."

"Is that why we had to get here so early?"

I smiled and dropped her hand to wrap an arm around her and press my face into her hair.

"Yes. I know you like this kind of thing."

She fisted my jacket in her hand, drawing me closer.

"Cole... I don't know what to say."

"All you have to do is enjoy it."

When she'd given me a chance, I'd spent a long time looking at places I could take her. The thing I knew Meredith loved was the theatre, so giving her this seemed apt even if I had no idea whether or not she'd been before. Judging by her reaction, she hadn't.

"Thank you."

She let me lead her into the building and find where the tour started. Meredith had the biggest smile on her face. It made planning this and getting up early worthwhile.

Whilst we toured the theatre, she looked around with rapt interest and asked the guide a ton of questions. I don't think I'd ever seen her so animated about anything. Meredith was usually either cutting people down with her smart mouth or remaining as far away from others as she could. Here, she was open and free. Her smiles were genuine and easy. The appreciation she had for me bringing her here written all over her face.

What a fucking sight to behold.

Nothing could prepare me for this feeling in my chest. I made this moment possible. It wasn't me bullshitting to get what I wanted or telling her what to do, although I couldn't wait for when I could indulge in the latter.

"You okay?" she asked as we were looking at the set being built for a new show.

"Yeah."

"I know it's not that interesting."

I took her hand and gave it a squeeze.

"I'm not bored. Besides, making you happy is all I want."

Her green eyes softened.

"I am happy. It's just…"

"Just what?"

She shrugged and looked away.

"Being here reminds me of my dad."

I knew from Raphi her dad had died four years ago from a heart attack.

"He brought me here when I was younger. We always used to see plays together. It was our thing... I miss him."

The sadness lacing her tone made my heart hurt. Losing him must've hurt her deeply.

"Is that why you want to do this for a living?"

"Yeah. I've always liked painting and designing. I used to drive my brother crazy by insisting on making all these little backdrops, then stealing his Lego men to perform plays with them."

Her expression became pained when she mentioned her brother. She shook it off the next moment but something about it bothered me.

"Siblings, eh?"

She chuckled.

"Yeah, though you must have it worse with three."

I shrugged and reached out for her hand, lacing our fingers together. The tour was moving on, so we followed the group.

"Sometimes, but being the baby has its perks."

"Oh, I'm sure... didn't Raphi call you a mummy's boy?"

I scowled. My damn brother. Meredith hadn't yet seen me interact with my parents other than at dinner. My dad asked me about her the first time she'd come over. I hadn't told him what happened between us in my room, despite his questions. I'm sure he knew I liked her, even if it wasn't obvious to anyone else. He had a way of seeing right through me, which meant I couldn't hide a single thing from him. Plus, it didn't help how alike we were.

"Yes."

"It's okay, I was a daddy's girl until…" her voice got all small and distant as she trailed off.

I squeezed her hand, not wanting her to be upset. We were silent as the guide explained something about the stage we were standing on, but my attention was on Meredith. Her green eyes were full of unspoken emotions. Sadness. Regret. I wanted to soothe her. I just didn't know how when we were surrounded by people.

She visibly shook herself the next moment and smiled up at me, obviously trying to hide her emotions from me. I wasn't fooled but pressing the matter wouldn't help. Instead, I leant down and pressed my lips to her hair, reassuring her it was okay.

When the tour was over, the two of us walked over to the railings by the Thames and looked out across the water towards the other side. I wrapped an arm around her waist, drawing her closer to me since it was cold. She tucked herself between me and the railing, letting me wrap my arms around her.

"Thank you for this. It was amazing to get to see behind the scenes. One day that'll be me back there… I hope anyway."

"It will be. I know you'll succeed."

She didn't speak, just tilted her head back and stared up at me. This girl fit so perfectly to me. I thought I might have more of an uphill battle to get Meredith to date me. It wouldn't have stopped me anyway. Nothing would. Meredith was mine. No one else could have her. Getting to know more about her only made me all the more certain. I'd got past the tough girl act and saw the real girl inside. The one who had vulnerabilities and insecurities. The raw and emotional Meredith who was scared to let anyone else in.

"I never imagined you'd be like this."

I raised an eyebrow.

"Like what?"

"Thoughtful, kind, a good listener."

I grinned.

"It may come as a surprise, but I'm not actually a dick, Meredith. And that stuff… I get it from my dad."

"I never thought you were a dick. Arrogant and cocky are the words which spring to mind."

"I won't dispute that."

She lowered her head down again, staring out across the water.

"You're lucky I like those things about you."

Leaning down, I nuzzled her ear, making her squirm.

"So you weren't lying when you said you're into me last night. Tell me what else you like."

Her hand curled around my arm situated across her chest.

"I'll have to add narcissism to the list of not so sexy attributes."

I chuckled.

"I'll happily list everything I like about you in exchange."

"You're like a dog with a bone… that's another thing to go on the minus list."

"Just tell me."

She turned around in my arms and stared up at me, those green eyes telling me she wasn't particularly impressed right now.

"Fine." She waved a hand at me. "You're very attractive. Like out of my league attractive and you can spare me the 'oh, am I? I hadn't noticed' routine. I don't think any of your parents would be capable of making ugly babies."

"Out of your league?"

"Yes, Cole. You are way, way out of my league, which is why I've had a hard time understanding what it is you see in me."

I raised an eyebrow. She was right. I did notice the way girls looked at me like I was a piece of meat they wanted to devour. I knew I was a good-looking boy, but she failed to see she was just as attractive as me if not more.

"What I see in you? Meredith, I've told you already, you're beautiful, like so fucking beautiful it drives me crazy every time I look at you." I leant closer, staring into her eyes so she could see the truth of my words. "I like that you're smart, outspoken and so fucking brave. You take risks even if they could backfire on you. And the way you've opened up to me, showing me who you really are, fuck, that makes you all the more stunning inside and out."

Her lips parted, a small exhale escaping them.

"I'm not out of your league. If anything you're out of mine, but I don't give a shit. You call me arrogant and cocky, I call it knowing what I want and going after it. I want you and if we weren't in public right now, I'd show you exactly how much."

She swallowed and closed her mouth. Perhaps I'd been a little intense, but she needed to know how much I desired her. How much I wanted to make her mine completely. Every part of her. It wasn't about how much I wanted to ravage her either. Protecting her was just as important. Making sure she was happy and cared for. Giving her everything she needed.

I wanted to be Meredith's friend, confidant, protector and lover.

If only she could see how serious I am about her.

I'd have to prove it to her over and over again until she got it into her head.

"Now, it's chilly as fuck out today so why don't we go grab a hot drink, hey?"

She nodded slowly. Pulling away, I took her hand and pulled her along the South Bank. Determined to make sure the rest of our date would show Meredith I wasn't fucking about. She and I were going to be together as a couple. She just had to catch up and get on board with it.

CHAPTER FOURTEEN

Meredith

The rest of Cole and I's date was spent in a coffee shop exchanging stories about our childhoods and not addressing what he'd said to me after the tour of the theatre. The intensity of his words and the look in his eyes told me he was very serious about me. I couldn't keep pushing back against him and letting my insecurities ruin this. No matter how much trouble being with Cole could cause me, especially when Jonah found out, I wanted to make it work. I wanted this with him. To be… his.

After we'd had a spot of lunch, we headed back to Kensington on the tube. I didn't want our date to end and was happy when Cole decided he'd walk me home. He'd made me feel special today, especially choosing to take me on a backstage tour. Of all the things he could've picked, that was the very last thing I expected.

"You worried about your exams?" I asked as we walked up my street.

Exam season would be on upon us soon.

"No, I'll do fine. Not almost top of the class for no reason."

I smiled. Not sure what else I expected as a response. Cole didn't seem to let anything faze him in life.

"There's that arrogance again."

"What you call arrogant, I call confident in my own abilities."

"Oh yeah? Then why aren't you top of the class?"

He looked down at me, his hazel eyes darkening.

"Don't need to be."

"It'd tarnish your bad boy persona, that's why."

For a moment, I thought he might snap back at me for that. Instead, he threw back his head and laughed.

"Can't have that or you wouldn't like me anymore."

I shoved him in the shoulder with my free hand.

"Shut up, I'm not that shallow."

His eyebrow rose.

"No? Is that not why you're into me? For my... what did you say earlier... out of your league attractiveness?"

I scowled.

"No, Cole, I like you for you. The outer package is a bonus as far as I'm concerned."

He leant closer and waved a hand at himself.

"More than a bonus when the only person in this world who gets all of this is you."

I bit my lip, pulling him to a halt as we reached my house.

"Is that supposed to make me feel grateful?"

"Very."

"You are so…"

I fought to find the right words. He made it difficult to fit him in a box. Cole was like a walking contradiction. He could be so bloody cocky, but he didn't make me feel as though my insecurities were invalid. He fought against them by showing me they were baseless. For all his arrogance and pushiness, he'd respected my wishes about not telling anyone about us and giving me time to come to terms with us. Showing me I didn't need to be scared of what we were.

"I'm so what, Meredith?"

He stepped closer to me, his hand coming up to cup the back of my head.

"Everything you never knew you needed?" he continued.

"Yes," I whispered. "That."

His face moved closer until his lips were inches from mine.

"You can say no."

After our near-perfect date, I wanted him to kiss me. It had nothing to do with never having been kissed or needing to get it over with and everything to do with wanting the boy in front of me.

You make me feel alive, Cole Carter. I've never wanted anything as much as I want you.

"Cole."

"Yeah?"

"Stop talking and kiss me."

The way his hazel eyes darkened set my blood on fire, but it was nothing compared to the way my lips tingled in anticipation. His hand at the back of my neck, stroked across my skin, making me want to arch into him.

The press of his mouth against mine sent a spark of pleasure down my spine. His lips were soft, moulding against mine as he moved them ever so gently, testing the waters. This was, after all, the first time either of us had experienced a kiss. It was everything and nothing like I expected. The feelings exploding in my chest over having *him* kiss me almost overwhelmed all my senses. Cole showed me with that simple touch just how much he wanted this. Wanted me. Wanted us.

I wanted it to go on and on, so when he pulled back, my mouth followed his, my body swaying forward. I put my hands out, steadying myself against him. It wasn't enough. No, I wanted more of Cole's mouth against mine. I needed to explore every inch of him.

"Do you want to come in?"

The words came out in a rush. My need to keep him here bulldozing any of my fears about what this meant. How letting this boy kiss me would change everything irrevocably. How I set us on a path neither of us expected to walk down.

"Yes."

There was no hesitation on his part. His eyes searched mine all the same as if making sure I was serious. There was no way in hell I was inviting him in so we could sleep together. This was entirely about wanting to kiss him in the privacy of my bedroom where my neighbours wouldn't be looking out and getting an eyeful.

Cole let me go and I dug around in my bag for my house key. I unlocked the door and the two of us walked in, shutting it behind us.

"Um, wait here a sec. Just need to check where my mum and Grandma are."

I didn't wait for his response, walking down the hallway and checking the living room finding it unoccupied. Carrying along the hall, I went into the kitchen and discovered they'd rubbed the note I left on the fridge away, replacing it with something else.

Gone to Leonard's. Your mum is out with the girls. Sort your own dinner out. Grandma.

My grandmother was visiting her 'friend' who I knew was actually her boyfriend. I rolled my eyes before backtracking back into the hall. Cole stood waiting, his eyes roaming across me in a distinctly predatory way. It made me shiver.

"We have the place to ourselves," I shrugged.

I only had to reach out my hand for him to take it. Leading him towards the stairs, we went up together. I pushed open my bedroom door and noted the way he looked around, taking everything in. Closing the door, I slipped out of my shoes and took off my coat, hanging it over the back of my desk chair, placing my bag down with it. I put my hand out and he took off his coat, giving it to me. I turned away and placed it on top of mine.

Cole was at my back the next moment, leaning down as his hands curled around my waist. His breath fluttered against my neck, making my skin prickle.

"I think you owe me something, Meredith."

"What's that?"

"Did you forget what you promised if you let me kiss you?"

I shivered. I couldn't forget. Saying those words felt dangerous. Admitting this was real out loud meant I really had broken my promise to my brother. Cole had no idea what I'd risked for him. How much trouble it would cause when Jonah found out. And there was no doubt in my mind he would.

"No, I didn't."

"Say it."

He planted his lips on my neck, pulling a gasp from my lips.

"Cole…"

"Say. It."

He went from gentle and sweet to demanding so quickly. I couldn't help the way it made me ache for more of his commands.

"You want me to kiss you again. That's why you asked me in. You tell me what I want to hear and I'll give you what you want."

I turned in his embrace, planting my hand on his chest as I stared up into his eyes brimming with repressed desire. It didn't scare me knowing how much Cole wanted me.

"I… I'm yours," I whispered.

I didn't think his eyes could get any darker but they did.

"What does that make me?"

"My boyfriend."

My heart tightened at the words escaping my lips.

"And what does it make you?"

"Your girlfriend."

"That's right, little queen… you are mine."

I don't know why those words made me swoon inside, but they did. Especially when he flattened a palm across my back and pulled me against him. I could feel every inch of his body and it was fucking glorious.

When he leant down and claimed my mouth, my hands travelled upwards and wrapped around his neck. Cole's free one was in my hair, directing how this would go. This time he wasn't gentle. He kissed me like he meant every swipe of his mouth against mine. Every touch of our lips drove me higher until I was clutching him, drowning in the intensity of his kiss.

"Cole," I moaned against his mouth, unable to help myself.

He took that as an invitation to part my lips with his tongue and delve inside my mouth. At first, it was a little messy as we attempted to find some kind of natural rhythm. He tasted faintly of mint, tea and something else I couldn't put my finger on.

He backed me away towards my bed whilst our tongues tangled and our hands grasped each other. I landed with my back on the mattress and him on top of me. Neither of us wanted to let go. Cole's mouth left mine and trailed down my neck, making me tremble below him. My fingers dug into his shoulders, desperate for more of this feeling. More of him.

"Don't stop," I panted, my rationality leaving me completely.

"What do you want?" he murmured against my skin.

"You."

"You already have me. Be specific."

He'd barely touched me, only lightly pressing his body to mine with one hand planted by our heads and the other in my hair. I needed more but I wasn't ready for it. For everything with him. Despite wanting Cole with such desperation, it drove me crazy, so much played on repeat in the back of my mind. My insecurities about myself and my appearance. My broken promise to my brother. Cole being only sixteen. None of this was easy or simple.

"I don't know what I want."

"I think you do, you're just scared to ask for it."

I hated him for being right. This thing with him terrified me. Trust didn't come easy to me. I'd never let anyone in, but Cole chipped his way through my walls, shattering them one by one.

"I'm not ready," I whispered.

"I wasn't under any illusions you were ready for *that*." He shifted back, staring down at me as he stroked my face with one finger. "Trust me, I'm not expecting anything here. It doesn't matter how much I want you, it's your decision if and when you want to go further."

"Then what am I scared of asking you for?"

His lip curved up at one side.

"You want me to touch you."

I licked my own lip since I didn't have an answer to that. Lying to Cole would be stupid. He'd see right through it and I'd told him no more lies.

"I won't unless you ask for it, Meredith."

"What if I want you to take away those decisions for me?"

He eyed me for a long moment.

"You want to give me control?"

I nodded. If Cole took the decision out of my hands, I wouldn't feel so conflicted about what we were doing. He knew very well I wanted him but my fears kept me from asking for everything.

"You have no idea how tempting that is, but I can't. Not yet. Not until you're fully in this with me. That means you have to make the decision."

He leant down and pressed his lips to mine briefly before he shifted off me. Cole lay on his side and stroked his fingers down the centre of my chest, making me swallow hard as I watched his progress to my stomach. He stopped just above my jeans and didn't move any further.

"Tell me why you're scared."

"Of what?"

"All of this. What made you so scared of having a relationship?"

I stiffened then exhaled as he laid his hand across my stomach, stroking his fingers along the strip of skin exposed where my blouse had ridden up.

"Celia did."

His eyebrow raised. I felt stupid. My supposed best friend had all but destroyed me the week before we went back to school. Her revelation had rocked me to my very core. I should've seen it coming, but I'd trusted her.

You were a fool to think she wasn't a horrible person.

All the signs had been there, but I'd ignored them as her mean streak was never directed at me. Until it was.

"What did she do to you?"

"She… lied to me, made a boy humiliate me when we were sixteen, all the while pretending she had nothing to do with it and a multitude of other horrible things to make me feel nothing but small and insignificant."

My heart fractured at the memories. They seemed so stupid now, but they'd given me a complex about myself. It was bad enough that ever since Dad died, Mum and Grandma had done nothing but make me feel shit about myself, but to have this on top of it. Well, it was the icing on the cake.

"We were at this party when we were sixteen, playing spin the bottle and because I was embarrassed about never having kissed anyone, I didn't want to do it in front of people. So, we went in a cupboard, me and Owen Blackburn, but instead of kissing me, he told me no boy could ever be attracted to me because I'm a ginger bitch who thinks she's better than anyone else. And he'd rather kiss Amanda Phelps than touch me with a bargepole. Then he forced me to lie about it by saying he'd spread it around that I was a prude if I told anyone the truth."

My eyes were focused on Cole's hand so I didn't have to look at his expression.

"It sounds so childish now and it was, but it really hurt me. I've already been bullied for being a redhead most of my life so I guess I took his words to heart. And it was made worse when I found out two years later Celia had told him to say those things to me as she knew exactly what would hurt me the most."

I took a breath, trying to hold back the tears springing behind my eyelids as I closed them. Explaining the truth would never be easy, but Cole wouldn't understand why I was so fucked up about myself unless I did.

"You see, the thing is ever since my dad died four years ago, my mum and grandma have done nothing but say nasty things to me about my appearance, calling me fat and unattractive. They even accuse me of wearing certain things to be deliberately provocative towards men since I can't attract them any other way. Celia knows this and she used it against me out of jealousy."

I opened my eyes and finally turned my head to look at Cole. His eyes were dark with anger but there was also compassion there.

"I ignore Mum and Grandma most of the time, but their barbs get to me. It's why it's been harder for me since Jonah left for university. He used to protect me from it, but he's not here any longer. And after Celia revealed what a backstabbing bitch she is, I felt so alone. The only person who's been there for me since it happened is your brother. Raphi and I have always been casual friends, but when I broke down and told him about Celia, we became closer. He helped me with it all."

It would never be anything more than friendship between the two of us. Not least because Raphi had some history with my brother. One day, I'd get the full details of what happened out of Jonah. Until then, I was reserving judgement on the whole situation.

Cole raised his hand from my stomach, cupping my face and turning it fully towards him. Then he leant down and pressed his forehead to mine. My lips parted as I waited for him to speak. My heart hammered wildly in my chest. I'd admitted my darkest secrets to him. I had no idea how he felt about any of it, but I knew telling him was the right thing to do. The only thing I could do in this situation. If I was ever going to move past this shit, then I had to let someone in. And I wanted it to be Cole Carter. The boy who'd swept me off my feet with his cocky attitude and innate kindness. He was who I wanted to give everything to.

"I'm sorry you have to deal with that shit. No one should put you down like that. If they can't see this intelligent girl who's so full of life in front of me, then they aren't worth your time or energy. They don't deserve you."

CHAPTER FIFTEEN

Cole

The knowledge of what Meredith had to go through cut me deeply. No one should ever make her feel small or give her a complex about her own worth. If I ever met her mother and grandmother, I'm not sure I could refrain from giving them hell for treating her the way they did. Not to mention fucking Celia. Now more than ever I wanted to give that girl a taste of her own medicine. Duke chucking her after he was done wasn't enough. No, Celia needed to be punished for the way she'd treated *my girl*.

Meredith was fucking well mine. She'd admitted it. Confirmed we were a couple. I would stop at nothing to destroy the people who'd tried to tear her down.

Then again, I had made sure Celia wouldn't say another word about Meredith. I doubted my girl wanted nor needed me to do anything else. She didn't seem like she wanted revenge, just to move on with her life. And I would not be responsible for bringing more trouble to her door.

I stroked her cheek, keeping my forehead pressed to hers. Reassuring her I was here for her now. She never had to be afraid again. I'd be her protector.

"Thank you for telling me. You don't have to be alone anymore. I'm right here," I told her. "I'll always be here."

Her bottom lip trembled. Fuck, her lips. Kissing her had been the single greatest moment of my life. She tasted sweet with a hint of cinnamon from the chai latte she'd consumed earlier. And as much as I wanted to relieve the intolerable ache touching her brought on, it was her decision. She had to take the first step. Only when Meredith was ready would I strip her bare and sink into her.

"I never thought you'd be so… understanding."

"Why wouldn't I understand? It's not your fault people have decided to be dickheads towards you. That's on them."

Her eyes searched mine. Whatever she saw there had her rolling over, her hands pressed to my chest as she shoved me on my back. I didn't stop her when she leant over and kissed me. My hands went to her hair despite wanting to run them down her body. My fingers itched to touch every inch of her. Kissing had to be enough.

Her hand landed on my chest and stroked downwards as if exploring the contours of my body. I held back from groaning at her touch. Meredith had no idea how much self-restraint I had to exert right then. Every part of me screamed to take her hand and press it to me so she could feel how hard I was for her. The torment never ended when I was in her presence. It was already bad enough outside of it when I was alone with thoughts of her.

Her hand curled under my t-shirt, stroking across my bare stomach. I didn't hold back a moan then. My hand dropped from her hair, skimming down her shoulder and stroking across her collarbone. It only made her press closer as if starved of my touch.

Fuck, stop tempting me, little queen.

She was mine to take if I wanted. And I wanted so fucking bad.

"Meredith, you have to stop," I all but panted against her lips.

She drew back an inch, staring at me with fully dilated pupils. I'd messed up her hair a little with my hands in it and her face was flushed.

"What's wrong?"

"Nothing's wrong. You're merely testing my self-restraint to its limits."

She remained still for a moment then a smile spread across her face. She looked down my body towards where the obvious state of my arousal strained against my zipper.

"So I see."

"Is my discomfort funny to you?"

Her eyes snapped back to mine.

"No, Not funny. Did you want me to help you with that?"

My eyebrows shot up.

"Help me how?"

Her blush spread down her chest in the most adorable fucking way.

"I… well…"

I reached down and pried her hand off my stomach pulling it down and hovering it over my confined cock.

"I told you I'd show you it's not small."

"Cole…"

I lifted my hand off hers.

"I'm not going to make you do anything. I told you, this is your choice."

Her eyes had turned a vibrant green with her obvious desire for me. I could see it in her expression even if she also felt scared.

"I don't want to make it worse for you."

"Trust me, nothing about you touching me will make it worse."

She snatched her hand back and shook her head before burying it in my shoulder.

"I'm nervous about all of this," she mumbled, her words muffled by my t-shirt.

I stroked her hair.

"I know. It's okay, you can be scared. We'll take all the time you need. I'm not going anywhere, Meredith. I'd wait forever for you."

"You mean that?"

"Yes, you mean so much to me. I never want to let you go."

She turned her head, laying on my chest as she wrapped her arm around me, curling up against my side.

"Can we just stay like this?" she whispered. "I don't want you to go anywhere."

My lips curved upwards into a smile as I wrapped my arm around her.

"I'll stay as long as you want me here."

She let out a sigh, stroking her fingers down my side. I kissed the top of her head, reassuring her I was right here and would be until the end. Meredith had no idea of the sheer depth of my devotion to her. How I'd waited five fucking years to be old enough for her to even consider me an option. I'd do anything to keep her by my side now I had her.

"That's the problem, Cole. I don't think I ever want you to leave. You're under my skin and it fucking terrifies me. We barely know each other and yet... I want everything with you."

"Then what do you want to know? I'm an open book. All you have to do is ask."

Her words made me nervous. She'd told me many of her secrets, but I didn't think that was the end of it. Something else kept her from letting go. I didn't want to push her into telling me after everything today.

"Why do you hang out with the troublemakers at school?"

I snorted.

"They're not vapid idiots who only care about whether or not they look good in a selfie."

She chuckled, shifting against me a little.

"No, but seriously, everyone thinks you're trouble too."

"I am. Quinn grounds me every time the school phones them about something I did. You're lucky I was even allowed out today after what I did to Penelope Stokes in chemistry. I'm surprised the school didn't suspend me."

"Do I even want to know?"

"Probably not."

Penelope hadn't made any further snide remarks, so she'd got the message. Don't give me shit about my parents and I won't fuck you up. Pretty simple if you thought about it.

"Are you going to keep getting in trouble? You know, it'll be hard for us to see each other if you're grounded and is yet another reminder of the fact I'm an adult and you're not."

I wanted to tell her I didn't need to be an adult to make this work, except Meredith had a point. She wasn't beholden to her mother in the same way I was to my parents. No matter how much my mum indulged me, I didn't think 'just because' would be an acceptable reason for why I should be allowed out when I was grounded. Although, I'm not sure telling them I wanted to see my girlfriend would help my cause either. Meredith had rendered it impossible for me to tell them the truth. I didn't like it. Lying to my mum and dad wasn't something I often did.

"I'll try not to."

She raised her head off my chest and stared at me.

"I'm serious. You want this with me, you have to act like it. That means being responsible for your actions."

No way in hell I wanted to mess anything up between Meredith and me.

"I said I'll try, Meredith. Don't ask me to promise you I won't fuck up, okay? I'm not a saint. You know that."

She looked at me for a long time before her expression softened and became vulnerable. Her hand reached up and she traced her fingertip along my bottom lip.

"Just make sure I can still see you," she murmured. "That's all I'm asking for."

I kissed her fingertip, my hand winding into her hair and pulling her closer until our noses touched.

"Always, my little queen."

Her cheeks flushed at my term of endearment. She was smaller than me and my queen. Perhaps it had something to do with my dad calling my mum, little star. It just felt right. My beautiful, fiery girl needed a crown nestled in her strawberry blonde hair.

"I won't tell anyone how sweet you are to me."

"Don't want to cramp my style like my brother does."

A smile graced her lips and she chuckled.

"Exactly."

I pressed a kiss to the side of her mouth, stroking her scalp with my fingers. The urge to fist her hair in my hand and hold her down so I could ravage her pretty mouth drove through me but I resisted the impulse.

"Do you have any other surprise perfect dates up your sleeve?" she asked as she pulled back slightly.

"Perhaps. If you continue to be good for me, I'll make sure to reward you."

Her eyebrow curved up.

"And if I'm not?"

I slid my hand from the back of her head to the front, brushing my fingers along her cheekbone.

"Then I'll have to…"

"Have to what, Cole? Punish me?"

I noticed the way her pupils dilated at the word punish.

"Is that what you want?"

"No."

I gripped her chin.

"See, now, Meredith, I know you're lying and you promised me you wouldn't."

Her lips parted, a low pant escaping them.

"I don't want you to hurt me."

I smiled.

"Who said anything about me hurting you?"

"Isn't that how you'd punish me?"

"No." I pressed my thumb against her lips, forcing it in her mouth. Her eyes widened at the gesture. "I'd make you beg and plead for what you want until you can't take it any longer. That's how I'd punish you."

Her mouth closed around my thumb, her eyes turning into molten pools of desire. I dared her to go one step further with my own. It only took her a second to swirl her tongue around the tip. I could only imagine what her hot, wet mouth would feel like around my cock.

"I think you like the idea of that."

She didn't need to respond with words. Her eyes told me everything. I popped my thumb out of her mouth and ran it along her lip, leaving it glistening. Leaning forward, I captured her mouth in mine before she had a chance to speak.

This girl would be the fucking death of me at this rate. I ached to have her. And I would when she let me. When she was ready. Meredith would give me every part of her.

"You make it very hard to resist you," she whispered against my mouth.

"Good."

"So arrogant."

I smiled.

"You wouldn't have me any other way."

Pulling away, she smirked.

"You're probably right about that."

Then she laid her head on my chest again, right over my heart thumping against my ribcage. Her hand rested next to her.

"Stay for dinner?"

"You sure?"

"I'm sure I want to spend as much time with you as possible when I don't have to hide what we are."

I wanted to tell her we didn't have to hide anything, but somehow, I knew that line of conversation would be a mistake. Meredith was keeping something from me. And only a delicate hand would get her to open up about it. For now, I'd bide my time and let her keep us a secret. I couldn't afford to lose her now I had her. That would make me fucking miserable.

"Okay. I just have to tell Mum I won't be home."

Meredith said nothing to that. She didn't have to. And for the first time, after our conversation, I truly felt the divide in our ages.

Would I let it keep me from her?

No, but I had to remind myself of how hard this might end up being on both of us when people did eventually find out we were together.

I don't care how difficult it all is. Meredith is meant to be mine. She belongs with me.

When you wanted something in life, you had to fight for it. I'd go to war to remain right here with her. Now I knew how she felt in my arms and her lips on mine, there'd be no going back. I'd claim every inch of Meredith. Branding myself on her skin. On her fucking heart. She'd never be free of me. Just as I hadn't been free of her for five fucking long years.

The fucking thing is she'd already branded her name on my chest long before she even knew I existed. I belonged to her. For a long time, I'd hated it. Now, I was determined to have her completely. So she'd feel every moment of torment I had. So she'd sink so deep into the abyss with me, she'd never be able to pull herself out.

I shoved my wayward thoughts away. Concentrating on being here with her was more important than thinking about the years I'd waited for her to be mine.

Because now… she was.

And I'd make damn fucking sure it stayed that way.

CHAPTER SIXTEEN

Cole

The knock on my bedroom door followed by it opening had me turning my head towards it. My mum and dad walked in, taking in me sat at my desk fiddling with a suspension strut. I'd been taking it apart so I could put it back together. I learnt by doing when it came to cars.

The two of them sat on the edge of my bed. Sighing, I turned, dropping the parts on my desk and spun my chair around.

"Are you here to give me a lecture?"

Mum frowned and Dad's eyes flicked to her then back to me.

"No," she said. "We were wondering where you've been all day."

I crossed my arms over my chest.

"Out."

Not the answer she wanted judging by the flash of irritation in her blue eyes.

"Cole."

"What?"

"This has to stop."

"What does?"

Dad put a hand on her knee as if reassuring her.

"Your attitude. We've all noticed it and I've had enough."

And they said they weren't here to lecture me.

"Really, Mum? I won't tell you where I've been and suddenly I have an attitude."

Her brow furrowed further.

"This isn't about today. You've been in a lot of trouble at school for the past year. You won't talk to any of us about what's going on nor why your behaviour has only got worse."

I looked to my dad but his expression remained neutral.

"I wasn't in trouble last week."

"That isn't the point." She sighed. "Cole, I realise I may have allowed you too much freedom, but I am still your mother. I do not appreciate the way you're acting towards everyone around you."

I didn't like the sadness in her eyes. It cut me deeper than I expected.

"You used to be close to your brothers and sister. Now you give everyone, including me, the cold shoulder. Did I do something wrong? Is that why you don't come to me any longer?"

I looked away. The guilt ate at me. I knew I'd been acting out, but they should already know why. It was fucking obvious if they thought about it.

"No," I mumbled.

"Then what is it? Because I'd like my son back. The one I know is still in there."

I could trace it back to the day after I turned fifteen. When all five of them sat me down and told me the truth about their past. I don't know why it bothered me so much, but it did. And the fact Raphi, Duke and Aurora were all told before me. I hadn't been deemed old enough. The baby. They all still treated me like that. And I hated it. I wasn't a fucking child even if I was still deemed one in the eyes of the law.

Maybe it's why I was so determined to prove myself to Meredith. To show her we could work even if I was only sixteen. I'd had to grow up fast in the past year. Learning your parents had come from a legacy of blood and corruption, well… that was royally fucked up.

"Is it so wrong for me to miss my baby boy?"

The way her voice shook on those words had me uncrossing my arms, leaning forward and taking her hand in mine.

"No, Mum."

She tugged me closer, reaching out with her other hand to stroke my hair back from my face. Her eyes searched mine for a long minute.

"Tell me what's wrong."

I couldn't stop the truth spilling out.

"Everything."

"Oh, Cole."

I found myself wrapped up in her arms the next second.

"This is about what we told you last year," my dad said, his voice quiet and measured.

I didn't have to respond. He'd known even if she didn't. I wondered for a moment why he hadn't said anything. Then I remembered, this was my dad. He didn't like to talk unless it was necessary and perhaps he'd been waiting for me to come to him. Pity this wasn't something I felt like talking about with either of them. What did I even say? I don't know who you are any longer since I found out you've killed people? Yeah, that would go down well. I mean, fundamentally it hadn't changed how I saw them. They were still my parents. All five of them. They'd raised me to be the person I was today. I still loved them all deeply even if I hardly ever said it.

It had changed how I viewed them in other ways. Knowing my mother had been groomed to rule over a criminal empire was a little unsettling, to say the least.

"I'm sorry we had to put that on you," Mum whispered.

I couldn't exactly say it was okay. Whilst they'd raised us in a household full of love, there were still things lingering from the past. Ones I couldn't ignore.

"I already get shit from people about the five of you. I constantly have to defend it." I pulled away, staring at the two of them. "How do you think it makes me feel knowing what you all did? It makes it worse. So much fucking worse."

As I took in their expressions, my heart hurt and all I wanted was the one person in my life who wasn't part of this bullshit.

Meredith. My beautiful, sweet, fiery little queen.

I ached to have her back in my arms. Leaving her earlier had been physically painful. Sharing kisses with her half the afternoon and her making me dinner was the icing on the cake. She was so fucking warm and full of life. A far cry from the coldness she showed to other people. And learning more about her had only deepened my feelings towards her.

"We felt we owed you all the truth. I know it's not what you want to hear, Cole, but it's the only way we can protect you."

"From what exactly? You said you left that life behind."

"We did, but it doesn't mean it left us behind."

I looked away. I understood what she was telling me, but I didn't have to like it.

"That doesn't make me feel any better."

Nothing would. It was something I had to learn to accept and I'd been having a hard time doing that.

"Will you tell me where you were today?"

I stared hard out the window overlooking the garden where the meadow of wildflowers grew beyond my dad's conservatory.

"I hung out with a friend."

"Cole…"

"I'm telling you the truth, Mum."

I felt her hand on mine, squeezing it but I didn't look at her. Meredith was technically my friend so I wasn't lying, just missing out the part about her being my girlfriend.

"Does this friend have a name?"

"Does it matter? I didn't get into any trouble if that's what you're worried about."

I heard her sigh.

"Can you deal with this?"

I glanced back at them to find her turned to my dad with a desperate plea written all over her features. He merely gave her thigh a squeeze as he nodded.

"Thank you, Ror," she whispered, kissing his cheek before she got up and left the room.

I hated upsetting my mum and yet I didn't know if I was angry, upset or disappointed in them after what they'd revealed. Perhaps it was all three.

"Nothing you say will change how I feel about it," I said before he could open his mouth.

"You don't like knowing what we've done."

"Now, where did you get that idea from?"

He didn't even blink as he continued to stare at me.

"You're lashing out at the world. I understand that and it's okay, Cole, but I don't like seeing Ash upset. Especially not over you."

"And you think I do?"

"With the way you talk to her, it makes me wonder."

I looked at my hands. My dad never scolded me, not in the way Quinn did. When his tone became laced with disappointment, I felt it deep in my bones. And I hated it.

"I do love her but she's so overbearing. I'm not a baby."

"Then don't act like one."

"I'm not," I bit back even though I knew he wouldn't have said it without cause.

My dad got up and gripped my shoulder, leaning down to press a kiss to the top of my head.

"I know who you were with today," he said, his voice quiet. "Will you tell me why you're keeping it a secret?"

I wanted to say no. I didn't have to ask how he knew. Dad clearly saw the way I looked at Meredith. He knew I had feelings for her. I'd given up getting angry with him over his tendency to read me and everyone around him so well.

"She asked me to."

"I can see why you like her. Don't mess it up and don't hurt her... and your mother would want me to tell you to make sure you're using protection if she knew you had a girlfriend."

"Dad!"

I do not need another lecture off my dad about sex! They already gave me that talk before my fucking birthday.

He pulled away and dropped his hand, smiling at me.

"Is she your girlfriend?"

I crossed my arms over my chest and glared. He raised an eyebrow.

"Yes, she is."

No point lying because he would get it out of me one way or another.

"Then what I said stands."

"Are you going to tell Mum?"

"No, but you should."

Meredith would kill me. She might already if she found out my dad knew about us.

"I can't. I promised."

He sat back down on my bed and eyed me for a long moment.

"Is it because you're sixteen?"

I rolled my eyes.

"Not you as well. I waited until I was old enough before pursuing her."

He gave me a smile.

"I don't care if you're dating a girl who's older than you, Cole. I care about your happiness."

I looked away, rubbing my arm.

"Sorry… it's just the only way she agreed to give me a chance was if I promised not to tell anyone. She doesn't want anyone judging her or gossiping about it. I hate it though, Dad. I really fucking hate it." Just thinking about it made my fist clench. "She's mine and I'm hers. I don't want to be a secret. It makes it feel like we're doing something wrong."

He said nothing for a long moment. When I looked back at him, his eyes shone with pride and I was about to question it when he spoke, "You're so like your mother. I'm glad there's more of her in you than me."

I blinked, not expecting that statement to come out of his mouth.

"What?"

"Ash never wanted to keep our relationship a secret. She's always been proud to be with the four of us and wanted the world to know who she belonged to. She's stubborn, fierce and opinionated. You look like me, but everything else, that's all Ash."

I snorted.

"I wouldn't be so sure of that if I was you," I muttered under my breath.

"No?"

My face felt hot at the thought of the type of relationship I wanted with Meredith when she finally let go. The way I wanted to take control of everything.

"I'm so not having this discussion with you."

My dad smirked, cottoning on immediately as usual.

"I see… you *can* talk to me about that if you want."

I scrunched up my face. Who the hell wanted to think about their parent's sex life let alone talk about it? Not me.

"Hell no, that's gross."

"I wasn't going to discuss what I do with your mother."

I put my hand over my face, wanting the ground to swallow me whole.

"Dad!"

"I'm only saying…"

"Please, stop. I cannot talk about that with you. I'd rather die or even talk to Xav about it."

"Shall I get him for you?"

Now I knew he was winding me up.

"You're twisted, you know that, right?"

I dropped my hand to find him shrugging.

"No, you're right, you're better off talking to E. He won't take the piss out of you."

I couldn't deal with him any longer.

"You can leave now."

"I'm not sure I'd recommend Quinn if that's who you're considering."

"Dad!"

I spun around in my chair and rolled it back to my desk. This conversation was officially over. I picked up the strut and turned it over in my hands. I heard movement behind me before he ruffled my hair.

"You know where to find me when you're ready."

He squeezed my shoulder and left the room, closing the door behind him. If I was ever going to discuss that subject with anyone, it would be with him. What I did with Meredith would be between me and her. The thought of having to tell her my dad knew about us filled me with anxiety. I didn't want to give her a reason to run or end things with me. But I knew I couldn't keep secrets from her either. Not if we were going to work in the long run.

I wouldn't tell her tonight, though. Perhaps tomorrow.

I pulled out my phone and fired off a text to her.

Cole: I wish I could hold you whilst you fall asleep x

I got an immediate response.

Meredith: I wish you could too x

Cole: You in bed?

Meredith: Yes... why?

Cole: What are you wearing?

I could imagine her expression and I bit my lip.

Meredith: None of your business. Mind out of the gutter.

Cole: I wasn't asking you to send me a picture but if you wanted to make me happy...

Meredith: Not happening.

Cole: That's okay. The memory of your lips is more than enough material for me.

I didn't get an immediate response. I got up, ambling off to the bathroom to get ready for bed. By the time I got back and stripped down to my boxers, she'd texted me back. I slipped into bed and read it.

Meredith: Are you doing what I think you are right now?

Cole: No, but I can be if you wanted me to. Does the thought of it turn you on?

Meredith: Are we ever going to have a conversation you don't turn sexual?

Cole: Yes... we had one earlier.

Meredith: Don't be smart!

I grinned and switched off my bedside lamp, tucking myself under the covers properly.

Cole: If I was there, I'd hold you close and watch you fall asleep.

Meredith: I really do wish you were here.

Cole: Me too.

Meredith: And yes... the thought of you doing that does turn me on in case you were wondering, but don't let it go to your head!

I called her rather than responding. She answered after a couple of rings.

"Cole…"

"I just want to wish you goodnight properly."

"You sure about that?"

"Yes. I already told you earlier, everything we do is your choice. I'm not going to push you."

Well, perhaps I would a little, but only because I liked seeing her riled up over me.

"If I told you I wanted you to do that right now, would you?"

"Do what?"

I knew exactly what she was asking but I played dumb. Perhaps Meredith would say the words I wanted spilling out of her mouth.

"T… touch yourself."

"You want me to wrap my hand around my cock and stroke one out to you on the phone so you can hear me?"

"I…"

"Say it, Meredith. Ask what you want."

"Cole…"

"If you don't, I'm going to say goodnight and hang up."

She let out a little huff. I couldn't prevent the smile forming on my face. The way she got embarrassed over this made her so fucking endearing.

"Goodnight."

I smiled wider.

"Night, little queen, sweet dreams."

"Call me tomorrow."

"I will."

"I miss you."

My heart tightened at the vulnerability in her voice.

"Miss you too."

She hung up. I dropped my phone on my chest and thought about her squirming in her bed right now. I could picture it vividly having had her wriggling beneath me earlier whilst I'd kissed her. My phone vibrated.

Meredith: You have to be patient with me. I'm nervous.

Cole: I will be, I promise.

Meredith: I want you to be my first in everything.

Her words made me feel on top of the fucking world.

Cole: You get my firsts too. Don't forget that.

Meredith: I know. It makes me feel special. Night Cole xxx

Cole: Sleep tight xxx

I smiled as I plugged my phone in to charge and turned over. We'd get there, eventually. Meredith had to let me in completely so I could gain her trust. And then we'd experience the rest of our firsts together. Just like I'd always hoped for.

CHAPTER SEVENTEEN

Meredith

Two weeks of sneaking around with Cole had started to grate on me. Hiding the truth had been my idea because of his age and my broken promise to Jonah, but it became harder for me to stay away from him. Not to mention he'd started taking risks at school just to be near me.

The library was quiet for a Tuesday afternoon. I wandered along the shelves trying to find a reference book I needed when two hands banded around my waist and tugged me against a solid chest.

"Little queen," came his voice, all breathy against my ear.

I wrenched away from him, very aware of our surroundings. As I turned to face him, I took in his scowl.

"What are you doing?" I hissed.

He tugged me against him with no compunction, stroking a thumb down my cheek.

"No one is around," he murmured as he leant down. "I've missed you."

I hadn't seen him at all yesterday, but I hadn't expected to either. And I didn't have time to protest as he kissed me. Bringing my hands up, I shoved against his chest, but Cole didn't let me go. In response, he deepened the kiss as his hand drifted down my back, pressing me closer. My thoughts got all tangled up as our tongues lashed against each other.

Why did I try to reject this again? Oh yeah, shit, we're in the fucking library.

"Cole," I managed to say, pushing harder against him with my hands.

He put a few precious inches between our mouths.

"Stop fighting me."

"You're not supposed to kiss me at school."

"I can't help myself."

I extracted myself from his grasp, putting more space between us.

"We've talked about this. If someone sees us…"

He rolled his eyes and crossed his arms over his chest.

"No one else is here. Would you quit being so paranoid?"

He wasn't the one who would get shit for us dating. I would. Everyone would judge me and make out like I was robbing the cradle. Cole was barely sixteen.

Staring up at him, I saw the hurt in his eyes over my reaction to him kissing me. I hated that look. And I hated how guilty I felt for forcing him to keep us a secret.

Reaching out, I pulled his hand away from his chest and laced our fingers together.

"I'm sorry."

His eyes softened in the way they only did for me. Cole was usually aloof to those around him, but with me, he was real. He laughed, made stupid comments and gave me his truths.

"I don't like not being able to touch you when I want to."

I stepped closer, running my hand up his chest.

"I know."

The two of us had grown so much closer over the past couple of weeks. Whilst we'd not done anything sexual yet, I felt more and more ready to take that step with him. I trusted Cole to take care of me. Not to mention it would be his first time too so if it got awkward or went wrong, we could put it down to that.

Going up on my tiptoes, I pressed my mouth to his ear.

"I've been thinking…"

"About what?"

"When we're alone, I want to touch you…" And so there were no misunderstandings, I ran my hand lower and tucked my fingers into the waistband of his trousers, running them over his bare skin. "… intimately."

His harsh breath made me shiver.

"Meredith…"

"Before you ask, I'm sure. You've been patient. I want to do this."

His hand dug into my hair, fingers stroking down the base of my skull.

"You're killing me right now," he hissed before tugging my head back and pressing his mouth to mine.

I didn't object this time, kissing him back as my body melted into his. When he pulled back, we were both out of breath.

"I have to tell you something."

"What?"

"You have to promise not to get upset with me."

I stiffened. What had he done?

"Cole…"

"My dad knows about us."

He promised he wouldn't tell anyone.

"You told him!"

"I didn't have to tell him, Meredith, he is the most observant person on the planet. He put two and two together, okay? I should've told you before, but I didn't want you to be angry."

I didn't let him go, but I wasn't happy either. His dad knowing didn't bode well.

"So what? You're telling me now I've said I want to go further?"

"No, that's not why. I don't like keeping secrets, especially not from you."

I saw the conflict in his expression. This had been eating him up. Without thinking, I cupped his cheek.

"It's okay. I believe you."

I didn't want to get into a fight. Arguing over it seemed futile.

"He hasn't told anyone. We can trust him, I swear."

"Okay. When can we see each other outside of school?"

His eyebrow raised.

156

"I thought you would've put up more of a fuss."

I sighed.

"What would be the point? It's not like we can do anything about him knowing now."

Cole rested his forehead against mine.

"The weekend?"

It felt like a lifetime away to wait until then, but it was difficult for us to spend time with each other after school on weekdays. At the weekend, my mum and Grandma were usually out so I could have Cole at mine without them knowing. I didn't want it getting back to Jonah under any circumstances.

"Okay. I need to get back to studying."

He pressed another kiss to my lips and let me go, giving me a smirk.

"I look forward to it."

He backed away, shoving his hands in his pockets. I rolled my eyes and turned to the shelves, watching him walk away out of the corner of my eye. He had more of a cocky swagger to his step. Given what I'd promised him, it hardly surprised me. That boy's ego had to be the biggest one in the school.

For the rest of the afternoon, my thoughts were so consumed by what we would be doing this weekend, I barely paid attention in lesson. And even less so when I walked towards the school gates. Probably why someone had a chance to sneak up on me. An arm slung around my shoulder and I jumped, turning to them with a rebuttal.

"I told you not... oh... it's you."

I stared at Raphi who was grinning at me as he prodded my nose.

"Yeah, it's me. Why? Were you expecting my brother?"

I let out a forced laugh.

What does he mean?

"No, why on earth would I be expecting him?"

Raphi's eyebrow curled upwards and his smile didn't falter.

"Well, for starters, you stare at him all the time whenever he's around and… the two of you were all over each other in the library."

I stopped dead in my tracks and turned to him fully.

"You… you saw that?"

Damn it, Cole! You told me there was no one around!

"Uhuh, but don't worry, I don't think anyone else did."

"Fuck," I muttered.

He eyed me for a long moment.

"I don't care if you're dating Cole, I knew you had a crush on him… but you could've told me, you know."

I blinked.

Raphi doesn't care? And he knew I had a crush on his brother? I want to die right now. This is so embarrassing.

"I… oh… it doesn't bother you?"

"No." He pulled me towards the gates. "My brother might be trouble, but he's not a complete tool."

Raphi's casual reaction to the news I was dating his brother took me off guard.

"My only question is why are you keeping it a secret?"

"Have you forgotten I'm two years older than him?"

"No, I just don't think age is a big deal."

I eyed him. Considering something had gone on between him and my brother, I supposed Raphi wouldn't care about age gaps. And perhaps it's also why he'd not got weird about me and Cole.

"You might not, but I don't need people gossiping about me."

We came to a standstill near where the line of cars sat waiting to pick up kids. Raphi didn't release me, his arm still slung around my shoulder.

"You got any plans right now?"

"Um no."

"Good. You're coming over and we can tell the family you're Cole's girlfriend. I mean, you are actually dating each other, right?"

I choked on my own breath, shoving Raphi off me.

"Excuse me, what?"

"Well, you want me to keep it a secret at school, the least you can do is be honest with my family, then you can come over without them getting suspicious."

I scowled. What the hell did Raphi think he was playing at?

"This sounds like blackmail."

He waved a hand, shoving his glasses back up his nose.

"It is."

"What the fuck, Raphi?"

I had to tell Cole about this. Like right now.

"That's the deal, Mer."

I tugged my phone out of my bag.

"And here I thought you were the nice one out of your siblings. Clearly, I'm wrong."

He put a hand on his chest in mock outrage.

"I *am* nice."

"Whatever."

I fired off a text to Cole.

Meredith: Raphi saw us kissing in the library and is now insisting I come over so I can be properly introduced as your girlfriend to your family.

"You telling your mother you won't be home until later?"

I rolled my eyes.

"I see I'm not getting out of this."

I had no choice. Raphi wouldn't tell anyone, but in all honesty, I didn't like this sneaking around business. Besides, if his family knew then going over to his wouldn't be an issue. We wouldn't have to wait until the weekend.

"No, you're not."

I sent a text to my mum, knowing she didn't care if I wasn't coming home for dinner. Since Cole and I had started dating, I'd ignored her and Grandma's comments. Instead of crying down the phone to Jonah about them, I texted Cole, who always made me feel better about myself. Who knew if my brother questioned why I hadn't been in contact with him as much, but he was busy with uni. Perhaps it was a good thing.

Raphi's parents' car pulled up and he opened the door for me. I scooted across the seat as Raphi climbed in behind me.

"Oh, hey, Rory… where's Dad?" Raphi said as I noted who was in the driver's seat.

Rory's eyes were on me through the rearview mirror. I remembered Cole told me his dad knew about us.

Well, this is just great.

"Busy with Xav."

"And Mum?"

"With Quinn."

Raphi scrunched up his face.

"Seriously? Gross."

I looked between them, the implications of Raphi's reaction dawning on me. His parents were spending *time* together.

"Oh, Meredith's coming over... hope that's okay."

"Yes. Hello, Meredith."

I shifted in my seat under his gaze.

"Hello, Rory."

This is officially awkward. And why aren't we setting off?

I realised why the next moment when the door next to Raphi was ripped open and Cole stuck his head in.

"Move," he grunted.

Raphi glanced at him.

"Excuse me?"

"Get out and sit in the front."

"I already have my seatbelt on."

Cole glared at him, then he pulled away and slammed the door shut. A minute later, my door was opened and I had Cole's hands on my face, turning me towards him.

"Are you okay?" he whispered as he leant his forehead against mine.

"Um, yes, I'm fine."

What else could I say? It's not like I was going to completely lose my shit over Cole's family finding out about us. In the back of my mind, I'd known it would happen, eventually. Besides, his presence soothed me. Cole had a way of making everything okay when he was right there next to me.

"Will you move over so I can sit next to you… please?"

When he let me go, I scooted into the middle and he climbed in, shutting the door behind him. He took my hand after we'd put our belts on, running his thumb down mine.

Rory pulled away from the curb and Cole leant over me, giving his brother daggers.

"I do not appreciate you butting into my relationship and making decisions about when we tell everyone else."

Raphi merely grinned at him.

"What? I'm trying to help you two out. Don't you want to spend more time with Mer?"

"How is that any of your business?"

I put my hand on Cole's chest and pushed him back, not wanting an argument to start in the car.

"You're dating *my* friend."

"So what? She's *my* girlfriend."

"Both of you shut up," I interjected. "I would rather you not have a pissing contest over me."

I glanced at Cole's dad, finding him rolling his eyes at the scene in the back of the car.

"What? We're not…" Raphi started then closed his mouth.

I looked at Cole finding the reason why Raphi had stopped talking. His brother looked downright murderous.

"Look, I realise I said I didn't want anyone to find out, but I'm okay with this, Cole." I glanced at Raphi. "And you, don't think I've forgotten about your attempt at blackmail."

Raphi put his hands up before Cole launched across me and strangled his brother. I stroked my hand down Cole's chest, trying to soothe him. His hazel eye met mine and softened.

"As long as you're really okay with this."

"I am."

He leant over and pressed his lips to my temple.

I had no idea what the rest of his family would say when we told them, but if Raphi and Cole's dad were okay with it, then surely the rest of them should be, shouldn't they?

CHAPTER EIGHTEEN

Cole

I could kill my brother. The fact he'd seen us irritated me, but to find out he'd forced Meredith into coming home with us so I could introduce her as my girlfriend… that made me angrier than ever. Just as well she was okay with it or Raphi would be in for a world of pain. And she wouldn't be happy if I hurt him so I kept my hands to myself.

When Dad pulled up at the house, I dragged Meredith up the steps with me and away into my room before Raphi could say a word. After the shit he'd pulled, I didn't care what he thought. She could see my family later. Right now, I wanted to be alone with my girl.

Meredith stared up at me from where I'd pinned her against the wall, my hands either side of her head.

"Cole?"

"Are you sure you want to do this?"

"Well no, but this would at least allow us to see each other more often, wouldn't it?"

"Yes."

The two of us wouldn't have to sneak around. She could come here and none of them would bat an eyelid. Plus, I didn't like lying to my mum. Perhaps it would go some way to healing the rift between us.

Meredith reached up and placed her hand on my heart.

"Then I'm sure."

I leant towards her, capturing her mouth as my hand curled around her waist, tugging her away from the wall. Her hand left my chest and wrapped around my back. I pulled her towards my bed, kissing those beautiful lips before I pressed her down on it. Meredith's hands roamed down me as I held her face, keeping her positioned exactly how I wanted her.

"We're alone," I murmured against her mouth.

"What about your family?"

"Later."

I'd locked my door before I'd put her against the wall. No one would interrupt us. Nothing would stop me from having her, just as she'd promised me earlier. The thought of it had plagued me all afternoon. Knowing I would have to wait until the weekend to have her hands on me had been pure torture. I guess I did have to thank my brother for bringing this to fruition sooner. My irritation with Raphi evaporated, leaving only desire for Meredith in its place.

I pried her hands from me and sat up, pulling my school jumper off. My hands went to my shirt buttons next, flicking them open one by one. Meredith watched me, her mouth slightly parted with no protests falling from it. Her eyes widened the moment I threw my shirt off. For a second, neither of us moved. Her hands came up and ran across my stomach as I leant over her.

"Do you want me to touch you too?" I asked, letting her explore to her heart's content.

"Yes."

The lack of hesitation on her part made my heart thump. She let me pull her jumper off, followed by her t-shirt, leaving her in a plain black bra. My hand closed around her breast as hers drifted lower and brushed across my cock. She laid her hand firmly on it, showing me she wasn't scared. Her touch sent my pulse spiking.

I hadn't pushed her in the past two weeks. The less pressure I put on her, the braver she became. Besides, I'd made her aware on our first date after she'd let go and trusted me with her firsts, then I'd take control and she'd submit. I could wait, knowing it would be so fucking sweet when it happened.

"Do you want me to show you how I like it?" I murmured.

"Please."

I unzipped my trousers and pulled them down a little way. Meredith's hand stroked across my stomach before dipping below the waistband of my boxers and curling around my cock. I grunted, trying not to curse at the softness of her skin against mine.

"I believe you now," she whispered.

"About what?"

"It not being small."

I grinned, helping her pull me out of my boxers and wrapping my hand around hers. Her eyes were on my face rather than what we were doing.

"Don't you want to look?"

I tugged her hand away and waited. Her eyes roamed down my chest and fell on what we'd exposed.

"Oh."

"Is that all you have to say?"

I bit my lip as she looked at me again. When she realised I was trying to hide a smile, she scowled.

"Shut up. I have seen a dick before, Cole, I'm not *that* innocent."

I wrapped her hand around it again and showed her exactly how I wanted her to stroke me. Nothing could prepare me for the way it felt to have it be her doing this. When I let go of her hand, she continued, watching me with darkened green eyes.

"Am I doing it right?" she whispered.

"Yes," I ground out. "Don't stop."

I leant down and kissed her, needing to feel her mouth on mine. Whilst I kissed her, my hand slid under her bra strap and tugged it down her arm. I peeled down the cup and ran my thumb over her nipple. She arched into me, not faltering in her strokes.

"Fuck, Meredith," I groaned against her mouth.

"More," she whimpered.

I kissed down her neck before trailing my tongue across her chest. Reaching her breast, I sucked her nipple into my mouth. Her gasp and pant were delectable. Her hand tightened around me, making me grunt. I tried to think of anything but her half-naked body below me and her hand around my dick. That happened to be impossible.

I let go of her nipple and pressed my forehead against hers. Her pupils dilated, breath coming fast and seeing it sent me over the edge.

"Fuck, little queen, I'm going to…"

Meredith didn't falter. I erupted, shooting sticky streams over her hand and bare stomach.

"Shit!"

I hadn't wanted to come so fast but everything about this girl intoxicated me. Panting, I found her smiling up at me, her green eyes bright.

"Did I make you lose control?"

I wrapped my hand around her face and forced her chin up.

"You should learn to keep that smart mouth shut."

"Never."

I kissed her, pressing my tongue in her mouth and making her submit to my touch. She moaned in my mouth when I stroked her nipple again.

"Shall I make you come, Meredith?" I murmured when I pulled away.

"Do you even know how?"

I smiled.

"I'm sure you can tell me if I'm doing it wrong."

I leant over and grabbed the tissue box, pulling some out. Cleaning up her stomach and hand, I chucked them on the bedside table to dispose of later.

My hands went to her black jeans, unbuttoning and unzipping. She swallowed as I ran my finger along her underwear. Getting to touch her like this made my heart hammer wildly in my chest.

"Do you want to keep these on?"

She shook her head, reaching around and unhooking her bra. I stared at her bare chest for a long moment. Her tits mesmerised me. They were perfect.

"You're beautiful."

Her cheeks flushed.

"I want you to see all of me."

I dragged her jeans down her legs, stopping to take her shoes off. I kicked mine off, forgetting I still had them on. Peeling her underwear off, I sat back and looked at her. My stunning girl in all her glory.

"You are… perfect," I murmured, leaning over and kissing my way down her chest.

"I want to see you."

My lips curled up.

"As you wish."

I removed the rest of my clothes, aware the sight of her had made me hard all over again.

"How are you mine?"

I paused in the act of leaning over her.

"I just am. Why? Do you like what you see?"

"Yes."

I stroked my fingers down her chest.

"Good."

Reaching her curls, I dipped my fingers lower. Meredith felt hot and wet. All for me. I explored, finding her clit and stroking it lightly. Her hips arched up, hands wrapping around my back and her gasp echoing in my ear. I wanted to make this good for her even if I'd never done it before. The internet had given me a lot to go on.

I ran my fingers lower, circling her entrance.

"Can I?"

She nodded, biting down on her lip. I pressed my finger inside her. There was little resistance. Her pussy felt hot and tight, giving me vivid images of how it would be around my cock when I fucked her.

"You don't have to be so gentle," she whispered. "I have used toys."

I stared at her.

"What?"

The red of her cheeks deepened.

"Well, a girl has needs, Cole. I wanted to know what it felt like since I had no idea when I'd experience the real thing."

I slid a second finger inside her, causing her back to arch and a hiss to leave her lips.

"You've had a fake dick inside you?"

"Yes."

"I'm a little jealous."

She smiled.

"It's not as big as yours."

"I should fucking well hope not."

I pulled my fingers back and thrust them inside her. Meredith moaned my name. Leaning down, I sucked her earlobe into my mouth.

"You've only made me want you more, little queen."

Her hands tightened around me.

"I want you too."

"Now?"

"Maybe if you make me come…"

"There's a challenge I'll willingly accept."

My thumb landed on her clit, stroking the little nub.

"Tell me what to do," I demanded.

"A little harder and to the left."

I did as she asked. Her mewls in response made me smile.

"Yes, Cole," she moaned. "There, god, right there."

She kept directing me. Her hips bucked and her back arched every time I hit the right spot.

"Oh, oh, fuck, Cole."

I felt her clench around my fingers and her eyes closed. Her body trembled. Her fingers tightened on my back, nails biting my skin.

When she opened her eyes, they were shining.

"You do that so much better than me."

I cocked an eyebrow.

"Is that so?"

"Maybe it feels better to have someone else touch me."

"I concur."

I pulled my fingers from her and settled on the bed on my side. Meredith reached out, lacing our fingers together on her chest.

"How am I going to face your family now? I probably look like a mess."

In my mind, she looked happy and satisfied. But I didn't want anyone else seeing her like this. I owned that expression on her face. I made it happen.

"You're always beautiful to me."

"Is it okay if we don't?"

I kissed her forehead.

"I told you. It's your choice when we do."

"Okay. Should we clean up and see your family now?"

I pressed my lips to hers.

"After I kiss you senseless."

"How can I say no to that?"

Meredith let me hold her, our bodies pressed tightly together as our tongues danced. For the first time in a long while, I felt peaceful. Meredith belonged here in my arms. My girl. My queen.

And I was fucking proud she was going to let me introduce her as my girlfriend. I had no idea what Mum would think since I was her baby boy. She'd soon see why I couldn't do anything but give Meredith every part of me.

You own me. Now. Forever.

CHAPTER NINETEEN

Cole

Meredith's hand shook in mine as we entered the living room finding Duke alone watching TV. He didn't look up, probably having not noticed we were there.

"Where is everyone?"

Duke looked over the sofa and his eyes immediately landed on mine and Meredith's joined hands. The smirk on his face made my eyes narrow.

"Fucking."

I cocked an eyebrow.

"Is that a serious answer?"

"Dad said it's his date night with E."

I scrunched my face up. Our parents were far too open about their relationships. It's not like it bothered me. The fact they wouldn't stop going on about their sex lives in front of us? That grossed me out.

"Hey, Meredith."

"Duke."

He grinned wider.

"So you're screwing my baby brother?"

Her cheeks went pink.

"Shut up, Duke," I grunted. "Don't embarrass her."

"We're in a relationship," Meredith said, tugging me closer to her by my hand. "But I'm sure you wouldn't know what one of those is even if it slapped you around the face."

I laughed and Duke shook his head, turning back to the TV. Meredith knew all about my brother's reputation. A player through and through. He hadn't always been like that, but life had handed him a shit deal. Couldn't really blame Duke for the way he coped with it.

"I would give you a high-five for scoring an older girl, but I'm not sure your *girlfriend* would appreciate that."

"Feel free. I don't care," she told him, rolling her eyes.

Meredith wasn't about to take any shit off Duke. I smiled and shook my head, tugging her away towards the kitchen where I found Quinn and my mum standing side by side next to the stove. The low murmur of voices stopped when we walked in. Mum turned her head and glanced at us, looking up at Quinn then back at me and Meredith. Her eyes fell on our hands. I couldn't read her expression.

"Hello again, Meredith," Quinn said as he turned and crossed his arms over his chest, levelling his gaze on both of us.

"Hello," she said, shifting on her feet.

I rubbed the back of my neck with my free hand. Might as well just get it over with.

"Meredith and I are dating… so you'll be seeing a lot more of her."

Quinn's lips curved upwards.

"Well, you are welcome here any time, Meredith. Especially if you keep this one in line."

He pointed at me. I didn't comment on it considering I'd caused my parents more than enough trouble over the past year.

"I will," Meredith replied. "He does tend to get a little out of hand at times."

Quinn's grin widened and he laughed. I glanced at my girlfriend whose eyes were twinkling.

"I like you already."

Mum didn't say a word, just continued to stare at the two of us. I wasn't sure if that signalled danger or not. My dad chose that moment to walk in. His eyes flicked between us before he strolled over to Mum and kissed her temple. She didn't look at him, her eyes fixed on me.

"Mum?"

"Is Meredith staying for dinner?" were the only words out of her mouth.

"Yes."

"Okay."

She turned back to the stove. Quinn and my dad looked at her with some concern.

"What's wrong, little girl?" Quinn murmured as he leant closer to her.

"Nothing."

Meredith glanced at me, her eyes wide. I'd got used to my parents and their terms of endearment for each other. It must seem weird to her. Then again, this might have more to do with my mum's reaction or lack thereof to the news her baby boy had a girlfriend.

"No? You sure it has nothing to do with your baby growing up?"

"Quinn." The warning note in her voice had him frowning. "Not now."

"We should go," I hissed at Meredith who nodded.

The two of us crept away into the games room, finding Raphi stretched out across one of the sofas with his homework.

"Do I even want to know what you two have been up to?" he asked without looking up.

"No," Meredith said.

No way in hell I'd be declaring to my brother I'd had his friend naked in my bed. What she and I did was strictly between us.

I pulled her over to the other sofa and we sat down. She leant her head on my shoulder after I grabbed the remote and turned the TV on.

"How did the family take the news?"

"Okay, I guess," I said. "Though I don't know if Mum is happy about it."

I handed Meredith the remote and she flicked through the channels.

"Ha, of course, she isn't. Her baby has a girlfriend. She doesn't like you growing up one bit."

"Shut up."

"Does she hate me?" Meredith whispered.

I wrapped an arm around her.

"No. It's not you. I don't think it'd matter who I brought home."

"Mum will get over it," Raphi said. "You're lucky Quinn isn't Cole's dad, or you'd have to deal with the inquisition."

"He didn't seem surprised or bothered by it," Meredith said. "I don't see why you two keep going on about how overbearing he is with discipline."

"None of us has done anything to earn his ire whilst you've been here."

She raised an eyebrow, her expression entirely sceptical.

"Trust me, you don't want to see that side of him," I muttered.

Having been on the receiving end of Quinn's version of discipline many times, I didn't wish it on anyone. He'd been particularly strict when we were younger. Now, he treated us like adults and made sure we took responsibility for our actions.

"I'm more interested in what your dad thinks."

"Of us?"

She nodded.

"He basically told me not to fuck it up. Oh, and let's not forget about the whole using protection lecture."

Raphi snorted. Meredith's cheeks flushed.

"You should've been on the receiving end of the sex talk I had to endure from Dad and Xav. That was hell on earth."

I glanced at my brother.

"Was Mum not there?"

"No, but I wish she was, then I might not have had Xav explaining the ins and outs in such graphic detail."

I could well imagine. It made my experience seem tame in comparison.

"Your parents are an interesting bunch," Meredith said, grinning.

Reaching up, I stroked her cheek. The way her eyes lit up when she smiled made my chest tighten.

"You can say that again," Raphi muttered.

I didn't want her to find out about my parent's past. Meredith didn't deserve to get dragged into that shit after everything she'd already been through.

"You mind staying here whilst I go to talk to my mum?"

Clearing the air with her sooner rather than later would be best. I didn't think leaving it would do me any favours.

"Yeah, okay."

I kissed her before getting up and ambling away towards the kitchen, pausing before I reached the doorway when I heard voices.

"I just don't see why you're so upset about it," came Quinn's deep voice.

"He's my baby and she's two years older than him," Mum said.

"And that's a problem?"

"I don't want anyone taking advantage of him."

I clenched my fists. What the hell kind of opinion had she formed of Meredith?

"If you think anyone could take advantage of Cole, then you clearly don't know your own son very well."

"She didn't pursue him," Dad murmured. "This is very much Cole's doing."

"And how would you know that?"

I heard Quinn scoff.

"Did you forget this one spends his whole time watching instead of talking?"

"How long have you known about this?"

I took another step towards the kitchen, unsure whether I should interrupt them or not. Eavesdropping wasn't exactly my style, but they were talking about me and Meredith.

"A couple of weeks. He told me when I asked him about it," Dad replied.

"Why didn't you tell me?"

"He asked me not to."

"We're supposed to be in this together, Ror. You can't keep secrets from me."

"If I told you, I'd have betrayed his trust, little star."

"That's hardly the point."

I needed to put a stop to this conversation.

"I think it's very much the point, little girl. Do you want Cole to think he can't come to any of us? If you don't let him live his life, then you're only setting yourself up for disappointment," Quinn said.

I did trust my parents with my secrets, but I hadn't been prepared to break a promise to Meredith by telling them about her.

"Oh yes, because you're going to win parenting award of the year with the way you behaved when Rora got involved with Logan."

"That's different."

"How is it different, Quinn?"

"Cole can take care of himself."

Mum had to be rolling her eyes right now.

"Rora can handle herself, you saw to that. Take your own advice for once in your life."

"You've clearly forgotten how he treated her. If that boy ever goes near our daughter again, I will kill him."

I walked into the kitchen with a raised eyebrow.

"Can I talk to you, Mum?"

The three of them whipped their heads around. Dad's lip twitched. He knew I'd heard them. Quinn crossed his arms over his chest and Mum's cheeks flushed.

"Of course." She turned to Quinn and pointed at a saucepan on the stove. "Make sure this doesn't boil over."

He rolled his eyes.

"Yes, sweetheart."

Mum came over and the two of us retreated into the dining room. I leant against the table, trying to think of what I could say to make this better.

"Are you upset about me having a girlfriend?"

She took a step towards me.

"No."

"You seem upset."

"I don't want you getting hurt."

I gripped the edges of the table. Meredith wouldn't hurt me. Underneath those walls she put up, she was sweet and kind. The girl was my fucking sun.

"What is your problem with Meredith?"

Her blue eyes softened and she took another step towards me.

"I don't have a problem with her."

"So you don't think she's going to take advantage of me because she's older?"

She put a hand on my arm, her expression falling.

"You overhead us."

"You weren't exactly being quiet."

"I'm sorry. We shouldn't have been discussing you like that. I just worry, Cole, you're only sixteen."

I hated how everyone used my age against me. It drove me fucking crazy.

"I really wish you would stop treating me like a baby, Mum. And for your information, I promised Meredith I wouldn't tell anyone about us. I don't think telling my mother constitutes a reason to break my girlfriend's trust."

She reached up and cupped my cheek. Her eyes betrayed her inner turmoil and made me feel horrible for pushing her away all the time.

"I know I can be terribly overbearing and protective. I'm sorry. I promised myself I wouldn't be anything like... the man who raised me with my own children. After everything we went through, I know the value of family and how important it is to make sure nothing happens to the ones I love."

She stroked a thumb down my cheek.

"You are especially important to me, Cole. Ror giving me you was a gift I never imagined I'd receive. Not after everything he went through. That's not to say I don't love your brothers and sister just as much. You're all equally precious to me. I want you to know my concerns come from a place of love."

My heart ached. They'd told me about my father's childhood and it hurt worse than I could ever imagine. Yet, he'd found happiness in my mother and our family had stuck together through thick and thin.

"I want you to be happy and if she makes you happy, then that's all that really matters."

I let her wrap her arms around me and hold me tight.

"She does, Mum. She's the only girl I've ever wanted." *Do I admit the truth to her? Will she understand?* "It's been her since I was eleven… it will always be her."

She pulled back and smiled.

"That long, hey?"

I nodded, feeling my face growing hot.

"Well, I look forward to getting to know her. Why don't you invite her to Sunday dinner? Grandpa's bringing Lily."

I rolled my eyes.

"Are you sure that's a good idea with Grandma coming too?"

"Yes, well… that can't really be helped."

I snorted. Grandma couldn't stand Lily. Grandpa had met her twelve years ago and they'd got married a few years later. I think Grandma hated how we'd all taken to Lily like a duck to water. Not to mention the way Grandpa doted on his wife.

"Fine, I'll ask Meredith."

Mum stepped back, giving me a smile.

"Good. Now, I best go finish dinner before Quinn burns the place down."

I shook my head as I watched her retreat into the kitchen. At least I'd cleared the air with her. And I had to hope she'd do what she said and get to know my girlfriend. A girlfriend I should really be getting back to.

I smiled as I walked out into the hallway. Perhaps Meredith would enjoy the shitshow that was family Sunday dinners with my grandparents. The monthly gatherings were never dull. I wondered what type of madness would ensue this time. And I could only hope it didn't make my girlfriend want to run far, far away from us.

CHAPTER TWENTY

Meredith

I knocked on Cole's front door and wiped down my sweaty palms on my skirt. Checking myself over one last time, I hoped I'd dressed appropriately for Sunday dinner with my boyfriend's entire family. When Cole asked me to attend, I'd been more than a little apprehensive. He told me it would go some way to reassuring his mum we were serious about each other.

The door opened, revealing Raphi's dad, Eric, on the threshold.

"Hello, Meredith. Come in."

"Hi, Eric."

He gave me a smile as he stepped back and let me walk into the house. I shrugged off my coat and he hung it up.

"Nervous?"

I gave him a weak smile.

"It's not like I haven't met you before."

He led me into the living room where Duke, Aurora and Raphi were with Xav, Rory, Quinn and two people I didn't know.

"I'll go turf Cole out of his room," Eric murmured before disappearing.

Raphi got up and came over to me.

"Since grumpy isn't here, I'll introduce you."

He pulled me over towards the older gentleman with blonde hair and blue eyes and the lady with beautiful dark straight hair flowing down her back and glasses standing next to him. They were both dressed impeccably, making me feel a little inadequate in comparison.

"Grandpa, this is Cole's girlfriend. Meredith, this is Viktor."

The older man reached out and took my hand, pressing a kiss to my knuckles. I felt my face growing hot.

"This is my wife, Lily," came the accent tones of Cole's grandfather.

"It's nice to meet you both."

"The pleasure is all ours, I assure you."

I put my hand out to Lily, but she batted it away and gave me a hug instead.

"You are stunning. Cole is a very lucky boy."

I bit my lip, my face feeling as though it was on fire as she let me go. Lily's expression was so kind and open.

An arm curled around my waist, tugging me against a solid body next to me. I looked up, finding Cole staring down at me with happiness blooming in his hazel eyes. He leant down and kissed my cheek.

"You look beautiful," he whispered in my ear.

I wanted to hide away from all the compliments. I wasn't used to them. At all.

"Thank you."

The doorbell went and someone behind us stepped out of the room. Cole looked around before his expression turned grim.

"That'll be Grandma."

Raphi raised an eyebrow.

"Well, this will be fun," he muttered.

I looked between the two of them, wondering what that meant. Cole hadn't mentioned anything about his grandparents to me.

A minute later a woman bustled in with greying blonde hair and Eric trailing after her. She looked exactly like Cole's mother, except older and far more put together. Not that Ash wasn't, it's just Cole's grandmother had an air of superiority surrounding her.

Duke and Aurora got up and were embraced before the woman came over to us. Her eyes fell on Lily and Viktor, narrowing to slits.

"Afternoon," she gritted out.

"Isabella," Viktor nodded with a neutral expression on his face.

I stared at Cole, whose eyes were on his grandmother. The next moment, she looked at us, her eyes softening. Reaching up, she squished his cheek with her fingers. That made him scowl, but he didn't bat her hand away.

"And how is my littlest grandson?"

189

Cole wasn't exactly little, so I wondered at that. It seemed his mother wasn't the only one who treated him like he was still the baby.

"Fine, Grandma."

Her eyes fell on me.

"And who is this?"

"My girlfriend, Meredith."

His grandmother stepped forward and gave me two air-kisses. I stood there, unsure of what the hell to do or say.

"Charmed. You may call me Bella."

"It's nice to meet you," I mumbled.

Isabella moved onto Raphi, and Cole drew me away towards the window.

"You're about to witness my family at their worst," he whispered as he leant closer.

"I am?"

"Grandma doesn't like Lily, be prepared for scathing remarks."

I watched as Isabella said hello to Cole's dads one by one.

"Why the family meals then?"

"Mum likes to see her dad regularly, but if she didn't invite Grandma, then there would be more trouble. Trust me, it's really not worth the hassle."

I nodded as Ash came in and hustled over to her father, embracing him, followed by Lily. Her mother's eyes narrowed again. I could see what Cole meant. There were clearly jealousy issues going on.

"Lunch is ready, everyone," Ash said as she pulled away from Lily.

Everyone moved towards the dining room whilst Ash said hello to Isabella. Cole took my hand and pulled me along towards where the table was filling up. It was just as well they had a huge dining table so they could fit everyone around it. I sat in between Cole and Rory, which had my nerves spiking.

Food was passed around and the general chatter soon became deafening. I didn't bother attempting to listen to the various conversations going on. Cole wasn't either. He placed his hand on my leg, giving it a squeeze as he eyed me.

"Suppose you don't have big gatherings like this," he murmured.

"Never. It's just me, Grandma, Mum and Jonah."

I tried not to flinch at mentioning my brother. He'd called me yesterday. I had to be very careful about what I said to him. Jonah could read me like the back of his hand. Our closeness combined with his sensitivity to emotions made it impossible for me to keep many things from him. He'd be coming home in a few weeks for half term, something I was dreading. I was in no doubt he'd get it out of me that I was dating Cole and then things would fall apart.

"We take some getting used to," Rory said, glancing over at me.

"I can see that."

He smiled, which put me at ease.

"You didn't tell me Cole had a girlfriend," Cole's grandmother's voice filtered through the noise.

She sat in between Ash and Duke, who didn't look like he wanted to be there at all.

"I didn't have time, Mum," Ash said.

"Oh, and I suppose you had time to tell your father."

"No, I didn't tell him either."

Isabella looked sceptical. Cole's hand on my leg tightened.

"Well, are you going to tell me about her?"

"For fuck's sake," Cole muttered.

"What do you want to know, Mum?" Ash asked, her lips thinning.

"Why, everything."

I wanted to shrink back in my seat. When I'd been here on Tuesday, Ash had made an effort to talk to me over dinner, asking all sorts of questions. I hadn't minded since Cole told me she only wanted to get to know me. This was different. Being talked about didn't sit well with me.

"Well, she's in sixth form with Raphi—" Ash started.

Isabella's eyebrows shot up.

"Excuse me? She's Raphi's age?"

"She's eighteen."

"And you're allowing your son to date someone older than him?"

"Like you can say anything, Mum. You had an affair with Dad and he's younger than you."

"That's different, we were adults. Cole is still a child."

Cole stiffened next to me. I was well aware he hated people treating him like a kid.

"I'm not going to tell my son who he can and can't date."

"Cole doesn't let anyone tell him what to do," Duke said, eying his grandmother with a smirk. "Don't you know your own grandson?"

Isabella turned to Duke, a scowl appearing on her face.

"Of course, I know my own grandson. You need to mind your own business, young man."

Duke nudged Isabella's arm with his.

"Whatever, Grandma, lighten up a bit, eh? Meredith's a solid girl."

Isabella's face fell further.

"Here we go," Cole snorted next to me.

"Did you hear what your son just said to me?" Isabella ground out through her teeth.

"I did," Ash replied.

This was like watching a car crash. I couldn't stop myself from smiling at the way Duke rolled his eyes and ignored his grandmother's pointed stare.

"And are you not going to do anything about it?"

"No."

Cole's shoulders shook next to me.

"I don't know why I'm surprised considering which one of your men his father is."

Ash's face fell and her mouth thinned into a hard line.

"Leave Xav out of this."

"He never takes anything seriously."

"I'm warning you, don't start on him. I won't have it. He took raising Duke very seriously and is a wonderful father, so just don't."

I leant closer to Cole, wondering if this was a normal occurrence.

"Is she always this protective?"

"Pretty much. Grandma is always going off on one about someone in our family. Last time she got annoyed with Quinn and that almost turned into a screaming match between her and Mum."

I dreaded to think what that would be like. After seeing this, I could well imagine what kind of madness ensued in Cole's family.

"Sounds like this is a tame Sunday lunch then."

"You could say that. Are you okay or are we scaring you off?"

I smiled and reached up, running my fingers through his hair.

"No… I like how close you all are."

Cole leant closer, turning his head towards me. His hazel eyes were full of affection. I momentarily forgot we were with his family. The way he looked at me made my heart swell. This boy was absolutely beautiful. And he was mine.

"Don't look at me like that," he murmured.

"Like what?"

"Like you want me to kiss you."

"Maybe I do."

Cole's lips curved up.

"And get told off by Grandma for PDA at the table… well, that might be worth it."

His words made me drop my hand from his hair and straighten in my seat. No way in hell I wanted to make a poor impression on his grandmother after what she said. Cole's grin widened and he turned back to his own food.

The rest of the meal passed without further outbursts. It seemed Ash's warning to her mother had stuck. Rory had asked me a few questions about my plans for the future, particularly about where I'd applied for university. I was hoping to attend one in London as I didn't want to leave the city, unlike Jonah.

Cole's parents and grandparents retired to the living room, leaving us kids in the dining room to clear up. I helped Cole take the dishes into the kitchen.

"You not running off screaming over our crazy family yet?" Duke asked, winking at me as he walked by with some serving dishes.

"You're not that bad."

Duke's eyebrow raised.

"Don't let this one escape, Cole. If she can put up with our family, she's a keeper."

Cole looked at me.

"I know she is."

I shuffled on my feet, feeling a little embarrassed by Cole's assertion in front of his siblings. Aurora came through and looked between me, Duke and Cole.

"You giving her the 'don't fuck with my little brother' talk?"

"Nah, I was leaving that for you, Rora," Duke said, bending down to put stuff in the dishwasher.

"You don't need to give me that talk," I said, eying their sister.

Aurora popped the plates she was carrying on the counter as Raphi came through.

"No?"

I crossed my arms over my chest. I wasn't afraid of Aurora Knox.

"No. I don't intend to hurt your brother... also, our relationship is no one else's business but our own."

Duke straightened and chuckled whilst Aurora's dark eyebrows shot up. Raphi dropped some more plates on the counter and nudged me with his shoulder.

"Careful, Mer, you'll be getting the full force of Rora's wrath in a minute."

Cole watched us silently, his eyes betraying his admiration for me standing up to his sister.

I dared Aurora with my eyes to say something else, but she merely smiled.

"Don't fuck it up with this one, Cole."

And with that, she left the room.

"Well, I'll be damned," Raphi said.

"That means Rora approves," Duke put in as he continued to stack the dishwasher.

Cole came around and took my hand, pulling me towards the door.

"Hey, you're meant to be helping us clean up," Raphi called after us as Cole dragged me into the hallway.

"I'm sure you and Duke can manage," Cole threw over his shoulder.

The way his eyes roamed across me spoke volumes. Cole couldn't wait any longer to kiss me. And to be quite honest... neither could I.

CHAPTER TWENTY ONE

Cole

I tugged Meredith into my room, shutting the door before I turned the lock. My mouth descended on hers, my hands tangling in her hair the next minute. No doubt I wanted my girlfriend on my bed and writhing beneath me.

My parents probably expected us back in the living room after cleaning up the kitchen. I couldn't wait any longer. I wanted Meredith. She'd held her own today. It'd made me fall so much harder for her. Even Grandma's remarks no longer seemed important in light of the way my girl had looked at me and how my dad's eyes told me he approved of her.

"Cole," she moaned against my mouth, her hands fisting my t-shirt.

Since we'd shared intimacies on Tuesday, all I could think about was being inside her for the first time. I wouldn't put pressure on her. My beautiful girl could take all the time she needed. Didn't stop me growing hard from our kiss. And when she noticed, her hand uncurled from my t-shirt and slipped between us. I grunted when her hand brushed over me.

"Meredith…"

"I want you."

I pulled back, looking at her for signs she didn't mean it.

"Want me how?"

Her face flushed but she didn't look away.

"Cole…"

"Tell me what you want."

I backed her away towards the bed, my fingers digging into her scalp.

"You… all of you…"

I smiled, wondering why she couldn't bring herself to say the words. My heart hammered in my chest as I pressed her down on my covers.

"Aren't we supposed to be back with your family?"

My hand drifted under her skirt, brushing up her inner thighs. Meredith squirmed, her green eyes darkening with heat.

"Maybe," I murmured, leaning down to kiss the skin above her breasts where her pretty pale green top rode low.

"Then we can't… you know."

"I don't know, Meredith, why don't you enlighten me?"

Her hands curled around my shoulders as my fingers brushed over her underwear.

"Have sex," she whimpered.

"Is that what you want?"

"Yes," she breathed.

I tugged her underwear down her legs, not caring about my family whatsoever. Why the fuck would I when the girl of my dreams had admitted she wanted us to sleep together finally?

"Then I'm going to give it to you, little queen."

"Cole—"

I cut her off with my mouth on hers. No more waiting. No more excuses. We were going to do this. My cock throbbed at the thought of being inside her. My fingers went to her clit, stroking along the little bud. She pushed her hips up against me, making it very clear what she wanted.

"That's it. Let me make you feel good."

"Please," she breathed.

I slid two fingers inside her tight heat, adoring how wet she felt already. How I fucking wished I could feel her around me. Encasing me completely. I couldn't stop myself thrusting against her hip, grinding my cock into her to gain the friction I craved. Her nails dug into my shoulders through my t-shirt as she moaned my name.

"I want to be inside you," I whispered in her ear. "Do you want that? Do you want me to give it to you?"

"Yes," she panted. "Cole, please."

Pulling away, I scrambled to strip her down. I needed to feel her body against mine without barriers. My clothes came next, chucked off the side of my bed haphazardly in our desperation to be as close as possible. I reached over to my bedside table and pulled open the drawer, fishing out a condom. I almost grimaced, remembering how I'd had Xav knocking at my door and giving me a knowing smile before he handed over four boxes to me two days ago. He told me to use them wisely, and if I needed more or anything else, I only had to ask. I didn't know what to say to that. I'd muttered my thanks and stowed them away. My parents could be so embarrassing sometimes.

Ripping open the foil, I rolled it on, watching Meredith whose cheeks were flushed. I hoped I wouldn't mess this up either by hurting her or coming too quickly. Though the latter might happen with it being my first time and me being so fucking pent up.

I shifted over her, taking in the nervousness in her expression. Reaching up, I stroked her cheek.

"Are you sure you want to?"

"Yes," she whispered. "I don't want to wait."

I kissed her, wanting to reassure her I'd be careful and gentle. She opened her legs wider, allowing me to settle between them. Wrapping a hand around my cock, I released her mouth, looking down so I could see what the fuck I was doing. The moment the tip of my cock met her soft, warm little pussy, I held back from groaning. I pressed forward, meeting some resistance until I slid into her. Meredith let out a high-pitched squeak, making me go still. I looked at her, finding her eyes wide as her hands gripped my shoulders.

"Are you okay?"

I tried not to move despite how tightly she gripped me. Fuck, it felt heavenly already and I'd only got a couple of inches inside her. Nothing could compare or prepare me for how warm she was. How the sensations almost blinded me with pleasure.

"I… I'm okay."

I searched her eyes, trying to find the truth in them.

"Am I hurting you?"

"No, it's just… uncomfortable."

I leant closer, resting my forehead against hers as I cupped her face with my free hand.

"I'm sorry."

Her lips curved upwards.

"It's okay, Cole, I wasn't expecting it to be magical the first time."

"Can I move?"

She nodded. I watched her face scrunch up a little as I pushed deeper, but she didn't tell me to stop. Concentrating on going slow and trying not to hurt her helped me stave off the need to come, which kept threatening to consume me whole. When I'd hit halfway, I pulled back before starting to thrust inside her.

"Is this okay?"

I couldn't help asking. Even if she'd told me she didn't expect it to be amazing, I still wanted her to feel good.

"Uhuh," she breathed out. "Don't stop."

Her nails dug into my skin, but she moved with me, encouraging me to delve deeper inside her. I gritted my teeth, trying to hold back from my urge to hammer into her. I'd promised myself I'd be gentle and make sure she was enjoying herself.

Fuck. Fuck. She feels fucking amazing. Shit!

"Cole," she moaned. "More… please."

"That feel good, little queen?" I ground out.

"Yes, yes… god, yes. Don't stop, please don't stop."

As if there was any chance of me stopping. Not when it felt this fucking good to be inside the girl I'd coveted since I was eleven years old. My thrust grew deeper and more erratic as the overwhelming need to spill inside her pounded in my veins.

"Fuck, you feel so fucking good," I groaned, burying my face in her neck and kissing her flushed skin.

She chanted my name as I drove into her, knowing I was on a one-way train to bliss and I couldn't fucking get off. All of it hit me hard, making me impale her completely as I erupted.

"Fuck, Meredith."

Wave after wave washed over me as my cock pulsed deep inside her tight pussy. Hell, nothing felt like this. Nothing at all.

I panted against her skin when it ended, not being able to move. Meredith stroked her hand down my back, kissing the top of my head.

"You okay?" she whispered.

"I should be asking you that."

She laughed.

"I'm fine."

"You sure? Not uncomfortable still?"

She stroked my hair.

"No, not at all… it felt great."

I raised my head, staring down at the beautiful girl who I'd given my firsts to.

"I think the term you're looking for is fucking amazing."

She grinned and shook her head.

"If you say so."

I cocked my head to the side, realising I needed to make sure my girl had her pleasure too. Pulling out of her, I got up to dispose of the condom before crawling over her again. I ran my fingers down the centre of her chest, leaning down to take a nipple in my mouth. She gasped, staring at me with wide eyes.

"What are you doing?"

"Making you come."

Her lips parted, but no sound came out. My hand travelled lower, between her legs. My fingers met her clit, stroking it in the exact way she'd told me to last time. Meredith moaned and bucked, writhing against me within minutes.

"Cole," she panted. "Fuck."

"You going to come for me, little queen?"

"Yes, god, yes, don't stop!"

I stroked her faster, adoring the way she mewled and cried out my name as her body trembled with her release. Watching her come apart was the most fucking magical experience. No doubt about it, Meredith was the most beautiful girl I'd ever seen in my life. No one else would match up to her in my eyes. The way her strawberry blonde hair lay across my covers and the spark of happiness in her green eyes. All of it made my heart fucking ache with the need to be as close to her as possible.

I leant down and kissed her when she was spent, removing my fingers from her clit and stroking her side instead.

"Cole," she whispered against my lips. "You mean the world to me… I hope you know that."

"I do now." I kissed her again. "And you mean everything to me too."

She meant more than she'd ever know. Meredith still had no idea how long I'd waited for her. It didn't seem relevant anyway. I wanted to stay in the here and now with her. We did need to get back to my family, but I could afford a few more minutes wrapped up in her like this. Kissing her soft lips in the afterglow of our first time together.

Life had taught me to savour each moment because you have no fucking clue when it might all fall apart. I was going to try my damned hardest not to mess this up with her. Especially now we'd cemented our relationship with each other.

I pulled back and stared down at her.

"I'm never letting you go, Meredith. You're mine forever."

Her eyes shone with happiness.

"You're mine too, Cole Carter. Always."

CHAPTER TWENTY TWO

Meredith

I equal parts dreaded and longed for the day my brother came home. I missed Jonah like nothing else, but I also didn't want him to find out about my relationship with Cole, who had no idea what I'd promised my brother. Something I sorely regretted. I should have been honest and open with the both of them.

Cole and I's relationship had been blissful since we'd finally slept together. I'd spent the night at his last weekend, something his parents hadn't minded me doing. I swear they knew Cole and I were having sex, but no one had made a comment about it. Raphi avoided anything to do with that side of my relationship with Cole. I could hardly blame him. Cole was his little brother.

I'd told Cole about Jonah coming home and wanting to spend time with him, which he understood. My reluctance to introduce them properly showed, but Cole hadn't pushed me.

He was sweet that way. Never asking too much from me. Allowing everything to be on my terms. Sometimes I wondered if he really was this easy-going or if he was holding back. There was a certain darkness in Cole, which I had yet to see in its entirety.

As soon as I heard the front door open, I stormed down the stairs and right into my brother's arms. He'd barely had time to get in the house.

"Well, hello to you too."

"I missed you," I whispered into his chest.

He let out a chuckle.

"You sure? You've barely spoken to me in weeks."

I'd been lax in calling him, all my spare time being occupied by my boyfriend and studying. Exams would be happening soon. I couldn't afford to fuck up if I wanted to get into the right university.

"You know I hate being without you."

I pulled away in time to see him smile.

"And I suppose it is coming up to exam season."

Something which stressed me out no end but having Cole in my life made everything easier. I could rely on him in ways I'd never experienced before. He gave me solace, comfort and understanding.

I took Jonah's suitcase and rolled it towards the bottom of the stairs before traipsing into the kitchen to make us both a drink.

"Where's Mum and Grandma?" he asked as he followed me in.

"Grandma is with Leonard and Mum is out with the girls, so you're stuck with me tonight."

"Oh no, what a chore."

I stuck my tongue out at him, opening the fridge and grabbing some tonic water. Jonah sat at the kitchen table whilst I mixed us up two gin and tonics with lime slices. I handed him his drink as I set mine on the table.

"You hungry?"

"A little. All I've had is shitty train food since breakfast."

"We can't have that. Hold on, let me see what we have."

I searched through the cupboards before deciding on chicken alfredo. Jonah leant his hands on his chin as he watched me.

"How's Robin and Damien?" I asked, setting some water on to boil for the pasta.

"You're actually calling them by their names?"

I stuck my finger up at him whilst I prepared the ingredients for the sauce.

"Would you rather I continued calling them the player and the straitlaced one?"

He rolled his eyes.

"They're fine. Although, I had to persuade Robin that coming home with me for half-term was not a good idea."

"Why not?"

"He's been going on about wanting to meet you now you've turned eighteen."

"Ugh, gross. He's probably ridden with STIs."

Jonah snorted.

"Well, you say that… he did actually catch one recently."

I whipped my head around.

"No way! You're not serious? What one?"

"Crabs."

I scoffed and turned back to the chopping board.

"Grim. I bet he had to shave his pubes."

"You know, I didn't ask. He's been moping around the flat ever since."

"And Damien? He caught anything he shouldn't?"

I popped a pan on the stove to start the sauce, turning the hob on in the process.

"No. He rarely leaves his room. I doubt he even knows what girls look like."

I grinned. One day I might meet his flatmates. Jonah had told me a lot about them, even though he didn't spend a ton of time with Robin and Damien.

We chatted a little more about his studies whilst I finished making dinner. I sat at the table after I'd plated up and tucked in. When I realised Jonah hadn't started, I looked up with a mouthful of pasta.

"How are things really, Mer?"

I chewed and swallowed, not sure how to answer that.

"They're good."

He raised an eyebrow. I looked down at my plate and twirled some pasta around my fork.

"You're going to ask what's going on with me," I muttered.

"Something clearly is considering you've been cagey since my last visit."

One way or another, Jonah would make me admit the truth. We didn't keep big secrets from each other. At least, I thought we didn't. Jonah's reluctance to tell me what really happened with Raphi was exactly the same as me not wanting to tell him about Cole.

"I have a boyfriend."

I peeked up at my brother, who's grin got wide.

"You do?"

I nodded.

"That's amazing, Mer. I'm so happy for you." Then his face fell. "But why didn't you want to tell me?"

And that was the kicker. I stuffed more food in my mouth to save me from answering straight away. How did I tell Jonah I'd broken the promise I made to him and dated Cole anyway? All the guilt built up inside me, making me feel awful. It was time to face the music and deal with the consequences of my actions. Swallowing hard, I looked down at my plate.

"I broke my promise," I told him in a small voice.

Jonah said nothing for a long moment. I didn't dare look up at him. I couldn't face his disappointment in me.

"Meredith…"

"I'm sorry, J, you have no idea how sorry I am about keeping this from you and lying and breaking my promise, but… but he's good to me. He's good for me and… and I think I'm falling in love with him so please don't hate me for all of this. Cole makes me happy. Please forgive me."

Tears pricked at the corners of my eyes, but I held them back. My heart tightened in my chest at what I'd admitted. I was falling in love with Cole. How could I not? He was everything I ever wanted. He'd broken down all my walls and barriers, showing me what it meant to be cared for and appreciated.

"I'm not upset."

I peered up at my brother, wondering if I'd heard him right. His expression was grim, but his eyes betrayed his understanding.

"Do you know about his family?"

I blinked. What did Cole's family have to do with my relationship with him?

"What do you mean?"

"They're dangerous, Mer, that's why I told you not to go near him. I don't want you getting mixed up in it."

Why on earth would his family be dangerous? They weren't mixed up in anything nefarious, were they? That didn't make any sense. They'd all been so nice. Cole hadn't said anything to me about me being any danger. Then again, what did I really know about his family other than what he and Raphi had revealed to me?

"Dangerous how?"

Jonah shook his head, looking away as he fiddled with his pasta.

"I can't tell you."

"Hold on, that's not fair, J. You can't tell me Cole's family is dangerous and then not say how."

He stuck some food in his mouth and chewed. I waited, wondering if he would say anything or not. When he swallowed, he put his fork down and stared at his plate.

"All I'm going to tell you is you need to look up the name Frank Russo."

I frowned.

"Why?"

"Their mother is… was his daughter."

"But I've met Ash's father, his name is Viktor."

Jonah shook his head.

"She didn't meet her biological father until she was twenty-one. Just look up the name, Mer. I shouldn't really be saying this to you in the first place, but I'm worried… that family… they're…"

I didn't understand Jonah's problem with them. Yes, he had an issue with Raphi, but why did his grudge extend to his entire family?

"They're what, Jonah? Whatever it is you think you can't tell me, it's clearly in the past. What matters to me is Cole, not his family." I let out a breath, not really wanting to bring this up, but knowing I had to. "You've never told me why you and Raphi fell out other than the fact you liked him and he rejected you. Is this about that?"

Jonah's eyes darted to mine again and the anger in them startled me.

"No, it has nothing to do with Raphael."

I dropped my fork and crossed my arms over my chest.

"Yes, it does. You've never been the same since. What did he do to you?"

"I can't tell you."

He said the same thing every time. I'd got sick of it. Either he told me what happened or I'd have to go to Raphi. I was tired of being in the middle of this.

"For fuck's sake, J, whatever happened you need to let it go. I'm done with this and I won't let you sabotage my relationship with Cole because of your grudge against Raphi."

I hadn't meant to say it, but my frustration had bubbled over. Jonah's eyes widened and his expression turned contrite.

"I don't want to sabotage your relationship… but I don't want you to be with him either."

"You don't even know Cole, how can you say that?"

"I don't want you getting hurt, Mer."

"He's not going to hurt me. Cole isn't his family and you'd know that if you hadn't forced me into making a promise I couldn't keep."

Jonah's expression turned dark.

"Did you forget he's only sixteen? You seemed to be very worried about that when you last spoke to me."

"Things change, Jonah. I gave him a chance to prove to me he was worth my time and he did."

This was going so horribly wrong. I didn't like fighting with my brother, but he was being incredibly unreasonable right now. He had no right to dictate to me who I could and couldn't date. He wasn't our father and I was an adult.

A sharp stabbing pain erupted at that thought.

Dad.

I missed him so damn much. If he was here, we wouldn't be in this situation. Dad would have liked Cole.

Jonah rose from the table after chucking his fork on his plate. He stalked from the room, leaving me staring after him. I didn't know if I should go after him and continue to have this out or not, but he came back a minute later with his tablet.

He sat down, fiddled with it and then placed it on the table in front of me.

"Read it."

"Why should I?" I shot back, annoyed by this whole discussion.

"You might begin to understand why I don't want you involved with that family."

"Who'd have thought you would be so judgemental."

He sighed and pointed at the tablet.

"Please. For me."

I placed my fork down and picked the tablet up, scanning the text. It was an article about the London crime boss, Frank Russo and his rule over the city. The more I read about the man, the more my mind whirled with questions about Cole's family. There were descriptions of how people disappeared after working with him. How his business was a front for drugs and illicit dealings. And his ultimate demise, which the tabloids had branded '*The Massacre at Instinct Investments*'.

"Who… who killed him?" I asked, my voice shaking as I noted his killers had never been found.

"I think you know."

I shook my head, placing the tablet down. I felt sick. His family had seemed so nice and yet they'd been involved in some nefarious shit.

"How do you know about this?"

"Raphael."

My hand raised to my mouth, holding back bile rising in my throat. Did Cole know what his family had done? Were they still involved in all this shit? Would I be in danger by being Cole's girlfriend?

I stood up, realising the only way I'd get answers was by going straight to the source.

"I… I need to talk to Cole."

"Meredith…"

"No, you've done enough. This… this is between me and Cole. It's my decision whether or not I'm with him, okay? It's not yours."

I started to walk away, but he reached out and stopped me with a hand on my arm.

"I'm sorry you had to find out like this, please believe me when I tell you I never wanted you to know. I never wanted to do this, but I mean it, I don't want you around them. You don't need to be wrapped in that."

I looked down at him.

"I understand your concerns, but this isn't to do with that and you know it. It's to do with your shit with Raphi. If you don't want to tell me, then fine, but don't pretend this is anything else other than that."

I ripped my arm away and stalked out of the room. A minute later, I slumped down on the stairs, holding onto the bannister as I tried not to hurl my dinner up.

Did this mean Cole's parents were killers? That was seriously fucked up if so.

I pulled my phone from my pocket and dialled Cole's number. I couldn't cope with this revelation. It was too much.

"I didn't expect to hear from you this evening," came his voice when he answered.

It made my heart ache with longing. A longing for him.

Fuck. I'm not just falling for him. I'm in love with him. I love Cole.

I didn't have time to process that right now.

"Cole… is… is it true that your mother was raised by Frank Russo?"

The silence on the end of the line told me everything I needed to know. There was no question. My stomach roiled in protest.

"How do you know that name?" he finally said and his voice was cold. It sent a chill down my spine.

"Is it true?"

"Yes."

"Was it them… did they do it, Cole?" I whispered.

I had to ask. It might change everything depending on how he answered.

"Meredith, this isn't a conversation I want to have with you over the phone."

"I need to know."

"Then I'm coming over."

"What?"

I didn't know if I was prepared to see him. Not after what he'd just said.

"I'm coming over and we're going to talk about this."

"You can't—"

"I'll see you in ten minutes."

He hung up without letting me object any further. I let my hand drop to my side, clutching my phone tightly in my fingers. How was I going to face him? What would he tell me

when he got here? Was I ready for all of this? And if I wasn't...
did it mean Cole and I would be over?

I don't know if I can handle this. Not... not when I love him.

Fuck.

I was in love with Cole Carter.

But was love enough to overlook the shit his family had
done? The shit they might still be involved in.

I had no clue. None at all.

CHAPTER TWENTY THREE

Cole

I don't know how the fuck Meredith found out about my parent's past, but I couldn't let her freak out over it. I had to see her. Had to explain properly. There was no fucking way I was losing the girl of my dreams over this shit. The brokenness of her tone on the phone cut me deeply. All I wanted was to wrap her up in my arms and never let her go. Kiss away any of her fears and reassure her there was nothing to be afraid of. That shit was in the past and it wouldn't affect us. It couldn't. I wouldn't allow it to.

I didn't stop to tell anyone where I was going, just rushed out of the house and jumped on the bus. It would take too long to walk. Meredith needed me there whether or not she knew it.

How the hell had she found out about it? She had no reason to go searching for that kind of information. Few people knew who my mother had been raised by these days. Who my grandmother's husband had been. It's not something I ever wanted Meredith to know about. I mean, fuck, it affected me enough without involving my girlfriend.

When I got to her house, I felt distress and anxiety taking over. My palms were sweaty and my heart raced at a hundred miles an hour. A sense of dread washed over me. I couldn't let her disappear from my life. No matter what.

I rang the doorbell, tapping my foot on the step to calm my nerves, but it wasn't working. The need to see her and make sure we got through this drove through me.

The moment she opened the door I pulled her into me, framing her face with both my hands. Those green eyes were so full of hesitation and fear. Emotions I never wanted to see in her expression ever again.

"Cole," she breathed.

I dipped my head to hers, capturing her lips in a gentle kiss. Her hands went to my arms, clutching me as if her life depended it on it. Our kiss deepened, tongues clashing together in a mess because neither one of us could resist the pull. I backed her into the house, pushing her up against the wall as the door slammed shut.

"We should talk," I whispered, pulling away slightly.

"I need you," she whimpered, her hands clutching my forearms tighter, keeping me close.

The agony in her voice cut me into tiny pieces. How on earth could I deny Meredith anything she wanted from me? My heart couldn't take her expression. I grabbed her hand and pulled her towards the stairs.

"Is your brother back?"

"I don't want to talk about Jonah."

That made me suspicious. Jonah was important to her and the two of them were very close.

"Why not?"

She didn't respond. I looked back to find tears welling in her eyes. What the fuck happened between them?

"Meredith."

She merely shook her head, blinking away the tears as if she didn't want to cry at all. I took her upstairs to her room and shut the door behind both of us. She tried to reach for me, but I held her back with one hand on her shoulder.

"Cole…"

"No. You're going to tell me what happened and then I'll answer any questions you have about my family. That's why I'm here."

Meredith hung her head.

"I didn't tell Jonah we were dating and he's not happy about it. The thing is I told him you liked me before anything really happened between us. He made me promise not to get involved with you, then I broke that promise by agreeing to give you a chance."

I frowned. Why on earth would her brother have a problem with the two of us? That seemed odd.

"What's his problem with me?"

She sighed and paced away from me. I dropped my hand, knowing I should let her tell me in her own time.

"It's not really you, he has a problem with… it's Raphi."

Wait, what?

"Raphi?"

She nodded, rubbing her face as she walked back and forth in front of me.

"Something happened between them when we were fifteen. Jonah won't tell me exactly what, he merely said Raphi rejected him, but I know there's far more to it than that. The point is he's held a grudge against your brother ever since."

She stopped and looked up at me, her eyes full of pain.

I had absolutely no idea something had gone on between Raphi and Jonah. I'd known he'd withdrawn into himself when he turned fifteen and I'd since assumed it's when our parents revealed their past to him. Besides, we'd all been going through it at that time with Duke.

Raphi never really talked about relationships with me. He'd always been far closer to Duke. I wondered if he knew what went down. Perhaps not. Duke had been wrapped up in his own problems back then.

"Jonah showed me an article about Frank Russo... he said Raphi told him about your family, but I didn't ask any further details because I wanted to talk to you. I don't know how to feel about any of this, Cole. My brother doesn't support me in this. He doesn't want us together. He's the only person in my life who really loves me, the only one who was there for me after Dad died. I can't fall out with my brother."

A tear fell down her cheek. The urge to brush it away drove through me, but I kept my arms at my sides. Her words filled me with apprehension. I had no idea what the outcome of our conversation would be. It's not as if I ever wanted to come between her and her brother. The thought of that killed me. Meredith needed Jonah.

"But he can't tell me who I can and can't be with. He doesn't get to dictate that. I'm an adult. I make my own decisions and I did that when I decided I wanted to try with you. Now… now I'm so confused. I don't know what to think or say or even do."

I reached out and took her hand, leading her over to her bed. We sat down on the edge of it. I kept a hold of her hand, anchoring her to me. I needed it as much as she did.

"I never wanted you to find out about my parent's past, Meredith. They only told me last year and it really fucked with me. It's not what you think though… well, I guess it is because you asked me if it was them and the answer is yes."

I didn't want to lie to her about it. She deserved the truth.

"I'm going to explain it to you because I trust you with this, but you do realise this has to stay between you and me… and I suppose your brother since apparently he also knows."

"If Jonah hasn't told anyone about it by now, then he won't and you can trust me."

I turned her hand over and traced my fingers down the lines running across her palm.

"If you've read about Frank, then you'll know what kind of fucked up shit he did. He was never going to let Mum go, not after everything they went through, so they had to do it. They had to end it. As insane as this sounds, some people in this world can only be stopped if they're no longer among us."

At least that's how they'd explained it to me.

"They wanted to be free to live without the fear of him coming after them. They don't come from the same world we do. They fought so hard to get away from the life of poverty they grew up in... my dads, I mean. They all came from horrible situations which were a result of their families being involved in Russo's empire. I'm not saying I agree with any of it or that it's okay, but they wanted to end the cycle of corruption and greed... death."

I looked into her eyes but I couldn't read her expression.

"They're not bad people, Meredith, they're kind, caring and would do anything to keep their family safe. It's not the world they live in any longer. They put that behind them, but they told all of us to protect us. Some days I wish they hadn't. Knowing what they did has been a hard pill to swallow."

She stared at me for a long time before she looked away.

"Am I in danger by being with you?"

"No... I swear to god, Meredith, you're not." Reaching out, I turned her face back towards me, cupping her cheek. "You're never in danger with me. I'll keep you safe. Always."

"I don't know how I feel knowing that about your parents."

"Trust me when I say I understand, but how do you feel about me... about us?"

She raised her hand and placed it on my heart. I swear she could feel how hard it was pounding from my fear she would ask me to leave and that this would never work between us.

"I don't want to be without you," she whispered. "Being with you has made me braver and stronger. You make me so happy, Cole. I need you... I... I just really need you."

Leaning forward, I captured her mouth, needing to reassure myself she was still mine even after her words warmed my entire fucking soul.

"I need you too," I murmured as I pushed her down on the bed, sliding over her body with mine.

Her hands tangled in my hair, tugging me fully against her. I groaned in her mouth when she rubbed herself against me. I took her hands, pinning them to the bed and shifted back, severing the contact between our bodies. Her green eyes were wide and she let out a breath.

"Are you mine, little queen? Completely mine?"

She nodded, biting her lip.

"Say it."

"I'm yours, Cole. All yours."

She'd never belong to anyone else but me. I'd claimed Meredith Veronica Pope as my own. Finally after all these years. I could see it in the way she looked at me. I had her completely.

"I'm yours too."

I planted kisses down her jaw, making her squirm as my lips trailed down her neck and I buried my face in her soft breasts.

"Cole," she panted. "Please."

"Tell me what you want."

"You inside me."

I grinned against her t-shirt, unable to help myself. She'd become so much more open about sex ever since our first time, no longer afraid to tell me what she needed.

I let go of her hands and tugged at her clothes, pulling them off her beautiful body until she lay bare beneath me. Mine came next so we could be skin on skin. So I could feel every inch of her body against mine as I buried myself inside her. As we kissed, I stroked her clit which made her moan and her hands wrapped around my back, clutching me to her. She got wetter and wetter as I touched her until she begged me to give her my cock.

I pulled back, grabbing a condom from her drawer and sliding it on, having given her a box Xav had provided me with a couple of weeks ago so we wouldn't have to worry. She tugged me over her, fitting me between her legs with desire shining in her green eyes. I never wanted to leave the warmth of her body as I entered her slowly, making sure she was comfortable.

"Don't hold back," she whispered. "Give me everything."

I thrust forward, impaling her completely. A groan tore from my mouth as she let out a little mewl. Then there was nothing holding me back. I gripped her leg, pushing it up her chest and set a punishing pace, watching her come apart below me. She bucked and trembled, her hands gripping me as if her life depended on it.

"Cole, god, please," she moaned. "Harder… please, harder."

This felt fucking amazing. Being able to let go and her loving every moment. I wanted to stay with her like this forever. Just the two of us. Nothing could intrude on our little world when we were together.

"Fuck, Meredith," I groaned, feeling so close already.

We both let go together, all our pent-up emotions spilling out. She cried out my name as I moaned and came inside her, feeling her pussy contract around me with each pulse. I knew then Meredith was my forever girl. I loved her. She owned my fucking heart. I think she had done since I'd laid eyes on her five years ago.

After we cleaned up, Meredith pulled on some shorts and a t-shirt whilst I got dressed again. We held each other on her bed for a while, neither of us talking. It surprised me how calm she'd been about my parents, but she'd never really been the judgemental type. Besides, I think she was still processing it and perhaps it wouldn't hit her until later. It had taken a long time for me to come to terms with the whole thing.

"I have to speak to Jonah," she whispered.

I stroked her hair, wishing we didn't have this situation to deal with. It had never been my intention to come between Meredith and her brother.

"Okay... do you want me there?"

"I think I need to do this alone."

I nodded. As much as I wanted to take away Meredith's burdens, I respected her decisions. She could do this.

The two of us got up and I shoved my shoes back on. I took her hand, leading her back downstairs. I was leaning down to kiss her when her brother walked out of the kitchen. Jonah's eyes flashed with annoyance. I had a feeling what came next wouldn't be pleasant.

"Meredith."

She turned and looked at Jonah. As she stiffened, I wrapped a hand around her waist so she knew I was still there for her.

"Cole's just leaving."

"Good."

"Jonah…"

He shook his head.

"You know my feelings on it."

Meredith stepped away from me, reaching out to her brother.

"And I told you it's my decision. We talked about it. I need time to process, but I'm not in danger by being with Cole. Please, can't you respect that?"

He stared at her for a long moment, conflicting emotions flying across his face until it settled into annoyance.

"No, Mer. I can't." Then he turned his gaze on me. "I don't know you, but I don't trust you with my sister. I don't trust anyone in your family and you're never going to convince me otherwise."

"Jonah—" Meredith started but he raised his hand, cutting her off.

"I'm not done. Meredith is an adult so she can make her own choices, but you're not. You're sixteen years old. Can you really tell me you'll protect my sister and keep her safe? Can you truly promise me your family isn't involved in any more shit like they were in the past? Can you?"

Jonah's words slammed into me, reminding me of the differences in our ages. Reminding me I wasn't an adult yet.

Just like Meredith had feared in the beginning would come between us. And yet, here it was, doing exactly that.

"No. I can't promise you they aren't," I said. "I can't promise that because I don't know."

"Then you can't protect her. That's not good enough. My sister means everything to me. I don't want her wrapped up in that shit. And before she says anything, it has nothing to do with your brother, which no doubt she told you about. It has everything to do with me wanting Meredith to do well at school, get good grades and have a future. If she's with you, that's in jeopardy. She kept you a secret from me and she never does that. It's not even about her breaking her promise, it's the fact she knew I wouldn't be happy about it and she did it anyway." He clenched his fist at his side. "I'm her family. I've cared for her our whole lives. I love her more than anything else in this world and all I want is for her to be happy. If you care an ounce for Meredith, you'll let her go."

I wanted to tell him he was wrong. I wanted to fight against it, but if I did that, if I pushed… I might force Meredith into making a choice between me and her brother. That was something I could never do. And Jonah was right. My family's past would always lurk in the shadows and as a sixteen-year-old boy, there was nothing I could do about it. I wasn't old enough to be with her. Not really. Not when in six months, she'd go off to university and I'd still be in school.

"What the hell, J? My future is not in jeopardy. Don't talk shit."

"It is. Don't you see? You're distracted and keeping secrets from the people who care about you. You lied to me because of him."

"You forced me into making that promise."

"It was for your own good."

I didn't like seeing her fighting with him. The stark reality of our situation slammed into me. It broke me. The knowledge of what I'd have to do to protect her.

For the first time since I'd started down this path, I saw things clearly. As much as I wanted Meredith, it was too soon. I needed to be an adult to put us on even ground with each other. She'd asked me to prove to her I was responsible. I had to put her needs first. I had to put her first. And that meant letting her go.

"He's right," I murmured. "I can't give you what you need right now."

Meredith's head whipped around, eyes wide.

"What?"

"I care about you too much to come between you and him… I'm sorry, little queen, but I think he's right. We can't do this anymore."

She stared at me, tears beginning to fill her eyes all over again. The sight split me in two. I bit the inside of my cheek to stop myself from taking my words back.

"That's not true. You make me happy, Cole. You make me so much better."

I shook my head, knowing I had to do this no matter how broken I felt on the inside.

"I know you think that, but you need your family more than you need me."

A tear slid down her cheek.

"No. I need you."

I took a step back knowing if I stayed, I would crumble and my resolve would be shot to pieces.

"I'm sorry."

"No, don't do this. You promised you'd be here for me."

I shook my head, taking another step back towards the front door.

"I'm sorry, Meredith."

She closed the distance between us as I continued to back away.

"Please, Cole… I… I love you. I'm in love with you. If you leave me now, you'll break my heart. Do you understand? You'll break me."

Of all the things she could have said to me, that was the absolute worst. I wanted so much to wipe those tears away from her face, take her in my arms and kiss her senseless. Tell her I loved her too, but I'd only hurt her even more if I did that.

"I'm sorry," I whispered.

Then I turned, opened the door and walked out.

"Cole!"

I didn't look back, walking down the street with my heart shattering into tiny pieces with every step. Never did I think someone else would come between me and Meredith, but I knew this wasn't the end. I had to be patient and bide my time until I turned eighteen. Until I was an adult and could make all my own decisions. She might not see it now, but this was best for both of us.

I promise I'll come back for you, Meredith. I promise I'll make this right. This is only temporary. We only have to be apart for a while, then we'll be together again. And next time, it'll be forever.

PART II

revive

verb, re·vived, re·viv·ing.

to activate, set in motion, or take up again; renew.

CHAPTER TWENTY FOUR

Meredith

Two years later

I should really be downstairs right now. It was a party for me, after all. I didn't feel much like celebrating, hence why I was hauled up on my bed with Rhys. He lay with one hand behind his head on the pillows with his fingers stroking down my bare arm as I curled up by his side. The base pumped through the floorboards, but neither of us cared much about the noise.

I let out a long sigh, knowing we couldn't hide up here forever.

"Why did we agree to let them throw us a party again?" I asked.

"They use any excuse to throw one, you know that."

Rhys and I had both turned twenty over the Christmas holidays, so this was technically our birthday celebration. We'd become fast friends when we met in the union bar of our university in first year. We'd moved into a student house with Jazz, Alfie and Martin at the beginning of second year. It was too bad they were all party animals whilst the two of us preferred to get drunk alone without crowds of people. Thankfully, Rhys and I had bedrooms on the top floor and could escape the madness of the rest of the household.

"We should've found better housemates."

He snorted. I looked up at my best friend, watching him roll those dark eyes of his. His hair was a mess of curls and he had a smile on his face.

"You're telling me."

I was lucky to have met Rhys King. We were such opposites, but that's why we worked so well. I pushed him out of his comfort zone and he kept me from doing anything too stupid. I felt a kinship with him I'd never had with anyone else, except perhaps my brother.

"You sure you don't want to go cruising for guys with me downstairs?"

Not that I'd dated since school. The less I thought about what happened back then, the better.

"Definitely not. I'd rather poke my eyes out with a soldering iron."

I grinned and batted his chest.

"Yeah, okay, whatever. You're such a spoilsport. Never there when I need you to be my wingman."

"I don't think you'd be attracting the right sort of guys with me as a wingman, just saying."

"Okay, true, I'm not looking for a guy to be my beard."

He rolled his eyes again.

"I thought that's what you used me for."

"Ha-fucking-ha."

I may have used him once to get rid of this guy who wouldn't leave me alone, but it was Rhys who'd started it by putting his arm around me. And I loved him for it. He knew what I needed and vice versa. The two of us looked out for each other.

"Come on, Mer, you're always keeping men at arm's length."

I had a good reason for it.

"All right, beard, let's go get a drink, hey?"

"You really are a pain in my arse."

I grinned and hopped off my bed, giving him a wink.

"You love me."

"Yeah, well, sometimes I wonder why."

He got up, straightening his shirt and running a hand through his hair before strolling towards the door.

"I'll be down in a sec, just going to put some more lippy on."

"Fine, but don't leave me alone for too long."

I waved a hand at him, grabbing my lipstick from my dresser and leaning down to my mirror.

"Just down a few shots and you'll loosen up enough to talk to people."

"Mer…"

"Don't be a baby, Rhys."

The boy might be demisexual and find it hard to be around people he didn't know well, but I pushed him to get out of his own head and socialise. He needed to live a little.

"You're so annoying."

"And you'll thank me for it later, now go drink."

He left the room, but not without flipping me the finger on his way out. I smiled before applying my lipstick, followed by lip gloss. Once I was happy, I tousled my hair again and checked out my short green dress in the mirror. Rhys told me I looked pretty, but I didn't always believe people when they said that. He wouldn't lie to me though.

I walked out of my room and downstairs to the first floor. The corridor was crowded with people in line for the toilet and a few people chatting with drinks in their hands. I had no idea how many people the other three had invited, but I had to weave through several people to get to the second set of stairs. Just as I reached it, I glanced down and froze in place. My entire world fell out from underneath me. My skin prickled and I swear my heart just about stopped.

Standing on the bottom step with a bottle of beer hanging from his fingers was someone I hadn't seen since I'd graduated from secondary school. And even then, I'd barely spoken to him for the final term.

I couldn't believe my fucking eyes. It'd been a year and a half, and in that time, he'd grown into himself. A scruff of a beard framed his face, those hazel eyes unmistakable as they drew me in all over again, and his dirty blonde hair was messy. The white t-shirt he wore hugged his muscular body. Dark jeans, trainers and a chequered shirt clutched in his other hand completed his look.

Cole Carter stood on my bottom step.

Cole Carter, who'd broken my heart two years ago when he'd ended our relationship after my brother had interfered.

Cole Carter, who I'd never gotten over no matter how hard I tried. And I'd really tried hard to dispel the memory of him and me together.

I had no idea what to do, say or even think.

Fuck. Fuck. Fuck.

I might have forgiven Jonah for what happened because he'd only been protecting me, but I'd never forgiven Cole. And even though I wanted to hate him, I couldn't. On some level, I understood why he'd walked away.

It didn't stop my heart aching and pumping wildly in my chest at the sight of him now. I gripped the stair bannister as my knees threatened to give way.

What the hell was he doing here? Why? How did he know where I lived? What the fuck was happening right now?

Wait, he's drinking. Shit. I forgot. He's just turned eighteen.

I had too many thoughts and questions running through my mind, overwhelming me with the way they blared in my head. No way I could do this. Being near him. Seeing him. Talking to him.

I turned and fought my way back through the people in the hallway, needing to be as far away from the boy who broke my heart as possible. I couldn't breathe properly as I rubbed my chest, the pain almost crippling me.

Why? Why are you here, Cole?

This could not be happening. Not now. I wasn't ready to see him.

When I reached the stairs to the second floor, I felt his presence, but I couldn't look back. I practically clawed my way up the flight of stairs, reaching my room and flinging the door open. As I turned to shut it, a hand slammed against it, keeping it open. I raised my head slowly and met those hazel eyes which had captivated me when I'd been eighteen. And they still did so now. The heat and intensity in them set my blood on fire.

I opened my mouth and shut it again, the words bubbling up in my throat sticking there.

He dropped his hand from the door, stepping forward into my personal space. I walked backwards, finding him following me. He kicked my door shut and chucked his shirt on the dresser. The back of my legs hit my bed. I had nowhere else to go. Nowhere else to run. And a part of me didn't want to.

Cole didn't hesitate to wrap his arm carrying the beer bottle around my back, pressing me against him as he cupped my face with his other hand. No words needed to be said. I could see it in his eyes and I was sure he could read my thoughts in mine.

I missed you. I still love you. Show me you missed me too.

"Little queen," he murmured before his lips descended on mine.

I let him kiss me, helpless against the onslaught of his mouth, his tongue and his touch. My hands curled around his neck, pulling him closer, moulding to him just as I'd always done. We might have only been together for a short time, but

238

Cole Carter had won me over, heart and soul. He'd ruined me for anyone else because he'd made me feel alive, happy and free.

"Cole," I whimpered against his mouth before he bit down on my bottom lip, making me buck into him.

I should stop this. He'd hurt me, ripping my heart right out of my chest when I'd admitted the truth. When I told him I loved him and he walked away. What the hell was he doing here now? And why couldn't I think about anything else other than letting him strip me down and fuck me senseless?

Cole pulled away, his hand falling from my face to my throat. He caressed my skin with his thumb, staring at me as desire flickered in those hazel depths.

"Did you forget who you belong to, Meredith?"

The way he said my name had me surrendering completely.

"No."

"Good."

He pulled me away from the bed and turned me around, shoving me up against the wall with a hand on my neck. I should be scared shitless of what he was doing, but I'd always trusted Cole not to hurt me. Until he did.

Placing the beer bottle on my dresser, he pressed his body flush with mine, showing me how much he still wanted me. I could feel his cock hard against my back and it only made me shiver. He brushed my hair away from my face, tucking it behind my ear.

"Are you going to let me have control?" he whispered in my ear, his teeth grazing down my earlobe. "Let me do anything I want to you."

Rationality had fled the building. Right then, I didn't give a shit because Cole was here. Cole, who my heart longed for every second of every minute of every day since he'd walked away from us. He felt good against me. He felt so fucking right. I should put up a fight... but I didn't want to.

"Yes," I breathed.

Cole tugged up my skirt, bunching it around my waist. His fingers slid into my knickers and he pulled them down my legs.

"I'm going to fuck you, little queen, fuck you the way I should've two years ago."

I trembled at his words. I'd flirted and kissed other guys at uni, but I'd never slept with anyone else. It never went that far because I was still so hung up on this boy... no, man behind me. Cole was an adult now, even if he was still two years my junior.

He kissed down my neck, his fingers finding their way between my legs and stroking me. I whimpered when he groaned at the feel of me.

"So wet," he whispered against my skin. "So ready for me."

I didn't have it in me to object.

He wrapped a hand around my hip, tugging me back whilst keeping my chest against the wall. The base still pumped through the floorboards, but all I could hear was our mutual harsh breath. All I could feel was him against me and the promise of the pleasure he'd bring.

He shifted back slightly, his hand between us tugging at his zipper. A few moments later, I felt his cock brushing against the bare skin of my behind. He continued to shift around, the rip of foil ringing in my ears. Cole pressed his cock between my legs, sliding against my pussy as he notched it to me. I barely had a chance to take a breath when he thrust in. The delicious sensation only made me ache for him to be fully seated in me.

"Cole," I moaned, feeling the stretch as he pushed in deeper.

"That's it, little queen," he murmured. "Take it."

He adjusted me so I was angled better for him and then he thrust up, making me cry out. My hands pressed against the wall, my breathing erratic as my pussy tried to adjust to his size and girth. It's not as if I couldn't take it before, but we'd never had sex in this position. He felt so much bigger this way.

"Fuck, you feel so good," he grunted.

His hand wrapped around my stomach as he pulled out and thrust in again, setting a pace I was hard-pressed to keep up with. My dress stuck to my back with my sweaty skin and having him against me only made it worse. My body was burning and I knew there'd be no let-up.

"Please," I whimpered, which only prompted him to fuck me harder.

He grunted which each thrust, his breath harsh against my neck as he buried his face in it. I never wanted this to end. I'd missed him so much. The feel of him. The taste of him. Everything.

"More, give me more."

His hand slid down my stomach, fingers finding my clit and stroking. He thrust deeper and I couldn't do anything but take what he gave me. I'd asked for it. I wanted it.

"Did you miss me?" he murmured, kissing my neck.

"Yes."

Lying to him seemed pointless. It was obvious I had from the way I'd allowed him to kiss me, push me up against a wall and stick his dick in me.

"I missed you."

My heart ached with those words. It slammed against my ribcage, pain radiating outwards, but I didn't care. Cole fucking me even whilst I hurt gave me the sweetest damn high.

"You're still mine. You're always going to be mine, Meredith, always."

He bit down on my bare shoulder, making me cry out. The extra sensation sent me over the edge. I bucked, trembled and chanted his name, my climax overtaking everything.

"Good girl," he whispered. "You always come so sweetly."

He hammered into me, drawing out every moment until I couldn't take any more. I slumped against the wall, letting him continue to take me with ruthless thrusts because I couldn't tell him to stop. I needed Cole to drive the pain away. And he did. He fucked me hard, his fingers still on my clit, pushing me to my limits.

"Again," he grunted. "You're going to come again."

I let him take me under, drowning me in the sea of bliss and years of hurt. Years I wanted to forget but couldn't. The memory of us haunted my every waking moment and taunted me in my dreams.

"Fuck, Meredith."

As I continued to pulse around him, he came, his hand gripping my hip in an iron hold as his fingers dropped from my clit. He almost collapsed against my back, pushing me harder against the wall. I didn't have it in me to say anything about it. All my senses had come alive when he'd given it to me Now, the crushing weight of everything which happened between us almost decimated me.

"Cole," I whispered. "Why are you here?"

He didn't speak for a long moment. The only sounds in the air were both of us panting from our vigorous fuck against the wall. I had no idea what he was going to say. No idea how I'd feel either way. All I knew is I'd probably made a huge mistake by letting him fuck me without us having a conversation. Without ranting and raving at him about how he'd broken my heart. The thing is, I don't think I ever had any willpower when it came to Cole Carter. No matter how much I'd fought against him when we were both teenagers, I'd still given in every single time.

I couldn't keep doing that, could I?

Cole let go of my hip and raised his hand to my neck, stroking his hand down my sweaty skin.

"I want you back. I never should've let you go."

CHAPTER TWENTY FIVE

Cole

I'd come here with the sole intention of making Meredith mine again. It'd taken me a few weeks of pestering until Raphi finally gave in and told me where she lived. Told me they were having a party tonight. The two of them were still friends and saw each other regularly despite everything which happened between me and Meredith and Raphi and Jonah. Raphi refused to talk to me about it, even though I told him I knew. Whatever went down between the two of them, it had only got worse after Meredith and I broke up. I didn't want to pry if he wasn't ready to tell me.

I'd finally turned eighteen a few weeks back. That had been one of Jonah's main objections to me being with his sister. Me not being an adult. And the shit with my family? Well, I couldn't change that. However, I could promise there was no reason for him to worry about her not being safe. I'd protect Meredith from everything. I was a grown man now.

I'd been patient and bided my time until I could be the one she needed. The one who would give her everything. There were no more reasons for us to be apart. I was taking back what was mine. Her. Meredith fucking well belonged to me and I to her. Being without her had been pure agony, but I'd endured it all so I could have this moment again. So I could have her.

"You want me back?" she whispered, her body trembling against mine.

"Yes."

She let out a shuddering breath.

"Cole."

"Yes?"

"Let me go."

My heart physically ached at her words. If she thought for a second, I would allow her any room to run, she was mistaken. It'd been too long.

"No."

"No?"

"I haven't been able to touch you for two years. I need this. I need you."

Meredith had to forgive me. She had to know I'd done it to keep her safe. To protect her. I'd broken it off because it was the right thing to do at the time, even if it killed me. I hated hurting her. Hated the way she'd looked at me. It burnt a hole in my chest, ripping my heart right out of it. I couldn't let her go. Having her against me after all this time felt so right.

Being with her like this. Having her give into me. It made up for all the time we'd been apart. All the time I'd spent hating every minute of my life and my decision to leave her.

I've missed you. I love you, Meredith. So. Fucking. Much.

"You need me? What the fuck, Cole?"

She shoved against me. I reluctantly let her go, stepping back to give her some space. She spun around, tugging her skirt down. Her green eyes were full of fire and fury. A reaction I wasn't expecting.

"Where the fuck were you when I needed you? Huh? You left me! You walked away from me when I needed you, so don't you dare tell me you need me."

"Meredith—"

"No! I don't want to hear it. You can't just walk back in my life and… and fuck me like that and expect me to forgive you."

I reached for her but she moved out of my grasp, tearing away from the wall and pacing towards her bed. Knowing she needed a minute, I tugged the condom off and looked around for a bin, throwing it away when I spied it. Then I zipped myself back up and turned to her. Meredith paced the floor, her hands in her hair and her expression hadn't changed. She was pissed as hell.

"I'm really sorry, you must know I never wanted to hurt you," I said, sticking my hands in my pockets to stop myself from reaching for her.

She dropped her hands from her head.

"Sorry isn't good enough, Cole. Sorry doesn't change the fact you walked out on us without a backwards fucking glance." She stopped, raising her eyes to mine. The pain in them destroyed me. "What kind of person walks away when their girlfriend tells them she loves them? Huh? What kind of person does that? You broke my fucking heart."

My chest burnt. I'd done that. I wasn't proud of it. Not at all. Hurting her was my biggest regret. She meant the whole world to me. I'd loved her since I was eleven. Time hadn't changed that. It hadn't dulled the feeling. If anything, her absence from my life had only made it grow, latching itself onto me like a leech determined to suck the life out of me. Meredith had infected every part of me. I had no reason to tear her out. Not when she was fucking well mine forever, even if she was angry at me right now. I deserved her ire, even as it cut me.

"Meredith—"

"No. No, I won't listen to any excuses coming out of your mouth, Cole. I won't. I want you to leave. I want you to go and never come back. I can't do this with you. It's not fair. You broke me. You broke everything after you promised me forever, so do not stand there and tell me you're sorry and you didn't mean to hurt me, because you did. And I hate you for it. I hate you for all the time I had to spend seeing you at school whilst my heart lay in fucking pieces at my feet. I hate the fact that you came here after all this time. And I hate myself for letting you fuck me."

The way her body shook as she threw those words at me made the ache in my chest worse. I wanted to hold her and kiss away all the pain I'd caused, but I knew she wouldn't let me. And she really wouldn't forgive me if I tried to comfort her now.

"I want you to leave. I don't want you to come back here ever again, you hear me? Don't come back. I don't want to see you."

I shook my head. There was no way I could promise her that. No way I would give up on her. I never had, even when everything had got so fucked up between us. But she wasn't ready to hear that. Not yet. Meredith needed time and I'd give it to her. It was the only thing I could do.

"Okay, I'll go... but this isn't over, Meredith. Not by a long shot."

"It is fucking over, Cole. It was over the day you walked out on me and it's over now."

"I get you're angry at me, but I'm not giving up on you. I'm never going to give up."

She pointed at the door.

"Get. Out."

I put my hands up, edging away as I grabbed my shirt and beer. Meredith stared at me with no small amount of hatred in her eyes. That was worse than anything else. Knowing she actually felt hate for me right then. I didn't know how I could convince her to forgive me, but I knew I had to try.

I left her room, slumping against the wall outside before swigging from the beer bottle in an attempt to regain some semblance of control. It had never been my intention to have her up against the wall when I saw her again, but lust had taken over. She set me on fire and I needed to be in her. When she'd let me kiss her, wrapping herself around me, all thoughts of a conversation and an apology had gone out the window. Meredith consumed me and I couldn't hold back. I needed my girl close. I needed to hear her crying out my name in ecstasy. And I really needed to fuck her in the ways I'd been imagining for years.

There'd never been anyone else but Meredith in my eyes. Girls had tried to come onto me, but I'd not given them the time of day. Hell, way too many people wanted a piece of me. I didn't care. None of them were Meredith. I'd remained true to her even though we weren't together.

I loved that fucking girl to death. She'd been the only thing on my mind since the day I'd walked out. It'd been as hard for me seeing her at school as it had been for her. Not to pull her into me and kiss away all the pain in her eyes. To tell her how much I loved her. But I didn't want to ruin her relationship with her brother. I wanted her to be happy. Now I knew she wasn't happy without me. She'd been miserable. And so had I.

I sighed, trudging back downstairs and pushing my way through the crowd as I downed the rest of the beer. I dumped it in the living room before grabbing my jacket and helmet and walking out of the house. If Meredith didn't want me here, I'd respect her wishes. But I'd be back to reclaim her. She could only stay angry for so long. And she would hear me out one way or another.

I stared up at the house as I tugged my jacket on and sat astride my motorbike.

I promise you, Meredith, I'll make this right. We'll have forever with each other. Mark my words.

Jamming my helmet on, I turned the key and kicked my motorbike into gear. I pulled away from the curb knowing this was only temporary and soon, Meredith would be mine again.

CHAPTER TWENTY SIX

Meredith

hy had I been so stupid? Watching Cole walk out on me again tore into my heart in a way I hadn't experienced since the last time he'd left me. Except this time Cole told me it wasn't over and I wanted it to be. I wanted to be done with this shit between us.

You know it's not done. It will never be done.

I hated myself for still loving him. What was wrong with me? Cole had hurt me. He didn't deserve a second chance. He deserved nothing from me.

I bloody hoped he'd left like I told him to. If he was still here, I didn't think I could take it. And the only person I wanted right then was Rhys.

I found my underwear and pulled it back on before staring at myself in the mirror. My face was flushed with anger and my neck still red from the sex I'd just had. My skin felt clammy, but I looked okay for the most part. Deciding I no longer cared about my appearance, I walked out of my room, glad the landing was empty. Fighting my way downstairs was another matter, people were everywhere and drunker than ever. It took me a few minutes to reach the kitchen, finding Rhys leaning up against the counter with what I assumed was a rum and coke in his hand.

My heart couldn't take it. I dashed across the room and barrelled my way into his chest, wrapping my arms around his back.

"Jesus, Mer, what the fuck?"

A pitiful sob erupted from my lips in response. I felt his arm come around me.

"Hey, hey, what's wrong? I was getting worried about you."

I didn't know how to tell him about Cole. We'd never really gone there about past relationships. I didn't want to talk about my shit and he'd been cagey about his own. Now wasn't the time to hold back. My best friend would help me through this. Rhys had been there for me since the day we'd met, even though it had taken me two months to wear him down and actually admit we were friends. I swear to god he was the most difficult and stubborn boy I'd ever met in my life, but I loved him to bits.

"My ex," I mumbled into his t-shirt.

"Your ex?"

"He was here… and… and fuck, Rhys, I can't do this. I can't be here."

"Shh, shh, it's okay. Why don't we go outside? I know it's freezing, but it's fucking stuffy in here and the music is too loud."

I pulled away from him, nodding. The two of us got coats and shoes on before grabbing a bottle of vodka and making our way outside into the garden. We sat in two of the garden chairs on the patio. My legs were already beginning to feel the chill in the air since it was winter, but I didn't care. Rhys handed me the vodka and I swigged from the bottle, feeling the burn as the liquid slid down my throat. I gave it back to him, dropping my chin onto my chest.

"So your ex turned up. Is there some horror story there?"

I nodded, feeling the weight of what happened overloading my senses. Why the hell had I allowed him to just take control of the situation like that? Damn Cole and his fucking sexy-as-sin-self playing havoc with all of my self-control. I hated the fact he'd become so much more attractive since I'd last laid eyes on him.

Damn him. Damn his hotness. Damn those bloody hazel eyes of his. Damn everything about him.

"Do you want to talk about it?"

I shook my head. Rhys put the bottle back in my hand and I took another large gulp, almost choking on it. Who gave a shit? I wanted to drown out the noise in my head. Drown out Cole Carter so I didn't have to think about how much I'd fucked up.

"He broke my heart," I blurted out.

"Well, I kind of assumed that might be the case."

I waved the bottle at him, feeling the alcohol buzz already. Maybe I should've had more to eat at dinner.

"He's a bastard, Rhys. An absolute bastard! I hate him and… and I… I still love him."

"Does this bastard have a name?"

"Cole… Cole fucking Carter."

I drank more, wanting to disappear into a hole where no one could find me ever again. Where the shit with Cole wasn't at the forefront of my mind. God, why the hell did I let him fuck me against my bedroom wall? How would I ever even look at that stupid wall the same way again?

"Can I sleep in your bed tonight?"

I looked over at Rhys, whose eyebrow quirked up.

"Why?"

"Cole fucked me against the wall of my bedroom and I can't be in there."

A smile spread across his face.

"Well, you've had quite the adventure in the last half an hour."

Dick.

"Shut up. I don't know what came over me, except I haven't had sex in two years since we broke up and I missed him… and I wanted him so much. God, Rhys, I really fucked up."

He took the bottle from me and swigged from it.

"Jesus, this shit is strong."

I laughed, unable to help myself. The alcohol had gone to my head far too quickly.

"Yeah, it is. Shit, I slept with my ex… who sleeps with their ex? I'm an idiot."

"We all do dumb things with people we shouldn't when feelings are involved. I mean shit, look at Alfie and Sienna. That is getting so old."

I snorted. Alfie and his on and off girlfriend, Sienna were annoying as hell. Always arguing with each other and then having very loud sex afterwards. I swear to god we all needed earplugs with the way she kept screaming. No doubt they'd be at it later.

"Those two need to end it for good, then we might actually get some sleep."

"You're telling me. Is makeup sex really that good?"

"I wouldn't know."

Rhys swigged from the vodka bottle before handing back to me. I took another gulp.

"No? You never fought with your ex and fucked afterwards?"

"Nope. We were happy until Jonah interfered in our relationship and Cole left me. And then tonight… well… fuck knows what that was."

Rhys looked over at me with a frown.

"Your brother ruined your relationship?"

"Well, technically he objected to the whole Cole being sixteen and me eighteen thing, along with some shit to do with Cole's family. You know my friend, Raphi? That's Cole's older brother… and there's bad blood between him and Jonah, so it's all kinds of fucked up."

"You're still friends with your ex's older brother?"

I waved a hand at him.

"Raphi isn't like Cole in any way shape or form. Besides, they have different dads, but their mum is still with both of them."

Rhys' eyes went wide.

"Hold on, what did you just say?"

I drank from the bottle again before handing back to him.

"Oh well, their mum, Ash, she has four partners and a kid with each of them. I know it sounds weird, but it works for them. Plus Raphi's dad is also in a relationship with his older brother, Duke's dad."

"Jesus Christ."

He downed some more vodka and I laughed again. Yeah, their family was completely unorthodox, but I'd never judged them for it. Especially not after I'd met them all.

"Right? I was a bit taken aback when I first found out, but honestly, you should see them together. They have this amazing bond. It's pretty special, you know, especially how they've made it work for so many years."

I envied their relationship in so many ways. The openness they must have with each other in order to make it work. And, judging by what Cole had told me, they had a fucked up beginning and were still together despite it. It was inspiring in a lot of ways. Not that I wanted to be involved with four men at the same time or anything.

"Well, cheers to them, eh?" He raised the bottle to the sky and then downed some before giving it to me to do the same. "Hold on, hold on, did you say Cole is two years younger than you? Damn, Mer, you had a toyboy."

I snorted and shoved him in the arm.

"Fuck off."

"No, but seriously, did you take his v-plates?"

"You are such a dick sometimes."

Rhys grinned and I instantly forgave him.

"We were each other's firsts, okay? It was special."

He reached over and stroked my hair back from my face. Rhys' eyes were full of understanding as if he knew exactly what I meant. It made me wonder about his own past. I knew he'd lost his virginity, but that was the extent of my knowledge of his relationship history.

"You really loved him."

I nodded, feeling tears welling all over again. Crying over Cole after all this time seemed stupid, but I couldn't help it.

"Aw, Mer, come here."

He put his arms out. I set the bottle of vodka down and slid off my chair into his lap, letting Rhys hold me as the tears started to fall.

"I miss him so much," I sniffled. "Why'd he have to come back, Rhys? Why'd he have to remind me of how much I still love him? Why did I let him fuck me? I hate him… he… he…"

"Shh, it's okay."

Rhys stroked my hair, attempting to soothe me, but all it did was make me cry harder. The stupid part of me wanted Cole so much it blazed like an inferno. I couldn't turn off what my heart yearned for. Him. All of him. Surrounding me. Consuming me. Proving to me why I'd always belonged to him and him to me.

"He… he walked away after I told him I love him. It devastated me and I was angry at Jonah for all of it, but I was so upset, I couldn't even bring myself to shout at him. J was only protecting me… he was only looking out for me… god… it hurt so fucking much, Rhys, so much. It still hurts. Who leaves their girlfriend right after she says I love you for the first time? I still don't understand why he broke my heart. I don't understand any of it."

Rhys' arms around me tightened.

"I'm sorry, Mer," he murmured. "That's a really shitty thing for him to do. You don't deserve to be treated that way by anyone."

I placed my hand on my best friend's heart, feeling the emotion in his words hit me right in the chest. He knew exactly how I felt, but I didn't dare press him as to why. If Rhys didn't want to talk about it, I wouldn't force him.

"Do you think we ever forget our first loves?"

"No, I don't think we do, especially if that first love destroyed us."

I pulled away and leant down, reaching for the vodka bottle which I raised in the air.

"Here's to shitty first loves."

A smile crossed his features even though his eyes were still sad. I drank deeply, knowing I was on the fast track to getting completely wasted. Rhys took the bottle from me.

"And to never letting them hurt us again."

He knocked back the bottle as, by then, we'd almost consumed the entire thing. We were going to feel this in the morning. Thank fuck it was the weekend or going to lectures would be hell.

As the two of us stumbled back in the house together, grabbing a bottle of water from the fridge and attempting to navigate our way to his room, I couldn't help wondering if we'd stick to that goal. Seeing Cole again had hurt me. And some part of me, deep down, knew what was between us was in no way done.

Cole had promised me he'd be back and I didn't know whether I should dread him pursuing me all over again or not. Only time would tell.

CHAPTER TWENTY SEVEN

Cole

As I washed my grease-stained hands in the sink, I glanced over at Anthony Jason or AJ as he was known by most people, who was stripping off his overalls by the lockers. The moment I left school, I'd started an apprenticeship at a garage which my grandfather helped set up for me. I was close to finishing now since I'd almost got my qualifications. I was expecting them to offer me a full-time position when I was done, but I could get a job elsewhere if it didn't work out.

"Hey, you up for getting a drink? Today has been long, man."

I used to think AJ was an okay guy, but since I'd turned eighteen, he'd been on at me to go out with him and the boys after work. To be honest, I wasn't so keen knowing what type of shit they were involved in outside of work. Whilst I knew about Grandpa's connections to the Russian Mafia, I wasn't meant to know the garage I worked at was under their protection. Nor that a few of the guys who worked here were members.

"I would, but I've got something to do," I replied, shutting the tap off.

Besides, I didn't think Mum and Dad would want me hanging out with anyone from here. I'd tried to stay out of trouble since Meredith and I broke up. If I was ever going to prove I was a good man for her, I had to keep on the straight and narrow. Turning my life around had taken time, but I was getting there. My parents were proud of me, which made it all worth it. Now all I had to do was convince Meredith to give me a second chance.

"You never come out with us, Cole. You should. It'll be fun."

I shrugged, walking over to my locker and grabbing my shit from it.

"I really have something to do tonight."

It'd been a week since I'd gone to Meredith's party. I'd given her time to cool off. Raphi told me he'd had an earful off Meredith over me turning up unannounced. He hadn't wanted to lie to her about being the one who told me where she lived. I'd sworn up and down I wouldn't hurt her again. He understood why I'd done it since he knew what Jonah was like. How much he loved and cared about his sister. Raphi hadn't been happy, but at least he didn't blame me entirely for how everything had gone down.

"Oh yeah? Hot date or something?"

"Or something."

AJ gave me a wink.

"Oh damn, well, if you're getting some action, I can't blame you for not wanting to come out with us."

I rolled my eyes and nodded. Better he thought that than the actual truth. I didn't want anyone here finding out about Meredith. The less they knew about my personal life, the better. I might have worked with these guys for a year and a half, but that didn't mean I trusted any of them.

Shrugging on my jacket, I left the staff room with my helmet dangling from my fingers. Mum hated the fact I had a motorbike. Always worrying about her baby getting hurt. I'd promised her I would be safe, but she still fretted all the same.

Now I was eighteen, I did my own thing and my parents mostly accepted that. All us kids had grown up. Only Duke and I still lived at home. Aurora lived with her boyfriend and Raphi moved out when he started uni, wanting some independence of his own.

I sat astride my motorbike when I reached it. Out of the corner of my eye, I saw AJ leave the garage. Two huge, burly looking men in suits approached him. He shook their hands and then they exchanged something between them that looked awfully like bags of pills and money. I shoved my helmet on, not wanting to get involved. This was why I never accepted AJ's offers of going out for a drink. I knew he was dealing drugs on the side and I wasn't down with that shit. If Demetri, the owner caught wind of it, I'm not sure he'd appreciate AJ's extra-curricular activities occurring in his place of business. Especially not since he was mafia. AJ should know better.

"Idiot," I muttered under my breath as I kicked the motorbike into gear and pulled out of the back carpark.

It didn't take me too long to get to Meredith's house despite it being rush hour as I could weave in and out of the traffic. I parked up and made my way to her front door, my helmet dangling from my fingers. Pressing down on the doorbell, I waited. Whilst she told me never to come back here, I wasn't giving up on her. I didn't think she'd want me turning up at her university. This was a slightly safer bet.

The door was pulled open a minute later revealing a shortish guy with blonde hair and glasses.

"Hello, is Meredith in?" I asked.

"Nah, man, she isn't home yet."

Shit, I was hoping she'd be here.

The guy looked me over with a frown as if he expected me to say something else.

"Would it be okay if I waited for her? I'm an old friend."

Not sure Meredith would describe me like that but I didn't care. I wasn't leaving until I'd got to speak to her.

The guy shrugged and pulled the door open wider.

"Sure, whatever. She should be back soon."

He walked away, leaving me standing on the doorstep. I shook my head, stepping in. Meredith would probably have words with her housemate over this. I shut the front door behind me and looked around the hallway, wondering if I should wait downstairs or go up to her room. She'd be more pissed if she found me on her bed. Deciding that wouldn't be a good idea, I strolled down the hallway the way her housemate had gone and entered the kitchen. He was mixing a drink at the counter.

"How do you know Meredith?" he asked without turning around.

I set my helmet down on the kitchen table.

"From school."

"Nice. She doesn't really talk about herself much, always hauled up with Rhys. Those two are like super close and shit. Oh, fuck, sorry, I'm Alfie, by the way."

Who the fuck is Rhys?

Raphi had not mentioned Meredith having a boyfriend so I sure as fuck hoped this guy was just a friend.

"Cole."

He turned around and leant against the counter, taking a sip of his drink.

"You want tea or coffee or something?"

"Um, sure. Tea would be nice. Thanks."

He gave me a smile and flipped the kettle on. I shrugged off my jacket and hung it over the back of the chair before taking a seat.

"How do you take it?"

"Milk, one sugar."

Alfie set about making me a tea and handed it to me when he was done. He looked like he was about to say something when we heard the front door open and voices filter down the hallway.

"Okay, let me get this straight, a guy asked you out in class?" That was Meredith.

"Yes and I very politely declined," came a male voice. "It was so fucking embarrassing. Who does that, Mer? Like seriously."

The door slammed shut and the voices grew closer. I set the tea down on the table and stood up, knowing Meredith would not be happy to see me at all.

"Some people are way too forward. He could've waited until afterwards."

"That wouldn't have been any better. I'm not dating. Ever."

"All right, fuckface, I know, don't get your knickers in a twist."

"Oh shut up, you know how awkward it is for me."

The two of them appeared in the doorway. My breath caught at the sight of her. How her strawberry blonde hair was now dyed this pale pink colour and she had a thick white knitted jumper on. She must've done that during the week because her hair was still red when I'd seen her. The guy she was with was tall with curly dark hair.

"I'm so sorry people finding you attractive is such a chore for you."

"You will be fucking sorry."

"Oh yeah, try—" she stopped mid-sentence as she spied me standing there, her mouth dropping open.

"Hey, Meredith, your friend dropped by," Alfie said. "All right, Rhys?"

"Hey, Alfie," the guy Meredith was with said, looking between me and her with a raised eyebrow.

Meredith's mouth snapped shut. She pointed at me, her face contorting with anger, "What the fuck are you doing here?"

I took a step towards her, putting my hands up.

"Meredith."

"I thought I told you never to come back here. Do you not understand the fucking concept of I don't want to see you again, Cole?"

"Oh, so this is the ex," her friend said.

I didn't appreciate having an audience for this, but it couldn't be helped.

"I know what you said, but I told you I'm not giving up."

"Okay, well, I'm just going to…" Alfie said, pointing at the doorway before he slipped by Meredith and the other guy with his drink. She collared him before he could escape, holding onto his arm.

"You let him in our house?"

"He said he was an old friend."

He pulled his arm out of her grasp before she could respond and dashed away. Meredith threw her arms up and turned back to me. Even though she was mad as hell, to me, she looked beautiful. I couldn't help wanting to pull her against me and kiss away the anger in her eyes. Kiss her even whilst she struggled to get away. Kiss her until she gave in and let me soothe her.

"I want you to leave."

"I want to talk to you."

"I don't want to talk to you."

"I get that, but if you just hear me out, please."

She shook her head.

"No. I told you, I don't want your excuses."

"I'm not going to give you excuses."

Her eyebrow shot up.

"Oh so you're not going to make up a bunch of bullshit lies as to why you broke up with me, huh?"

I dug my hand in my pocket to stop myself from going over to her.

"You already know why that happened. I didn't want to come between you and Jonah."

"He would've got over it, Cole! And I chose you. I picked you, but you didn't pick me."

I shook my head.

"You have that all wrong. I did choose you. I put you first."

She scoffed.

"Oh yeah and how do you figure that?"

Meredith's attention was so intent on me, she didn't notice her friend disappearing from the room to give us space. I was thankful for that much. The two of us needed to have this out alone.

"You lied to your brother about me, Meredith. How is that a healthy relationship when you have to lie to the person you care about, huh? It's not one. I was coming in between you and him and that wasn't okay, but I had no idea because you didn't tell me either. You didn't confide in me about what was going on, so how the fuck was I to know what damage I was causing? It was better for us to be apart before we destroyed everything around us."

She took a step back as if my words had physically struck her. I wasn't the only one to blame in this situation. Yes, I'd hurt her by walking away and I took full responsibility for that. It was on me. I'd apologised for it. Her lying to her brother and breaking her promise to him? That was on her.

"I'm sorry for everything that happened, but this isn't all on me."

"Are… are you saying it's my fault you broke up with me?"

"No. I'm not saying that all."

"Then what the hell are you saying?"

I couldn't take the agony in her expression. My feet carried me over to her and my hands curled around her arms, holding her in place. Meredith stared up at me with hurt and heartbreak in her eyes.

"I'm sorry. I'm just really fucking sorry I walked away from us. I didn't want to be the reason you and Jonah fell out. I didn't want to be the reason we fell apart completely because we were already imploding right before my eyes. I walked away to save us… to save you. And it killed me. You think it didn't hurt when you told me you loved me? You think I really wanted to walk out on you after that? Because I didn't. I really fucking didn't, but you once told me I had to be an adult and prove to you I could be responsible. Well, that's what I did. I took responsibility for us. For everything. I did it for you because I care about you so fucking much, little queen. I still do."

A tear slid down her cheek. I reached up and wiped it away, hating that I'd made her cry. Hating that I'd hurt her. Hating every part of this.

"You mean everything to me, Meredith. You always have. I never stopped wanting you. Every day without you has been absolute torture. I need you. Please give me a chance."

More tears spilt down her face.

"You really hurt me," she whispered. "You broke my heart."

"I'm sorry."

"I hate you for it."

"I know and trust me, I deserve it."

I stroked her cheek, needing her to come around. Needing her to give me a chance to show her how sorry I was. To prove to her I'd never hurt her again. Never.

"I don't know if I can forgive you."

"You don't have to, just give me a chance. One chance… please."

CHAPTER TWENTY EIGHT

Meredith

I didn't know what to say to Cole. It never occurred to me that he could have valid reasons as to why he walked out on us. I couldn't see past my own pain when it came to him. And he was right. I had lied to Jonah. Kept a secret from the person who'd always been there for me no matter what. Jonah had taken care of me throughout my heartbreak, soothing away the pain even if it hurt him to do so. He was sensitive to other people's feelings. Being around me when I cried my heart out had only caused him more distress. But Jonah would never leave me in the dark to deal with it all on my own. He was the best big brother a girl could have.

"I don't know if I can," I whispered. "How do I trust you won't walk away again when things are too hard or we lose our way? I can't go through that again, Cole. I just can't."

I would not put myself in the position to get my heart broken by him again. How could I? Being in love with someone didn't mean you let them walk all over you. Didn't mean you allowed them to treat you like shit.

"I'm right here. I'm staying by your side even when everything gets dark. You have me. All of me. I've always been yours. I'm so sorry, little queen. I'm sorry for everything I put you through. You deserved better from me. So much fucking better. I want to make it up to you. Please let me prove I can be what you need now."

My heart cracked and all my walls came crashing down. The sincerity in his voice and expression ruined me. I wanted to give him a chance. So badly. The truth was I'd missed Cole more than life itself. He'd played such an important role in my life. He was my first for everything when it came to a relationship with a man. This boy had torn my walls apart, given me hope and a new lease on life. And then he'd destroyed me in the worst possible way.

"I want to… I want to, but I'm scared."

He leant closer, making my heart pound harder in my chest and rested his forehead against mine. His thumb kept soothingly stroking my cheek, making me melt further.

"I'm not going to make you any promises. All you need to know is you are my priority. I want to make you happy. I'd do anything for you."

"Cole," I whispered, reaching out to him because I couldn't not. He was so close.

The moment my hands landed on his sides, curling around his waist, I knew I couldn't throw him out of my house. I couldn't tell him to go. I wanted him here.

"Please don't leave me again."

His hand dropped from my face and instead, he wrapped his arms around me, tugging me against him. Being close to him felt so good. That solid body pressed to mine. Cole had only grown more handsome in the past two years. I couldn't help staring into those hazel eyes and wondering how I could forgive him. How I could let go of the past and allow him to heal the heart he'd wounded.

"I won't."

"This doesn't mean you're forgiven or that we're back together."

He smiled and hell if it didn't light my entire body on fire.

"I can live with that. Now, are you going to let me kiss you or do I have to earn that again too?"

I trembled in his embrace, thoughts running rampant at the way he'd kissed me at the party last week. The way he'd fucked me up against my bedroom wall without any shame or mercy.

"I…"

Cole angled me closer, his mouth brushing against mine. I couldn't think straight with him so close and my body reacting to his like it belonged to him.

"Yes or no?"

There was no logical reason for me not to let him kiss me. Yes, this boy had hurt me so fucking much, but it didn't stop me wanting him.

"Yes."

His mouth sealed over mine the moment the word left my lips. My ability to do anything but hold on whilst he kissed me got shot to pieces when he pressed my lips open and slid his tongue against mine. Cole's kiss was hard and unyielding. He took and I gave. He'd told me when I was ready, I'd give him everything and I supposed he was right. I had done the night of the party. I'd allowed him to fuck me the way he wanted. And it had been the hottest experience of my life.

His hand on my back drifted lower, curling around my behind and pressing me closer to his body. There was no space between us any longer. I could feel all the hard planes of his muscles. It was intoxicating and glorious. But there was no way in hell I would let him take me up to bed and have his way with me. Not yet. Cole needed to prove to me he wasn't going anywhere first.

His lips left mine, pressing down my jaw and making my knees buckle. Cole's arms around me kept me from falling down at his feet.

"You taste like home, little queen," he breathed against my skin and I swear to god, I was lost. Utterly lost in a sea of Cole Carter who made my body blaze and melt at the same time. Who made my heart pound so hard in my chest, I thought it might explode.

And then the first thought in my head came out in a rush, "Have you tasted anyone else?"

I shouldn't have asked that considering I'd kissed other boys, but he couldn't blame me for that when he walked out on us. It was simply me trying to move on from him. Futile since my heart belonged to Cole. He'd inked himself onto the flesh. I couldn't erase him no matter what I did.

"No."

"But we've been apart for two years."

He pulled back. The look in his eyes almost made me flinch.

"Doesn't matter. There's only one you."

The seriousness of his tone made me feel guilty for even considering anyone else other than him. But it was guilt I shouldn't be feeling. He left me. He ended our relationship.

"And I don't care if you have. Nothing matters but the here and now."

"Cole…"

"I don't need you to tell me."

I slid my hands up his waist, along his chest and wrapped them around his neck. Despite his words, I still wanted him to know the truth.

"I haven't slept with anyone else."

His hands tightened around me and a dark look crossed his features before it cleared.

"Okay… I won't deny being happy about that."

I shook my head and half-smiled before I stepped back, forcing him into letting me go. Even though I didn't want to be out of Cole's arms, he wasn't forgiven yet.

"What now?"

He cocked his head to the side.

"What do you want to do now?"

I shrugged and dragged my toe along the lino floor.

"Rhys and I planned on going to the pub down the road, they have an open mic night every week… you can join us if you want."

Cole's eyes narrowed.

"Rhys?"

"Yeah, he came in with me earlier." I noticed Cole's hand clench into a fist. It made me aware of what he might be thinking. Reaching out, I coaxed him into unclenching it by prying his fingers back and linking them with mine. "Cole… Rhys is my best friend, there's no reason for you to be jealous."

"I'm not."

The way his jaw clenched shut on his words made it very obvious that wasn't the case. And as much as jealousy and possessiveness pissed me off, seeing Cole worked up over the thought of another guy being close to me made me aware of how much he still cared for me.

"Did I forget to mention he's gay, demisexual and refuses to date anyone like… ever?"

Cole's eyebrow curled upwards.

"Yes, you did."

I reached up and patted his face.

"Don't worry so much, hey?"

Before he had a chance to say anything more, I pulled him out of the kitchen and along the hallway to the living room. Rhys was sat watching TV, but he looked up when we entered the room.

"Cole, this is Rhys… Rhys, Cole."

Rhys' eyes ran up and down my ex.

"Hey," he murmured.

"It's okay if he comes with us to the White Hart, right?"

Rhys nodded although scepticism crossed his features. Considering the last time I'd mentioned Cole was when I'd been drunk in the aftermath of seeing him again, it didn't surprise me. I'd talk to him about it properly later.

"Okay, well, I'm going to get ready."

"Don't be long."

I rolled my eyes as I considered whether to ask Cole to wait here. Deciding against it, I pulled him out of the living room.

"I'm coming upstairs with you?" he asked as I started down the hallway.

"Yes."

"Can I get the tea your housemate made me?"

I stopped, letting go of his hand and giving him a look.

"Alfie made you tea?"

He shrugged so I waved a hand. Cole ambled back down to the kitchen before reappearing with a mug in his hand. The two of us walked upstairs with Cole clearly checking me out the entire way up. I didn't comment on it.

He sat on my bed when we reached my room. I walked over to my cupboards, pulling the doors open.

"So, what are you doing these days?" I asked as I rifled through my clothes for an appropriate outfit.

"I started an apprenticeship at a garage which I'll be done with soon, just need to finish getting my qualifications."

I smiled. Cole had told me he wanted to be a mechanic. He liked working with his hands and he was always fiddling with car parts when I was around his. At least, when his attention hadn't been on me.

Even though I'd kept in touch with Raphi, I never asked what Cole was doing. We always stuck to topics unrelated to our families for obvious reasons.

"Well, I'm glad you're getting to do your dream job."

I looked over my shoulder, finding him sipping at his tea.

"Yeah, keeps me busy and out of trouble."

"You've ditched your troublemaker ways, have you?"

He shrugged, cupping the mug to his chest with his big hands. I'd felt the callouses on them earlier. The thought of him bent over an engine with sweat running down his bare chest made my pulse spike. Okay, so Cole wouldn't do his job without a shirt, but a girl could dream, couldn't she?

"You could say that."

"I always kind of liked that you were a bad boy."

His lips curved up as he looked at me.

"I'll always be bad for you, little queen."

Those hazel eyes simmered with danger and I swallowed hard, turning back to my cupboards as my face heated. Having dirty thoughts about Cole would not do me any favours right now. I'd told myself I wasn't going to let us get that far until I knew he wouldn't leave. Giving him a chance was only fair, but time would tell if it was a mistake for me to have done so.

I grabbed my black skinny jeans, a white almost see-through short-sleeved blouse with little black rabbits on it and a cardigan since it was still winter and cold as fuck outside. Turning around, I found Cole still watching me.

"You know, it's rude to stare at a girl when she's about to change."

The smirk gracing his lips set my blood on fire.

"You did invite me up here."

"Cole!"

He closed his eyes, but the smirk remained. I shook my head and stripped out of my clothes.

"It's not as if I haven't seen everything before, you know," he murmured, keeping his eyes shut.

"That's not the point."

"Don't tell me you've got shy and self-conscious about yourself again."

Cole had explored every inch of me with his fingers and his tongue when we'd been together. He'd made me feel special. His care had allowed me to see myself as someone attractive and desirable, but I didn't think my insecurities would ever leave me. Not really.

"No… at least, not as bad as before anyway."

I stood there in my underwear, feeling vulnerable as hell even though he still had his eyes closed. A part of me wanted him to open them and remind me of why I never had to worry about my appearance. Whenever his hazel eyes had roamed over me, I felt beautiful, wanted, needed.

"You're still the most stunning girl I've ever laid eyes on. Nothing will ever change that."

"Hmm, yeah, okay."

He put a hand out to me. The other was still curled around the handle of the mug which was resting on his knee. I approached him with caution, wondering what on earth he planned to do. His fingers enclosed around mine when I stood before him and knocked my hand against his. He brought my hand up to his lips and kissed my fingertips.

"You don't believe me?"

He turned his face up towards me even whilst keeping his eyes closed.

"It's hard for me to accept compliments, you know that."

Cole flattened my palm against his face and placed a kiss in the centre of it, making my breath hitch.

"You have never been anything but beautiful to me, Meredith. Even with your pink hair."

I couldn't help smiling. Rhys had called me crazy when I'd come home from the hairdresser a couple of days ago. I wanted something different, especially after my encounter with Cole at the party.

"You like the pink?"

"It suits you."

"Well, it's staying… at least for now."

I pulled my hand away from him and walked back over to where I'd left my clothes on a chair. After I tugged them on, I looked in the mirror, feeling good about myself.

"You can open your eyes now."

I picked up my hairbrush and sorted my hair out. Glancing in the mirror again, I could see Cole watching me silently. I braided my hair down both sides and tied it up in a bun at the back before applying a little makeup. When I was done, I turned around and put my hands on my hips.

"Well?"

He stood up and walked over to me, his hazel eyes glinting. I raised an eyebrow. He reached up and stroked a finger down my cheek.

"You are the most perfect girl in the world to me."

Dropping his hand, he stepped away towards the door. My heart melted into a pile of goo on the floor. Cole needed to stop saying shit like that to me. I was in real danger of throwing caution to the wind and allowing him to drown me all over again.

"We going?"

I nodded, following him out and downstairs.

What am I going to do with you, Cole Carter?

I had no idea. My heart still belonged to him, but my mind kept me from doing something stupid… like telling him that. He had a lot of shit to make up for and prove to me before I did. And I hoped I could learn how to forgive him because I didn't think I could survive going through another ending with this boy. It would ruin me completely.

CHAPTER TWENTY NINE

Cole

Meredith let me hold her hand as we walked up her street with her friend tagging along behind us. I don't know what she told him, but he kept giving me the eye as if he wasn't sure whether he should be okay with her bringing me or not. If Rhys was important to her, I'd have to make sure I proved to him I was good for her. That I wouldn't ever hurt Meredith again.

"Can I ask you something?" she piped up a moment later.

"You can ask me anything."

"Is that motorbike outside my house yours?"

I grinned. I'd seen her eying it as we left to walk up to the pub.

"Uhuh."

She glanced up at me, her green eyes full of amusement.

"And Ash is okay with you having that?"

I snorted and shook my head.

"My dads bought it for me for my eighteenth birthday. She doesn't like it at all."

Dad told me they had an uphill battle getting her to agree to it, but he, Eric, Quinn and Xav had ganged up on her over it. It was the only thing I'd asked for since I'd got my licence a while ago. I'd had a smaller one before when I was learning, but I'd wanted a Ducati for as long as I could remember.

"Will you take me out on it?"

I raised an eyebrow.

"You want to straddle my bike, do you? Feel all that power between your thighs."

She shoved my arm with her free hand.

"Shut up."

I bit my lip before smiling.

"Yes, Meredith, I'll take you out on it."

Honestly, I would love it. Having her cling to me whilst I rode, her slight frame wrapped around mine.

"I look forward to it."

I hadn't been sure she would let me do anything with her when I came here to speak to her today. Even whilst I'd been determined to make her see I was sorry, she'd been adamant when I last saw her about never wanting to see me again. I hadn't given up on her when we'd been younger, not really, and I wouldn't now. She was mine even if she wasn't ready for us to get back together yet. I'd meant it when I told her I could live with that. As long as she let me spend time with her. Show her I was serious and wouldn't do anything to jeopardise us again.

The three of us walked into the White Hart five minutes later. Meredith looked around before a girl with bright orange hair put her hand up and waved at us. Rhys huffed next to us and Meredith rolled her eyes.

"Here we go," she muttered as we approached the table the orange-haired girl sat at with another guy.

"Who are they?" I asked, leaning closer to her.

"Our other housemates. If Jazz is here, it's going to get messy."

"She doesn't take no for an answer when it comes to doing shots," Rhys said, shaking his head.

The three of us reached the table. The guy Jazz was with had long hair tied back in a ponytail and bright blue eyes.

"All right, guys?" Jazz said, raising a glass to us.

"Yes. We didn't know you'd be here," Meredith replied.

"Oh well, you know we can't miss an open mic night." Jazz looked at me, raising her eyebrow. "And this is?"

"My… friend, Cole. Cole, this is Jazz and Martin."

Jazz jumped up and came around the table before throwing herself at me.

"Nice to meet you."

I patted her back, but I didn't particularly want to be hugging a random woman I'd never met before. When she pulled away, I eyed Meredith who only rolled her eyes as if to say this was normal. I rubbed the back of my neck when Jazz sat back down.

"Drinks?" I asked.

"I know what they want, I'll come help," Meredith replied before tugging me away from the table.

We approached the bar and waited for the other customers to be served.

"You know, it's weird to think you can buy alcohol now," she murmured, leaning against me.

"It's only been a few weeks. My dads took me and Duke out on my birthday, made me buy all the drinks. Mum wasn't happy at the condition they brought me home in."

Meredith chuckled.

"Oh, I can well imagine. What did she do about it?"

"They were all in the doghouse, moping around the house feeling sorry for themselves whilst there's me and Duke with hangovers and Mum taking care of our every need. She was all 'my babies need their mother', I swear my dads gave us so many evils. Mum rules the roost no matter what they say. You should've seen their faces after she had a go at them."

I glanced over, finding Meredith grinning and shaking her head. When we'd been together, my parents had treated my girl like one of the family after Mum had got over the age difference business. The only person I'd confided in about the real reason for our breakup was Dad. He understood why and didn't have a go at me over it. Then again, he respected my decisions. I'd had a whole load of grief off Mum, but I took it, knowing I deserved it.

Meredith and I ordered drinks for everyone and took them back to the table. The two of us got settled on the last two free seats next to each other. I rested my arm over the back of her chair, which she made no objections to, but her friend certainly gave me a look. There was no way in hell I would let anyone force me to back off from Meredith. As far as I was concerned, she was still mine.

I leant over to her when everyone else was distracted.

"I don't think your friend is happy about me being here."

She looked up at me, her green eyes wide.

"Rhys?"

I nodded.

"I haven't had a chance to talk to him yet."

"What did you tell him about me?"

She looked away, her hand curling around her glass.

"The truth."

I suppressed a sigh.

"You know I'm not proud of what I did to you."

Her hand dropped from the glass onto my thigh, giving it a squeeze.

"I know you're not and that you're sorry. I'll talk to him, I promise. Just not tonight. Let's relax and enjoy ourselves."

I stroked my fingers down her hand, reassuring her I planned on behaving myself. We were here to drink and listen to some music, not to further discuss what went wrong between us. It's a topic we could exhaust ourselves on.

Meredith smiled at me, picking up her glass with her other hand and taking a sip. I wanted to get on the good side of her friends. And I sincerely hoped I wouldn't get any grief off her brother again.

The rest of the evening followed with copious amounts of alcohol, some mediocre singing along with a few good ones thrown in. True to what Rhys had said, Jazz didn't take no for an answer when it came to shots. I refrained from drinking too much since I wanted to remain clear-headed for the most part, but by the time midnight came around, Meredith was a giggling mess. And she was all over me.

"I missed you," she told me, wrapping herself around me as I tried to stand up from the chair.

"I know, little queen, but it's time to get you home, yeah?"

Rhys rolled his eyes and pried Meredith off me. He wasn't quite as drunk as she was. The two of us got her up and out of the pub with Jazz and Martin trailing along behind us. They seemed to be holding each other up.

Meredith leant heavily against me as we walked up the street, but I didn't mind too much.

"I don't want you to go anywhere, Cole. Stay with me."

I wrapped an arm around her.

"You sure about that?"

I wasn't exactly in a fit state to drive myself home. My plan was to bug Duke to come to pick me up and I'd get my motorbike tomorrow.

"I want you."

She reached up and ran her fingers down my chest, her eyebrow quirking up in a rather suggestive way.

"You're drunk."

"So?"

I shook my head. I wouldn't take advantage of her when she was wasted. No, I'd put her to bed.

"You need to sleep it off."

She argued with me the whole way back to her place, but I wouldn't budge on the subject. No way would I do anything to jeopardise my relationship with her or her friend's opinion of me.

Rhys unlocked the front door. Meredith practically fell into the house, making me wary of her ability to get upstairs. Instead of asking, I picked her up and carried her. She giggled, staring up at me with a bright smile.

"You're so strong."

"Comes with hauling car parts and tyres around."

"I bet you get all dirty from it… grease stains everywhere… that's so hot."

I eyed her as I took her up the second flight of stairs with Rhys trailing along behind us.

"If you say so."

"Everything you do is hot."

Meredith clearly had no filter when she'd been drinking. I looked behind me.

"Is she always like this?" I asked Rhys.

"Pretty much, I can't shut her up when she's had a few too many," he replied, shrugging as we reached the second-floor landing. "I'll let you take care of her. Guess this is goodnight."

He squeezed Meredith's shoulder, gave me a nod and walked into his own room, shutting the door behind him. I carried her into her room and set her down on the bed. She grabbed my hand and pulled me onto it. Planting my hands down so I wouldn't crush her, I stared down at the girl who I'd been enraptured by since I was eleven.

"Stay with me."

"Meredith…"

"Please, Cole. Don't leave me again."

How could I say no to that? Saying no to her now felt wrong.

I pulled away and sat up.

"Okay, but we're just sleeping. Let me help you get comfortable."

She didn't object when I helped her out of her clothes. When she tried to pull me to her, I resisted. A sober Meredith would regret us sleeping together tonight. So even whilst she pouted over it, I helped her into a long t-shirt and tucked her up under the covers.

I left her to get some water, finding the house quiet now everyone had retired to their rooms. When I returned, she had fallen asleep. I stared down at her. The way her pale pink hair had come loose from her braids and the bun. She looked peaceful.

I set the glass on her bedside table, stripped down and turned out the lights before crawling in next to her. Reaching up, I stroked her face, but she didn't stir.

"I've missed you so much, Meredith," I whispered. "Being here with you tonight made me so fucking happy. I hope you can learn to forgive me… I love you."

I kissed her forehead before getting settled and closing my eyes. Admitting it out loud even if she was asleep made my heart tighten. This girl was my whole damn world. And I'd spend the rest of my life proving it to her if I had to.

CHAPTER THIRTY

Meredith

My head hurt and my mouth felt like cotton wool when I surfaced from a deep sleep. Opening my eyes felt like a whole load of effort. What on earth did I do last night? If I was this hungover, then no doubt Jazz was involved. Rhys and I hated going out with her since she was always trying to ply us with more alcohol no matter our objections.

A loud sound echoed around my skull. It took a second for me to register what it was. Someone was knocking on my door. I groaned and opened my eyes, turning my head towards it in time to note Rhys walking in with two mugs in his hands. He came over and set one down on my side of the bed before walking around the other side and setting the other down. I blinked, wondering why he'd made two.

Rhys came around to my side again when he noticed I was awake.

"Hey, sleepyhead," he murmured.

"Why do I feel like I got hit by a lorry?"

"Jazz and Jägermeister."

"Oh god. Why did you let me do that?"

Rhys snorted and rolled his eyes.

"I wasn't at the bar with you."

I rubbed my face, wishing I hadn't allowed Jazz to bulldoze over me last night.

"I'm making some breakfast, you think your ex will want some?"

"Huh?" I turned my head, noticing I wasn't alone. "Oh shit."

Cole was fast asleep next to me, his dirty blonde hair mussed and his face completely at peace. So that was why Rhys had made two teas.

"You were pretty insistent about not wanting him to leave," Rhys said, making me turn my attention back to him.

"I don't know what I was thinking."

Rhys shook his head.

"You were drunk."

"That shouldn't be an excuse."

"Should I make him something or not?"

I slapped a hand over my face, wishing I wasn't alive because my head was pounding so hard.

"Please do. I'll wake him up and we'll be down soon."

I couldn't remember what happened last night. I had no idea if Cole and I had done anything with each other. It's not as if I thought he would take advantage of me in a drunken state.

"I left painkillers in your drawer last time so you know, you might want to take some."

I heard Rhys shuffle out of my room. Dropping my hand, I looked at Cole again. What on earth was I going to do with this boy? I reached over and prodded his arm.

"Cole."

He murmured in his sleep but otherwise didn't open his eyes. I prodded him harder, which made him bat my hand away.

"Cole."

"What?" he muttered.

"What happened last night?"

He opened his eyes, a grin spreading across his features.

"Nothing."

"Why don't I believe that?"

He raised an eyebrow before reaching out and stroking my cheek.

"You told me not to leave you so I didn't."

Cole wouldn't bullshit me about that kind of thing. Even if I couldn't remember everything about last night, I believed him.

"And you didn't do anything to me?"

"No, not even when you tried to kiss me numerous times."

I wanted to curl up in a ball and die from mortification, but Cole looked nonplussed as if me wanting him wasn't a big deal. I supposed in his mind, it wasn't. He wanted us to get back together.

"I feel like shit."

He smiled wider and pulled his hand away.

"Need me to take care of you?"

I almost rolled my eyes before shifting away and pulling myself up into sitting position. My head hurt worse with the movement.

"No, Rhys brought us tea and is making breakfast."

I opened my bedside drawer and pulled out the painkillers Rhys had stashed in there for me. Popping two out, I knocked them back with my tea. I sat back against the headboard and watched Cole sit up, rubbing his face before he grabbed his own mug.

"Does he take care of you a lot then?"

"Yeah, we take care of each other no matter what."

Rhys was the one person in my life who hadn't let me down. I couldn't even say that about my brother after all the shit between me, him and Cole. He might be an incredibly private person, but Rhys cared deeply. It'd taken time for him to learn to trust me to be there for him in return. Somehow I knew he had old wounds festering away inside him, but I would never press him on the subject. He would tell me in his own time, even if it took years. I'd be there when he was ready.

"So it's not always you getting wasted?"

I shook my head, taking another sip of my tea.

"He didn't drink at all when I first met him. He grew up with a lot of shit in his life, his dad being an alcoholic didn't help matters. I certainly never forced him, but he kind of came to it on his own. Like he knew he wouldn't ever get in the same state as his father, you know."

His dad had also been abusive towards him and his mum. Rhys had opened up to me about it one night about six months into our friendship. Not long after that, he introduced me to his mum. I think she was happy he'd found a friend at university and she'd welcomed me into their family with open arms.

"It sounds like he means a lot to you."

"He does."

Cole reached out and laced our fingers together, rubbing his thumb along the back of my hand.

"I'm glad you have someone looking out for you."

He may have got a little jealous over Rhys yesterday until I set him straight, but Cole would never begrudge me having a friend. He'd never tried to run my life when we were younger, only ever encouraging me to go after what I wanted out of life.

"I want to forgive you," I whispered. "I want us to go back to the way we were, but I don't know if that's possible."

"I'm not asking to go back to the way we were, Meredith. We're not the same as we were two years ago, at least, I'm not. I did a lot of growing up and now I want to move forward. I hope you want to do that with me."

I had no idea how Cole always knew the right things to say to me. My eyes met his beautiful hazel ones. All I could see was his earnestness and affection for me. Even as my head still hurt, I couldn't stop myself from placing my mug on the bedside table before taking his from his hands and popping it down too. I moved towards him, straddling his thighs as I cupped his face with one hand and ran my fingers through the hair at the back of his head with the other. Cole stared up at me without moving or attempting to touch me back.

"My feelings for you have never disappeared or lessened. You were my first for everything."

I traced a line across his jaw with my fingers, my eyes fixed on their path. On the way his lips parted and how I couldn't look away from him. This beautiful boy who'd captured my heart two years ago and had kept it ever since. His lips curved upwards and his eyes grew softer. Even though my mind was still plagued with doubts and insecurities and Cole still had a ton of shit to make up to me, I wanted and needed him.

"Do you still love me?" he asked, his voice barely above a whisper.

I nodded, not willing to say the words out loud yet. Not until I could be sure I'd let go of the pain he'd inflicted on my heart.

"Move forward with me, little queen. Let me be what you need."

I didn't answer him with words. Leaning forward, I pressed my mouth to his. His hands wrapped around my thighs. He did nothing else but let me kiss him. When I pulled away, I rested my forehead against his.

"I'll try to."

He smiled, setting my world on fire even though I still felt like shit physically, what with the hangover raging through my system.

"Will you let me take you out? Just the two of us, to reacquaint ourselves with each other."

I nodded, not wanting to let him go. No one would care about our age difference now. It wouldn't hold us back any longer. Only my heart would, but in time, I hoped I could learn to trust him again.

Our lips met again, but this time the kiss became urgent. His hands moved from my thighs, curling around my behind as I gripped his head with mine.

"Cole," my moan vibrated across his mouth, my hips grinding into his.

All of my senses came alive at his touch. The aftereffects of drinking no longer seemed to matter when I had him between my legs. All the feelings I had two years ago when Cole and I were together rushed back. The want. The need. The craving. He was so familiar. So real.

My hands dropped from his head, running down his chest and sliding under his t-shirt. All his hard muscles remained. Just like I remembered. I'd always loved the way his skin felt under my fingertips.

"Do you want me?" he murmured.

I shouldn't. Now wasn't the time to get lost in him. And yet, I didn't want to stop either. I didn't have to ask if he wanted me. That much was clear by the way he'd hardened between my legs. I pulled away, staring at him as my chest heaved with each breath.

"I do, but I don't think we should… not yet."

He nodded, reaching up and stroking my cheek.

"Breakfast then?"

I stared at him in wonder. Sometimes he surprised me with how considerate of my feelings he could be. Yes, he'd hurt me, but before that, he'd always made sure I was happy with anything he did.

"Yeah, breakfast."

I crawled off him and got up, rubbing my head before I went over to my cupboards and pulled out a pair of jogging bottoms and a hoodie. Tugging them on, I shuffled back over to the bed and picked up my mug. Cole had got up and pulled his clothes on. The two of us went downstairs and into the kitchen, finding Rhys had cooked us up some bacon sandwiches.

"Oh my god, you are a lifesaver," I told him as I went over and wrapped my arm around his waist, leaning against his side. Rhys placed a kiss on my forehead and ruffled my hair, which was still half up in a bun and braids.

"You seem a little perkier."

"Tea helped." *And Cole's kisses. Those made me feel alive.*

He raised an eyebrow.

"Hmm, why don't I believe that is the only reason?"

"Shut up," I muttered, pulling away and going to sit beside Cole, who put his hand on my knee.

Rhys sat across from us with his own plate. The three of us ate in a companionable silence. Cole turned to me when he was done, leaning back in his chair.

"I need to get going, but I'd like to know when I can take you out."

I looked at my plate, feeling a little awkward with Rhys being here and having not talked to him about Cole properly.

"Depends on what you have in mind."

"Well, I was hoping you'd let me take you to dinner. It would also be nice if you wanted to come over at some point. I'm sure my parents would be happy to see you."

"Dinner during the week would be okay. I'd like to see them too."

Cole pulled out his phone and made me put my new number in it. Then he got up, placing a kiss on top of my head before gathering up his stuff.

"I'll call you later, yeah?"

I nodded, capturing him by the hand before he disappeared. He raised an eyebrow at me. I got up out of my chair and wrapped my arms around his waist, pressing my face into his chest. Cole hugged me back, leaning his chin on the top of my head.

"Monday," I whispered. "Dinner on Monday."

I didn't want to wait long to see him. Honestly, I didn't want him to go at all, but I knew it would be better for me to get my head straight first.

"Okay, little queen, Monday it is."

He pulled away and smiled at me. I gave him an awkward shrug before he walked away. A minute later, I heard the front door slam. Dropping back into my chair, I pushed my plate away and planted my arms on the table, leaning my head against them.

"So… you're just forgiving him?" Rhys asked.

"Not exactly."

"And that means?"

Rhys didn't look like he disapproved, but I sometimes couldn't tell with him.

"He explained why he left me and apologised for it, but it doesn't mean I forgive him for it or trust him not to hurt me again."

"And yet you're making plans with him anyway."

I closed my eyes. My head still hurt and I didn't like the way Rhys sounded as if I was making a huge mistake.

"Just because someone hurt you, doesn't mean you can just stop loving them or turn your feelings off."

"Trust me, I'm aware of that, but you ended for a reason. Do you really think he deserves a second chance after the way he treated you?"

"He didn't leave to deliberately hurt me. He didn't want to come between me and Jonah. He ended our relationship to protect me from that, and honestly, it was too hard with our age difference back then. It's so stupid. If he was the older one, it wouldn't be a thing, but as the older woman, there's this stigma attached. You should've heard the way Cole's grandmother went off on his mum about it all."

I buried my face in my arms, wishing I didn't have to justify my actions to my best friend.

"I still love Cole, Rhys. I never stopped. He is kind, caring, considerate and wants to make it up to me. Shouldn't I give the person who showed me I was beautiful and helped me overcome my fears and insecurities about myself a chance to prove he's sorry? I don't want to live with regrets or grudges. I just... I just want him. I can't help it. I want Cole. I need Cole. I love him so fucking much."

The truth slammed into me. No matter what he'd done, I couldn't let him go. My first love. I couldn't walk away from what the two of us shared. It didn't work like that for me. It didn't feel right to throw it away. Our connection had remained despite the circumstances of our breakup. And I wanted that closeness with him. I wanted him back as much as he wanted me.

I felt Rhys' hand on my arm, giving it a gentle squeeze.

"Loving someone isn't always enough."

The sadness in his voice tugged at my heart. Rhys spoke as if he knew exactly what it felt like to love someone so fiercely you think you can't live without them and yet... love hadn't been enough. I wished he'd tell me what happened to him. Why he'd closed his heart to the possibility of a relationship with another person.

"It's enough for me to know I need to try. I want to forgive him. I want to put the past behind us and look to the future." I raised my head, looking into his dark eyes and realising he was merely worried for me. He wanted me to be sure of what I was doing. "I need to do this. Can you understand that? Understand that if I don't try, I'll spend the rest of my life with regrets and what ifs."

It took a minute for his eyes to soften and for him to nod.

"Yeah, Mer, I can understand that."

I smiled and hoped beyond hope giving Cole a chance wouldn't backfire on me. I hoped I wouldn't end up regretting this more than anything else. I didn't care what Rhys said. Right now, love was enough for me. It had to be.

Cole might never have said those words to me, but why else would he be back if he didn't feel that way about me?

If he didn't love me?

The simple answer was he wouldn't.

Love had to be enough. I couldn't live without Cole Carter again. I just... couldn't.

CHAPTER THIRTY ONE

Meredith

I fidgeted on the sofa, nerves prickling across my skin. It wasn't going on a date with Cole, which had my stomach in knots. It was the fact he told me he'd be picking me up on his motorbike. Whilst I'd told him I'd love to go on the back of it sometime, I had not expected him to suggest it straight away. In preparation, I'd put on my warmest pair of jeans and a thick jumper to go on underneath my coat.

I jumped up the moment the doorbell rang before anyone else could answer it. My mouth went dry at the sight of Cole standing outside with a helmet and a motorcycle jacket in his hands, his dirty blonde hair tousled and a sly smile on his face.

"Evening."

"Hi," I all but whispered.

He held up the jacket and the helmet. I stared at them for a moment, noticing he was already wearing a jacket himself.

"Are those for me?"

"I didn't want you to get cold."

My heart went haywire in my chest, but I kept my cool, giving him a smile.

"Well, thank you."

I took the jacket from him and shrugged it on, not wanting to ask why it was in my size and fit me perfectly. Cole had gone out of his way to get this for me. He tucked the helmet under his arm and zipped it up for me. Then he carefully put the helmet over my head, securing the strap. I'd braided my hair so it wouldn't get ruined.

Cole took my hand, allowing me to shut the front door behind me before leading me over to his motorbike. He placed his own helmet on and sat astride it. I hooked my leg over and sat behind him, wrapping my arms around his waist instinctively.

"You need to hold on tighter than that," he told me. "Don't let go, no matter what."

I obliged, squeezing my arms around him. He started the motorbike and I felt it rumble beneath my thighs. Equal parts nervous and excited, I pressed harder against his back, knowing he would keep me safe.

I almost let out a squeal when we set off. Cole didn't go too fast, but it didn't stop the adrenaline pumping through my veins at the experience of being on the back of a motorbike for the first time in my life.

We weaved in and out of the rush hour traffic, making our way to wherever he was taking me to dinner. I completely understood why Cole wanted to ride one of these, but I didn't think I'd have the guts to do it on my own. I was thankful for the helmet so the wind didn't whip around my face. And the jacket he'd got me was warm, keeping the chill in the air at bay.

By the time we stopped, I was so hyped up from the whole experience, I was practically vibrating with it. Hastily, I pulled off the helmet and when Cole took his own off, I couldn't help myself. I went up on my tiptoes, wrapping my arm around his neck and planting my lips on his. He was a little startled by my sudden, bold movement, but his arm came around me after a moment. His kiss wasn't in any way gentle and I didn't want it to be.

When we pulled apart, his breathing was a tad laboured and his eyes were dark with heat. He smirked at me, setting my blood on fire.

"I take it you enjoyed that."

I nodded, licking my lip and staring at his mouth. He chuckled, pulling away so he could wrap an arm around me, dragging me away towards the pay station for the car park.

"Who'd have thought my little queen would be a speed demon."

"Shut up."

"Oh no, I like it… a lot."

I felt my face growing hot as images of us fucking on his motorbike flittered across my mind. That would never happen, of course, but thinking about it was hot. Honestly, I hadn't been able to get thoughts of me and Cole naked together out of my head. Before we'd seen each other again, it'd been two years since I had sex. Cole was too hot for words. Currently, his hair was falling in his eyes as he paid for our parking. And here I was, trying not to drool all over him like some rabid nympho.

I managed to get my thoughts under control as we walked to the restaurant. It was this Moroccan place and had all these low tables with benches and cushions for us to sit on. I couldn't help looking around in awe at all the colourful artwork and mosaics.

"You like?" Cole asked, taking my hand.

He sat next to me, something I was happy about. Being close to him made me feel alive.

"Yes, definitely."

He sat back, smiling at me.

"Mum and Dad took me to Morocco for my seventeenth birthday."

I raised an eyebrow.

"They did? I didn't think your dad would be up for flying, what with all the people and stuff."

Cole shrugged. He'd told me a little about his dad and how he wasn't so keen on crowds or being around people in general.

"He was okay with it, though he only agreed for me and Mum. Think flying first-class helped. It was hot as fuck there, but we had a good time. I think the rest of my dads appreciated Mum's tan when we got back." He shuddered as he said it. "Honestly, her reunion with Quinn, Xav and Eric was kind of sickening to watch."

I snorted, well aware of how open his parents were around their kids when it came to their love for each other.

"They have no shame."

"Zero. No point me complaining since they'd only tell me it's their house and they can do what they want in it. Duke exited the room pretty quickly after telling them they'd destroyed his innocence."

"Duke and innocent are two words I never thought I'd hear in the same sentence."

Cole chuckled, stroking a thumb down the back of my hand.

"Oh no, the most innocent one out of us is Raphi."

"I wouldn't be so sure about that if I was you."

Cole's eyebrows shot up.

"No?"

I'd heard a few stories from Raphi about what he'd been getting up to at university. Some of it concerned me since further shit had gone down between him and my brother in the intervening years. It hadn't helped their friendship, relationship or whatever it was in the slightest. If anything, it was worse now.

"I don't know what he's told you about him and Jonah."

Cole rolled his eyes.

"Nothing. Every time I've mentioned anything to do with Jonah, Raphi gets pissy and changes the subject. He doesn't want to talk about it at all."

I wasn't sure whether or not to tell Cole what I knew. Raphi had told me a few things after I'd pestered him, considering Jonah was still being very tight-lipped. Those two needed their heads bashing together, in my opinion.

"I think I know why he and Jonah are so fucked up about each other, but if Raphi hasn't told you anything, then I can't really say what it is."

Cole gave me a sad smile.

"It's okay, you don't have to tell me. Wouldn't want you to betray either of them."

"Oh, Jonah is still adamant he's never telling me what went down, but Raphi gave me some clues. He called me the Inquisition when I was grilling him about it."

Cole's smile turned brighter.

"I can well imagine. You are like a dog with a bone sometimes."

I shrugged. Saying it like it was made some people uncomfortable, but I wasn't the type of person to beat around the bush. Rhys often told me my honesty was refreshing and my pestering incredibly irritating.

The waiter came over to us and I realised I hadn't even looked at the menu. Cole merely grinned and said he'd pick a selection of things for the both of us. As he was driving, the two of us ordered mocktails. I often tried to restrict my drinking until the weekends so I could be fresh for uni. Some students got pissed most nights of the week and were barely sober during classes.

"How's uni going?" Cole asked when he'd finished speaking to the waiter.

"Good, keeps me busy and I'm learning a lot."

"Still want to work in stage production then?"

I nodded, grinning.

"Definitely. I can't wait."

Cole knew all about my dream to work in the West End. He'd actively encouraged me in pursuing it as a career.

"So, if I got us tickets for the theatre, you'd be up for it?"

Instead of answering with words, I leant over and kissed his cheek, running my hand down his chest. As I pulled away, I caught his smirk. Cole knew exactly where to take me out. The boy was nothing if not thoughtful. My interests hadn't changed much in the past two years. I would never turn down a trip to the theatre.

"What would you prefer, a musical or something more serious?"

"Well, if you take me to the Globe, you'd be guaranteed to get lucky afterwards."

His hazel eyes darkened and it made me shiver.

"Is that so?"

"Uhuh."

He leant closer, resting his hand on my thigh. I fought hard not to react, even though everything about him turned me on and I'd had very dirty thoughts about him earlier.

"And tonight?"

I bit my lip.

"Perhaps."

Honestly, I'd forgotten all the reasons why I shouldn't let Cole into my bed. He made me want him so fucking bad just by being his sexy-self. I couldn't help it. I mean, we weren't back together. I wasn't sure what it would take to help me trust him again, but it didn't stop my body needing his. Being close to Cole and knowing he was still mine if I wanted him was far too much of a temptation.

"I can see it in your eyes, Meredith," he murmured.

"See what?"

"How much you want me."

I didn't look away from him.

"So?"

"So, you don't have to do anything you're not ready to. I'm willing to wait as long as it takes."

Why did that only make me want him more? His consideration of my feelings and needs took my breath away at times. It's not as if it would be some casual thing. I still loved Cole. Not sure I knew how to stop even though he'd hurt me.

"What if I am ready?"

He reached over and brushed his fingers down the side of my face. The simple touch set all my nerve endings on fire.

"I want you, Meredith, I won't deny that. However, I don't want to screw up or have you regretting the second chance you've given me."

The sincerity in his eyes made my heart melt.

"I would never use that against you when it's my decision. All you've ever done is given me choices. It's never been about force or coercion. Trust me, Cole, when I let you back into my bed, it's because I want it to happen. It's on me."

He didn't respond as the waiter came over with our drinks, but I caught the relief in his eyes before he dropped his hand and thanked the man.

I'd learnt a strong lesson from our breakup. One about responsibility and making sure you accepted your part in things. It was my decision to lie to Jonah, which had almost guaranteed the failure of my relationship with Cole in the first place. I was fully aware of how protective Jonah was over me. I was his baby sister. The one he'd taken care of when our father died and our mother had decided we could fend for ourselves. Whilst Cole had walked away from us, I played a huge part in our ending. My actions were the catalyst. I couldn't place all the blame on him for our demise because it simply wasn't all his fault.

That's why in that restaurant, on our second first date, I silently vowed to myself I would always take responsibility for my own actions.

And that's the moment I forgave Cole for hurting me two years ago when everything fell apart between us.

CHAPTER THIRTY TWO

Cole

My date with Meredith honestly couldn't have gone better. We talked, laughed and enjoyed each other's company. It almost felt as if no time had passed and we were a couple again. It wasn't quite the same as we'd both grown up in the last two years. Things had inevitably changed. We were still Cole and Meredith though, two people who shared a connection. Who cared and deep down wanted each other for life.

Meredith turned to me at her front door, her green eyes shining and my heart lurched in my chest.

"Want to come in?"

I rubbed the back of my neck with my free hand as the other clutched my helmet. I had intended to drop her home and leave regardless of what she'd said at the restaurant.

"You sure I should?"

I had a feeling I knew what would happen if I did go in with her.

"Would I invite you in if I wasn't?"

"Meredith, I told you, there's no rush."

She unlocked the door and took my hand, pulling me in with her. I didn't protest any further, following her upstairs to her room. I wouldn't lie and say I didn't want to strip her down and fuck her. The thought of it made my cock harden. I'd missed everything about her. The time at her house party wasn't enough. Having to spend the night next to her on Friday hadn't helped matters either. She was so fucking tempting. I only had so much patience and restraint.

She popped the helmets down on her desk after taking mine from me. Then she tugged off the jacket I'd bought her. I didn't want her getting cold when I took her out on the Ducati. Her hands were on mine next, unzipping it and making me shrug out of it. She set those on her desk chair and stepped towards me.

"Cole," she murmured, reaching for my waist. "I want you to take control like you did at the party."

I swallowed hard, staring down at her. Fuck, I was so scared of messing everything up. Allowing that fear to hold me back would only end up in disaster. I had to trust this was what she wanted. The way her eyes darkened with heat and longing decided it for me. Turning her down would be fucking stupid.

Reaching up, I held onto her pink braid. I tugged her closer and tipped her face up to me. She let out a gasp as if not expecting me to be rough in my handling of her.

"You liked that, did you?"

"Yes."

Leaning closer, I brushed my mouth over hers.

"You want me to fuck you with no mercy?"

She squirmed against me, biting her lip.

"Answer the question."

"Yes… please," she whispered.

My fingers itched in anticipation, not to mention my dick. I was sure she could feel it now, how much I craved her. I had done for as long as I'd known her. The craving had differed when I was younger, but it was still there. The need for her in my life. I couldn't imagine a world where she didn't exist.

I'm never going to love anyone the way I love you, Meredith Pope. You are my first thought in the morning and my last at night. You are my one.

"Since you asked so nicely."

Who the fuck was I kidding? Even if she hadn't said please, I would give it to her anyway.

I forced her to step backwards until her legs hit the bed, then my mouth was on hers, tongue delving between her lips and tasting her. Meredith moaned in my mouth, her hands tightening around my waist. The sound encouraged me. My hands drifted down, tugging at her jumper. She raised her arms to allow me to pull it off, followed by her t-shirt and bra. My hand closed around her breast as I kissed down her neck. I swiped a thumb over her nipple, only eliciting another moan from her.

I needed her bare for me. My fingers were unbuttoning her jeans and tugging them off as she arched into me. Her knickers came next, followed by her socks and shoes so I could get everything else off. I pulled back to stare down at her. Her pale skin was luminescent in the low light. It'd been so long since I'd seen her like this. But here she was. The girl of my fucking dreams. And she wanted me.

"Kneel for me."

Meredith lowered herself, watching me with wide eyes. My hand curled around her braid again, forcing her head up.

"I think you know what I want you to do."

"Tell me."

She wants to be told. Fuck, that's so hot.

"Take my dick out and wrap your lips around it."

Meredith reached for me, tugging open my fly and digging her hands into my boxers. I let out a grunt when she wrapped her fingers around my hard cock, pulling it out. She leant closer and ran her tongue up the shaft. I still had a hold of her braid so I tugged on it.

"Don't make me wait."

Her hot, wet mouth enclosed around the head of my dick and I was in fucking heaven. I watched her take more with rapt attention. All my focus was on her. Her beautiful, naked body and the way she wrapped her fist around the base of my dick. Her eyes flicked up to mine whilst she sucked, giving me full access to her emotions. They just about fucking killed me. Those green eyes burning with all her pent up need for me. I didn't know how the fuck I could last with her staring at me like that. And I didn't want to. Her mouth around me was amazing.

I hadn't been lying to her when I said it wouldn't have bothered me if she'd been with other people. Knowing I'd been the only one who gave her this only made me harder. I wanted to keep her for life this time around. Make her mine completely. In heart. In body. And in name.

It might be too soon to thinking those things, but hell, I wanted everything with her. Absolutely everything.

"That's it, show me how much you want it, little queen. Make me spill in your hot little mouth."

Meredith didn't let up. She worked me faster and took me a little deeper. I held back from groaning as my fist tightened around her braid. I could feel it building. My mouth parted and my body tensed. This time I let a groan escape as I erupted in her mouth. Pleasure bloomed all over my body, intensified by knowing it was her who'd given it to me. Nothing would match up to being with her.

When the pulses faded, she pulled away and swallowed without me telling her to. It's not as if Meredith hadn't gone down on me when we'd been together before, but something about having her kneeling for me made this experience so much hotter.

"Mmm, I think it's time you got a reward for being a good girl." I pointed at the bed. "Lie back for me."

She released me and crawled on it, settling herself down in the middle.

"Spread your legs."

A flush spread down her cheeks but she did as I asked, raising her legs up and opening them wide. I couldn't help staring at her perfect pussy, just waiting for me to devour it. I knelt on the bed, running my hands down her legs as I leant over her. I pressed a kiss to her stomach, watching her squirm under my touch. Moving lower, I couldn't fucking wait to feast on her.

I didn't want to rush this, not like the last time when I'd fucked her up against the wall. That couldn't be helped. Seeing her again had all my feelings and needs boiling over. I had to have her. And she'd needed me too even if it'd left her in a mess of emotions afterwards.

"Cole," she cried out the moment my tongue brushed along her clit. "Oh, oh, fuck."

My hands banded around her thighs, spreading her wider for me. I went straight for the kill, flicking my tongue over her clit in the exact way I knew she liked. I'd memorised every inch of Meredith's body and all her tells. Most teenage boys would be too interested in getting laid to do so, but not me. I wanted to make sure I pleased her. I learnt everything I could. Knowing what buttons to press and when to make her come.

"Cole, don't stop, oh god."

I watched her body shake and tremble, her hands fisting in the covers. Her back arched off the bed when I slid two fingers inside her. Hooking them upwards, I found the right spot and almost smiled when the volume of her moaning increased.

"Fuck, Cole."

Her pussy clenched around my fingers as she came. Such a fucking beautiful sight. The way she unfolded for me, her body undulating and writhing. Her eyes were squeezed shut, her mouth open and my name kept spilling from it.

She lay there when she'd come down, panting hard as her fingers uncurled from the covers. I was fucking hard as stone again. I stripped out of my clothes whilst she was still recovering, digging a condom out of my pocket. Just because I hadn't planned on fucking her this evening, didn't mean I'd come unprepared. Rolling it on, I slid between her legs, making her open her eyes. I took both her hands and pinned them above her head with one of mine, locking her wrists together.

"You can struggle, but I'm not letting you go," I murmured, running my other hand down her chest and circling her nipple with my finger.

She let out a pant in response.

"You have no idea how long I've wanted to have you had my mercy. No matter what you say, you're mine, Meredith. No one else will make you feel the way I do. I'm your first… your last… your everything."

The fire in her eyes flickered. She wanted to rebel, but her mouth closed. She relinquished control. Meredith knew the truth. Forgetting what we shared would be impossible for both of us. No matter what happened in the future, this would remain. It would never be destroyed or burn out.

I ran my free hand down her stomach, watching her squirm all over again. No doubt, she knew what was coming. Gripping my cock, I guided it to her and pressed forward. Her choked moan when I slid inside made me smile. Fuck, I would never get over how tight she was.

Leaning down, I brushed my mouth against hers.

"Cole," her moan vibrated across my lips.

"You going to show me how much you want to get fucked hard?"

"Yes."

Her lips bucked, forcing me deeper. I kissed her, swallowing the resulting whimper. My hand around her wrists tightened as she pressed against me. I gripped her hip with my other as an anchor so I could pull back and press inside again. I wasn't gentle. I gave it to her without restraint. She couldn't escape me and I was high off the thrill of it. High off her submitting to me. Her whimpers in my mouth fed me. They prompted me to go faster, only making her tremble against me. She needed this. Wanted it. I gave her the freedom to let go. I made her feel alive. Kissing down her jaw, I listened to her moans and pants, the way she cried out my name with her pleasure.

"That's it, little queen, take it."

"Cole, please, more."

"Oh, am I not giving you enough?"

"You are, I just… I need more."

This position didn't allow me the space to fuck her with the ruthlessness she was asking for. I let go of her hands and sat up. She let out a mewl of distress as if me withdrawing from her wasn't what she wanted.

"I want you to turn over, get up on your knees and grip the headboard."

She scrambled to obey, clearly desperate to have me back inside her. I moved closer, leaning over her so I could kiss her shoulder. I wrapped a hand around her body, locking her against me as I slid back inside her wet, warm pussy. My other hand circled around her neck, giving me the leverage I needed to go to town on her. I didn't hold her too tight since I wasn't into any kinky shit like restricting her airway.

"Cole, oh god," she cried out when I began to fuck her, thrusting hard and deep without warning.

"This is what you wanted," I told her, biting down on her earlobe. "You wanted to get fucked hard."

"Yes, I want it, oh god, fuck."

My arm around her body loosened so I could run my hand down her stomach and between her legs. It only made her buck and tremble when my fingers worked her clit, driving her higher with my brutal pounding. Having come in her mouth earlier, I was more able to control myself this time. The need to climax was still there, but I wanted to draw this out. To make her so needy, she didn't know what was up or down.

The moment I felt her tipping over the edge, I released her clit. Meredith let out a hissing noise as if my denial of her orgasm pissed her off. She didn't tell me off, just submitted to what I wanted. When she'd backed off the edge, I resumed stroking her whilst I kept slamming into her. The sounds of our skin slapping together permeated the air, mixing with her moans and pants.

"You missed this, didn't you?" I grunted in her ear. "Missed the way I fuck you."

"Yes."

"You only have to say the word, Meredith, and you'll have access to this cock whenever you want it. I'll fuck you six ways from fucking Sunday if you ask me for it. Only you may have to beg. Beg me for my cock."

"Oh god, Cole."

"Mmm, does the thought of that turn you on?"

I could see her knuckles had gone white from gripping the headboard, but she didn't move them. She was such a good girl.

"Yes, oh fuck, yes."

"Do you want to come, little queen?"

She arched back into me.

"Yes, please let me come, Cole. Please. I want it so bad."

I wasn't sure she'd had enough yet and I wanted more of this. More of her. It'd been too fucking long since I'd been able to have Meredith. Her submission this evening had fed me, riling me up.

"Not yet. Patience."

My fingers around her neck tightened a fraction, showing her who was in charge. Her breathing was erratic and I could feel her pulse hammering against her skin. I kept fucking her, sending her closer to oblivion, but not allowing her to fall away into it.

"Cole, please… god, please."

"No."

"God, fuck, please, I need to come so much."

I pressed my cheek against hers, giving her everything I had.

"Do you?"

"Yes, please, Cole. I can't take it."

The need was building in me too. I couldn't help it any longer. The sensations had me spiralling higher. And I wanted her right there with me.

"Let go," I whispered. "Come for me."

The moment her pussy clenched around my cock, I exploded. Spots formed in my vision with the violence of it. Her cries echoed around my skull as a guttural moan escaped my lips. There was nothing fucking for it but to give in to it all. I let the waves carry both of us under, never wanting to come up for air.

We collapsed in a heap on the bed when we came down. Meredith couldn't hold herself up any longer. I couldn't blame her after the brutal pounding she'd received at my hands.

"Holy shit," she panted out. "I didn't know that's how you wanted to fuck me."

I kissed her shoulder, rolling us both over so we were on our sides. I tucked her against my chest, holding her close.

"You can't tell me you didn't enjoy it."

"Oh, trust me, I did, but that was intense." She stroked her fingers along my arm. "And I want you to do it again."

"Right now?"

She giggled.

"No, you've worn me out. I have to get up early for uni. I can't really be getting fucked by you all night."

It was my turn to laugh.

"Maybe we'll save that for the weekend."

"I'm going to hold you to that."

I nuzzled her neck before kissing her skin.

"I hope so."

She let out a sigh, wrapping her hand around my arm.

"Getting back together is a big step, Cole. I want to be sure."

"I know. I'll wait. I told you that."

She nodded, her body relaxing into mine.

"Did you want to stay?"

I wished I could, but I had to go to college tomorrow as part of my apprenticeship to get my qualifications. It would be a massive pain to get there from here first thing.

"I kind of need to get back."

"Oh… okay."

"I want to, Meredith, but I've got college in the morning and it's important."

She turned her head towards me, her eyes full of understanding.

"It's okay. I know, but do you have to leave yet?"

I shook my head.

"No, I can stay a little longer."

"Will you hold me for a while?"

I kissed her cheek.

"Of course, I will."

She gave me a smile before setting her head back on the pillow. Getting to be close to her like this was everything to me. I'd never turn that opportunity down.

"Mum wants to know if you'll come to dinner on Friday."

Not everyone would be there since we mostly only came together once a month on Sundays now. I'd told my parents about seeing Meredith again. Mum had been pestering me ever since.

"Friday? Sure, I can do that."

"It'll just be my parents. Hope that's okay."

Duke was going to be out. He seemed high strung right now. I wondered what the fuck was going on with him. I had asked Xav, but he didn't seem to know either.

"Yeah, it'll be nice to see them."

"I'll let her know when I get back."

We fell silent after that, content to just be with each other. Mum would be ecstatic to have Meredith for dinner. In fact, the whole family would love it if we got back together. They adored Meredith, treating her like she was one of the family. Perhaps I could ask Meredith if she'd actually told her brother we were in contact again. I didn't want things going downhill like they had done last time.

I didn't need Jonah to approve of me, but I did need him to stay out of my relationship with Meredith. I would not allow him to interfere a second time. As far as I was concerned, Meredith was mine and it was going to stay that way whether or not he liked it.

CHAPTER THIRTY THREE

Cole

I eyed AJ as I lowered the car I'd been working on down. He stood in the open doorway of the garage talking to a man who looked a little shifty to me. I couldn't hear what they were saying, but I couldn't imagine it was anything good considering the guy wasn't a customer. AJ had no shame. I swear he was growing more audacious by the day. And when I saw them exchange something, I knew he was up to no good.

He said goodbye to the man and walked towards the staff room, passing me on the way.

"You do realise if they find out what you're doing, you won't be around much longer," I muttered.

AJ stopped and turned to me, his eyes dark.

"I'm not doing anything."

"Yeah, okay, AJ. Whatever you say."

He took a step towards me as his fist clenched into a ball at his side.

"Listen here, Cole, I'm not doing shit and if I find out you've said a word to the boss, you won't like the consequences."

I almost scoffed but knew better than to antagonise him.

"If I can see what you're doing, don't doubt someone else will have noticed. You're skating on thin ice. I'm just warning you to be careful since I don't want to get dragged into your shit."

It's not like I would tell anyone. No way I wanted any trouble with the Russian mafia. Especially not since my grandfather wasn't in the country. He and Lily had decided to visit all the countries they'd missed out on when they'd been young. They were doing a worldwide tour. So yeah, I didn't want to rock the boat.

"Goody-two-shoes doesn't want to run with the big players?"

I wasn't going to rise to the bait.

"No."

"Granddaddy not around to bail you out if things go wrong?"

I walked away towards the bench to grab a couple of things I needed to finish the work on the car. It pissed me off him knowing I'd got my apprenticeship because of my grandfather. The work I did here was on my own fucking merit. I had to stay calm and not get riled up by AJ and his bullshit. I had a few months left until I got my qualifications and finished up my apprenticeship. Then I could move onto somewhere else. Whilst it would've been nice to continue working here since I got on with everyone else, the threat of AJ and the fact it was run by people in the mafia made me wary. I didn't want to get involved with that side of things or put anyone I knew in jeopardy.

"None of your business."

"You know, if you'd come out with us, I could show you the high life."

I rolled my eyes, but my back was to him so he couldn't see.

"If I wanted to live the high life, I wouldn't be working here."

I'd be working with my parents at the casino if I wanted that. It's not as if I ever had to worry about money since we'd all been set up with trust funds, but I wanted to make it on my own. Rely on myself for everything I needed. Mum had instilled that in us. She never wanted us to grow up with a sense of entitlement. The world didn't owe me anything.

Don't get me wrong, I appreciated the privileges I was afforded by them, but I'd never let it go to my head. I wasn't better than anyone else just because I came from money. If anything, my parents' dark past put a dampener on that idea.

"Huh… well, if you're not going to play nice, then don't expect me to do you any favours."

"As if I'd ever ask you for anything," I said under my breath.

I watched him stroll away to the staff room out of the corner of my eye. I'd made a mistake thinking he was a decent bloke. The guy had changed his tune when I kept refusing to go out with him and the boys. I really had more important things to be doing. Like getting Meredith back. That was my top priority.

I smiled to myself as I finished up with the car. She was coming over tonight. I couldn't wait since she'd agreed to stay over. Having her to myself all night would be heaven.

She'd told me her friend, Rhys, was still sceptical about me and whether I'd end up hurting her again. Meredith suspected he'd had his heart broken and that's why he was perpetually single as well as being wary of me. It's not like I could blame him. However, my breakup with Meredith wasn't simple nor did I hold all the fault. The timing and circumstances weren't on our side.

If I could avoid hurting Meredith, I'd do it in a heartbeat. I wanted to look after her. Treat her like the queen she was. My little queen who ruled over my heart. I wasn't sure when I'd tell her, but it wasn't going to be now. Not when I wasn't sure if she would take me back or not. I didn't want that to be a deciding factor. Meredith had to want to be with me of her own volition.

When I was done with the car, I got one of the others to make sure it was all good before taking the keys along to reception and handing them off to Jim who ran the office. I was about to walk towards the staff room since it was clocking off time when Demetri, my boss, stuck his head around the office door.

"Cole."

I turned, raising an eyebrow.

"Yes?"

"Come."

I followed him in, shutting the door behind me. Demetri walked over to his desk and sat behind it. He was a big guy with dark hair and a monobrow. I respected him since he'd always been good to me. Also as he was mafia, I wasn't going to be anything but polite and courteous towards him. I valued my life far too much.

"Take a seat."

I did as he told me, wondering what on earth he had to speak to me about.

"Your apprenticeship is coming to an end soon." He leant forward, resting his elbows on his desk. "The men tell me you are doing good work."

"I do try."

"Yes, yes, we all see your work ethic." He waved a hand at me. "This is not what I wished to speak to you of."

I rubbed my thigh.

"Okay…"

"Viktor speaks very highly of you. Very proud man."

I glanced away, wondering what my grandfather had to do with any of this. It's not as if I didn't know he was proud of me, but the way Demetri said it made me uncomfortable. Something about this conversation didn't sit right with me. Demetri and Viktor knew each other, yes, but they weren't close or anything. So why was he acting like Viktor was some kind of wonderful man who could do no wrong?

This feels… wrong.

"You are very capable, Cole, very capable. And you know what we do here."

I tried not to let my suspicions show as I gave him a smile. Demetri wasn't usually so free with compliments unless he wanted something.

"I… do."

"Cole, I want you to know you can come to me if you see anything that is… how should I say… not quite right."

A part of me wanted to straight-up tell him about the shit AJ was doing, but the other half didn't want to get involved with any of it.

"I do know that."

Demetri nodded his head.

"Good. Good. Of course, you do. But if you do see something, you will tell me, yes?"

"Um yeah, sure."

I didn't think not agreeing with him would do me any favours.

"Otherwise I will not know what to think of your… loyalties."

The threatening undercurrent of his tone set me on edge. Did he know something was going on? Did he suspect I was involved? Hell, I would never do anything like that under his nose.

"I haven't seen anything. I try to stay out of trouble, you know, for my mum and all that. She doesn't like it and I want to keep her happy."

He gave me a bright smile.

"Ah yes, a strong woman, your mother."

That was an understatement. Mum was a force to be reckoned with. I was sure Viktor had told him about my parents and their relationship. It was common knowledge. They weren't celebrities by any means, but in the criminal underworld, they were notorious for what they'd done to Frank Russo. Not to mention them owning the Syndicate and it catering to a highly exclusive clientele. The rich and powerful elite.

"Yeah, she is."

Demetri leant back.

"Tell me, Cole, do you have a woman?"

I did not want Meredith involved in any of this shit. I wasn't about to tell anyone here about her. That part of my life had nothing to do with my career.

"No. Too young to be tied down, you know how it is."

He laughed.

"Oh yes, I remember those days. Well, let me give you a piece of advice for when you do find yourself shackled to one. Keep her happy. Better for you that way. Women can make trouble for you. Too much trouble."

I gave him a half-smile. Didn't I know it? Meredith could be a handful at times, but I wasn't fazed by it. I liked that about her. She didn't take anyone else's shit and wasn't afraid to speak her own mind.

"I'll certainly try."

He slapped his hands down on the desk, making me jolt.

"Well, I'm sure I've kept you long enough. Have a good weekend… and make sure to keep it wrapped up if you're out on the prowl, yes? Wouldn't want to have any unexpected arrivals."

I let out a pained laugh as if that was funny when it wasn't. As if I'd ever put myself in a position to knock a girl up.

"Yeah, wouldn't want that."

I stood up.

"Well, yes, my children are my life, but I was not wanting them, you understand. Very young we were. Too young."

Now I knew why he'd said it. He didn't want me getting into the same situation he found himself in.

"Don't worry, Demetri, I'm always careful. You have a good weekend too and say hello to Magda for me."

He waved me away, giving me another smile and I left his office, feeling unnerved by our conversation. If I didn't tell him about AJ, would I end up in the shit? That concerned me, but not enough for me to go back and dob AJ in. It wasn't any of my business.

Stay out of trouble, remember? Just get your apprenticeship done, get your qualifications and then you can get out of here.

I kept that mantra up whilst I got myself ready to go home. I was not going to get dragged into other people's drama. AJ could do himself in as far as I was concerned. The guy didn't need me to interfere.

I shoved it from my mind when I straddled my motorbike. It was time I got home and had a shower before Meredith arrived. Tonight I was going to enjoy our time together even if we did have to endure dinner with my parents. Afterwards, I'd have her all to myself. And that's what I was most looking forward to. Time alone with Meredith so I could ravage her all over again.

CHAPTER THIRTY FOUR

Meredith

I'd been looking forward to seeing Cole since Monday. We'd been texting each other, but that wasn't the same as being next to him. Not even Rhys lecturing me over it had stopped my excitement. I swear he was far too concerned about me getting back together with Cole than he should be. Whatever had happened to him clouded his judgement. Cole had done nothing but show me he wanted to make things right.

I rang the doorbell as I waited on the steps of his parents' house having come straight from uni. As I was staying over I had my overnight bag with me. I was looking forward to a repeat of Monday night when Cole had fucked me with ruthless abandon. I couldn't deny him taking charge turned me on to the point of pain. I needed it again. Him saying dirty things in my ear whilst he pounded my pussy.

The door was pulled open to reveal a rather casually dressed Quinn in a white polo and navy chinos. He cocked his head to the side as he took me in. Considering every time I'd seen him two years ago, he was always wearing a shirt, to see him in something less formal was a turn up for the books.

"Hello, Meredith."

"Hey."

He stepped back, allowing me in and shutting the door behind me.

"How have you been?" he asked as I hung my coat up in the hall cupboard.

Cole's family had always told me to make myself at home. I didn't think that had changed.

"Okay thanks, you?"

"Well enough."

I nodded and followed him into the living room. I'd been closest to Cole's mum, but I liked all his parents as they treated me like I was family.

"Cole's still in the shower."

"Oh, okay."

Xav was sat watching TV, but he perked up when Quinn and I entered, giving me a grin.

"Well, hello again."

"Hey, Xav."

I dropped my bag down by the side of the sofa and sat down. Next thing I knew, he'd wrapped an arm around my shoulder and gave me a hug. He gave the best hugs in the world, not that I would tell Cole. It reminded me of the bear hugs my dad used to give me. I supposed that's why I loved coming around here so much. Cole was lucky to have four fathers who loved him, supported him and made sure he could want for nothing.

"We've missed you around here."

I bit my lip as he let me go. I'd missed them too. Cole's family was so welcoming and close-knit. Knowing what they'd done in the past and what they'd been through didn't bother me. They weren't bad people. Not really. Just had hard lives and made sure they secured their future. Having got to know them when Cole and I were together, I couldn't see them as anything other than a family who'd do anything for each other.

"Yeah, me too… what we watching?"

"Xav's obsessed with some new detective show," Quinn said as he sat down in an armchair and waved at the TV.

"You say that like you aren't in here watching it with me every time I put it on," Xav said, grinning, which only made Quinn scowl at him.

"That's beside the point."

"It is the point if you're ashamed of liking the same TV show as me."

"I'm not."

"Hmm, yes because you just had to go make a point of it being something *I'm* obsessed with as opposed to you asking me when I'm watching it again on a daily basis. You're not fooling anyone, Quinn."

"Shut up, Xav."

Xav nudged me with his shoulder, nodding his head towards Quinn with a sly smile on his face. I shook my head and sat back. The two of them had an odd love-hate relationship. Cole told me it'd always been like this.

"Nothing's changed then," I murmured.

"Nah, never will. Some days I wonder why I still hang out with this guy, but then I remember it's almost been fifty years so he can't be that bad."

I snorted, watching Quinn glare at Xav some more.

"You have no choice in the matter."

Xav raised an eyebrow.

"No?"

"If you want to tell Ash why you're leaving our quintet then, by all means, go ahead. Don't expect me to give you any sympathy when she has a go at you."

"Damn, Quinn, that's cold." Xav leant over to me. "Don't worry, he doesn't mean it. He wouldn't know what to do without me winding him up all the time."

"I'd have a fucking less stressful life."

"Aw, no need to put on a brave face. I know you'd miss me."

Quinn put his finger up at Xav.

"I'd ask if you two are giving each other shit again, but I think I already know the answer," Eric said as he walked in. He leant over the back of the sofa when he reached me and planted a kiss on my forehead. "It's nice to see you, Meredith."

"You too," I replied, grinning up at him as he straightened.

I'd always liked Raphi's dad. He was the sweetest one out of the lot of them and took an interest in what I was doing. Not that the others didn't, but he always made a point to engage me in conversation and find out how I was doing with schoolwork.

He came around and sat next to Xav who wrapped an arm around him.

"Who's doing dinner?" I asked.

"Ash and Rory," Eric replied with a shrug, leaning into Xav's hold.

I stared at him for a long moment.

"Rory is helping make dinner?"

Eric grinned.

"He's turning over a new leaf."

The whole time I'd known Cole's dad, he'd actively avoided getting involved with making meals for their family.

"I thought you said nothing had changed," I replied, directing my comment at Xav.

He winked at me.

"Well, nothing between me and Quinn. Rory's been trying lots of new things since you were last here. He said now the kids are grown up, he wants to start doing things for himself."

Cole mentioned them going on holiday together.

"Raphi didn't tell me any of this."

"My son is too busy spreading his wings to notice what we're doing," Eric said with an eye roll. "Last time I spoke to him, he said he was finally free of the tyrannical rule of his mother watching his every move."

I snorted. Raphi could be dramatic at times.

"Oh, I'm sure you didn't tell Ash that."

"God no. We argue enough in this family without that."

"Raphi is a cheeky little monkey like his father, always has been," Xav put in, giving Eric a squeeze.

"You love it."

"I didn't love it so much when he was running riot around the house as a toddler. I swear to god he wore me out every single day."

I could well imagine a green-eyed Raphi running circles around them. He might be the quietest of the four kids, but he had a wicked sense of humour and got up to mischief his parents didn't know about.

"Aw, Xavi, you were the best babysitter our kids ever had."

Xav scowled and flicked Eric's ear.

"Babysitter? Fuck off, I'm their father."

"Did you want me to start referring to you as Daddy X then?"

"You... Jesus, you know what, no, I'm not rising to any more of your shit today."

Eric grinned wide. Seeing them all interact with each other made me realise how much I'd lost when Cole and I broke up. Not just him, but his entire family who I absolutely adored.

I noticed Cole walking in, his dirty blonde hair all wet from his shower. He made a beeline for me the moment he saw me. I shuffled closer to Xav to make room for him on the sofa.

"I didn't know you were here already," he murmured as he sat down and leant towards me. I felt him nuzzle my ear. "Sorry if I left you with them for too long."

"I'm fine, you know I love your family."

He pulled away and smiled at me.

"How was your day?"

I shrugged.

"Okay, I suppose."

"Same."

I leant my head on his shoulder, staring up at his profile.

"I'm glad I'm here now."

Cole smiled down at me, which made my heart thump against my chest.

"See, why can't Aurora and Logan be as cute as these two?" Xav said in a low voice.

"Don't say that too loudly or Quinn might go off on one," Eric replied.

Cole rolled his eyes as I frowned.

"Who's Logan?" I whispered to him.

"Rora's boyfriend."

"And Quinn doesn't like him?"

"Well, it's more of a case of no one will ever be good enough for Rora as far as he's concerned. I'll explain later, they have a bit of a… history."

I nodded. Whilst I knew Quinn the least out of Cole's dads, he and Raphi had told me more than enough to give me an impression of the man. And that was incredibly overprotective and strict.

All of us lapsed into silence, our attention falling on the TV. I kept my head on Cole's shoulder, not wanting to be too far away from him. I'd had a lot of time to think during the week. To consider what I really wanted. Our date on Monday had reminded me of exactly why we worked so well together. Being with him was easy. He made me smile. Never failed to take care of my needs. Not that I had anyone else to compare

343

him to, but in the bedroom, Cole was hot as fuck. Every time I remembered the way he'd pinned me down and fucked me, I found my face growing hot and an ache started in my core.

I guess you could say I'd made up my mind about him and me. Perhaps it was too soon. Perhaps it was crazy. But it all came down to one very simple thing, as I'd told Rhys last night. I loved Cole. And even if he hadn't said it yet, I knew he loved me.

Rhys hadn't exactly been super supportive of my decision. He told me it was my life and he respected what I wanted, but he wished I'd take more time to see if Cole was genuinely going to stick by his word or not. Patience wasn't exactly my strong point.

The truth was I wanted Cole to be mine again and for me to be his.

"Dinner's ready," came Ash's voice, pulling me from my thoughts.

I glanced over to the dining room, finding her standing in the doorway with a bright smile on her face. As much as I wanted to say hello to her, I had something to say to Cole first. Whilst everyone else got up, I put a hand on his arm. He glanced at me for a long moment.

"We'll be along in a minute, Mum," he said, waving a hand at her.

Ash gave him a nod before leaving the room with the rest of Cole's parents and shutting the door to give us some privacy. Cole looked at me, his eyes full of caution.

"What is it, little queen?"

My heart fluttered at his term of endearment. I took his hand in both of mine, staring down at it as I stroked my fingers along his palm.

"I have… I have something to tell you."

"Okay."

It took me a minute to compose myself. I wanted this to come out the right way even though it should be simple for me to say.

"Cole… I…"

Swallowing, I took a deep breath and started again. My eyes flicked up to his, knowing I couldn't be a coward and shy away from confronting this.

"I forgive you for what happened. And I want us to be together again because the truth is… I love you, Cole. You're important to me. I don't want to have regrets about not taking this chance. So… so I wanted you to know that. And before you ask me, yes, I have told Jonah."

Before I'd had a conversation with Rhys whilst the two of us were tucked up in his bed, I'd had dinner with my brother. He'd been very understanding, although Jonah usually was. He admitted his feud with Raphi had been partially clouding his judgement when it came to Cole. Whilst him and Raphi still weren't okay by any stretch of the imagination, he wasn't going to let that affect his feelings about me and Cole any longer. Especially not now Cole was eighteen and legally an adult. Having Jonah's blessing had made my choice to be with Cole that much easier.

"You have?"

Cole's expression was neutral. I didn't know how he felt about my declaration. I hoped he'd be happy since it's what he wanted.

"Yeah. He's happy for me... for us... if there is going to be an us."

For a moment he said nothing. My stomach was in knots. All I wanted was for him to smile at me. Reassure me in some way.

He reached up with his free hand and stroked my face with his fingertips. The depth of emotion he was feeling finally showed through in his hazel eyes. The adoration he felt towards me slammed into my chest, making me giddy.

"There's an us, Meredith, there'll always be an us. You're mine and I'm yours."

"So... we're back together then?" I whispered, needing him to say the words.

"Yes," he murmured, leaning closer. "I'm not letting you go again."

I smiled before he kissed me. His lips on mine reassured me. He made me feel on top of the world. I let go of his hand to tangle mine in his hair, wanting this kiss to go on forever. And feeling bereft when he broke it off.

Cole rose to his feet and took my hand, pulling me up.

"Ready to have dinner with my family, my beautiful little queen?"

I stared up at him.

"Yeah." I stepped closer, wrapping a hand around his waist. "And I'm ready for the next chapter in our lives... starting now."

Cole's smile set my whole world on fire. And I hoped we wouldn't have to tackle too many issues from here on out.

It's just a pity I couldn't predict the future. Because the future always has a way of throwing you off course and setting you on a different path. And it was not one I would have ever chosen for myself and Cole.

Not at all.

Not one bit.

PART III

crumble

verb, crum·bled, crum·bling.

to fall into small pieces; break or part into small fragments.

CHAPTER THIRTY FIVE

Cole

The past few months had gone by in a blur of work, college, Meredith and sex. A lot of sex. She and I had made up for lost time any which way we could. Getting to be with my girl without anything hanging over our heads was like a breath of fresh fucking air.

I'd just rung her doorbell as we were celebrating tonight. I'd officially passed my assessments to get my qualifications, which meant I'd be finishing up my apprenticeship soon. Something I was glad of, considering how much I couldn't stand being around AJ any longer. I needed to find a new garage to work at no matter what. No way I wanted to put anyone I knew at risk, especially not my girlfriend.

Meredith had been insistent regarding us having our own personal celebration. My parents were taking us out tomorrow to some fancy restaurant.

The door was pulled open to reveal Rhys. He gave me a nod and stepped back, letting me walk in.

"Hey."

"Meredith's in the kitchen," he told me, waving at it as he walked away into the living room.

Rhys didn't entirely approve of me. I didn't hold any animosity towards him for it. I had made the effort to get to know him. He was a decent guy and cared a lot about my girl. Meredith told me he liked me well enough, but the fact I'd hurt her had left a black mark against my name as far as he was concerned.

I hung up my jacket and popped my helmet on the rack above the coats next to hers. She loved going out on the Ducati with me. I dumped my bag down as well since I'd take it up to her room later. Then I walked along the hallway until I reached the kitchen, finding Meredith by the stove with her back to me. She had an apron tied at her back and was wearing a rather short pale blue dress. I took a second to admire her as she had soft music tinkling out of her phone. She was still sporting her pink hair and it fell down her back in waves. Fuck, she was beautiful and all mine.

"Little queen."

She turned her head and smiled at me.

"Hold on, let me just get this."

Meredith shuffled back and opened the oven, bending down to get something out of it. I swallowed hard when her dress rode up, revealing she had very skimpy lace knickers on underneath. Plans formed in mind involving pulling her into my lap and ripping them off her so I could make her sink down on my cock. The way her tits would bounce whilst she rode me. The little pants and moans she'd make. And the way she'd cry out my name when she reached climax. Those had me reaching down to adjust myself.

Fuck.

I had plenty of time to enact those ideas later.

Meredith straightened and set a dish on top of the stove before tugging off the oven gloves and setting them on the counter. Then she turned and practically ran towards me. I had to take a step back when she launched herself into my arms, curling hers around my neck before she kissed me.

"Hello to you too," I murmured when she pulled back slightly to nuzzle her nose with mine.

"I'm so proud of you."

I smiled.

"Oh yeah?"

"Yeah, you're officially my hot mechanic boyfriend and that's pretty damn amazing."

I kissed her, feeling my heart fucking swell at her words. Despite us being back together for months, I still hadn't yet told her I loved her. I don't know what was holding me back. It never felt like the right time to say those words, even as she told me every day how much she loved me. Meredith had never pushed me to admit my feelings.

I guess in a lot of ways it was hard for me to express it verbally. I preferred to show her in the way I made love to her, gave her the things she wanted and took her to the places which made her happy. Perhaps I was like my dad in that respect. He had a tendency of showing how much he cared and loved us as opposed to saying it all the time. Don't get me wrong, he said the words 'I love you', but it was rare and more meaningful when it did happen. I'd always been okay with it. It was just his way.

Meredith pulled back and patted my shoulder.

"Okay, you need to go sit outside and I'll bring dinner out."

I raised an eyebrow.

"Oh?"

"I'm treating you as we're celebrating." She waved me towards the back door. "Now go."

I put my hands up and walked towards it. I gave her a wink before I disappeared. Out on the patio in the garden, Meredith had set the table complete with candles, flowers in a vase and a bottle of wine. I fought hard not to smile but failed. I took a seat and poured a glass for each of us before pulling out my phone when it buzzed.

Mum: So proud of you, baby boy!

Cole: Thank you.

Mum: I hope you have a lovely night with Mer.

Cole: She's made me dinner so I'm sure we will.

Mum: Oh, that's so sweet of her. See you both tomorrow. Don't be late.

I rolled my eyes. As if I would ever be late to a meal with them. Quinn would go off on one, and then the entire night would be soured. Duke had done it once on his own birthday.

We'd never heard the end of it. Since then, Mum always reminded us to be on time.

I tucked my phone away when Meredith came out, minus the apron, carrying two plates piled high with lasagne accompanied with salad and garlic bread. She set them down and kissed my temple before taking her own seat.

"That lot in there can serve themselves," she told me as she picked up her wine glass.

"You made dinner for everyone?"

"Well, it's not like we can eat an entire lasagne between us."

I grinned, reaching out to take her free hand.

"I could try."

Meredith shook her head before tilting her glass towards me. I picked up my own.

"To you passing all your assessments and almost finishing your apprenticeship."

We clinked our glasses together before drinking from them. Then we tucked into the meal she'd made, which was amazing. Meredith had told me she had to learn to cook because her mum and grandmother left her and Jonah to fend for themselves a lot after her dad died. She didn't see either of them much, but she did meet up with her brother at least once a week. Sometimes I'd join her. He was a lovely guy who cared about his sister deeply. It made me wonder what on earth my own brother had been thinking when he fucked things up between them. Honestly, I was with Meredith on this point. The two of them needed to sort their shit out.

"So, your brother wants us to come out with him next week," Meredith said as she leant back in her seat with a piece of garlic bread between her fingers.

"Does he now?"

"Just drinks, not clubbing or anything."

"Raphi doesn't want me to show him up with my dance moves."

She snorted and rolled her eyes as I busted out a move whilst still seated, waving my arms in the air.

"With moves like that, you'll have Raphi bowing down to your superior skill."

I gave her a wink. She knew I could dance. We'd been dragged out clubbing with Jazz several times. We always got lost in our little world with each other under the strobe lights and loud music.

"He's got two left feet."

"Poor Raphi, not his fault he's uncoordinated sometimes."

"I don't know where he gets it from. I genuinely think E is the best dancer out of all of my dads."

She cocked an eyebrow.

"When have you had to watch your parents dancing?"

"Oh, we went to one of their employee's weddings last year, but there's been a few times before that. As you can imagine, Xav was out there straight away with Mum, followed by E... Dad and Quinn hated it when Mum made them get involved too. You know they have a hard time saying no to her."

"Ash certainly keeps your dads in check."

I grinned. My mum definitely ruled our household. I don't think my dads would have it any other way.

Meredith and I continued talking about my parents for the rest of our dinner. She gathered up the plates when we were done and took them into the kitchen. When she came back out, she grabbed her glass and curled up in my lap. The two of us sat watching the fading light, just content to be in each other's company for a long while.

"Cole," she murmured from where her head was resting on my chest.

"Mmm?"

"I have another treat for you."

"Oh yeah?"

She looked up at me with a sly smile on her face.

"It's in my bedroom."

I had a feeling I knew where this would be going.

"Did you get me a gift?"

She bit her lip before sliding off me and taking my hand, pulling me up.

"If you consider what's under this dress a gift."

I watched her pick up our discarded wine glasses and the half-empty bottle.

"It's a gift only I get to see."

She winked at me over her shoulder as she sauntered back towards the house.

"Coming to get your gift then?"

No way in hell I'd be turning that shit down.

"You better run or I'll be tempted to unwrap it before we're alone."

She squealed as I chased her into the house and up the stairs. I definitely couldn't wait to unwrap my gift and take full advantage of her.

CHAPTER THIRTY SIX

Meredith

ole caught me as we made it to my bedroom. He plucked the glasses and wine bottle out of my hands, placing them down on my desk before shoving me towards my bed. The boy had this look in his eyes which told me I would be getting no mercy from him. And fuck, if it didn't turn me on.

His hands ran down my body to grab hold of the dress and pull it off me. I put my arms up to help him out. Cole's eyes roamed over me, taking in my lacy pink underwear. It was new and I'd bought it especially for this evening, having gone shopping earlier since I didn't have classes on Friday afternoons.

I'd meant what I said to him. I was so proud of him for passing his assessments and gaining his qualifications. Cole loved working with cars and his hands. And I couldn't deny I loved the feel of his calloused fingers against my skin.

"Undress me," he said in that commanding voice he used when we were in the bedroom.

I complied immediately. I absolutely adored the dynamic we shared behind closed doors. Cole telling me what to do and taking control got me all hot and bothered.

When I'd pulled off all his clothes, I couldn't help staring. Cole was too hot for words. He liked to go running with Eric, something he'd taken up in the past couple of years, and did weights with Xav. It meant he was beautifully toned and I really couldn't get enough. I wanted to reach for him, but I kept my hands by my sides, knowing I had to wait for him to tell me what to do next. Cole smirked as he rounded the bed and sat down up against the headboard.

"Come here."

I crawled on the bed and straddled his thighs. Cole reached over to my bedside drawer and pulled out a condom before rolling it on. It hadn't escaped my notice how hard he was. He reached behind me and unhooked my bra, tossing it away. His fingers fell to my underwear, stroking along the waistband.

"Don't ruin them, they're new," I whispered, immediately realising his intention.

"Take them off then, little queen, I want you on my cock."

I hurriedly stood up and shimmied them down my legs, throwing them off the bed before kneeling over him again. Cole wrapped his hand around my behind, tugging me closer. I let out a little pant when he made me sink down on him, my hands landing on his shoulders to steady myself. It didn't take much for Cole to rile me up and get me going.

His fingers tangled in my hair, pulling my face closer so he could kiss me. I moaned in his mouth as he continued to push me down on his cock until I'd taken him all the way.

"Ride me," he murmured. "Show me exactly how good you can be."

His other hand curled around my behind, making me rock on him. Using his shoulders as an anchor, I rose and fell, watching him intently. This beautiful boy who was all mine. I couldn't believe how happy we'd been for the past few months. Cole gave me everything I needed and so much more. We fit together perfectly like we were made for one another.

I got to see him twice a week, if not more. He'd taken me to the theatre a few times and we rode out of the city on his motorbike every weekend. I'd never felt so free and alive as I did when I was clutching him tightly whilst we sped down the motorway. I'd never let anything tear us apart again. Cole was it for me. I wanted us together forever. Even if my best friend still had reservations about my relationship.

Rhys liked Cole. The two of them got on, but Rhys was also overprotective in his own way. It's not like he outwardly disapproved of Cole, but the fact my boyfriend hurt me two years ago still made him wary. No matter how many times I explained what happened, Rhys still stuck to his guns. He kept telling me you had to be careful of who you let into your heart because they could tear it into shreds at the drop of the hat. My suspicions about what happened to him grew with each remark, but my best friend was tight-lipped about his past. And I didn't dare let on I was sure someone had broken his heart in the worst way possible.

I needed to stay in the moment with my boyfriend. He deserved my full attention tonight.

"Cole," I moaned, going faster as his hands tightened around me.

He leant forward and kissed my breast, his tongue soon finding the nipple even as I continued to fuck him. I cried out when he bit down on it. The exquisite blissful feeling of pleasure and pain surrounding me. Ever since we'd got back together, we'd pushed the boundaries of sex to see what made each other tick. My favourite times were when he told me what to do, demanding I get on my knees for him and give him everything. I would never let him talk to me like that outside of the bedroom. He never tried anyway. Cole respected the fact I made my own decisions. He let me be me without asking for too much or demanding anything. In return, I gave him my devotion and love.

Love.

I did love this boy. Everything about him. His overconfidence. His ambitions. The way he never gave up. I admired his kind and caring nature. Appreciated everything he did for me.

So him not admitting his own feelings verbally? I just had to be okay with it. It's not as if this girl didn't want to hear those three little words from her boyfriend, but it was the one thing I never pushed him on. Cole, whilst so like Ash in every way, also had a lot of Rory in him. And the one thing I knew about his dad was his stoicism. Cole assured me Rory could be open and talkative when he wanted to be. It just wasn't often and never with strangers. I had experienced some of it myself, but it had taken time for Rory to come out of his shell around me.

"So perfect," Cole murmured into my skin. "No one is as beautiful as you in my eyes."

I felt my face heat up. My whole body was already burning up from our lovemaking, but Cole's compliments no doubt had made my skin red.

My hands travelled up from his shoulders into his hair, pulling his face from my chest. I stared into those hazel eyes of his.

"You're not so bad yourself."

His eyebrow curved upwards.

"Here I thought you considered me hot as fuck."

"Shut up."

He grinned.

"Say it, Meredith."

I almost scowled but the way his eyes twinkled rendered it impossible for me to be mad at him.

"You're hot as fuck, Cole, and I can't get enough of you."

His hand left my hip and fell between my legs, thumb brushing over my clit.

"And you may come for being a good girl who does as she's told."

I moaned in response, increasing my pace as Cole's touch drove me higher. His cock felt so good as did his thumb on my clit. I couldn't hold back for long. I clutched him as I came, crying his name and feeling the sensations wash over my skin.

I slumped against him, panting as I came down. He stroked my hair and kissed the top of my head, whilst still encouraging me to fuck him with his other hand.

"I love you," I whispered into his neck.

Cole didn't respond. I didn't expect him to. He kissed my head again as if showing me he felt the same way. My heart ached a little at his lack of reciprocation, but I shoved aside my bruised feelings over it. Instead, I kissed up his neck and along his jaw until I met his mouth.

"Shall I make you come?"

His grunt before he kissed me told me he wanted it. I rocked my hips harder in the way I knew he liked. When he released my mouth, I ran my tongue along his jaw and met his ear. My teeth grazed along the lobe, making him moan. His hands banded around my hips, telling me I was driving him crazy. I'd found out how sensitive his ears were a few weeks ago. I took full advantage of it when I wanted to make him come.

"Meredith," he hissed as I bit down. "Fuck."

I sucked and he groaned louder. His fingers dug into my skin, keeping me captive as I continued to rise and fall on his cock. There was nothing like this high of giving him pleasure, driving him towards his own explosive ending. I loved every part of it.

"Fuck… fuck, little queen."

He erupted, panting hard as I felt him pulse inside me. I released his ear and pulled back, watching him close his eyes and lean his head back against the headboard. When he opened them again, he was smiling at me.

"That was some reward."

I smiled back.

"You deserve it for all your hard work."

He reached up and stroked my hair back from my face.

"I could get used to you taking care of me."

"We take care of each other, Cole. Always."

He kissed me again. My heart swelled. I was happy for the first time in a very long time. And nothing was going to put a dampener on that.

Nothing at all.

CHAPTER THIRTY SEVEN

Cole

I'd walked into the garage after taking a break in the back when I noticed those guys who always seemed to hang out with AJ standing in the corner. Glancing around, I couldn't see AJ anywhere. I thought it was his day off, so why these two were here was a mystery to me. And it really didn't bode well at all.

I ducked behind the car I'd been sent to work on, not wanting to disturb them or get involved. Danny, one of the other mechanics, had told me it needed a wheel change. For some reason, the rest of the floor was empty. It had been a slow day so far. Demetri hadn't left his office once, something I could only be glad of. He'd been on edge for the past week. Probably something mafia related going on. It had affected the whole mood of the garage. Everyone seemed a little more subdued. Well, everyone except AJ, but he was a fucking loose cannon these days.

AJ himself strolled in through the open doors a moment later with a fucking smirk on his face. I'd just picked up the impact driver and was going to raise the car up. I did not like this. Whatever AJ was up to, it couldn't be good.

"Lads, I told you to wait outside."

"It's fucking raining, fam."

AJ shrugged, flipping the hood of his coat down. I had been about to deal with the wheel nuts, but I stayed low, holding the impact driver like it was a weapon which would protect me. Outside, the rain hammered down on the concrete. It had been a pretty miserable day so far weather-wise.

"Whatever, let's get this shit done then."

My muscles tensed as I peered around the car at them after AJ disappeared out of view. The three of them were standing by one of the benches. One guy pulled something out of his coat pocket and slapped it down on the metal bench. My eyes went to the package. And my stomach sunk. If I wasn't mistaken, that looked a lot like it might be drugs. My suspicions were confirmed when the guy cut open the packaging to reveal the white powder within.

"Okay, we need to divvy this shit up and fast before anyone else comes back to work, you got it?" AJ said, glancing around.

I ducked back behind the car before he saw me.

What the fuck did he think he was doing? Cutting up drugs at the garage? Could he not do this somewhere else?

This was fucked up. I didn't want to be involved in his shit. He was taking a massive risk. Anyone could walk in. I was fucking well hiding behind a car so as not to get caught. I couldn't imagine what anyone would think if they saw me. Though, AJ would be the one getting in the shit since I wasn't anywhere near them or dealing with their drugs.

Fuck this.

I glanced around the car again, finding the three of them busy cutting up the drugs and placing the powder into baggies. I needed this to be over. I wanted to get back to work. If I made my presence known now, it would be worse for me. How the fuck did I get myself into this mess? I should have turned around and gone back to the staff room the moment I saw those two.

Ducking back behind the car, I shifted on my haunches as my legs were starting to hurt from being stuck in this position. I tried to be as quiet as possible, mindful of making sure my shoes didn't scrape across the concrete floor.

AJ had really taken this to a whole new level of fucked up. I'd promised myself I wouldn't get dragged into it, but now, having seen him and his friends cutting up drugs here, I didn't know if I could stay out of it. Demetri would fucking lose his shit if he knew about this. And if I didn't tell him, then I'd be in trouble too. It would look bad on me for keeping it a secret. It would make me look complicit.

Fuck.

The sooner I could wrap up my apprenticeship, the better. I had my qualifications so I could easily get another job. At this point, I really didn't care where it was. I couldn't stay here and be pulled into this mess. It put me in danger. And it would eventually put everyone else around me in it too. I wouldn't do that to Meredith. I'd promised her she wouldn't be in any danger with me two years ago, what with my family's past. Except it wasn't their past catching up with me. It was my grandfather's association with the fucking Russian mafia.

I should have never taken up his offer of help. It came with strings. Not from him, but from dangerous people who I didn't want to piss off under any circumstances. And if everything went south, Grandpa wasn't around to protect me. I was going to have to keep myself and Meredith safe. I was just fucking glad no one here knew about her. But if I didn't stay off the mafia's radar, it wouldn't remain that way.

"AJ, man, be careful. This is top-quality shit," came a voice from the other side of the car.

I stiffened.

"Shut up, Isaac. I know what I'm doing," AJ shot back.

"Mate, you sure we're good to do this here?" the other guy asked.

"Yeah, yeah, it's cool. Everyone's out on break."

Everyone except me.

"We gotta get this shit moved."

"I know, I know. It's urgent. It's cool."

It was not 'cool' at all. This was the worst. I internally kicked myself for not walking away sooner the whole time they were finishing up. And almost breathed a sigh of relief when the two guys left with all their baggies. AJ remained by the bench, fiddling with something.

I ducked back behind the car and waited until I heard retreating footsteps. Then I slumped down against the car, placing the impact driver on the ground. My legs burnt from squatting for so long. I stretched them out in front of me and rubbed my face before dragging my hands through my hair.

"Oh hello, Cole, didn't see you there before."

I almost jumped out of my skin. Looking up, I found AJ leaning on the car bonnet with a lighter in his hand. He twirled it around his fingers, making me feel uneasy.

"Um, hi… didn't know you were working today."

"I'm not."

He knew I'd been here the whole time. He fucking well knew. I could see it in his expression.

Not wanting to address the elephant in the room, I got to my feet, moving over to the controls to lift the car up.

"What you doing here then?"

"Need to talk to Demetri about switching some shifts."

I didn't believe that for a second.

"Oh, right."

AJ moved away from the car and I hit the button to raise it. When it was high enough, I dropped the controls and picked up the impact driver again.

"You know, whatever you think you saw, you didn't," he said in a low, but casual tone.

"I don't know what you're talking about."

"Just so we're clear."

"If something was happening, which I definitely didn't see, I suggest you don't do it again here."

If AJ pulled me in any deeper, I would be a dead man. No two ways about it. That couldn't happen under any circumstances.

"What Demetri doesn't know can't hurt him."

"It could hurt a whole host of people, AJ. I already told you, I saw nothing and I don't want to be involved. I'm not here for that shit."

I wanted this conversation to be over. And I'd have to have a long and hard fucking think about what I was going to do. Whatever AJ was involved in, he needed to keep it away from the garage. Demetri had been very clear about loyalties. I needed to remember that.

AJ gave me a nod and walked off. I got on with my work since I was here to do my job and not get involved with AJ's drug running.

By the time the day came to a close, I was tired and irritable, but I'd agreed to see my brother, Meredith and Rhys tonight. Demetri had already left for the day. Ronnie, his assistant manager, was closing up. I'd made up my mind throughout the afternoon. I didn't have to be directly involved, but I had to stop AJ from fucking up my life.

Walking into Demetri's empty office with a small note in my hand, which I hadn't signed, I placed it on his desk underneath his empty coffee cup. No doubt he'd find it in the morning. Then I left, feeling lighter than I had done earlier. Hopefully, this would make sure Demetri was aware of what was going on and I wouldn't get into trouble for it. The very last thing I wanted was the mafia on my back because they thought I was involved in AJ's schemes.

The note I'd left was the only thing that saved me. It's just turned my life into a complete nightmare too. One which tore apart everything I'd built for myself into tiny pieces, scattering like dust in the wind.

My life as I knew it was about to be over. And I wasn't ready for the fallout.

CHAPTER THIRTY EIGHT

Meredith

"So you and my brother are all loved up and shit? It's really going to work out this time, yeah?"

I gave Raphi the finger, which only made him laugh. Rhys, Raphi and I had got to the bar a little while ago. Cole wasn't here yet as he wanted to go home and shower first. I couldn't blame him considering the type of work he did.

"We are, though he hasn't said it yet."

I wasn't sure why I'd admitted it, but Cole's lack of verbal assurance was beginning to bother me. Rhys knew all about it. That didn't help matters between us. He told me it was a red flag, but I refused to believe it. I knew Cole. Knew he loved me. He showed me every day, but I wanted to hear those words out of his mouth. Desperately.

"What? He's not said he loves you?"

I shook my head, staring down into my mojito as it was kind of embarrassing.

"Well, he's an idiot."

"Shut up, don't be mean about your brother." I looked up in time to find Raphi grinning. "You are a dick sometimes, you know that, right?"

He shrugged, leaning back in his chair whilst Rhys shook his head.

"He's my baby brother, it's in the sibling code, we're allowed to be mean to each other."

"Glad I don't have siblings," Rhys muttered.

I refrained from bringing up my own considering the history between Raphi and Jonah. Something I'd mentioned to Rhys a few times. He knew when to keep his mouth shut too.

"No, you're just a loner boy," I said, giving him a wink.

"Fuck off."

"Aw, fuckface, you know I'll never leave you."

He scowled. I wrapped an arm around his shoulder and gave him a squeeze.

"For someone who professes to love me so much, you aren't half cruel."

"Me? Cruel?"

Rhys gave me a look.

"Calling your best friend, fuckface, isn't cruel?"

I smiled and nudged his nose with my finger.

"No, it shows how much I adore you."

"Whatever."

He smiled back even so.

"You two are cute as fuck," Raphi said.

"Ugh, shut up. We are not cute and don't let your brother hear you say that."

I let go of Rhys, who grabbed his drink and took a gulp.

"Oh, why? Does Cole get all jealous and possessive over you?"

"Maybe."

He wasn't that bad. Cole was secure in the knowledge I was his, so he had no need to be jealous. As for being possessive? Perhaps a little, but it didn't bother me in the slightest. I liked knowing he wanted me that much. It made me feel special. After all, I was the only girl Cole had ever been with. The only one he wanted. And I was sure he wanted it to stay that way.

"That does not surprise me. He gets it from Rory and Quinn."

I raised an eyebrow.

"What do you mean?"

Raphi rolled his eyes before tapping his fingers on the table.

"Oh well, according to my dad, when my parents were in the early stages of their relationship, Quinn was super possessive of Mum. Like on an extreme level. He calmed down after that, but you know what he's like."

I was well aware of Quinn's reputation. Strict and completely unyielding. And yet he loved his family in his own way. You could see it in the way they all interacted together.

"And Rory?"

"I think out of all of my dads, he's the most devoted to Mum. He would do anything for her, even stuff which makes him uncomfortable since like… you know what he's been through."

"Ash seems pretty devoted to him too."

Raphi smiled.

"She's devoted to all of them. I mean shit, they've been together for like basically twenty-seven years. Doubt anything could break my parents apart."

The fact that the five of them had stayed together this long and worked was no mean feat. I knew it was hard enough to maintain a relationship with one person let alone four. I admired Ash for that. And just in general. She was such a kind and caring soul.

"I do love your family. They're pretty amazing."

"But you love my brother the most."

I reached over the table and slapped his arm.

"Shut up."

Raphi laughed.

"What? It's true. And I'm happy for you. None of us liked it when you two broke up."

He looked away, his eyes hardening. I knew he was thinking about Jonah's involvement in it and my heart sunk. I wished those two would sort out their differences, but I had no idea what it would take. It was clear as day to me they both still had feelings for each other.

"Yeah, well, that's in the past now."

"What's in the past?"

I looked up to find Cole standing over me with that heart-stopping smile on his face. My heart thumped hard in my chest.

"Nothing."

He leant down and kissed me.

"Hmm, I don't believe you," came his murmured breath against my mouth.

"I'll tell you later."

He pulled away, ruffled my hair and smiled again.

"I'll get another round in. What are we all having?"

A few minutes later, with drinks duly noted, Cole walked off to the bar.

"You two are sickeningly in love," Raphi said.

"Would you stop it? Why is my love life the number one topic of conversation this evening?"

"Because me and Rhys have abysmal ones."

"You mean non-existent," Rhys said, fiddling with his straw.

"Harsh… but true."

Raphi had been going a bit crazy at uni with girls, but that had petered out recently. I think he'd got whatever was going on with him out of his system. At least I hoped so.

"This one views dating an anathema," I said, slapping Rhys on the shoulder.

Rhys crossed his arms over his chest and gave me a look.

"You know why."

"Okay, but being demi doesn't exclude you from ever feeling attracted to people. If you got to know a guy, you might find you like him and actually want to date him."

Rhys continued to stare at me.

"I'm never dating. Ever again. Not worth the hassle."

Cole placed a tray on the table before plonking himself down in the chair next to me and hooking his arm around the back of mine. I reached over and rubbed Rhys' arm. I didn't like to push him, but he got in his own way far too much.

"What are we talking about?"

"Dating," Raphi said.

"Well, that's a pointless topic considering you two are shit at it." He pointed at Rhys and Raphi in turn. "We should definitely talk about something else."

"Well, since you brought it up, you get to pick our topic."

Cole gave his brother the finger then leant closer to me, nuzzling my hair with his nose.

"I missed you," he whispered.

I squirmed in my seat.

"Me too."

Cole turned back to his brother with a sly smile. I had a weird feeling rush over me like someone was watching me, but no one was as I glanced around so I don't know where it came from.

"If you're that hard up for dates, I heard from Rora that Colleen's sister is still on the market."

Raphi's face drained of colour and his fist clenched around his glass. I snorted. Mimi Lintott had always had a crush on Raphi.

"Hell fucking no. I am not going there, not that desperate."

"I'm sure she'd let do all sorts of dirty things to her if you were that way inclined."

"Fuck off, Cole. I'm not... that's not... it's none of your business what I'm into. I'm not like our parents who put it all out there, thank you very much."

Cole snorted and put his hand on my shoulder, giving it a squeeze.

"No? Don't want the table to know the truth, huh?"

"Shut. Up."

Cole could hardly talk. He was dominant and controlling in the bedroom. Only last week he'd tied my hands to the bedposts with some of my scarves because I'd teased him too much over dinner. Not that I'd complained in the slightest since he proceeded to give me multiple orgasms before getting himself off by fucking me into oblivion.

"We're all aware you're into guys and girls, no one is judging."

Raphi looked like he wanted to kill Cole. That was an extremely touchy subject. I put a hand on Cole's thigh, warning him to drop it. I did not want tonight to devolve into an argument.

"Let me guess, Cole pissed you off again, am I right?"

We all looked up to find Duke standing there with his arms crossed over his chest and a grin on his face.

"Who invited you?" Raphi muttered.

"I invited myself when Cole told me where he was going. You forget to invite your big brother?"

Raphi shook his head whilst Duke grabbed a chair and sat down with us, popping the drink he'd bought down.

"I thought you were going out with—" Cole started.

"She's busy," Duke cut in.

I glanced between them. Cole had his eyebrow raised. Duke looked as if he was daring Cole to continue. And if he did, he wouldn't like the consequences.

"Who's busy?" Raphi asked, looking between them as well.

"No one."

"Have you got a secret girlfriend or something?"

"No. As if."

Cole snorted and rolled his eyes. Clearly, Duke was seeing someone and he didn't want to talk about it. That surprised me given how much of a player the boy was. It would take some woman to make Duke Scott settle down. Then again, according to Cole, Xav had been the same until he met Ash. Like father. Like son.

Raphi narrowed his eyes and pointed at his brother.

"I don't believe you."

"What's there not to believe?"

"For starters, Cole wouldn't bring it up if it was no one and secondly, you've been really cagey recently."

Duke shrugged and sipped his beer, eying Raphi with some amusement.

"I don't have to run shit by you, little bro. As if you confide in me about your love life."

"I don't have a love life."

"Hmm, yeah, okay. I'm sure you're not still pining over Meredith's brother like some lovesick fool who ruined the only good thing in his life."

The whole table went silent. Raphi looked like he was about to get up and storm out. Then he leant back and gave his brother a hard stare.

"At least I didn't fuck up a fourteen-year friendship with the only person who cared about me outside of my family."

Duke's face fell.

"Shut up."

"See? Not so nice to throw around accusations now, is it?"

The two of them continued to stare at each other. Cole's hand on my shoulder tightened and Rhys looked plain uncomfortable. Considering this was his first introduction to Duke, it didn't surprise me in the slightest.

Duke reached over and ruffled Raphi's hair.

"I'm sorry, man."

"Me too," Raphi replied, giving his brother a smile.

"Now, you going to introduce me to your friend here, Mer?" Duke asked, turning to me.

"Duke, this is Rhys. Rhys, this is Cole and Raphi's older brother," I said, waving between them.

Duke stuck his hand out which Rhys shook, although I could see the reluctance in his eyes. He didn't like touching people he didn't know, but Rhys was nothing if not polite, so he didn't object.

"Shall we get off the morbid and miserable topics and on to something far more interesting then?" Duke asked with a wink as he sat back.

"Yes, please," Raphi replied with a nod.

And thankfully, for the rest of the evening, there were no further arguments. I enjoyed spending time with Raphi and Duke, but I couldn't shake the feeling someone in the room was watching us. Every time I looked around, there was no one there. The last time I'd felt like this was two years ago when I'd been sat in the library at school and Cole was watching me. Except this time, Cole was right next to me so it couldn't be him.

I had no idea why I felt this way. And no matter how hard I tried, I couldn't shake the ominous feeling it gave me. I put it down to the weirdness of this evening. It'd set me on edge. Because no one could have any real interest in our little table, could they?

CHAPTER THIRTY NINE

Cole

I walked into the staff room completely knackered after the day I'd just had. It felt like everyone and their fucking son was trying to get their car repaired. We'd all been rushed off our feet with absolutely no let-up. I was looking forward to getting home as Meredith would be over for dinner. She would make everything better. All I wanted to do was curl up in bed with my girl and forget about the world for a few hours.

I walked over to my locker, wanting to get out of my overalls and into my regular clothes. Definitely needed a shower when I got in.

"Hey, Cole."

I stiffened when I realised it was AJ's voice.

What does this dickhead want?

"Hey, man," I murmured, pulling open my locker door.

"You up to much this weekend?"

I shrugged.

"Working tomorrow, so not really."

I glanced over at him. He was washing his hands in the sink, but he had this smile on his face which set me on edge. Like he knew something he shouldn't. The guy did my head in. I hadn't seen him do anything else since that day with his two friends, but I didn't trust him.

Demetri hadn't said anything about the note I'd left him. I hoped he'd got it and knew where it came from. I wasn't fucking loyal to the Russian mafia, but I valued my life. My loyalty was to Demetri as opposed to AJ. The guy deserved to be thrown under the bus.

"You sure about that? Seems like you have an active social life to me."

"I guess so."

I spent most of my time with my family, Meredith and her friends. That was it really. I'd lost touch with people I went to school with. It wasn't like we were close anyway. A lot of people didn't want to know me and my siblings because of our parents' relationship. Fucked up if you asked me. If they weren't willing to accept it, that was their problem, not mine. They weren't fucking welcome in my life. Judgemental dickheads could do one.

"You know, I saw you out with your friends a couple of nights ago."

And that's when I knew this conversation was going nowhere good.

How the fuck did he know that? Had this dickhead been spying on me?

"Oh?"

I didn't want to let on how uncomfortable this made me. AJ basically just admitted he followed me because there was no other reason he'd have known my whereabouts otherwise. I kept that shit to myself.

"Yeah. You go to bars a lot then? Thought that wasn't your scene since you always refuse to come out with me and the lads."

"Not really. My brother wanted to meet up is all."

I stripped off my overalls and started to change, wondering where the hell he was going with all of this.

"Which one's your brother?"

"Is that any of your business?"

He laughed, which grated on me.

"Nah, probably not."

I wasn't about to tell him anything else. We weren't friends. Hell, I wanted to be as far away from the guy as possible. I kept reminding myself I was going to see Meredith soon. My girl would make me feel better.

"When you said you didn't have a girlfriend, you were lying, right?"

My back went ramrod straight.

"What's that supposed to mean?"

"Come on, Cole, you know what I'm talking about. The pink-haired chick you were all cosy with. She's your girl, right?"

The last thing I wanted was for him to know about Meredith or how I felt about her.

"She's a girl I hang out with, doesn't mean we're together."

AJ shook his head as he walked over to the lockers.

"Yeah, yeah, you've been holding out on us. Keeping that stunner all to yourself."

I gritted my teeth. Yes, she was stunning, but I didn't like the way AJ was smiling nor the leering look in his eyes. Meredith was fucking well mine.

"What's it to you anyway?"

"What's it to me? Oh, Cole, don't you know?"

I slammed my locker closed having grabbed what I needed.

"Know what?"

"I've been trying to work out what will get you on side. You'd do well if you stuck with me. I could open doors for you."

I didn't want doors opened for me. I wanted to finish my apprenticeship and get the fuck away from these guys. Then and only then could I keep me and Meredith safe.

"So now I know you have a girl, who you clearly care deeply about judging by the way you're biting my head off, perhaps I can use that to my advantage."

I dumped my helmet and jacket down on the table nearby and stormed over to him, getting up in his face. I was slightly taller than AJ so the fucker had to look up at me.

"Listen here, AJ, you stay the fuck away from her, you hear me? If you lay a hand on her, I will fucking end you."

AJ's eyes widened. I never rose to his shit, but a threat against Meredith was something else. That girl was my entire world. I would go to the fucking ends of the earth to protect her. To keep her safe. She was mine. I wasn't about to let this fucking dickhead ruin anything between us.

"Oh really?"

"Yeah, fucking really. You will be a dead man walking if you go near her. I'm not letting you come up in here and threaten my girl. She has nothing to do with you or whatever shit you've got going. Just leave us the fuck alone. I've told you so many times, I'm not interested in being involved."

AJ smirked. He fucking smirked and it irritated me no end.

"Oh dear, have I hit a sore spot?"

"Fuck. You."

He stepped back, giving me a smile.

"Oh, Cole, you have no idea just how much I'm going to fuck up your life now, do you?"

"Whatever. You can do your worst to me but stay the fuck away from her. She is not a pawn for you to play with."

He shook his head, shoving his hands in his pockets as he strolled away towards the door. This fucker. He was un-fucking-believable.

"If you just joined up with me, you could have the world. But no, you're Granddaddy's golden boy, aren't you? Sitting up there on your throne of fucking self-righteousness. It's pathetic. Just you wait. You're going to regret turning me down. I'm going to destroy everything you hold dear."

And with that, he left. I stared at the open doorway. What the hell had just happened? That dickhead had used Meredith against me. This was exactly why I didn't want anyone finding out about my relationship with her. Especially not AJ.

Fuck. This is all so fucked.

I didn't know what the hell he was going to do, but it couldn't be anything good. He'd told me he was going to destroy my life. He could try, but he didn't know who he was dealing with. I wouldn't let him get away with shit.

Pulling out my phone, I checked the time. I was going to be late if I didn't get a move on. I grabbed my helmet and jacket, shrugging it on. The whole way home I stewed over what AJ had said. And no matter how hard I tried to be brave, the truth was, I was fucking scared. Mostly for Meredith. If I broke my promise about keeping her safe, it would be one broken promise too many. I'd already broken enough between us before.

I got in the shower when I arrived home, not bothering to go in search of my family to say hello. This mess was making me crazy. I felt like I was losing my fucking mind with worry.

AJ was involved with dangerous people. If the Russian mafia got wind of it before Demetri could deal with him, I was in no doubt I would be caught in the crossfire. AJ had it out for me even though I'd done nothing to do him. I didn't know why he was so insistent about me joining him. The guy was crazy as far as I was concerned. Clearly, he didn't like not getting his own way. And that shit he sprouted about me being Grandpa's golden grandchild? Well, I supposed he did dote on me, but he did that with all of us.

I didn't understand AJ's problem with me, but I had to do something to stop him dragging me down with him. Because if he fucked with Meredith, I would have no choice but to end him. No one messed with my girlfriend. Not on my fucking watch.

Everyone kept telling me I was more like my father than I knew. And in that moment, I finally understood why.

Once upon a time, Rory Carter had ended a man's life for Ash Bykov. And perhaps one day, his son would end one for the love of his life too.

CHAPTER FORTY

Meredith

For once when I rang the doorbell it was Cole who answered the door. It was usually his parents. The moment his eyes landed on me, I was tugged into the house and his face was buried in my hair. His arms tightened around me until I struggled to breathe properly.

"Little queen," he murmured.

I let him hold me for all of a minute until I shoved uselessly at his back.

"I can't breathe."

He loosened his hold but didn't let me go. This wasn't like him. Yes, Cole showered me with affection, but the way he held me felt... desperate. As if he was scared I'd disappear in an instant. I didn't know what to make of it.

"Cole?"

"Shh, don't say anything," he whispered. "Just let me hold you."

This had my stomach in knots. I could feel the tension in his body radiating off him. Instead of saying another word, I stroked his back, hoping I could soothe him in some way. Cole wasn't very open about things which bothered him. To be honest, he rarely let anything in life faze him. So this? This made me feel like something bad had happened.

Finally, after what seemed like a lifetime, he pulled away only to cup my face in both his hands. His hazel eyes were full of repressed emotion. I could see worry and agony there.

What happened to you, Cole?

"You're everything to me, you know that, right?"

I nodded. Cole had said those exact words many times. Only this time I felt the weight of them settle over us.

"And you love me, right?"

"Yes, Cole, I love you. You know that."

He leant down and kissed me. It was urgent and unyielding. I was completely swept away in those minutes his tongue was in my mouth, taking and taking as if he couldn't get enough. The moment he pulled away, I could see the shutters starting to come down.

"I'm going to protect you," he murmured, pressing his lips to my forehead. "Forever. I'll keep you safe."

I don't know whether he was directing that at me or to himself.

Cole stepped back. His whole demeanour was off. And he'd closed himself down.

"Cole… what's wrong?"

Seeing him like this worried me. I didn't care if he looked unapproachable. I wanted to be there for him. To show him he could rely on me if he needed to talk about something. I wished so many times Cole would be more open with me about his concerns and feelings. Just as he didn't push me, I didn't push him. We weren't like that with each other. But maybe I should be. Just this once, maybe I should press the subject.

"Nothing."

"Don't tell me it's nothing when you manhandled me the moment you opened the door."

"Can't I have missed you?"

I shook my head.

"Of course, you can, but this doesn't feel right."

He took my hand, dragging me towards the dining room.

"Come, dinner is already on the table."

"Hold on, let me take my coat off."

He stopped in his tracks and let go of my hand. The fact he was avoiding the subject told me many things. Firstly, Cole wasn't willing to share and that hurt. And secondly, it had to be something big for him to be this unnerved.

The moment I had my coat off and hung up, he grabbed my hand again and tugged me away. All his parents were seated at the dining table along with Duke.

"Ah, there you two are," Ash said with a bright smile. "We were just about to start."

Cole made me sit next to him and put a rather possessive palm on my knee. Plates had already been dished up and the chatter started up immediately. I kept glancing at Cole who didn't look up from his plate.

"So, Meredith, how's uni?" Eric asked.

He was sat next to me. Across from us were Rory, Xav and Duke. Ash and Quinn sat at either end. I wasn't the only one who'd noticed Cole was in a mood. Ash was looking at him with a frown.

"Oh, it's okay. I mean, it keeps me busy. Second year has been a lot tougher."

"They go easy on you for your first year."

I grinned.

"Oh yeah, my best friend, Rhys, keeps saying we got an easy ride before and now the real work is here. Who knows what it'll be like next year."

Eventually, I'd like Rhys to meet Cole's family since they'd basically adopted me. I was around here for dinner a lot more than I went to see my mum and Grandma. To be honest, if I never had to go around theirs again, it wouldn't bother me too much. Being away from their snide remarks had helped me immensely. Jonah agreed with me in that respect, although he was living at home with them at the moment since he'd moved back to London, something he hated. The two of us had talked about getting a place when I finished university, but now I was with Cole, I was hoping to move in with my boyfriend. It wasn't something Cole and I had discussed yet. There was no rush so I hadn't brought it up. I still had another year of uni to go.

"Yes, Raphi says he's got no more time for parties."

I chuckled.

"Oh yeah, right party animal your son is."

Eric grinned. Raphi might have gone through a string of girls, but he wasn't the life of the party. His idea of a good time was drinks at home whilst gaming, although he did like going out to bars on occasion too.

"Well, I'm sure his mother would disapprove if she found out he'd turned into a wild child like Duke."

"He's not a wild child, just a bit of a player," I murmured, not wanting anyone else but Eric and maybe Cole to hear me.

I saw the twinkle in Eric's green eyes. He knew what his son got up to. They all did. Duke made no secret of his lifestyle. Although, from what Cole had told me, Duke was seeing someone. One girl and no one else. And I had a sneaking suspicion I knew who it was after Raphi's comment at the bar.

"He'll settle down when he's ready. Though, it might be sooner than we all think."

I raised an eyebrow but Eric shrugged. He wasn't going to say anything more. I glanced at Duke but he seemed to be in deep conversation with his dad. Rory was talking to Quinn and Ash was watching Cole. I wanted to ask him what was going on with him, but I wouldn't in front of his family. He and I needed to talk about this in private.

By the time dinner was finished and we'd cleared up, Cole's parents were talking about retiring to the games room for a movie night. I was following them when Cole grabbed my hand and started pulling me away down towards his bedroom.

"Hey, what are you doing?" I hissed.

"Taking you to bed."

I ground to a halt, forcing him to stop.

"What is going on with you?"

His hazel eyes were dark when he turned on me.

"I told you, nothing."

"This, right here," I waved at him, "is not nothing. I'm worried, Cole. You're scaring me."

His face fell and he looked contrite.

"I'm sorry, didn't mean to scare you. I just don't really want to talk about it."

I stepped towards him, reaching up to cup his face.

"It's okay."

He shook his head.

"No, it's not. Nothing is okay right now."

The way his voice shook on those words made my chest tighten.

"Are you sure you won't tell me? I could help."

"No, you can't help me with this, little queen. I just want to go to bed… can we do that?"

I nodded and let him take me down to his bedroom. The moment we were in the room, he stripped us both down and pulled me over to the bed. I let him tuck me up under the covers and hold me against his chest. Whatever Cole needed tonight, I'd give it to him. I didn't like the way he was acting. It concerned me. Made me almost sick with worry. My stomach twisted and turned and I fought to keep my dinner down.

What had happened today to make him like this?

And why wouldn't he tell me what it was?

CHAPTER FORTY ONE

Cole

Seeing Meredith really fucked me up after what happened with AJ earlier. I wanted to lock her in my room and never let her out so he couldn't get to her. To keep her by my side at all times so no one could hurt her. Those were my irrational fears talking, but it didn't stop me being afraid of what he might do. Being so fucking afraid of losing her.

I didn't admit to being scared very often. The thought of being without her broke my fucking heart into tiny pieces. I couldn't stand it. The world felt like it had started to cave in on me. I'd done nothing to warrant AJ coming after me. Nothing.

"Cole," Meredith whispered, her breath fluttering against my chest where I had her pressed to it. "Please tell me how to help you."

I didn't know how to answer her. The fact she sounded so upset tore into my soul. I knew I wasn't being myself. How could I be? Someone had threatened my girl. All of my thoughts were consumed with it. Of what AJ might do to her in retaliation. Of how he might hurt her.

No one was going to hurt Meredith under my watch.

No one.

I would rather die than see her in pain. The agony in her eyes when I'd broken up with her two years ago still haunted me. We weren't going through that again. She needed to know I would lay down my life for her. That I would keep her out of harm's way. I would love her until the fucking end. Where she ended, I began. There was no in between. She was my heart and fucking soul. The reason that organ beat in my chest. I couldn't breathe if she wasn't a part of my world.

Instead of giving her words of how she could help me like she'd asked for, I shifted and caught her chin with my hand. Those green eyes stared up at me with such undying love, I couldn't fucking take it. I leant closer and captured her mouth with mine, kissing her softly at first. Feeling her against me ignited the pulsing desire I had for her. It drove through me. Demanding and unrelenting. I needed her. All of her. Always.

My hands went to her hair, tugging her closer so I could kiss her more thoroughly. She didn't utter any objections, letting me take what I desired. What I needed. What I fucking craved.

"Meredith," I whispered against her lips. "My little queen."

I flipped us over, pressing her down into the bed and covered her body with my own. I needed to be in her. To know she was still fucking well mine. I couldn't take this pain. This worry. This fucking agonising fear which kept me captive. The thought of losing her again was almost paralysing.

"You're mine." I kissed her, tongues clashing together in a war of who wanted who more. "You're all fucking well mine. No one is going to take you from me."

I didn't care if I wasn't making sense or that what I was saying might worry her further. She couldn't be torn away from me. She just fucking well couldn't.

My fingers went to her knickers, tugging them down her legs as they were the only stitch of clothing I'd left on her before I'd pulled her under the covers with me. My boxers came next, leaving us skin on skin. She felt so fucking good. Her skin was so soft under my fingertips and against my body.

Fuck. I love you so much, Meredith Veronica Pope. You are my everything.

"Meredith," I breathed, towering over her. "I don't want anything between us."

She stared up at me, her green eyes wide. I knew she'd gone on birth control in the intervening years, but we'd still used condoms anyway just in case. I needed this one night with her. My mind was too full. Meredith would take it away for me. I could get lost in her. She'd be my balm. My beginning. My end.

"Okay," she whispered. "I want to feel you too."

I spread her legs and fit myself between them. Kissing my way down her neck, I reached her breasts. My tongue ran around her nipple, making her gasp. Her hands threaded in my hair, encouraging me to continue. I wanted her soaking for me. Begging for me.

"Cole," she moaned, the word vibrating through her body.

"Tell me how you feel, little queen," I whispered against her skin.

"I love you."

The words sunk into me. Warming every inch of my body and soul.

"Again."

"I love you, Cole Carter."

If there were five words I'd never tire of hearing from her, those were it.

I couldn't wait any longer. I wanted to be wrapped up in Meredith.

Capturing her mouth again, I reached between us so I could fit myself to her. The moment I slid inside her tight, wet pussy, feeling her bare for the first time, I choked out a moan in her mouth. She felt fucking amazing. So perfect. Nothing would ever tarnish this girl in my eyes. She would always be everything I needed in this world no matter what happened next. No matter what shit tried to ruin us.

I pulled back and thrust deeper, groaning at the feel of her. The absolute ecstasy I felt at being with her like this.

"Cole," she cried out, turning her face from mine. "Cole, fuck."

"Does that feel good, little queen?"

"Yes, god, yes, please... more."

I gave her what she was asking for. I gave her all of me, adoring the way her green eyes glazed over with pleasure.

Knowing she was in this with me. Her beauty almost stopped me in my tracks. Her pink hair spilling all over my pillows in soft waves. Her perfect body pressed against mine. I needed to brand every inch of her into my memory so I'd never forget this moment. So I'd never forget her this way.

I caught her chin with my fingers, forcing her to look up at me whilst I continued to make love to her, my pace slow and measured.

"Meredith."

"Yes?" she whispered, her expression growing cautious.

"I need you not to speak, okay? I need you to listen."

She nodded, although she still looked worried about what I was going to say. She shouldn't be. Tonight was about letting go. Telling her the truth. The whole fucking truth. No more holding back. No more keeping things to myself. I had to let go.

"You are my everything. I can't live in a world where you and I aren't in existence next to each other. You belong to me, Meredith. Only me. You'll always belong to me just as I belong to you."

I took a breath, increasing my pace. Emotion clogged my throat, but I had to press on. Had to get this out.

"I was eleven years old when I first saw you... this beautiful strawberry blonde haired girl with green eyes. I couldn't fucking look away. And I knew then I wanted you despite not knowing a thing about you. I knew you were it for me. No one else could ever come close."

I could see tears welling in her eyes and I hoped they were happy ones.

"You are the one, little queen. My one… I love you. I've always loved you. And I'm never going to stop loving you until I take my last fucking breath."

I released her chin and took her hands, pressing them down on the bed, pinning her to it. I thrust harder, wanting to show her my words were true. To prove to them to her.

"We're going to have forever. I'm going to marry you. Have children with you. Give you all the things you deserve in life. I'll give you a home for the two of us and our future family. I'll make sure you never want for anything."

Tears slid down her cheeks. I wanted to kiss them away.

"You're enough for me. Just you and only you. I love you, Meredith Pope. Never forget that."

She let out a little choking sound as if she was trying to speak but couldn't. Leaning down, I kissed her wet cheeks, wanting to reassure her it was okay. I was right here. I pressed my forehead to hers, staring into those tear-filled eyes and hoping I hadn't gone too far in my brief impromptu speech.

"You want to marry me?" she whispered.

"Yes, in the future when we're both ready for that step."

"Oh, Cole." Her hands pressed against mine and I released them. Her fingers curled into my hair, holding me to her. "I want those things with you too. I love you so much"

We kissed again, pouring out all our feelings into each other. We drove each other higher, reaching that peak together. Coming apart with her like this felt incredible. It washed away all the shit I was going through, leaving me with just her. The girl I wanted to spend the rest of my life with. And as she lay curled up against me later that night, drifting off to sleep, I made a silent promise to myself that I'd do anything to make sure that happened.

"I love you, little queen," I whispered into her hair. "I'll give you the whole world and more, you'll see. One day, we'll have everything together and no one will threaten us or tear us apart again."

CHAPTER FORTY TWO

Cole

I literally dragged myself into work the next day, having not wanted to leave Meredith at all. She looked peaceful tucked up in my covers. I knew she was going to see her brother today and that made me happy, although I wished I could go with her. She always had the biggest smile on her face after she spent time with Jonah. Those two were so much closer than I was to my siblings. Although, over the past couple years I'd grown closer to Raphi and Duke. Aurora was always the odd one out being the only girl and a law unto herself. She had mellowed out a little since she'd moved in with Logan, thankfully.

I'd walked into the staff room and was stripping my jacket off when Demetri stuck his head around the door. His serious expression made me nervous.

"Cole, come with me."

I was about to put my stuff down but he shook his head. Now, I was worried as hell. Following him out into the hallway, we walked down to his office where he shut the door firmly behind us. Demetri indicated I should take a seat. I placed my stuff down in one of them and took a seat in the other. He sat behind his desk and steepled his hands.

I swallowed as he stared at me for a long moment.

"Cole, I like you. You are a good boy, this is why what I have to tell you is… difficult."

My hand curled around the arm of the chair.

"I will be very clear so you do not misunderstand. The people I work for… they wish for me to deal with you. They believe you have stolen from them and they do not take kindly to such things, yes?"

I stared at Demetri. The Russian mafia thought I'd stolen something from them.

What the fuck?

"Now, I know you would do no such thing, but there is evidence and I cannot refute what they say."

He slid a piece of paper across his desk towards me. I leant forward and picked it up. It was the note I'd written to him.

'AJ is dealing drugs out of the garage.'

"This tells me you are loyal, but you have angered someone who is dangerous. He knows you, how do I say… are a snitch. He does not like this nor that you would not join him."

I wanted to shred the note into tiny pieces. AJ told me he was going to fuck up my life. I just didn't realise it would be so fucking soon.

"What did he do?" I all but whispered.

"He's taken secrets and money… placing the blame on your doorstep. I cannot tell you too much more as it is not safe for you to be here."

I looked up at Demetri who had nothing but understanding and empathy in his eyes. He leant his elbows on his desk.

"It is not all about the money before you ask, it is pride. This can't be fixed easily. They won't harm you or your family because of Viktor, at least not yet, but they will harm those closest to you. They have placed a hit out on your… lady friend."

My heart fucking fractured in my chest.

Meredith.

"They know about Meredith, yes."

He must have seen the question in my eyes. The world fell out from underneath me. The Russian mafia had put a fucking hit out on my girlfriend. My girlfriend. Meredith.

Fuck.

"They… they're going to kill her?" I choked out.

"Yes, if you do not secure her safety."

I didn't know what the fuck to think, say or do. All of this was insane. AJ framing me for something I didn't do. And now Meredith was in fucking danger.

"I can't… I can't take her away from her life. She… she wants to… fuck."

Demetri nodded slowly.

"She isn't safe here, Cole."

"Why… why are you telling me all of this?"

I couldn't focus on Meredith right now. I didn't understand why Demetri would go to the trouble of telling me what was going on. Everything was such a fucking mess in my mind. I didn't know what was fucking up or down.

"Viktor saved my life a long time ago. He is a good man. I want to repay him. And you are a good boy." He leant back in his chair again. "And this… AJ. I do not like him. He is trouble but he has powerful friends. Ones who will protect him."

I nodded slowly. I took all of my emotions and shoved them in a box to deal with once I got out of here. No matter how much my skin prickled with anxiety and worry, I had to focus.

"What do I need to do?"

"Run. Leave the country and take her with you. Stay hidden from them."

"And if I don't go?"

"They will hunt you down, eventually. And they will kill her."

I couldn't let that happen. I'd promised to protect Meredith.

"Will I ever be able to come back?"

Demetri gave me a sad smile.

"I will do what I can, Cole. Proving you did not do this will be difficult. But I wish to help you. When you are safe, we will talk. We will find a way."

I nodded. The fact he was even helping me counted for a lot. And I'd have to thank Grandpa for saving Demetri when

I saw him. If I ever saw him. Right now, everything was up in the air.

I stood up, knowing I had to leave. Knowing I had to keep Meredith and me safe from all this shit. Demetri reached into his drawer and took out an envelope. He slid it across the table. I picked it up, turning it over in my hands.

"Open it when you are safe."

"Thank you, Demetri."

"Now go, you do not have much time. I have stalled them until tomorrow, but after that, they will expect me to kill her. You work for me, it is my responsibility to see to it."

I swallowed hard, understanding what he was telling me. Gathering up my things, I shrugged my jacket back on and walked out of the garage in a daze, thankfully not running into anyone. As I made my way home, I tried to work out what the hell I should do. How to fix this mess. It didn't seem real. It felt completely at odds with what I expected AJ to do. I should have known he'd use extreme measures. The guy was fucking arsehole. And apparently, one with a huge vendetta against me.

This doesn't make sense or add up right.

I unlocked the front door and walked in when I got home, dumping my helmet in the cupboard along with my jacket.

"Cole?" came my dad's voice, startling me as I shut the cupboard door. "I thought you had work."

"I did."

I looked over at him. My dad's expression was neutral but his eyes showed his concern. The weight of what Demetri told

411

me crashed into me. Pain radiated down my chest. My heart pounded against my chest. My skin felt clammy.

How the fuck do I deal with this?

"Dad… I'm… I'm in trouble."

"What do you mean?"

"The… the mafia put a hit out on Meredith."

"What?"

I couldn't take this. Everything fell apart in front of my eyes. I was completely lost.

"This guy at work… he's a drug dealer, but I think he's more than that and he wouldn't stop trying to get me involved. I kept telling him no, but he has it out for me. And… and he's framed me for something I didn't do. Now… now the Russian mafia is after me, but they won't kill me because of Grandpa. They will kill Meredith though… they'll hurt her."

A tear slid down my face. My hands shook by my sides as the violence of my emotions threatened to destroy me. My girlfriend would die if I didn't do something. If I didn't save her. All for something I didn't even fucking well do.

My dad was in front of me the next moment, putting his arms around me and holding me as the emotional dam broke. I sobbed into his shoulder, clutching his t-shirt because I couldn't take it. The thought of her being gone ruined me.

"Shh, it's okay, Cole. It's okay. We'll fix this, okay? I promise," Dad murmured.

"I have to run. I can't stay here… they'll come after me if I do. But I can't take her away from her life. It's not fair. She needs to stay and finish uni. She has to. It's her life. Her dream is to work on the West End. I can't rip that away from her,

Dad. I just can't. She deserves it. To make her dad proud even though he's not here any longer."

"I know. We'll make sure she's safe. You don't have to worry."

He held me tighter. I didn't know how he would fix any of this, but my family were nothing if not resourceful. They'd dealt with the criminal underworld before. It's why I'd not hesitated to tell Dad exactly what had gone on. I couldn't deal with it alone. I needed them. My family were the only ones who could help me.

"I love her. I love her so much. She's my whole world and I can't live without her, but I can't make her run away with me. It's not fair."

He pulled back and took my face in his hands, forcing me to look at him.

"Listen to me, Cole. We will find a way to keep her here and get you out of this shit, okay? Whatever it takes. You're my son, Meredith is your girl and I will protect both of you. Always. Do you understand me? I will make this okay even if it means you have to leave us for a while. Ash, Quinn, Xav, Eric and I will fix it because we love you. We're never going to let you fall."

I nodded. Dad looked so determined and each word he spoke soothed me a fraction. He wiped away my tears with the pads of his thumbs.

"Now, you go and clean up your face and come into the dining room afterwards. I'll get everyone else and we'll deal with this."

"She's not still here, is she?"

Dad gave me a sad smile.

"No, she left half an hour ago to see her brother."

My heart hurt, but Meredith being gone already could only be a good thing. I didn't want to disrupt her life with this shit. She needed to be kept out of it for her own protection.

"I told her I loved her for the first time last night… and now… now I have to leave her."

A fresh set of tears ran down my cheeks. Dad hugged me again, rubbing my back in slow circles until I calmed down enough to stop sniffling.

"She's a very special girl. One day, you'll make this right, but for now, we have to deal with what's going on." He pulled away and pushed me towards the bathroom. "Go. I promise we're going to find a way, Cole."

I believed him. My parents weren't people to be messed with. They protected each other and they'd do the same for me. It didn't stop my heart fracturing at the thought of leaving Meredith all over again. Didn't stop me from wanting to curl up in a ball until this all went away. I had to be strong. To face up to the situation. When I was safe, I could afford to break down. I could mourn the loss of the love of my life.

After I cleaned up my face, I walked into the dining room finding all of my parents standing around the table with grave expressions on their faces. Mum immediately came over to me and wrapped me up in her arms, burying her face against my chest.

"My baby boy," she whispered. "I love you so much."

I knew the thought of me having to leave would be eating her up inside. But I didn't see any other way around this.

"I love you too, Mum."

She pulled back and stroked my face before turning to my dads.

"We're going to protect him and Meredith, right?"

"Yes, little girl," Quinn replied, his expression darkening. "We're always going to keep our children safe."

The rest of them nodded, reassuring me they would go to the ends of the earth for me.

"How are we going to make sure she can stay and finish uni?" I asked.

Xav looked over at Quinn and then winked at me.

"We have our ways, Cole. Those Russian cunts aren't going to keep your girl from living her life, not on my fucking watch."

"You're not going to do something reckless, Xavi," Eric said.

"Don't worry, E, I wouldn't want you getting your knickers in a twist over me."

Eric scowled at him, which almost made me smile. I was going to miss my family so fucking much. They were the most caring people I knew except for Meredith. I'd miss her the most. Fuck. My heart would be eviscerated because of this, but the knowledge I'd be keeping her safe drove me. It gave me the strength to go through with it.

Dad walked over to me and put an arm around my shoulder, giving me a squeeze.

"I'm going to break her heart again," I whispered.

"One day, you'll be able to tell her why. Sometimes the best thing you can do for someone is to let them go."

I nodded even though I'd never be able to let Meredith go for good. She was the love of my life. It was for her I was doing this. To protect her. She wouldn't know that though. She wouldn't understand. That hurt worse than anything else.

I'm sorry, Meredith. You have no idea how much. I have to protect you. I have to keep you safe even if it means I rip your heart out in the process. You'll heal in time. I hope you don't forget what I told you last night. I hope you don't forget I love you.

I regretted a lot of things in my life. Especially what was about to happen next. But I didn't regret telling her I loved her last night along with my intentions for the future. It was all I had left to hold on to. All I had left to get me through the treacherous path I'd inadvertently stepped onto. Because the thought of leaving this all behind did nothing but wreck me inside.

CHAPTER FORTY THREE

Meredith

The fact I hadn't heard from Cole all day yesterday after he kissed me goodbye in the morning concerned me. I'd texted him a couple of times without a response and even tried calling him in the evening. It had gone straight to voicemail. What with the way he'd been acting, it left me feeling a little unsure and confused about what was going on.

I should be happy since he'd told me he loved me for the first time. Told me he wanted us to spend the rest of our lives together. Get married and have babies. All of it had filled my heart with joy. The openness and sincerity in his voice put to rest all my fears, doubts and insecurities. Having him finally tell me he loved me was everything I needed.

I'd just made it downstairs when the doorbell went. Walking over, I pulled it open and blinked when I found Cole's dad on the doorstep. Rory had a pensive expression on his face as if he wasn't comfortable being here. Considering none of Cole's parents had turned up at my door before, I felt a little unnerved.

Why is he here? Where's Cole?

"Uh, hi, Rory."

"Meredith… can I come in?"

I nodded and stepped back. Rory walked into the house, leaving me to shut the door behind him. I led him into the living room and waved at the sofa, indicating he could take a seat.

"Can I get you something to drink?"

"No, thank you."

He sat down, eying the place for a long moment before he levelled his gaze back on me.

"I think it might be best if you sat down too."

I shuffled over to the sofa and sat down next to him. The tone of his voice filled me with nervous anticipation. And not in a good way. It's not like I was super close with Cole's dad or anything so I didn't know what to make of this.

Rory dug into an inside pocket of his jacket and took out an envelope. He smoothed it out with his fingers. I stared at it, my stomach sinking with every passing second.

"Meredith, I don't come bearing good news. In all honesty, I'm sorry it has to be me."

He looked over at me, sadness radiating out of his hazel eyes. They reminded me so much of Cole's. And I knew then, whatever he had to tell me, it had everything to do with his son.

"This is for you, but I want you to know before I give it to you, it is the last thing any of us wanted, especially my son. Sometimes life leads us down a path none of us wants to walk along and we just have to deal with the consequences."

My heart tightened painfully in my chest. Whatever was in that letter, I wasn't sure I wanted to read it. Wasn't sure I was ready for what it would contain.

"What... what happened?"

His expression darkened and he shook his head. Then he held out the envelope to me. I took it with shaky fingers. Staring down at my name on the front in Cole's cursive, I felt hot and cold at the same time. I carefully opened the envelope and tugged out the page, unfurling it.

Meredith,

I don't think there are words which can express just how sorry I am for what I'm about to tell you. I need you to know everything I said to you the last time we saw each other is the truth. I want to spend the rest of my life with you. You are mine and I am yours. That will never change. No matter the circumstances. No matter the pain you will surely feel when I say what I have to say. Know I will love you forever. You are my one.

By the time you read this, I will be gone. I didn't want it to come to this, but I have to leave. It's for my own safety and yours. I wish I could have taken you with me, but I can't in any good conscience pull you away from your life. I want you to finish university and fulfil your dreams of working on the West End. I need you to go on living for me. To achieve all the things I know you can in life. You deserve to be happy.

I know this is difficult to read and to understand. I wish I could explain, but please know this is the only way. Please know I would never leave you if it wasn't absolutely necessary. I never wanted to hurt you the way I did before. I never want to cause you pain. I know I'm hurting you right now and it kills me, but I have no other choice. I will spend every day wishing I could have found another way where we could still be together.

For now, this is goodbye. I'm sorry I couldn't say it to you in person. I wish it didn't have to be this way.

I love you, Meredith. Never forget that.

Yours forever

Cole

Each word I read stabbed at my heart. It tore my insides apart, ripping me to shreds.

Cole was gone.

Cole had left me again.

I read the words over and over, trying to understand what would force him into this. To understand why he had to leave me. Why he had to go. But the letter didn't explain. It didn't tell me anything.

"Why… why… what… what made him leave?"

I looked over at Rory, trying desperately to hold it together. My heart burnt. My whole body ached. This was worse than last time. Much, much worse. This time I didn't understand his reasons for leaving me.

"I can't tell you that. I'm sorry, but I promised my son."

Rory reached into his pocket again and pulled out a little packet of tissues. He offered it to me. It's then I realised tears were falling down my cheeks. Each one echoed the agony I felt inside.

"But... but how could he leave me behind?"

Rory tugged a tissue out and moved closer to me. He took the letter out of my hand, placing it down beside him. Then he took my face in his hand and wiped my cheeks. Cole had once explained to me why his dad didn't like human contact with those he didn't know, so this came as a surprise to me.

"He didn't want to," Rory said in a quiet voice. "He never wanted it to be this way."

"But he loves me, how could he do this?"

I wanted to understand. I needed an explanation. Cole wouldn't tell me he loved me one day and leave me the next. That wasn't the Cole I knew. He had to have a reason.

"He's doing it because he loves you. All I can say is he wants to keep you safe and for you to live the life you deserve."

"I can't live without him. I don't want to."

My words came out on a sob and tears blurred my vision. Yes, I'd lived without Cole for two years before this, but he made me happy. He made me feel alive. I loved him. Just as he said I was his one, he was my one too. I didn't know how to be happy without him even if he'd asked me to be. How could I when my heart had been ripped out of my chest and the pieces lay on the floor in a bloody mess.

I was enfolded in a pair of arms. A hand stroked my hair as I buried my face in his shoulder. I felt ridiculous getting comfort from Cole's dad, but he was right there offering it to me. It made me wonder why he'd come as opposed to Ash. Perhaps it was because Cole trusted his dad not to tell me why he'd gone. And that made it all so much worse.

"I know this is hard and it hurts," Rory murmured. "I want you to know we care about you, Meredith. And if you ever need anything, we're here for you. All of us."

I sobbed into his shoulder harder. Cole's family were far too nice. I didn't want to lose them along with Cole. The thought of it made everything hurt worse.

"You promise?"

"I promise. Ash told me to let you know you're welcome at our house whenever you need. We might not be able to tell you what happened and where Cole is, but you are part of our family. That's never going to change."

It was too much. All of it. I could hardly breathe as the world around me crumbled. And there was only one person in this world I wanted.

"I… I… I need," I hiccupped. "I need Jonah."

"Your brother?"

I nodded against Rory's shoulder. Either Cole must have told him who Jonah was or he knew about Jonah and Raphi.

"My phone… pocket."

Somehow, I managed to dig my hand into my pocket and pull it out. Rory made me unlock the phone with my fingerprint and then he called my brother for me. I didn't listen to their conversation as my ears were ringing and my head felt stuffy. When Rory was done, he assured me Jonah was on his way.

"Can I get you anything? A cup of tea, maybe?"

I nodded. Rory stood up and pulled the blanket off the back of the sofa before tucking it around me. He left the tissues by my hand and walked out to find the kitchen, leaving me lost in my own thoughts. My own misery. I stared down at my lap, tears still flowing down my face.

I was lost without Cole. Utterly lost. And alone.

How the hell did you cope when the love of your life left you for a second time?

How was it possible to feel this much pain inside?

It ate at me. Destroying me.

It was nothing like before. I had no hope. No nothing. Cole had told me he wanted to spend the rest of his life with me and that hadn't changed. He'd left anyway. Did that mean he would come back for me eventually? And how would I feel if he did?

I had no idea. All these questions only made my heart ache more.

By the time Rory came back in, he had Rhys following along behind him. The moment my best friend saw me, he was by my side and taking me in his arms.

"I'm so sorry, Mer," he whispered. "Cole's dad told me what happened. It's okay, I'm right here."

I really appreciated his presence even though I wanted just my brother. Jonah had a way of repairing everything. It would be hard on him given his sensitivity to emotions, but he never complained when it came to me. My brother had been the only constant in my life after our father died. Even though he'd come between Cole and me before, he did it because he loved me, not because he wanted to hurt me in any way, shape or form.

I didn't say a word to Rhys, just cried on him because there wasn't anything else I could say. I felt broken. And by the time Jonah got there, I was a mess even though I'd drunk the tea Rory had made for me.

Jonah took one look at me before he was by my side and had his arm wrapped around my shoulder, kissing the top of my head.

"I know," he murmured. "I know."

He didn't need me to explain. My brother would help me. He would keep me from drowning completely even though the water threatened to take me under and keep me there.

I didn't hear Rory or Rhys leave. Not when Jonah was there, murmuring soothing words into my hair and being my shield.

"It hurts right now, Mer. It hurts and it will for a long time, but I'll be right here. Always. I love you. I'll make sure you get through this."

And my brother was the only thing that kept me from losing my mind that day. The only person who gave me a reprieve from the desolation which had set in the moment I discovered the love of my life had left me in the dark.

I love you, Cole Carter.

And I hate you at the same time.

Our Darkest Path

I hate that you've left me alone all over again.
I don't want you to come back this time.
Don't come back because I won't be waiting for you.

PART IV

rectify

verb, rec·ti·fied, rec·ti·fy·ing.

to make, put, or set right; remedy; correct.

CHAPTER FORTY FOUR

Meredith

Five years later

ou know when you should be out celebrating and being happy for your best friend? Well, I wasn't doing that. And it made me feel like absolute shit. As if I didn't feel bad enough already sitting here in a cubicle in the ladies' toilets crying my eyes out.

You are such a mess, you know that, right?

Don't get me wrong, I was thrilled for Rhys. This was his special day. His wedding. He deserved it after everything he'd been through. After all the heartache and pain, he'd found his way back to the love of his life. His best friend from his childhood, Aaron. The person Rhys was meant to be with. They made a beautiful couple. I didn't think two people could love each other more than they did each other. It was fucking magical to see.

My tears had nothing to do with Rhys. Well, in some ways it did. It was seeing him get married which set me off. And all the alcohol I'd consumed at the reception so far. They'd been a toxic combination, leading me down a path I didn't want to follow. At the end of that path lay only more fucking pain. I was done feeling pain. Done experiencing this never-ending agony deep inside my soul. Done trying to deny I couldn't get over it. Done with it all.

I sniffled, trying not to make too much noise. My chest hurt, constricting with each breath I took. It was stupid. I was stupid. A stupid girl who couldn't forget. One who still harboured someone she shouldn't in her heart. I never meant to. I'd intended to let go. But that boy had dug his claws in, latching onto the parts of me needed to keep me alive.

My heart was required to beat.

My lungs were required to fill with air.

My brain was required to keep me functioning right.

He stole my ability to let anyone into my heart.

He stole the breath from my lungs.

And he ruined me for anyone else.

Five years should have been enough to make me forget about him. Except it wasn't. I didn't know how long would be enough. At this rate, I could go the rest of my life nursing the shattered pieces of myself and never finding a way to fix them.

It's not as if I thought about him all the time. I'd got on with my life, finished university and started working in the West End and on film and TV sets. It was my absolute dream come true. It's just some days I got hit with the reminder this was the life I'd wanted to share with the love of my life. The person who'd promised me everything.

So yes, he was the reason I was crying my eyes out on my best friend's wedding day. He was the reason my heart had remained closed off to everyone and anyone all this time. He was the fucking reason I was a big baby who couldn't get her act together and move on.

I was meant to have a day like this. A wedding day with him. He was meant to give me this and yet, all he'd done was left me with nothing. Fucking nothing but a broken heart.

I mentally slapped myself. Crying in a toilet was pathetic. Absolutely pathetic and only went to show how *un*-over him I was. How no matter what I did, I could never escape that boy. Though I suppose he'd be a man now. A fully grown man of twenty-three. I tried not to think of what he looked like now. It would only make it worse for me.

Pull yourself the fuck together. You can't sit in here all night. You are not going to cry over him any longer, you hear me? No more of this self-pity and wallowing.

I pulled at the toilet paper, ripping off some sheets and dabbing my face with it. Standing up, I chucked them in the bin and unlocked the door. I peered around, finding the room unoccupied. Breathing a sigh of relief, I trotted out on my heels and spent a few minutes in front of the mirror sorting my face out. There was nothing I could do about my bloodshot eyes, but at least I didn't look like a sodden mess any longer.

You are going to walk out, put on a brave face and be there for your best friend, you hear me? Do not allow yourself to fall apart.

I straightened my spine, walked out of the toilets and into the function room they'd hired out in a fancy hotel. The dancing had started up in my absence. Rhys and Aaron had invited more people to the reception than the wedding itself, so the room was pretty full. I leant up against the wall, watching as my best friend and his new husband held each other. They wore matching blue suits and smiles only for each other. I'd never seen Rhys look so happy in all the years I'd known him.

"Those two are like the poster children for a fairy tale love story."

I looked to my right, finding my brother had joined me. He was watching my best friend and his new husband with a smile.

"You wouldn't say that if you knew what they'd been through together."

"Suppose everyone has their dark histories."

Whilst Rhys had never explained the exact circumstances surrounding his breakup with Aaron when they were teenagers, I knew how painful it'd been for the both of them.

"Hmm, yes, I could say that about some other people I know."

He glanced at me and shook his head.

"Hush you."

I smiled and nudged his shoulder with mine. Jonah deserved every piece of happiness that had come his way recently. I swear to god my brother had been put through the fucking wringer or at least his heart had. But, as he said to me a couple of weeks ago, the heart wants what it wants. And his

432

heart led him to the person I had always known he'd end up with, even if their journey had been perilous.

"What? You not seeing him after this?"

Jonah nudged the floor with his foot.

"I am."

"Well then, you know I'm happy for you."

He reached out and took my hand, tugging me away from the wall. I gave him a look.

"Jonah…"

"Come on, Mer, it's a wedding, you're going to dance with me."

I begrudgingly allowed my brother to pull me out on the dancefloor. He'd been my plus one today since I wasn't seeing anyone. And even if I had been, there's no way in hell I'd have brought them to Rhys' wedding. Only someone truly special would get this privilege.

I rested my head on Jonah's shoulder as he took my hand and wrapped an arm around me.

"Are you okay?" he murmured.

"No."

There was no point me lying to him. We didn't keep anything from each other these days, not after everything that had happened between us. You could say mutual heartbreak brought my brother and me closer together. That, and Jonah's ability to read my emotions so well. The man never ceased to pester me until I told him what was up with me.

"Is it…?"

"Yes."

"I'm sorry, Mer."

I didn't have to explain myself to him, nor Rhys when it came to me and men. Well, one man. I couldn't bring myself to think his name, let alone say it out loud.

"I feel like a shit friend right now, wallowing in my own misery when it's Rhys' day."

"You know, I'm relatively sure Rhys is too busy making gooey eyes at Aaron to notice, and even if he has, he knows as well as I do why this is hard for you."

Jonah was right. Rhys knew me like the back of his hand. I glanced over at him and Aaron. They looked so happy and at peace together. He likely had no idea I'd disappeared for a cry and it would stay that way. I wouldn't ruin his big day for anything.

"Besides, you were there for the important bit, supporting him at the ceremony. Best woman duties and all."

I sighed, burying my face back in his shoulder. What would I do without Jonah? He was my rock.

"I love you, J, you know that, right? I'm so grateful you're here."

"Love you too."

Jonah spun us away so we didn't bump into another couple.

"It is wrong for me to miss him after all this time?"

He kissed my hair, leaving me feeling vulnerable. I kept my face pressed against him. I didn't want to see his expression, or anyone else's for that matter.

"You still love him."

It wasn't a question, but a statement. I nodded anyway.

"It's not wrong, Mer. It's just how you feel. You never got any closure. I imagine a part of you will always wonder if you and him would have made it if he hadn't left."

As usual, Jonah saw everything with such clarity. I used to hate how bloody wise he was when I was younger, but not now. Besides, he knew how to talk to people. He'd been working as a counselling psychologist for the past three years after he'd done his postgraduate studies to become a Chartered Psychologist. I didn't know how he coped, given how sensitive to emotions he was, but Jonah liked to help people. He always had. That was his superpower. At least, to me it was.

"Can you be my brother instead of psychologist Jonah?"

He chuckled.

"As your brother, I would still tell you the same thing. You're allowed to feel the way you feel. Have I ever told you to just get over it?"

"No."

"Then stop beating yourself up."

"Ugh, you're annoying when you're right."

He squeezed my hand as the song ended and a more upbeat one started. I pulled back and stared up at him.

"Don't you want to go see your man?"

"He's not my man yet."

I rolled my eyes.

"It's only a matter of time."

He shrugged, letting go of me as we made our way off the dance floor.

"We'll see."

435

"You could just ask."

He shook his head, his eyes growing darker at the prospect of putting himself out there like that.

"You tell me to stop dating emotionally unavailable men, so I'm going to tell you to stop letting your fear of rejection get in the way."

"Can you blame me?"

I didn't answer him straight away. Jonah had every reason under the sun to be scared.

"No, but if you don't nail that man down and make sure he stays yours, you're an idiot."

"Thanks so much for the vote of confidence in me."

I nudged his arm.

"J, I adore you, but you suck at this shit so take my advice. Tell him either he commits to you or you're done for good."

We stopped near the door of the function room. Jonah looked back over the guests for a moment, then levelled his gaze on me.

"Fine, but if this goes to shit, I'm placing the blame at your door."

I shrugged.

"I'll take it."

He hugged me before giving my hand a squeeze and ambling out the door.

"I won't expect you back tonight," I called after him.

I could see him shaking his head as he made his way towards the front door of the hotel. I smiled to myself. Jonah always knew how to make me feel better.

I turned back to the room, determined not to allow that boy I should learn to forget any further time to ruin my night. Besides, my best friend had promised me a dance. It was high time I dragged him away from his new husband for five minutes and ask if his wedding day had been everything he hoped and so much more.

CHAPTER FORTY FIVE

Meredith

I unlocked the front door of my building, having caught a taxi home. It was midnight. Usually, I was the life and soul of the party, but after Rhys and Aaron disappeared, I wanted to be alone. Trudging up the stairs, I felt the weight of the world on my shoulders. I wanted to strip down, take off my makeup and crawl into bed. All of those plans went out the window the moment I reached the first-floor landing and found a figure sitting outside my front door with their head bowed to their chest.

I stood at the top of the stairs wondering who it was, how the fuck they got in here and why the hell they were sitting outside the door of the flat I shared with Jonah. Then I hit the light switch and everything came into focus.

My heart thundered in my ears and my skin prickled. It was a man. A man who had quite clearly been beaten up by the looks of the bruising starting to colour on the side of his face and the dried blood on his knuckles, which were hanging down from where his arms were resting on his bent knees.

I took a step closer, wondering if he was even awake. His chest rose and fell steadily. He was still alive. At least that was something. I didn't know what to make of this or him. But I'd never backed down from anything else in life, so I wasn't going to start here.

I walked over to my door and stood over him, trying to work out what I was going to do about the bloodied man.

"Um, hello?"

A couple of seconds later, my world dropped out from underneath me when he raised his head and opened his eyes. Hazel eyes I would recognise anywhere. His hair was darker and he had stubble dusting his cheeks, but there was no mistaking who was sitting by my door.

"C… Cole?"

"Meredith."

My heart fucking exploded in my chest. That's what it felt like anyway. As if it'd been working sluggishly for five years and now it beat properly again at the sight of the man who'd ripped it apart from the inside out.

Cole Carter was the very last person I was expecting to see. *What the fuck is happening?*

I didn't know how to unstick my tongue from the roof of my mouth or even how to articulate my shock at seeing him again. At him being here, bloodied and bruised outside my door. I expected to feel anger. Anger and hatred. Neither of those things happened. No, the only thing racing through my body was relief. Sweet, blissful relief.

Cole was here and he was alive. Cole, who I still loved so fucking fiercely, it physically hurt. The only person in this world I'd wanted forever with.

You idiot. This boy destroyed you. How can you feel relief? How can you not be angry?

I didn't know what I should be experiencing right now. It's like the world had heard my heart calling for him earlier and had granted me a reprieve. The world had given him back to me.

"What are you doing here?"

His lip curved up. His split lip which looked painful.

"Isn't it obvious?"

"No. I don't really have people from my past turning up like this." I waved at him. "Especially not ones who look like they just got the shit kicked out of them."

I couldn't leave him sitting outside like this no matter what my fucked up emotions were doing at seeing him again. The part of me that had always cared about Cole didn't give a crap what the other parts thought. She wanted to clean him up and bandage his wounds.

"Well, I kind of did. Guess it looks worse than it is."

"It looks pretty fucking bad from where I'm standing."

He looked over at me, his brows turning down. It made me feel self-conscious. Did he not like what he was seeing? Had I really changed that much in five years? I mean, I had gone back to my natural strawberry blonde hair, but otherwise, I'd remained pretty much the same as I'd always been. Perhaps I looked older, but then again, so did he.

Why on earth do you care?

"You been out somewhere?"

"Rhys got married today."

Cole shifted off the wall, setting his bloodied hands down on the floor and pushing himself up.

"Really? Thought he'd sworn off men for life."

I smiled despite myself.

"Well, he did until the love of his life walked back into it and then all bets were off."

The irony of that statement wasn't lost on me considering the love of mine had just landed on my doorstep after all this time.

Cole rose to his full height, almost dwarfing me in the process even in my heels. My mouth went dry. Even though his face was bruised, Cole was still undoubtedly the most handsome man I'd ever laid eyes on. And he really was all man. It only served to melt my insides even as I tried to command myself to stop reacting this way to him.

I should be angry. I should be throwing him out of here. And yet I couldn't bring myself to.

"Well, congratulations to him."

"You never answered my question."

"About why I'm here?"

I nodded, trying not to wring my hands in front of me.

"It's a long story." He reached up and rubbed the back of his neck. "Not that I want to impose on you, but I do need somewhere to lie low for tonight."

I let out a breath.

"Okay."

I moved closer to the door, sticking the keys I was still holding in the lock and turning it. Pushing the door open, I walked in, holding it for him. Cole hesitated for a few seconds, then followed me into my open plan living area. I flipped the light on and slid out of my coat, hanging it up by the door.

"Sit down at the table. I need to get the first aid kit."

I didn't stop to think about it or let him object. I set my handbag on the table and walked to the small hallway which led to the bedrooms and bathroom. First, I went into my bedroom and took off my dove-grey dress since I didn't want to get blood on it. I pulled on some PJ shorts and an oversized t-shirt. Then I padded out into the bathroom and grabbed the kit from the cupboard. Jonah kept it on hand for emergencies. My brother was always prepared for anything.

Carrying it back out into the living area, I found Cole had taken his jacket off and hung it over the back of the chair. He'd sat down and was staring at the table, running his fingers along the wood. He looked up when I approached. I set the kit on the table and moved one of the chairs around so I was facing him. Sitting down, I opened up the box and took out the things I needed almost methodically. It helped me remain outwardly calm since this situation had caused my emotions to run riot.

I fished out one of the antiseptic wipes. Reaching out, I took Cole's hand. A jolt ran up my arm and down my spine at the contact. I tried not to react, but my heart kept racing so hard in my chest. My entire body was on high alert being so close to him. I let out a shaky breath and cleaned his knuckles.

He hissed at the sting but otherwise made no complaint. I tried not to squirm under his intense gaze.

When his knuckles were clean, I bandaged them since they were split in places on both hands. I didn't want to ask who he was fighting with, even though I had a million and one questions about why he was back and why he'd come to me.

"Do you have any other injuries apart from your lip?" I asked, setting the gauze down.

"Nothing you need to attend to."

I raised an eyebrow.

"They're just bruises, Meredith, I promise."

I nodded, picking up another antiseptic wipe and leaning closer to him. I captured his jaw with one hand and used the other to dab at his lip, wiping away the blood. He went very still, watching me intently again. I could hardly breathe, but I concentrated on making sure I did a thorough job. Every part of me screamed out to crawl into his lap and hold him. To never let go so he wouldn't leave me yet again. The urge was idiotic, but my walls were down after my emotional breakdown at Rhys' wedding earlier and the alcohol I'd consumed.

When my hand dropped, Cole leaned closer, his gauze wrapped hand coming up to curl a lock of my hair around his fingers. My breath stuttered and my hands trembled.

"I've missed you," he whispered.

"Cole…"

"I know, little queen. Trust me, I know."

I exhaled, my body aching with the need for him. And his term of endearment almost decimated all of my rationality.

Especially when his cheek brushed against mine. Cole was here. Right here where I could touch him, see him, feel him against me.

God… I love you. I still love you so much.

"I've missed you too."

I didn't know what I was doing, but I couldn't help myself when it came to Cole Carter. I'd never been able to. He had this hold on me, which was unshakable despite what he'd done. Despite everything we'd gone through.

I pulled back abruptly, knowing I couldn't allow myself to get lost in him.

"You can stay in my room. Jonah shouldn't be back tonight so he won't mind if I take his bed."

"I don't want to put you out."

I didn't look at him, not wanting to see his expression.

"You're not. I'm just tired, it's been a long day. We can talk in the morning."

I stood up and started packing up the first aid kit. As I closed the box, Cole placed his hand over mine, stopping me from going anywhere. I turned my head, staring up into his hazel eyes. They were full of emotions I wasn't sure I was prepared to see. The appreciation and affection he still held for me. It tore my insides to shreds.

"Thank you."

"You're welcome."

He dropped his hand. My body almost swayed towards his, desperate for contact with him again. I shook myself and picked up the wipes, throwing them in the bin. Cole followed me down the small hallway after I turned out the lights and

445

into my bedroom. He hung back in the doorway as I switched on the bedside lamp.

"You don't have to give up your bed. I can stay on the sofa."

I shook my head.

"No, it's okay. It'll be more comfortable in here. You're hurt so…"

He came up behind me, making my heart go into overdrive again.

"Meredith…"

I turned away to walk towards the door but he caught me by the arm, spinning me around to face him.

"Don't go," he whispered.

I stared up at him, my mouth going completely dry.

"I… I can't stay in here with you."

It was the truth. If I did, I would give in to all the need I had for him. The urge to hold on to him. I wouldn't let him go and that could only end in disaster for me. This man had left me twice. Who was to say he wouldn't do it again?

He let go of my arm and stepped back.

"Okay."

I nodded and walked out, pulling the door closed. A quick trip to the bathroom had me cleaning off my makeup. Then I curled up under the covers in my brother's bed. Jonah wouldn't mind even if he came back and found me in here.

I wanted to fall asleep straight away, but my heart wouldn't stop pounding and my skin prickled. I lay there staring at the ceiling, knowing across the hallway my ex-boyfriend was in my bed.

Cole had been more than my boyfriend, he'd been my everything.

"Why are you here?" I whispered. "Why are you back?"

Curling up on my side, I tugged one of Jonah's spare pillows into my arms and hugged it. I had no idea how I was going to survive the rest of the night since my mind was in overdrive.

Cole Carter had shown up back in my life. And it was the last thing I'd ever expected to happen on my best friend's wedding day.

CHAPTER FORTY SIX

Cole

I opened my eyes, blinking at the morning light streaming in through a gap in the curtains. My body ached all over. Hardly surprising given I'd ended up fending off two guys last night who tried to beat the crap out of me. They got a few good hits in, but they failed to realise I was faster and bigger than them. All it had taken was me slamming one into a wall to knock him out before I subdued the other. I left both of them where they were, not wanting to attract any further attention considering I was still wanted by the mafia.

I had my reasons for coming home, not least of all because I wanted my girl back in my life. And I was planning to make sure AJ paid for stealing the last five years of my life. For rendering it impossible for me to return home... until now.

I heard the door open. Rolling over onto my back, I found Meredith bustling in with a mug and a plate in her hands. She came over and set them on the bedside table. Seeing her in the morning light made my heart twist painfully in my chest. It caught her strawberry blonde hair, making her look almost angelic.

Fuck.

I swear she'd grown more beautiful in the intervening years since I left the country. The last time I'd seen her, she had pink hair, but I'd always thought her natural colour suited her best. No one would ever be as stunning as her in my eyes.

"I made you some tea and toast." She pulled out a small packet from her pocket, placing it down next to the mug. "Thought you might want some painkillers too."

She didn't stop to look at me as she moved towards her wardrobe. I pulled myself up and sat back against the headboard, wincing as I did so. As much as I appreciated her taking care of me, I hated the way her voice shook.

"Meredith."

She froze in the process of opening her wardrobe door.

"Come here."

We needed a conversation. We'd needed one last night, but I hadn't pushed her considering she'd looked exhausted. Not surprising as she'd been at a wedding. Not just any wedding. Her best friend who'd sworn off relationships for life. Rhys certainly had changed his tune since I last saw him.

"I need to get a change of clothes."

I didn't want her to leave. Having been starved of her presence for five long fucking years, I needed her.

"Just come over here."

I wasn't about to get up and manhandle her. That wouldn't go down well. Especially not after I'd turned up unannounced in a bit of a state. She was likely confused and questioning everything. I would give her answers… eventually.

"I need to go take a shower."

I wouldn't let her deflect. She said we would talk in the morning. She couldn't run from this.

"Meredith."

"What?"

"Look at me."

It took her a second but she turned and met my eyes. I could tell immediately she'd not slept well as there were dark circles under her eyes. My chest hurt, and not because I had bruises all over it. It ached for her.

"How can you expect me to look at you like nothing happened? Like it hasn't been five years since you left without telling me why." She took a step towards the bed, her eyes flickering with pent up emotion. "Tell me how, Cole, because I really don't know how to handle this. I don't know how to deal with you being here nor how it makes me feel."

I didn't have time to respond. Meredith came around the bed, crawled into my lap and took my face in her hands.

"I must be crazy," she said right before her mouth pressed against mine with the gentlest of touches as if she didn't want to re-open my split lip.

Pleasure and pain blossomed all over me at her touch. Pain because my hands curled around her, tugging her closer, which jostled my chest. Pleasure because she was kissing me.

I hadn't expected her to. Honestly, I never expected her subdued reaction last night either. Meredith had always been fiery. I just wasn't sure where that side of her was at right then.

Was she that messed up by seeing me again?

Did she feel everything I did?

Did she still love me?

I sure as hell still fucking well loved her. It didn't matter how many years passed. How long I'd gone without seeing her face. It wouldn't have mattered if I'd waited a lifetime. I would always love Meredith Veronica Pope.

"Why the hell am I kissing you?" she murmured against my lips.

"You missed me."

"Doesn't make this okay."

Her hands dropped from my face, skimming down my chest and reaching the covers bunched around my waist. She tasted and felt exactly as I remembered. Heat blossomed all over my skin, desperately wanting more. Desperately wanting her. I didn't give a shit about how I was bruised all over. Not when I had her. Not when she was touching me. Not when she was fucking well kissing me.

She shifted, tugging out the covers from under her. I didn't know what she was acting on right now.

Instinct?

Desire?

Did it matter?

You know it matters. You don't want her to regret this.

My hands went to her hair, pulling her away from me. Her green eyes were wide and her mouth parted in surprise.

"We need to talk."

Her mouth shut abruptly and she scrambled backwards away from me.

"Oh god, what the fuck am I doing?" She buried her face in her hands. "I'm so sorry, Cole. I don't know what came over me."

"It's okay, not like I wasn't enjoying it."

She groaned.

"No, it's not okay. Jesus, you came here for my help and then I maul you like that's normal when it's not fucking well normal." She dropped her hands and waved them around like she was agitated and didn't know what to do with them. "I spent all night wondering what to say to you. Wondering why you're here. And then I kiss you since I apparently can't help myself around you. Fuck."

I shifted up on my knees and moved closer to her, grabbing her wrists to still her hands. Her head whipped up to me. Her eyes were conflicted and her body tense.

"I'm back because Aurora's getting married, I'm tired of running away, and you. Though, I should have said you first because you are the reason I'm right here, in your bed, with you."

"M… me?"

"Of course, you. Did you think I just arrived at your door because I had nowhere else to go?" I shook my head. "I'm staying with my sister and Logan, but I wanted to see you. You, Meredith. I wasn't lying last night, I've missed you so fucking much. There hasn't been a day I've not thought about you or wanted to come home so I could see you again."

I didn't know how to articulate how much I'd longed for her. How I'd spent the past five years on the run. And how I finally had a way to clear my name. Meredith didn't know about the shit I'd got myself into. What I'd done to survive. What I'd done to protect her. What I would do to make sure I never had to live in fear of my life or hers again.

"Where have you been?"

"Honestly? Everywhere but here. I've been around the world, probably twice over now, but I couldn't come home. It wasn't safe. Hell, it's not fucking safe now, but I don't care. I'm dealing with it."

The words were on the tip of my tongue about how AJ had framed me. How I'd had to move around from place to place so the Russian mafia didn't find me. How I'd had to do things I wasn't proud of just to survive. I didn't know how to tell her any of it or whether she'd even believe me. She did know about my family's past so it wouldn't be that much of a stretch. She just didn't realise how fucked up everything had become over the years.

"I don't understand. You never explained anything. Why isn't it safe?"

I sighed and let go of her.

"I told you once you weren't in any danger from my parents' past."

Meredith visibly swallowed at my words.

"I thought that was the case at the time, but it turns out the past has a funny way of catching up with you. Only it wasn't my parents' past, but my grandfather's. Trust me, Meredith, I want to explain it all to you, but I don't want to put you in any more danger. Just know I'm going to make sure this all goes away."

"Is… is that why you got beaten up?"

I nodded and she put her hand to her mouth as if holding back all of her questions. All of her words. Then she got off the bed and walked away.

"I should kick you out, you know," she said when her back was to me. "I should but won't." She let out a hollow laugh. "I promised myself the day you left I wouldn't be waiting for you if you ever came back. Funny that it's been impossible to forget you. To stop myself from wishing you'd come home. To stop hoping when you promised me forever, you actually meant it. It's so fucking funny that it's not funny at all." She dropped her face down into her hands again. "Deep down, I have been waiting, hoping and wishing for you because my heart never stopped believing everything you told me. I should be angry. I should be so fucking angry… but I'm not. I'm just not and that's fucked up."

My heart lurched and my fingers itched to touch her. To soothe her. I wanted to tell her I'd meant everything. I was always going to come back for her. I'd hoped she'd not found anyone else. I'd fucking well wished she'd wait even though it was unfair of me to ask it of her. That's why I'd never said it in the letter I'd written to her. Never asked anything of her but to remember I'd love her forever.

"I'm going to take a shower. You should take the painkillers and eat." She dropped her hands, walked towards the wardrobes and tugged out her clothes. "We'll talk properly when I get out."

She didn't let me respond, walking out of the room and not daring to look at me.

I didn't know how to feel about what she'd admitted. The Meredith I'd known five years ago would have raged at me. She would have got emotional and thrown all of my broken promises back in my face. But the Meredith in the here and now had changed. She'd laid all her feelings out on the table without accusations or irritation lacing her voice. It was more like resignation.

Had she really changed that much?

Did she just not know how to deal with me being here?

I stared down at my bandaged hands, closing them into fists. The movement hurt but it reminded me I had so much to fight for. I didn't care how much Meredith had changed. I would get to know her all over again if she let me. It didn't make a difference to the way I felt about her. She would always be the one no matter the time or distance. Her kissing me had confirmed it.

My heart still beat for her.

My soul ached for her.

And no matter what, this time I wasn't leaving or giving up.

This time I would destroy all those who stood in our way. I would make sure things didn't fuck up or go wrong. Because if Meredith still felt things for me, then I had hope.

Two months ago, I'd decided enough was enough when I'd got word from Demetri that he knew where to find the evidence I needed to prove I was innocent. To show AJ was the one who set me up. I would not stop until that worthless fucker was in the grave. Then and only then would I ask Meredith the only burning question I had. The one I'd wanted to ask her years ago before everything went to shit.

I haven't come back to make you empty promises, Meredith.
I've come back to make vows to you.
I've come back to make you my wife.

CHAPTER FORTY SEVEN

Meredith

I stood under the spray wondering how on earth I was going to sit and have a conversation with Cole without wanting to hold him close and kiss him again. It was stupid of me to have done that in the first place. The problem was my heart belonged to him. Hell, my whole damn soul belonged to the man in my bed. Seeing him again had only made me realise I still wanted him. I needed him because he was my air. I could finally breathe again after all these years of feeling as though I was drowning.

It was ridiculous. I shouldn't want him. I shouldn't need him. I shouldn't damn well forgive him for leaving me five years ago without any real explanation. And yet… and fucking yet… it's as if my heart and soul didn't care about those things. They didn't care about any of it. All they cared about was Cole being here. Cole being home. Because Cole was my home.

I slammed my hand against the tiles, frustrated with my conflicted feelings towards him. Cole and I had never been simple. We'd always been on this twisted path where our lives met and diverged repeatedly. But I didn't want us to diverge again. Why couldn't we be on the same track?

It would be a lie to say I didn't want to be with him. I didn't do lies or try to kid myself into believing anything but the truth. Yes, I wanted an explanation from him. One which didn't leave anything out. I deserved that much. It's just I didn't think it would change my feelings towards him. It wouldn't change how much I loved him.

Sometimes people change for the better and sometimes for the worst. I believed I was the former. I'd grown up. I'd learnt forgiveness and how to move on from the bad things in life. It was Rhys who taught me that lesson. Seeing him and Aaron come back together despite the hardships and betrayals. If Rhys could forgive the man who'd broken his heart, I sure as hell could forgive the one who'd broken mine. As long as he told me the truth. I needed that much from Cole if he wanted to be back in my life.

He'd said him leaving had something to do with his family. Considering their past, it didn't surprise me. It wouldn't matter to me because I loved his family. Even though five years had gone by, I'd kept in touch with them. I knew Aurora was getting married, but I didn't think Cole would come home for it. It didn't cross my mind when it should have. None of them had mentioned him when Ash told me about the wedding. Perhaps it was for the best. They knew talking about Cole was painful for me so we never did.

Some people might consider it crazy that I kept in touch with my ex-boyfriend's family. Cole and I breaking up hadn't changed how I felt about them. How they'd become more like my real family than my actual family had ever been, except for Jonah. When the two of us had got a place together, we stopped speaking to Mum and Grandma. It stung a little when neither of them seemed too bothered by us severing contact, but ultimately, Jonah and I didn't need them when we had each other.

I got out of the shower after washing my hair, dried myself and got dressed. It's not like I could stay in there all day avoiding Cole. My thoughts would only whirl around and around in my head. That wasn't particularly healthy nor would it get me anywhere.

I padded out into the open plan living area finding Cole had got dressed and was sat on the sofa fiddling with his phone. He put it down the moment he heard me. My hair was still damp, but I wasn't in the mood to sit and dry it. Instead of going over to him, I walked over to the kitchen and flipped the kettle on. If I was going to do this with him, I needed tea and breakfast.

A few minutes later, I was loaded up with two mugs and a plate of toast which I carried over to the sofa, setting them down on the coffee table. I sat down on the other end from him, not trusting myself to do something stupid. In the morning light, Cole's face looked worse, but he hadn't mentioned it hurting earlier.

"How are you feeling?" I asked as I picked up my plate and held it against my chest.

"Okay. I told you last night, it looks worse than it feels."

"So, I know you said you don't want to put me in danger, but I think I deserve an explanation."

He nodded slowly before letting out a sigh and reaching for the mug of tea I'd made him. He stared down into it, his expression darkening.

"I left because the Russian mafia is after me for something I didn't do and I had no other choice but to run in order to stay alive."

The Russian mafia? Holy shit. What the fuck?

"That's the short explanation anyway. I promise I'm going to tell you everything, but I want you to know leaving had nothing to do with you. It wasn't because I didn't want to be with you or I didn't mean anything I said. I meant those things and I still do."

My heart hammered wildly against my chest. Cole's admission he still wanted everything with me had me gripping the plate tighter.

"We haven't had it easy. I know that. I'm not going to ask you for more chances or forgiveness. You deserve more than that, so much more. You deserve someone who can give you everything, but I can't do that yet. Not until I clear my name. All I'm asking for is, when I've done that, you hear me out. That's it. Then it's your decision what happens after that. It will always be your decision what path we take. Whether we stay on the same one or we go our separate ways. Can you do that for me? Hear me out when I've handled everything?"

It took me a minute to process what he'd said. To fully understand the implications. He couldn't offer me everything yet. Not whilst his life was in danger. I don't know why it made me surer than ever of what I wanted. Perhaps because it made me realise, I wasn't the only one who'd grown up. Cole was only willing to offer himself to me when he felt worthy. That wasn't the Cole I'd known all those years ago. The one who took whatever he wanted because he wanted it. He'd pursued me and he didn't care about who or what got in his way. This time felt different. We weren't the same people, but we still shared the same feelings. The same connection. The one drawing us together. Putting us on a path to each other again and again.

I put my plate down on the coffee table, then I took the mug out of his hands, placing that down too. Carefully, I pushed him back against the cushions and crawled into his lap. My hands went to his shoulders and I stared down into those beautiful hazel eyes I'd always loved so much.

"I can do that, even though I already know what my answer will be. You've changed and so have I, but time hasn't altered this." My hand slid from his shoulder to his heart. "You still feel that, don't you? You feel what I feel."

The soft rise and fall of his chest echoed the thump of his heart against my fingertips. It echoed my heart beating for him and only him.

"I know you do. You might not be asking anything of me right now, but I'm going to ask something of you."

Cole's hands wrapped around my hips as if he knew what I was going to say. As if he understood what I wanted.

"Show me how you feel. Remind me of the way we were. Give me something to hold on to."

I knew he was injured and I shouldn't ask him for anything, but it all seemed so fucking useless to pretend. To act like he wasn't all I wanted. All I needed.

"Please."

His hand left my hip to cup the back of my neck. Cole tugged me forward and captured my mouth with his. It wasn't gentle, which had me worrying about his split lip, but he was so demanding. Just as I remembered him to be. He devoured my mouth, pushing me down on his rapidly hardening length. The moan escaping my mouth was involuntary.

Rationality be damned. I needed to feel him. To have him against me. Inside me. I wanted Cole to consume me.

He broke the kiss, leaving us both panting. His eyes were dark with arousal, making me shiver at the intensity of his expression.

"I don't want to hurt you," I said since I couldn't forget he was injured.

A smirk appeared on his face.

"Oh, little queen, I'm not about to let a few bruises get in the way of giving you what you asked for."

I swallowed as his hands went to the shorts I was wearing, peeling them down and making it very clear what his intentions were. I shifted off him so I could get rid of them and my underwear. Cole's eyes were on me, staring at my most intimate parts intently. It wasn't anything he hadn't seen before so I wasn't embarrassed. I let him look. He'd always made me feel beautiful. And his expression told me he liked what he saw. He fucking well loved it.

He reached out, grabbing my leg and tugging me back in his lap. Then his fingers ran up my inner thigh before meeting my pussy. He kissed me again, groaning when he felt me and how wet I'd grown for him already.

Should I be doing this with him?

Probably not.

I no longer wanted to question anything. I just wanted to feel.

As he found my clit and stroked me, my hips bucked, grinding against his fingers.

"Cole," I moaned in his mouth.

No one had known my body in the way he did. No one had given me the pleasure he did. Cole had discovered every erogenous zone I had and mastered it. He got off on giving me pleasure. On ordering me around and making me do exactly as he pleased.

"Take my cock out," he practically growled against my mouth whilst continuing to drive me higher.

I fumbled between us, almost desperate to free him. Wrapping my fist around his cock when I'd unzipped his jeans and tugged at his boxers, I stroked a hand down his length.

"Fuck," he groaned. "I need inside you."

I didn't hesitate, shifting higher and pressing myself down on him. It didn't occur to me to even think about protection when I was on birth control. His resulting moan only made me want more. Need more.

"Oh god," I cried out sinking lower, impaling myself inch by inch.

Cole felt so damn good. It felt like coming home. He and I fit so perfectly together. I'd been missing this high since he left. Missing out on him. No one would ever match up to Cole in my eyes.

I guess what they say about first loves is true. You give them a piece of yourself which you can never get back. It remains with them forever. They're the one you can't forget. The one you hope to have forever with because nothing ever consumes you in the way they do. Nothing ever fits quite right.

Cole Carter had all my firsts. I had all of his. That cemented us together. It bound us to each other. Acting as if we were anything other than soulmates would be futile.

I rested my forehead against his when he was fully seated inside me. My hand curled around his jaw, careful not to hold on too tight.

"I've never been able to forget you and I've never been able to let you go. Do whatever it is you need to do so you can come back to me."

"I will. Mark my words, little queen, I'm going to claim you as my fucking own when this is all over."

His hands clasped my hips, starting to move me up and down on his length. We stared at each other, our eyes saying more than we ever could with words.

You're my forever. I'll never let you go again. I love you.

I knew it was crazy to let this man back in my life after less than twenty-four hours of him being here. There was no logic. Love wasn't rational. It just was. You either follow your head or your heart. I decided on the latter. It didn't matter what anyone else thought. I didn't care if Rhys or my brother disapproved. Their feelings about my relationships had never factored into my decisions. Cole had taught me how to be secure in my own actions all those years ago. He'd shown me how to be fearless and always go after what you wanted.

I wanted him. And he wanted me.

The rest would fall into place in time.

Cole's hands left my hips, one wrapping around my back and the other my shoulder. He pulled me closer, our chests moving together as he thrust upwards. I gripped the back of the sofa with my free hand, turning my face from his and kissing down his jaw to his ear instead. My teeth grazed over it, only prompting him to thrust harder.

"Meredith," he groaned. "Fuck… fuck, I've missed you."

He said my name with such a desperate plea as if all these years without me had weighed on him. I knew the feeling because they'd cut me too.

"Harder," I whispered. "Fuck me harder."

His grip on me tightened, thrusts growing more erratic. My hand left his jaw and slid between us, fingers finding my sweet spot. My teeth dug into his ear, knowing exactly how to drive Cole insane. His guttural moan only made me want to feel him explode. I'd missed this man. The way he knew how to play me just right.

"Come for me," he grunted. "Fucking well come for me."

Something about him saying it set me off. Him giving me permission.

"Fuck, Cole," I moaned, shaking in his embrace as he continued to fuck me without mercy or restraint.

He shuddered when he let go, both of us high off each other. Both lost to the sensations and feelings. The bliss washing over us. The unending pleasure. It was everything I needed, desired and craved. Him. Just him and I.

My forehead dropped to his shoulder after he stilled, my breathing erratic as our hearts pounded against our chests. I didn't care to think about the consequences of doing this with him. Didn't really give a shit about anything other than holding him close and never letting Cole go again.

That's when I heard the key in the lock. My head snapped up in time to see my brother walking through the front door. It was lucky the back of the sofa was facing the door or he'd have seen way more than he ever needed to. As if he wasn't going to see enough already. It's not like I had any time to cover myself or Cole for that matter.

Jonah's eyebrows shot up when he spied me after he stepped in and shut the door behind him.

"Well, I've clearly caught you at an inopportune moment," he said, turning away but not before I saw his grin.

Cole looked back at my brother with no small amount of amusement in his expression. I didn't know why he found this funny. The last thing I wanted was for Jonah to come home and see me right after I'd fucked my ex-boyfriend.

"Um, hi, J… sorry, I didn't know when you would be back," I said, unsure of how to deal with the situation.

"No, no, it's fine," Jonah said, but I could hear the mirth in his voice. "About time one of us caught the other, eh?"

"Oh, shut up and go to your room. And keep your eyes averted!"

Jonah put his hand over his eyes and walked further into the flat. He was still smiling wide, which only irritated me. It's not as though I often brought people back to our flat and I'd certainly never slept with anyone outside of my bedroom. We didn't have rules or anything, it's just I didn't want Jonah catching me in the act.

When Jonah was in the small hallway, he turned back slightly, "I don't care if you fuck in the living room. Just make sure nothing gets on our sofa, eh?"

I grabbed a cushion and threw it at his head. Jonah laughed as he walked away into his bedroom. I buried my face in Cole's shoulder, feeling embarrassed and unsure of what I should say. Whilst I might be pretty out there with Rhys about all things to do with sex, it was a different story when it came to my brother. We rarely ever discussed that sort of thing.

"Why is this my life?" I muttered.

"Do you think he saw me?" Cole asked, stroking my back.

"No, or he would have said more."

"Guess he's in for another shock then."

I groaned, having forgotten all about that.

"Oh Jesus, don't remind me. Fuck."

"It's okay, I can leave before he comes out if you don't want him to know."

I shook my head. Jonah wouldn't judge. He knew how I felt about Cole. I doubted he'd be surprised I'd ended up sleeping with my ex within less than twenty-four hours of him being here.

"No. I'd rather get this over with now."

Cole kissed the top of my head.

"Okay, little queen, whatever you need."

What I needed was for my brother to have never gotten home yet, but we didn't always get what we wanted in life. Guess it was time to face the music. It would come out one way or another that Cole was back. I was going to be an adult and fess up to my brother. Cowardice wasn't my style. Besides, Jonah couldn't say a fucking thing. Not when he'd got back together with the person who broke his heart too.

Apparently, me, Jonah and Rhys were far too alike when it came to first loves. They were ink, permanently etched on our hearts, binding us to the one person in our lives we were meant to end up with. It didn't matter how much they'd hurt us, we couldn't help but be drawn back into their sphere. To need them like they were the essence of life we needed to keep breathing. We forgave them for the pain because of love.

I pulled back and looked at Cole. My one was right here. And I wasn't fucking well letting him go again. Not for anything.

CHAPTER FORTY EIGHT

Meredith

When Jonah emerged from his bedroom, Cole and I had sorted ourselves out and were both sat on the sofa, not touching. I'd wolfed down my cold toast and half my tea. Cole had certainly given me a workout and I'd been starving.

Jonah paused when he spied us, eyes roaming over Cole. His eyebrow raised slowly before he glanced at me with a knowing look on his face. I bit the inside of my cheek to prevent a retort falling out of my mouth. I hoped my brother would not make a smart remark.

"Well, this is a surprise. Hello, Cole... dare I ask why your face is all messed up?"

I glanced at Cole who merely smiled.

"Got into a fight. Your sister fixed me up."

Jonah frowned.

"Is this going to be a regular thing? You know how I feel about you getting Meredith in trouble."

"No, it's not. I'm dealing with it and it won't be an issue much longer."

I glanced between Cole and Jonah, wondering if this would turn into a huge confrontation. Jonah canted his head. I sucked in a breath.

"You here to make an honest woman out of my sister?"

"Jonah!" I hissed, wondering what the fuck my brother was playing at.

"If she lets me," Cole replied with a shrug.

"Good. It's about time."

"Glad to know I have your blessing."

What is happening? Why are my brother and my ex-boyfriend planning my fucking future right now?

I opened and closed my mouth. What did I even say to any of this?

"I'm pretty sure Mer would tell me to go fuck myself if I demanded you ask my permission. She's going to do what she wants regardless of my opinion."

Cole grinned. What on earth was with these two? Were they trying to gang up on me?

"Excuse me! I'm sitting right here in case you'd forgotten," I blurted out, annoyed by them acting as if I wasn't in the room.

"I hadn't," Jonah said. "But the look on your face is priceless."

"Why you little fu—"

My phone going off interrupted me before I could rip my brother a new one. I got up off the sofa, stomping over to the kitchen table and giving Jonah evils along the way. He winked at me. I ignored him as I picked up my bag and tugged out my phone. It was running low on battery. I'd forgotten to put it on charge last night. Fiddling with it, I checked my messages.

Rhys: I've been spoiled.

It was followed up with a photo of the spread Aaron had put on for them for breakfast. I rolled my eyes as another photo came through of the two of them. Aaron was kissing Rhys on the cheek. These two. I swear to god they were obsessed with each other and making my life hell by taunting me with their happy relationship. Not that I wasn't happy for them. Hell, I loved this new Rhys now he had Aaron.

Meredith: You two lovebirds make me sick.

Rhys: You're just annoyed I didn't send you a pic of us fucking.

I snorted. *Cheeky little fucker.*

Meredith: I would have to bleach my eyes if you did that!

Rhys: Oh, so you only like to hear all about it as opposed to seeing it?

Meredith: Go do dirty stuff to your new husband as opposed to harassing me.

Rhys: Oh, I intend to. The new Mr King needs a reward for all his hard work.

Why is he doing this to me? This man is not okay. I swear he's getting me back for all the times I divulged too much information about my sex life.

Meredith: I swear you've been hanging around me too much.

Rhys: You say that like it's a bad thing.

Meredith: In this case, it is. Love you.

Rhys: Love you more! A says hi and to keep corrupting me so he can reap the rewards.

Meredith: Tell A if he wants you to get all dominant Rhys on him, he needs to rearrange everything on your desk.

Rhys sent me back crying with laughter emojis. Well, it was true. Rhys hated people touching his desk. No doubt those two would be all over each other soon enough. They were leaving for their honeymoon in Thailand tomorrow, something Rhys had been looking forward to since it'd be his very first holiday outside of the country. In some ways, I was glad Rhys wouldn't be around so I didn't have to tell him about Cole yet. That was a conversation I was *not* looking forward to.

I felt a hand on my shoulder. Looking up, I found Jonah standing next to me with concern on his face.

"You okay?" he asked, his voice quiet.

"Yeah, it's just Rhys and he's fine."

I leant against my brother, putting my phone back down on the table.

"I meant about, you know."

I knew he was talking about Cole, but I didn't want to start a conversation about it with Jonah when my ex was still here.

"We'll talk about it later."

Jonah gave my shoulder a squeeze.

"I actually have to get going," came Cole's voice from behind me.

Both Jonah and I turned towards him. He'd stood up and was rubbing the back of his neck.

"Oh, okay," I mumbled.

I wanted Cole to stay. We had so many things to discuss, but I also knew he had shit to handle.

"I can come by tomorrow… if you'd like."

I let out a long sigh.

"I'm working. Not that I want to, but I took time off for Rhys' wedding and they need me. I'm around late evening though, like after nine."

Cole nodded slowly. I walked over to him, feeling Jonah's eyes on my back.

"If you give me your number, I'll text you, yeah?"

He handed me his phone and I added myself to his contacts. No doubt he'd had to get rid of his old number what with the trouble he was in. After he left, I'd texted him way too many times, hoping for a response and knowing I wouldn't get one. I didn't want to think about those months. How I'd had to go on with my life even though I'd fallen into a pit of despair. It was during that time I'd been truly grateful for Rhys and Jonah. Those two picked up my broken pieces and patched them up with tape. It was only temporary, but it was something.

Cole took his phone back and gave me a smile. The sight of it made my heart hurt. I hadn't had enough time with him yet. Hadn't had a chance to savour his presence. I internally shook myself. He said he'd see me tomorrow. I had to hope he'd stick by that. Don't think anyone could blame me for being wary about Cole turning up after the way he'd left me. Twice.

He leant down towards me and pressed a kiss to my forehead.

"I'm coming back," he whispered without pulling away.

"I know."

He reached up and brushed his fingers down my arm.

"I don't think you do. You're scared and I don't blame you for that, little queen. I won't ask you to trust me, but I am coming back to you."

My heart did a backflip at his serious tone. His reassurance. I looked up at him, trying to stop myself from having all these fears and doubts but failing miserably.

"Cole, if you don't… I won't survive it," I whispered, my voice shaking on each word. "I don't want to live without you."

His hazel eyes softened, melting my fucking heart into pieces. Here I was being vulnerable with him all over again because he made me that way. He held my whole fucking soul in the palm of his hand and could crush it if he chose to.

"When I've done what I need to do, I want you to be prepared for the question I'm going to ask you. You know what it is, Meredith. You know what I want. Think about your answer because I'm going to fight my way back to you if I have to. I *will* fight for you."

Both his hands came up and he cupped my face, pressing his lips to mine and sealing his words a kiss. When he pulled away, he assessed me for a long moment.

"I love you."

He kissed my forehead again and let me go, walking away to grab his jacket before he disappeared out the front door, giving me one last glance and a smile. I stared at the space he'd been in, my heart racing at a hundred miles an hour. The way he'd said it so casually as if I was supposed to know he still felt that way. I mean I did and I didn't. It wasn't as if I expected him to just come out with those three words. Cole had taken forever to say them last time.

"So, do I even ask if you're happy he's back?" came Jonah's voice from behind me.

"I... he... did he mean what I think he did?"

"About what?"

"He said I know what question he wants to ask me."

I heard Jonah chuckling. I turned and found him smiling at me.

"Please tell me you're joking."

I gave him a look. My mind was too full of everything to process what had happened. And I was probably being completely dense.

"Meredith, that boy has loved you since he was eleven. I think it's pretty obvious what he wants. He even told you the night before he left."

I'd confessed everything to Jonah. Every last detail because I'd over analysed it a million times since Cole left. Every word and action. So fucking futile, but my memories of Cole were the only things I had left to cling onto at the time.

"Please spell it out for me. Seeing him again has me all crazy, okay? I don't know what's up or down any longer."

Jonah walked over to me and put his hands on my arms. His green eyes twinkled with amusement.

"He wants to make you his wife."

"He what?"

"Cole wants to marry you. That's what he's going to ask you and the fact you can't see that…" Jonah shook his head. "Meredith, I love you, but you really are an idiot sometimes."

"Hey! My ex-boyfriend just landed on my doorstep after five years of no word, give me a break."

Jonah pulled me into his arms and held me against his chest. I relaxed into him, feeling all the stress and emotional turmoil spilling out of me. Jonah had a calming presence. He always knew how to make me feel better.

"Do you want him back?"

"Yes," I mumbled into his jumper.

"Then I think you already know the answer to the question he's going to pose."

I buried myself deeper into my brother's hold. The thought of Cole asking me to marry him gave me heart palpitations. As if my heart wasn't going crazy as it was.

"You're not going to tell me I'm insane for wanting to be with him after everything, are you?"

"No, because I know you wouldn't be considering it if Cole didn't have a good reason for leaving."

I shook my head, gripping Jonah tighter.

"The Russian mafia wants him dead for something he didn't do. That's all I know. He said he'd explain it all when he's dealt with it."

"I did tell you that family is trouble."

I smacked Jonah's back.

"Shut up. You cannot talk. Did you ask him last night?"

"This isn't about me."

I pulled back and looked up at my brother's smiling features.

"Jonah, I swear to god I will beat you up."

"Yes, I did ask."

"And? You are mean for leaving me in suspense. If you don't tell me, I'll just ask him."

Jonah bit his lip and then shook his head.

"He said yes, okay?"

For a moment, I just looked at him. Then I smiled.

"And did you tell him you love him?"

Jonah rolled his eyes.

"Yes."

"Did he say it back?"

"Yes."

I let go of him and clapped my hands together, which only made Jonah give me a look.

"You two are the cutest couple ever and I'm going to count down the days until I get to be your best woman. It's going to be so beautiful."

"Excuse me?"

"Oh, come on, J, you and him are going to get married and adopt beautiful babies. Just think, we'll have a real family then."

Jonah let me go abruptly and scowled.

"You need to quit getting crazy ideas in your head."

"You telling me you don't want to marry him?"

Jonah stalked away from me. I kept smiling because I knew exactly how my brother felt and what he wanted out of life.

"Fuck, you are annoying. Yes, yes I do want those things in the future and you need to keep that shit to yourself, got it? No telling him about any of it, because I only just got him back and I'm not going to lose him again."

I zipped my mouth shut. As if I would do anything to jeopardise their relationship. I'd encouraged Jonah to go after what he wanted when the opportunity presented itself.

"Your secrets are safe with me, J. Just don't give me shit about Cole and we're good."

Jonah considered my offer for a moment.

"Fine, deal. Just… be careful, yeah? I don't want you getting hurt."

I nodded. I'd be careful. Cole said he was going to handle things first. I guess I was going to have to be patient, wait for him to come back to me and hope I wouldn't lose my shit in the process.

What I'd said to Cole was true. I didn't want to live without him again.

It would break me.

Completely.

CHAPTER FORTY NINE

Cole

The moment I walked through the front door of the house I grew up in, I sucked in a breath and let it out. Five years away from my family. My home. The place which held my hopes and dreams. All of it weighed on me. Coming back here felt like the start of something new.

I'd only arrived back in the UK two days ago and had gone straight to Aurora and Logan's, so I hadn't seen my parents yet. My heart got tight thinking about how much I'd missed out on. Seeing Meredith again had only reminded me of how much that fucker, AJ, had stolen from me. He'd taken away my fucking life and I wasn't going to let him get away with it. He might think he was king in his castle, but he was nothing and nobody. I'd make sure he knew that before I destroyed him.

"My baby boy!"

I looked up in time to see a blur of blonde hair before my mum crashed into my chest, holding me as tight as she could.

"I've missed you so much," she sobbed.

I wrapped my arms around her, burying my face in her hair and breathing her in. Mum smelt just like home. It didn't bother me she was crying because I sort of felt like doing it too. It had been far too long.

"I've missed you too, Mum."

She pulled back and looked me over before reaching up to cup my face in her hands. She ran her fingers over my bruises. I'd pre-warned her about having got into an altercation last night so she'd been expecting it.

"You look so grown up and here you are towering over me like everyone else."

I smiled when I saw her own one plastered on her face even though tears were still falling down her cheeks.

"Well, clearly I got Dad's genes."

She laughed and hugged me again. It felt so good to see her. I'd kept in touch, but it'd been too dangerous to see them.

"Cole."

I looked up, finding all four of my dads standing by the living room doorway. Mum let me go, rubbing my arm after she'd turned to my dads with a smile.

"Our son is home."

I closed the distance. Quinn gave me a pat on the back at first, but then he hugged me.

"Welcome home," he whispered. "Your mother has been driving us half crazy for the past month since you told us you were coming back."

"I'll bet. I wasn't going to miss Rora's wedding. She'd throttle me."

"Hmm, yes, well, that boy has certainly taken his time in asking her."

I laughed and pulled back, catching Quinn's scowl.

"Did he ask you permission for her hand?"

"You do not want to know that story," Xav said, tugging me over to him and wrapping me up in his arms. "Trust me, all of us would rather forget it."

"That's not fair, I bet everyone else knows."

"Fine, we'll fill you in later at dinner, but it's not pretty."

"And yet he's marrying her anyway."

Xav laughed.

"Oh, you really have missed out on all the drama."

I wasn't sure if that was a good or bad thing. My family drama could be a lot, especially when all nine of us were together. Our family had grown since I'd left. Duke had his lady love. Aurora was getting married. And Raphi? Well, he had finally got his head out of his arse and stopped self-sabotaging his love life. All that was left was for me to get Meredith to agree to be my wife.

All in good time. First, I'm going to stick it to that scumbag who ruined my life, then I'm going to marry my little queen. Make her the happiest fucking woman alive.

Seeing the fear in her eyes before I left made me realise how much I'd put her through. The pain and agony. It only made me more determined to make sure it was safe for us to be together. This time we would be permanent. I'd make it so.

Xav let me go so I could hug Eric. He smiled at me before enfolding me in his arms.

"You've been missed around here."

"Missed you too."

"How is she?"

I smiled. He was asking me about Meredith. My family had kept in touch with her, but it was more in relation to how she felt about seeing me again.

"She's okay. Scared I'll leave again, but that's not going to happen."

Eric nodded as I pulled away and squeezed my shoulder. Finally, I stood in front of my dad. He looked me over before shaking his head.

"You've been through the wars."

"Like father, like son."

That made him snort. Dad hugged me and I tried my best to keep my emotions in check. Being without my family had been tough even though they'd been there for me in spirit. All these years away from everyone I loved left me feeling alone. Some days I lost all hope I'd ever be able to return.

"Did you get what we needed last night?" Dad murmured.

"Yes."

"I have what you asked me to get too."

Dad was well aware of my resolve to do what was necessary to end this once and for all. Not that my parents ever wanted this sort of life for me, but circumstances forced my hand. Forced me to become someone who fought tooth and nail just to survive.

"Thank you."

"Did you tell her?"

I pulled away and shook my head.

"Not the full story. She doesn't know what you did to keep her alive."

Dad gave my hand a squeeze. They'd kept it from her. Meredith hadn't needed to know the lengths my family had gone to in order to nullify the hit the mafia had put out on her. They did it so she could go on with her life here and fulfil her dreams. I knew she was doing what she loved because they told me. They watched over her for me because I couldn't do it myself. In so many ways it made everything worth the pain and hardships. It'd been my fault she was in danger in the first place. We'd done what we had to.

"Come, let's move this little reunion into the dining room, we have a lot to discuss," Quinn said.

The six of us walked through the house. I noticed they'd redecorated, brightening the place up with lighter colours. Unsurprising given five years had gone by and Mum would have wanted a change.

"I like what you've done to the place," I said to Mum who'd come to a standstill next to me in the dining room.

"I haven't touched your room. I know you don't want to move home, but there's always a place for you here."

I nodded as we took a seat next to each other at the table, placing my backpack down on the floor which I'd retrieved from Aurora's before I came here. It had everything I needed to show them regarding what I had discovered over the years.

"And Grandpa apologises for not being here."

Considering my grandfather was now in his seventies, had retired and disassociated himself from the Russian mafia after everything which went down with me, I was hardly surprised. He and Lily were enjoying their retirement and didn't need to be involved in this. My parents and I were more than capable of handling AJ.

"I'll see him at the wedding so it's fine."

Aurora's big day was only a couple of weeks away now. It was all hands on deck. I felt bad about pulling my parents away to help me with my shit. Aurora had told me not to be so stupid when I'd expressed my remorse over it the day I'd arrived home. She'd grown less temperamental since she'd been with Logan. I personally liked the guy. His family had a dark past like ours, so he could relate to the four of us in a way not many others could. Besides, he was just about the only person capable of handling my sister and her moods. That counted for something in my book.

"I wasn't sure Logan would ever propose," Mum sighed. "But here we are, my little girl is getting married."

"Well, at least you actually get to be there for this wedding."

She glanced at Xav for a moment before rolling her eyes.

"Yes, well, the less said about *that* the better."

I snorted. I was so not going to dig into that right now. Definitely something we didn't talk about or bring up often.

My attention was dragged away to my dad sliding a small box across the table towards me. His eyes twinkled as I picked it up, my hands shaking a little.

"You sure you got the right one?"

He gave me a look as if to say, 'what do you think?'

"Okay, okay. I trust you."

It didn't make me any less nervous about opening it up. I set it down on the table and flipped open the lid. Nestled inside the velvet interior was a white gold ring with a round cut emerald in the centre. The setting was carved and encrusted with diamonds. It was exactly what I'd asked for. I stared at it for a long time without speaking. The thought of presenting this to Meredith and asking her to be my wife made all my words stick in my throat.

Mum leant her head on my shoulder, giving my arm a squeeze.

"It's beautiful," she whispered.

"Do you think she'll like it?"

"I think she'll cry."

"I don't want her crying."

"Happy tears, baby boy, happy tears."

"We have to make sure I can stick around to give this to her first."

"Oh, we will. Your fathers and I want you home and safe."

It's not so much I didn't believe them, but five years on the run had eaten away at my hope this situation would ever end. AJ had a lot to answer for. A hell of a fucking lot.

I snapped the box shut and set it to the side. That ring symbolised everything I was fighting for. A life and a family of my own without this bullshit hanging over my head.

I picked up my backpack and pulled out my laptop, setting it on the desk along with the documents I'd kept all these years. The folder Demetri had given me was worn at the edges, but I couldn't let it go. I opened it up and set out the pages one by one. Most of them were photos of AJ and his dealings. There was AJ's criminal record. All of his associates. Everything Demetri had kept on him. Whilst this was useful, it didn't tell either of us how AJ had framed me. How he'd even managed to steal from the mafia in the first place.

Finally, I took out what I'd obtained last night. The USB stick which contained everything I needed to destroy AJ.

"This is everything I have."

My dads looked over what I'd given them. Going through all the files on the USB and familiarising themselves with all I had.

"What do you want to do, Cole?" Quinn asked, looking up at me.

"Are you asking me if I want to deal with it personally rather than handing this over to the mafia?"

He nodded. It wouldn't be enough for me to leave it to the mafia to deal with AJ. He'd stolen five years of my life. Perhaps what I'd gone through had twisted me, but I wanted to destroy him. Personally. Nothing else would do. It had to be me.

"No, I can't. He's taken too much from me."

"Never any doubt who spawned you," Xav said, giving me a wink.

"Do not start on Ror," Mum said, pointing at Xav.

"Oh, don't you worry, I wasn't talking about him, angel. I was referring to you."

Mum's eyebrows shot up.

"Me?"

"Yes, you. Miss I want to murder the man who raised me in cold blood."

"Xavier! Our children do not need to know about that."

Her face went pink. I eyed them all, wondering what he was talking about until it dawned on me.

"Wait, it was you?" I asked.

Mum gave Xav a dark look before turning to me.

"We never wanted you to know about this."

"Mum, did you kill him yourself?"

The whole table went silent. It's not that I didn't know my parents had taken lives before, but this little detail was news to me.

"Yes."

"Oh."

"Cole, it was—"

I put a hand up.

"You don't have to explain. You needed it for closure, right?"

She nodded.

"Then I get it. And you can understand why it has to be me."

Mum put a hand on my arm.

"I do, Cole. We all do."

"Then you're not going to stop me. I want to ruin his life like he ruined mine. I want him dead."

I glanced around the table and none of them said a word. It was their silent acceptance of what I wanted.

"So, shall we make a plan?"

My parents were always going to be on my side regarding matters of our safety. Whilst I'm sure none of them wanted me to have blood on my hands, I'd suffered enough. No one fucked with me and got away with it. No one fucked with the people I cared about. And no one would ever threaten the girl I loved again. Not while I still drew breath.

CHAPTER FIFTY

Cole

I t was just after nine when I arrived at Meredith's. I'd spent yesterday with my parents and today setting things in motion. It was only a matter of time now until I finished this shit for good. My plan was dangerous, but the risk was worth the reward if it worked. More than fucking well worth it. I'd be safe and so would Meredith. We could have our life together.

When she pulled the front door open, I could see the relief in her eyes. I didn't give her a chance to speak, pulling her into my arms and kissing her. She didn't object, clinging to me as if I was the very air she breathed and needed to survive. When I released her, she looked up at me with a sheepish expression on her face.

"Hey."

"I told you I'd be back."

Meredith bit her lip.

"Can you blame me for being afraid?"

I shook my head. She stepped back, letting me in her flat. She had the TV on but otherwise, the room was unoccupied.

"Where's Jonah?" I asked as we walked over to the sofa.

"In his room."

I raised an eyebrow.

"Alone?"

"Nope, not alone."

"Is it…?"

Meredith nodded, her eyes twinkling.

"And he didn't want to come say hello?"

She shrugged, sitting down. I took a seat next to her and Meredith immediately tucked herself under my arm, curling her legs up on the sofa.

"Have you not seen him since you got back?"

"No. He's been busy with your brother, but to be fair, I only flew in a few days ago."

Meredith shook her head, wrapping her arm around my waist. It felt like no time at all had passed between us even though it'd been years. I didn't know how to feel about her not getting annoyed with me over leaving her. It seemed all too easy. How could we just fall back into a relationship without addressing everything? Surely there would be more consequences for me with her than this? I didn't want to ask in case I rocked the boat or upset her. It wasn't like me to take things at face value. She might be okay now, but how would she feel when she knew the truth about everything?

"I saw my parents yesterday."

Meredith looked up at me with a smile.

"Yeah? How did that go?"

"It was nice. I missed them a lot whilst I was away and I can't really thank them enough since they saved us."

Her brow furrowed.

"Us?"

"I told you, I left to keep you safe."

She sat up, extracting herself from my grasp.

"I was in danger?"

I nodded, not liking how her voice had become strained.

"In danger how, Cole?"

I sat up straighter. She deserved to know even if I hadn't wanted to start this line of conversation right then. I had no option but to lay it all out on the table.

"The mafia knew about you... who you were to me."

She stared at me for a long moment without speaking.

"What does that mean?"

I looked away. This was the part she would hate, but I couldn't blame her for it. There was never going to be an easy way to reveal it.

"It means your life was under threat. They couldn't take me out because of their respect for my granddad."

Meredith got up off the sofa and paced away. I watched her drag her hands through her hair.

"Let me get this straight, Cole. They were going to kill me for being your girlfriend, is that what you're saying?"

I rubbed my thigh with my hand.

"Yes."

"Why the hell am I still here then?"

I let out a sigh. Her tone made it clear she wasn't happy with this revelation.

"My parents."

Meredith stopped and stared at me.

"Your parents? What did they do?"

"Meredith…"

"What. Did. They. Do?"

Her green eyes had darkened and narrowed to slits. If I didn't tell her, it would be worse for me.

"They paid them off so you could go on with your life, finish uni and fulfil your dreams."

Meredith sucked in a breath. Then she threw up her hands and paced away again.

"I cannot believe this," she muttered.

I watched her, unsure of whether or not to say more. It's not like I advocated throwing money at a situation to make it go away, but we'd had little time to make a deal in exchange for her life.

It took Meredith a minute to stop walking around the room but she didn't look any less agitated.

"Why would they do that?"

"For me… and because they love you and think of you as family."

She ran a hand over her chest as if hearing that physically pained her.

"How much?"

"You don't need to know that."

She took a step toward me.

"How much? How much was my life worth, Cole?"

I flinched. Meredith was priceless to me. She didn't understand how that world worked. I'd protected her from the harsh reality of a life of crime. It wasn't a world she belonged in. In all honesty, neither had I. Now? That was a different story, but I wasn't going to get dragged down by it. When this was over, I'd be done. No more bullshit.

Rubbing my face, I tried to think of a way I could explain this to her so she could understand.

"Meredith, trust me when I tell you this isn't about your worth. Their world doesn't work in the same way as ours does. It's about money, honour, debts and pride. It's not like anyone could put a price on you. Not really."

"How. Much?"

I looked down at my hands, resigned to the fact she was not going to back down.

"Two million. Half of it was what was stolen from them and the other half was to pay them off so they'd leave you alone."

The room was silent for a long time except for the noise coming from the TV. I finally looked up at Meredith when I couldn't stand it any longer. She was visibly shaking.

"Your… your parents paid the Russian mafia two million pounds to keep me safe?"

I nodded once.

"What the fuck, Cole? Where the hell did they get all of that money from? And why on earth would they spend that much on me? Are they insane?"

I stood up and stepped towards her. Her voice had got all loud and high pitched. I was worried her brother would hear.

It's not as if I thought Meredith wouldn't tell him, but this was something between the two of us. I didn't want an audience.

"They're incredibly wealthy. Like insanely so, okay? I mean, I don't know how much they're worth exactly, but it didn't make a dent in their finances. And I told you why already. There's nothing they wouldn't do for you because I love you."

She shook her head as if she couldn't believe a word coming out of my mouth.

"This is not normal. Parents don't pay off the mafia to protect their children's girlfriends." She threw up her hands again. "I can't believe they did this. Do you realise how this makes me feel? My life was fucking well bought. Bought! Like I'm some kind of fucking commodity. Jesus Christ, how am I ever going to face them again?"

My heart fractured at her words. I didn't see her that way. None of us did. We merely did what we had to so we could protect her. That was it. It wasn't about the money to my parents, it was about keeping her out of harm's way.

"Meredith—"

"No, I'm not fucking done. This is bullshit, Cole. Do you know that? You told me I was safe with you but clearly, I wasn't. Am I even safe now? Are they going to come after me again now you're back, huh?"

"No, of course, they aren't. They don't even know I'm here."

I took another step, wanting to reach out to her. The fury in her expression held me back.

"Oh, because that makes it so much better. Fuck! You just come here and drop this fucking huge bombshell on me like it's no big deal. Did you really not stop to think about how this would make me feel?"

I clenched my fist by my side.

"No, I didn't, Meredith. And you want to know why? I love you and my only fucking thought at the time was keeping you safe and allowing you to go on with your life. That's it. That's *all* that mattered to me. I would have done anything to make it so. *Anything.* I didn't want to tear you away from your life and force you into going on the run with me. Trust me, it was no fucking walk in the park."

She closed the distance between us, her green eyes full of fire and pointed a finger at my chest.

"You didn't give me a fucking choice. You didn't ask me. You just left. If you had told me, we wouldn't be in this situation." She let out a little noise of frustration. "Did your parents tell you I went and begged them to tell me where you were? I fucking begged, Cole. I told them I didn't care about my life or my dreams because you were it for me. You. My dreams and hopes were with you. Everything I've done has felt fucking meaningless because I didn't do it with you. I would have followed you to the ends of the earth. That's how much I fucking well love you."

The blows kept coming. Every word tormented me. I had no idea she'd gone to them. No fucking clue. But I wasn't upset with them for not saying anything. I don't think it would have done me any good if they had. It would have just hurt more. They knew how much this situation tortured me.

Meredith's hand curled into a fist, then she hit my chest with it. It didn't hurt, but I could feel her frustration in it. Feel how much I'd hurt her by leaving.

"God damn it, Cole. I love you. Don't you understand what that means? You don't just abandon the person you love because it gets fucking hard. You don't leave them. I would have been there for you. I would have done anything to be by your side. You say you did all this because you love me, but you didn't give me a chance to love you back. To show you what I'd have done for love. You took that away from me."

She hit me again. I didn't care. She could take her pain out on me if it made her feel better. Hell, all of this shit was on me.

"I. Love. You."

Each word was punctuated with her hand slamming against my chest. There were no tears in her eyes, only utter agony and it decimated me. She didn't stop me when I reached up and cupped her face.

"I'm sorry."

"You left me alone," she whispered, each word dripping with pain. "All alone in the dark without any hope. I couldn't breathe without you. I drowned. You should have told me. You should have given me a choice like you did about everything else."

I leant down, pressing my forehead to hers.

"I don't deserve you, Meredith. All I've done is hurt you and I can't do anything to make up for it. I can't offer you anything other than my love and that's not enough."

She shook her head, staring into my eyes with a wild intensity in hers.

"You don't get it. I don't care about you deserving me or any of those other things." Her hand flattened against my heart. "You are my soulmate and I love you. That's all that matters. It is all that has ever mattered between us. I can't escape from you. And the truth is, I don't want to. The only thing in this world I want… the only thing I have ever really wanted is you. Just you."

My heart was thumping so hard against my chest, I was sure she could feel it.

"You have me. You've always had me. I've belonged to you since the moment I laid eyes on you."

"I don't have you, Cole, that's the problem. You keep disappearing on me. I can't trust you to stay by my side. Especially not now when I know people are actively trying to kill you for something you say you didn't do."

I pressed myself closer to her, my hand around her face tightening.

"This isn't how I wanted to do this with you."

"Nothing in our lives is ever how we want things. They just are what they are."

It was the wrong time and the wrong place. Everything about this was fucked up, but I needed to prove to her I wasn't going anywhere this time. I would stay forever if she let me.

If she said… yes.

My other hand dug into my pocket. It was crazy of me to keep it in there, but I didn't care about crazy any longer.

Nothing about Meredith and I had ever been anything but messed up and insane.

"Are you sure you want to do this right now?"

"Do what, Cole? I wasn't aware we were doing anything but arguing."

I smiled despite the situation.

"No, Meredith, we're not arguing any longer. I hear what you're saying. You can't trust me to stay. I'm just hoping this will go some way to proving I'm not going anywhere."

She frowned.

"What will?"

I brushed my lips over hers, needing to feel her for a moment before I did this. Before I said those words. Because these words would change everything between us forever. Or at least... I hoped they would.

"You said I'm your soulmate... well, you're mine too. The thing is I've loved you for twelve years. You stole my heart when I was only eleven years old even though I knew nothing about you. Time and distance hasn't changed a single fucking thing. It will never change how I feel about you."

I stroked her cheek with my thumb.

"Meredith Veronica Pope... will you marry me?"

I tugged out the ring box from my pocket and held it up between us. Meredith's eyes fell on it, widening as her mouth dropped open. It wasn't how I planned it. I was going to go all out in a big romantic gesture. Nothing in our lives had ever gone to plan. Our path to each other had been treacherous and deadly. Who the fuck cared what the circumstances of my proposal were any longer. What mattered was I'd said it. I'd asked her to be my wife.

Meredith took the box from me as she pulled back slightly. Her shaking fingers flipped open the lid. For a long moment, she said nothing.

"Cole… I swear to god this is the most insane thing you've done yet. What the hell kind of timing is this?"

Her eyes flicked up to mine.

"It's us timing, little queen. We don't work to anyone else's schedule."

"What am I going to do with you?"

"You can start by giving me an answer."

Her eyes darted between the ring in the box and me several times.

"We barely know anything about each other now… it's been five years. I've changed. You've changed."

"I don't give a shit about five years, Meredith. You're still you and I'm still me. That will never change. I love you and I want you to be my wife. Now, would you please put me out of my fucking misery?"

Sweat had broken out on the back of my neck. I could feel the clamminess on my skin. Asking Meredith to be my wife was more terrifying than anything else I'd done. And I'd done a hell of a lot of shit just to stay alive for the past five years.

"Is this really how—"

"Meredith, answer the fucking question. Will you marry me?"

She blinked, her mouth still parted as if she was going to continue what she had to say. She sucked in a breath the next moment and closed it. Her eyes fell on the ring again.

"It's beautiful," she whispered.

"It reminded me of your eyes. That's why I chose it."

She picked it up out of the box and, to my utmost surprise, slid it onto her ring finger on her left hand. Her eyes met mine again and I could see the determination in them.

"Yes, Cole Carter… I'll marry you."

CHAPTER FIFTY ONE

Meredith

I think you could call me certifiable right now considering I'd just agreed to be Cole's wife only a couple of days after he'd landed back in my life. It was like Jonah had said. I'd already made up my mind about him. I'd always known how I felt about Cole Carter.

When you love someone, you'd do anything for them. And nothing would make me happier than to make that commitment to him. Not least because he would be making a commitment to me as well.

"You will?" he whispered as if he couldn't believe I'd said yes.

"Would I tell you yes if I didn't mean it? Has anything I've said to you in the past ten minutes actually got in your head, Cole?"

"It has… I heard you… you love me and you don't want me to leave again along with some other stuff about soulmates and how I didn't let you choose whether or not to come with me, which I'm still sorry about by the way."

"Well then, I think you have your answer."

He took the ring box from me and chucked it on the coffee table. Then his mouth was on mine, kissing me without any restraint. Cole's arms wrapped around me, holding me against him whilst he devoured my mouth. I surrendered to it. To him. All of him.

"You going to take me to bed and make love to me?" I murmured against his mouth when he pulled back slightly.

His hands banded around my thighs and he hoisted me up on his hips. I could do nothing but hold on to Cole as he carried me out of the living room, down the hallway into my bedroom. He kicked the door shut and pressed me against it.

"Make love? Fuck that, little queen. We don't do love, we do raw fucking emotion."

And with that, he was pulling my t-shirt off me, chucking it away whilst he almost ripped my bra cup down. His mouth was on my nipple, licking and sucking, making me gasp as my hands tightened on his shoulders.

"Cole, oh, oh god."

He bit down, making me arch into him. I needed him inside me, his hands and mouth all over me. He ground me into the door, rubbing his cock against me which only made me want more. My eyes went to the ring I'd placed on my finger minutes ago. The ring signifying Cole's intention to make me his wife. It was really the most beautiful and perfect ring imaginable. How the hell Cole even knew what my ring size was beyond me. I didn't even know when he had time to get this.

"You're wearing too many clothes," he grunted as he set me on my feet.

Cole tugged my shorts down, along with my knickers and unhooked my bra, tossing that away too. He worked his jeans open and freed his cock before lifting me up again and shoving me back against the door.

"Cole, what—"

Him sliding inside me cut off my words. He took my hand and pinned it against the door whilst he held my thigh with the other, keeping me against the wood. It took a few sharp thrusts until he was all the way inside me. The stretch made me choke out a moan as he pulled out and pushed back in.

"Fuck," he growled. "You always feel so fucking good. So tight."

He set a punishing rhythm, the door rattling under the onslaught. If Jonah hadn't heard us arguing in the living room, he would definitely hear this. I didn't know whether or not I should be embarrassed. He'd already caught Cole and me post-coital. Not sure I could take his teasing regarding making my bedroom door shake.

"They're going to hear us," I hissed even whilst I let Cole fuck me exactly the way he wanted.

"Mmm, should I make you scream then so they're in no doubt?"

"No!"

"Your protests are so cute, little queen."

He kissed me so I couldn't answer him and only proceeded to fuck me harder. I wrapped my legs tighter around his waist, unable to do anything but hold on for dear fucking life. What did I even say anyway? Cole wanted to have his wicked way with me no matter what I said. He wasn't going to stop so I might as well get on board with the program.

"Cole," I moaned against his mouth as his grip on me tightened. "Harder."

He responded to my request with vigour, driving me absolutely crazy.

"I'm totally going to have you screaming," he murmured against my skin as he buried his face in my neck.

"Please."

"Oh, you want that now, do you?"

He laced our fingers against the door together. I didn't want my brother hearing us fucking but honestly, at this point, I was too far gone to care about what Jonah would say in the morning. Cole and I were engaged. That craziness in itself would negate the awkwardness of our very loud sex.

"Fuck me, Cole. Fuck."

"Now you're just acting up for them on purpose."

I snorted, unable to help myself.

"So what if I am?"

"We can do better than that." He raised his head from my neck and smirked. "That's it, little queen, take it, fucking take it."

His voice was louder and I couldn't help smiling back at him.

"Oh god, fuck me harder. Give it to me," I called out, trying not to laugh.

Cole's eyes twinkled which only made it harder for me to keep my amusement in check. And right on cue, I heard my brother's bedroom door open followed by footsteps.

"I never thought I would have to say this to you, Mer, but can you maybe keep your... activities to a more reasonable noise level?" came Jonah's voice through the door. "Some of us have work early tomorrow."

"Sorry, J... feel free to make as much noise as you want with—"

"Don't even go there. Just shut up."

"Embarrassed?"

"You literally have no shame, Meredith. None."

"As if you'd have me any other way."

I could hear him huffing followed by his retreating footsteps and the door slamming shut behind him. Cole sniggered and I couldn't hold back any longer. He pulled me away from the door as I burst out laughing.

"That was so worth it," he said as he dropped me on the bed and tugged off his clothes.

"I'm the one who will have to deal with him complaining about it tomorrow."

"You say that like I'm not staying right here with you tonight."

I raised an eyebrow, watching him crawl over me and spread my legs wide.

"Are you?"

"If you don't want me to..."

I reached up and tugged him closer, forcing him in between my legs.

"I want you every day for the rest of our lives."

His smile was wicked as he slid back inside me, making me grip the covers below us. As he tugged my hands away and linked our fingers together, I couldn't believe we'd ended up like this. A few days ago, I was at Rhys' wedding crying over the loss of the love of my life, and now I was engaged to him.

Oh shit, what the hell is Rhys going to say to this?

I shoved my best friend out of my head. I'd have to deal with that when he and Aaron got back from Thailand. Maybe by then, Cole would have dealt with all the shit he was in. We still had a lot to talk about when it came to that. It's not as if I was happy about what his parents had done, but it wasn't like I could change it. Five years had gone by and it was like Cole said, they saved my life.

Cole stared down at me as he thrust inside me, his eyes soft and his expression so open.

"I love you."

"Show me how much."

He smiled, leaning down to kiss me. I let Cole take me under and drown me with each thrust. Each kiss. Each touch. Where I ended, he began. We were meant to be together like this. The world had tried its best to tear us apart, but we wouldn't let it do that again. We would fight. Together. I would fight for him.

"I love you," I whispered in his ear as he buried his face in my shoulder. "I love you forever."

We came together, each moaning the other's name. This man was going to be my husband. Just as he'd promised me five years ago when he'd declared his love for me. Before everything had been ripped away from us. I guess that's why I let bygones be bygones. Cole hadn't done any of this to deliberately hurt me. He'd not left me willingly. He'd been protecting me. Saving my life when I didn't even know I was in danger.

Cole flopped on his back next to me, breathing heavily with his arm planted over his eyes. I put my hand up in the air, staring at the ring on it. I ran my fingers along the stone, amazed at the clarity of it.

"When did you get this?"

Cole dropped his arm from his eyes and looked up at my hands.

"Technically I didn't."

I eyed him.

"What's that supposed to mean?"

"I told Dad what I wanted and he got it with Mum's help."

"Are your parents going to do everything for us?"

Cole shook his head, reaching up and dragging my hand closer to him. He stroked the ring, his lips curling upwards.

"No, but I didn't have time to do it myself. Not when I've got to handle the shit with the mafia." His eyes flicked to mine. "I'm doing that all by myself, little queen. They've just given me the tools."

"And what exactly are you going to do?"

He didn't speak for a long moment as if he was contemplating whether or not to tell me.

"Are you sure you want to know? It's not exactly safe."

I rolled onto my side and stared down at him.

"Not only am I sure I want to know, but I want to help you... you don't have to do any of this alone any longer."

He frowned.

"I'm not going to put you in danger."

I pulled my hand out of his and gripped his chin.

"You listen to me, and you listen good. I'm not letting you go running off on your own again. You're not going to shut me out, Cole. Let me help you. You saved me so it's high fucking time I return the favour. I'm not fragile nor am I going to let anyone get to my husband-to-be. This time, I'm fucking well making sure you stick around because I plan to walk down the aisle and vow to love you forever as your wife. Am I making myself clear?"

Cole's lip was caught between his teeth during my little speech. He released it and smiled at me.

"Crystal, little queen."

"Good. Now, how are we going to get the mafia off your back?"

He turned on his side and reached out, curling his fingers into my hair.

"Well..."

And for the rest of the night, Cole explained exactly what went down five years ago, not leaving anything out. Together, we decided on a course of action. We weren't going to rely on outside help or anyone else. It was the two of us against the fucking world. Just as it should have been before everything went to hell and Cole went on the run.

CHAPTER FIFTY TWO

Cole

The silence was oppressive and foreboding as I walked along the hallway of the building I'd just broken into. Sometimes you had to resort to doing shit you'd never consider otherwise. I reminded myself who I was doing this for. Why I was putting everything on the line.

My future. My happiness. My love.

It was time I ended this.

There was a light underneath a doorway up ahead. I let out a breath, clutching the knife hidden behind my palm tighter.

I'd thought long and hard about what path to take. Which way to go about this. And even though my parents had given me a solid plan, I had my own ideas. So what if it was dangerous and risky as fuck? I'd done nothing but get myself into dangerous situations for the past five years. Not that it was strictly on purpose. Sometimes you had to improvise when you had the mafia after you. Like the time I'd almost got caught out whilst crossing a border. It'd been a close fucking call involving me having to smuggle myself across rather than do it by legal means. That wasn't the sort of shit I enjoyed doing, entering another country illegally. It fucked up my plans royally. That's the kind of thing you dealt with on the run. It wasn't an easy life, but I'd survived. It made me tougher. Stronger. More resilient. It taught me how to rely solely on myself.

It was different now I'd come home. I had my support network who could drag me out of a sticky situation if necessary. Except I'd lived alone for too long. Always running. Always hiding. Now it was time to take a stand.

One way or another, I was going to destroy the man who forced me into leaving and everything he'd built. The fucker had only got stronger over the past five years. Moved up in the ranks to become the king. I almost scoffed. The king in his castle. More like the viper hidden in a nest of wolves, spewing his venom everywhere. Pity for him really. I might have been eighteen the last time we saw each other, but I'd grown up since then. I'd learnt how to be ruthless and smarter than my enemies.

I opened the door with the light underneath it. The room was empty as I stepped in. I smiled to myself, shaking my head. This guy clearly thought he was going to catch me out.

Stupid fucker.

I strolled towards the desk and sat down behind it, opening up the laptop sitting there. It took two minutes for me to hack in and less than thirty seconds to run the program I needed to execute my plan. Having one father who knew this shit inside out made this part easier. I leant down, picking the lock on the bottom drawer of the desk. Then I pulled it out, checking the contents.

Definitely a stupid fucker.

I barely looked up when I heard footsteps, palming what I needed and sliding it into my pocket. Closing the drawer, I sat up straight in the desk chair.

"Well, it's been a long time, hasn't it?"

"I'd say so," I replied, my eyes flicking up to the man who'd come to a standstill in front of the desk.

"I have wondered whether you would realise the truth or not."

I smiled. I don't think he realised how much he'd underestimated me.

"I knew the moment I opened the file on the plane when I left. You didn't think I was stupid, did you?"

He laughed, shaking his head as he stuck his hands in his pockets.

"No, I did not. You let me use you."

"You didn't exactly leave me with a choice. I had people to protect."

He tapped his fingers against the desk.

"Yes, that little girlfriend of yours. I wasn't really going to kill her. After all, she's an innocent just like you were. But you're not so innocent now, are you, Cole?"

I shrugged.

"You do know who my family is. The last thing you could call any of us is innocent."

I watched the screen of the laptop, knowing I had to stall him a little longer for this to work.

"Ah, but you were only a boy then. A man now, I see. All grown up and yet, still so reckless. If you were smart, you wouldn't have come alone. It's a shame it has to end like this, but I can't have you ruining everything."

"Ruining everything, am I? Is that why you decided to lure me back here? So you could take me out, hmm? Was I getting too close to discovering the truth?"

I rose to my feet, smiling down at the screen for a moment as it flashed for a moment to let me know the funds had been transferred. Taking back what we'd given him all those years ago and a little extra for the inconvenience of it all. Then I stepped out from behind the desk and cocked my head to the side. The man's eyes narrowed.

"You see, Demetri, I knew exactly what would happen this evening. I planned it all so meticulously. You should have known that considering who my fathers are."

His hand went to his side. I tutted and shook my head.

"I wouldn't do that if I was you. You could try to run, of course, but you wouldn't get very far. You see, I asked myself for a long time why you would double-cross the mafia in this way. Why would you go to all this trouble?"

I put my finger to my lip, stroking my thumb down the knife hidden within my palm.

"It all seemed so convoluted and unnecessary, but then I remembered a conversation we had a long time ago. One where you told me my grandfather saved you once and I thought to myself, did he? Did he really? Because the Viktor I know has only ever cared about his daughter and her children. Everyone else is… expendable. Even his own brother."

I'd never met my grandfather's brother for good reason. He'd died not long after I was born in a hail of gunfire. It was only when my parents explained their past, I learnt the true nature of his death. He'd betrayed his brother and that was unforgivable in my grandfather's eyes.

"He never saved you. He abandoned you. That's why you did this to us. You wanted revenge so you used me to force him to cut his ties with the mafia and then you climbed up the ranks without him standing in the way. He knew you were a snake."

I scoffed and eyed him with disgust.

"It must have been nice for you to live in luxury all this time thanks to my parents."

Demetri stared at me with a sort of newfound respect in his eyes. The man had tried to double-cross everyone and used those around him for his own ends. He'd made a grave error in judgement when it came to my family. A fucking huge error.

We didn't let people walk all over us. And we didn't fucking well allow anyone to take us down.

"You can try to call your men, but they won't be coming and you want to know why?"

Demetri dropped his hand.

"Why?"

"Because, Demetri… they're dead."

CHAPTER FIFTY THREE

Cole

Two hours earlier

My phone rang as I sat at my sister's dining table with my laptop and a snack beside me. Aurora and Logan were both at work and would be back later. None of my family knew I'd got engaged yet. I planned on telling them at our family Sunday dinner next week. Then all this bullshit with the mafia might have died down and we could celebrate properly.

I looked down at the caller display, smiling a little.

"Hello, little queen."

"Cole," came her frantic voice.

I dropped my hand on the table, my nerves going into high alert immediately.

"What's wrong?"

"You need to help me."

"What happened?"

I heard a muffled noise followed by Meredith making a noise of protest.

"Hello, Cole," came a voice which chilled me to my very core. "It seems you and I need a little talk, don't you say?"

I clenched my fist and stood up.

Don't rise to it. Remain calm. You've got this.

"What do you want?"

"Well, you're back when you shouldn't be for starters and clearly, you haven't forgotten what I did. If you want to see your little stunner alive, you'll meet me. I'll text you the address."

The phone went dead the next moment. I took a deep breath, summoning all my self-control. It would not do me any favours if I lost it right now. I had to remain calm and focused. My phone buzzed a moment later, telling me where they were. I stuffed it back in my pocket after firing off a message to someone else and made my way upstairs to the bedroom I was staying in. Methodically, I collected everything I needed before taking the stairs two by two and leaving the house.

The whole way over to the location, I reminded myself this was all going to be okay. He wasn't going to hurt Meredith. No one was going to hurt her. I had her back and she had mine. We were a team. Nothing would break us apart again. After all, she kept reminding me that we were engaged now. We had to stay alive so we could get married.

Yeah, it was probably crazy of us to get back together and engaged within a week of me returning to the UK. But when you know, you know. And we knew. Meredith and I had always been it for each other. It's not as if I'd wanted to leave her behind or fuck things up between us. None of what happened was really my fault. I'd been as much of a victim to other people's bullshit as she had. But I wasn't going to be a victim any longer. I was going to make sure we never had to be in fear again.

All Meredith and I wanted now was a normal life where both of us worked hard and had our own home together. That's it. A simple fucking life without shit like this hanging over us.

Today, I was ending this once and for all. I had no other option. It was time.

I parked up my Ducati, slid my helmet off and rested it on the seat. Two men were standing outside the warehouse. I cracked my neck before I walked towards them.

"Before you get all suspicious, I'm here to see your boss. He's expecting me."

Both men eyed me for a long moment as I came to a standstill in front of them.

"This way," one grunted.

The other opened a door to their left and I walked in. The first man followed me. We walked down a corridor but he stopped me at the end.

"Got to make sure you don't have anything on you."

I gave him a smile and put my arms out. The moment he reached for me, I grabbed his head and slammed it against the wall. The crack of his skull connecting with it rang through the corridor. He looked dazed as his head snapped back, so I did it again. Then he fell to the floor, completely out cold. I stepped over his body and opened the door in front of me, walking out into the warehouse. Only a few metres ahead was the man who'd decided to kidnap my fiancée. Meredith was sitting next to him in a chair, her hands tied behind her back.

I approached them with casual steps, not showing any fear. Because really... I wasn't scared of him or what he'd do.

"So, you have me here," I said, flicking a hand out.

I watched AJ's hands curl into fists at his sides. Three other men were standing nearby at various vantage points, watching me as I made my way over to them. My eyes fell on Meredith who just smiled at me. I didn't react when her face dropped and instead, fear showed through.

"Cole Carter. Aren't you a sight for sore eyes?" AJ said, venom dripping from his words.

"To you, perhaps."

AJ looked behind me as if expecting to see his man. His eyes narrowed when he realised I was alone.

"You should be dead."

I grinned at him. There'd been several attempts on my life over the years, but none of them were successful.

"Should I? Too bad for you, isn't it? That I'm not."

"What the fuck is that supposed to mean?"

I spread my hands as I stopped a few feet away.

Calm. Stay calm. You cannot lose your shit with him.

"It means you should have taken me out five years ago, AJ, when you had the chance."

He looked around at his men before scoffing.

"Didn't need you dead then, just gone."

I rolled my shoulders, sliding the knife under my sleeve into my palm.

"No, but you were just following orders, weren't you?"

AJ's eyes widened a fraction as if my response surprised him.

"I don't take orders from anyone."

I looked at Meredith again. She was eying AJ with disgust. He probably thought I'd run in here all frantic with worry over her. AJ was a fool. He had no fucking clue.

"Hmm, okay, you tell yourself that, but you can drop the act, you know, I'm aware of the truth."

AJ took a step towards Meredith as if he was going to do something to her.

"I ain't lying. And this isn't how this shit is going to go, Cole. I'm not letting this bitch go."

His hand enclosed over her shoulder, making Meredith flinch. I could see her shoulders working slightly as if she wanted him away from her.

"How what is going to go?"

AJ gave me a look, his eyes darkening.

"Why, don't you know? Both of you will die. Right here. Right now."

His hand slid from her shoulder to her neck. I clenched a fist. AJ had no fucking right to touch her like that.

Stop it. Breathe. Just breathe.

"Is that what you think? Oh, AJ, you were always the simple man. No wonder he used you for his own ends."

AJ's fingers tightened around Meredith's neck, causing her eyes to widen. I gave her an almost imperceptible nod.

"No one gave me fucking orders!"

He waved at his men, indicating me with his hands. Two of them started towards me, but before they could even get close, the ropes holding Meredith dropped to the floor. Less than thirty seconds later, AJ let out a howl of pain as my fierce little queen stabbed him in the thigh with a knife she'd kept hidden.

"Fuck, what the—?"

She was out of her chair and kicked him in the balls, making him fall to his knees and groan in pain.

The two guys reached me. I stepped back as one swung at me. It set him off balance. I took advantage of it, grabbing him and throwing him into the other man. They both grunted as they went down in a tangle of limbs. I darted away from them as the other guy in the room tried to come for me as well.

Meredith had run from the scene, I saw her red hair disappear behind some shelves. I'd told her to hide when she'd played her part. The girl was fucking determined to help me. Even though I hadn't wanted to put her in danger, her idea of playing bait had worked perfectly. AJ had fallen hook, line and fucking sinker. He couldn't resist the allure of taking me out by stealing her.

Idiot.

AJ was still groaning in pain, holding his leg as blood started to seep through his trousers from where Meredith had stabbed him. I reached him, hauling him up against my chest and facing the other men. I put the knife to AJ's throat.

"I suggest you back the fuck off unless you want me to kill him," I ground out.

The three men put their hands up, backing away from me slightly. The two who had fallen over were now on their feet.

"What are you doing?" AJ choked out. "Get him off me."

I dug the knife into AJ's neck until blood trickled down.

"I'm not fucking around," I said. "This is between me and him. I suggest you turn around and walk away."

"Get the girl!"

The knife dug in more, making AJ choke out a gasp.

"Do not fucking touch her, you hear me? I will end all of you if you go near her."

The men looked at AJ and then at me. I could see the conflict in their expressions.

"Walk away or you die alongside him."

"This shit ain't worth it," one of them said, glancing at the others.

"What the fuck? Where's your loyalty?" AJ practically screeched as the other two started to agree with the first guy.

One looked AJ up and down before pulling a face.

"You ain't worth shit, fam. Let's go."

"Hey, hey, Kel, get back here. All of you, get the fuck back here!"

I almost laughed as his men walked towards the doors, shaking their heads. They were as stupid as AJ. I dragged him towards the chair, keeping the knife at his throat.

"You and I need a little chat." I pressed him down into it and leant over him. "Just you, me and her now, AJ. And, you see, she knows what you did."

Meredith came out from her hiding place, walking towards us with a deadly expression on her face.

"You stole five years of our lives from us. I don't think you understand what you cost me."

Meredith reached us and dug her hand into AJ's pocket, pulling out his phone as she pressed her other hand against the knife handle sticking out of his leg. AJ let out a yelp and his hand went to the knife. She gripped one of his hands and forced him to unlock the phone with his fingerprint.

"Look in his photos… the ones in the cloud," I said.

She stepped back and fiddled with it.

"You like to keep evidence, don't you? To remind you of the shit you've done. At first, I thought I'd need it so the mafia could deal with you, but the thing is, you already work for them, don't you? You ran their drugs out of the garage."

AJ stiffened.

"No, I don't, I didn't," he said, his voice going up an octave.

"Yes, yes you fucking did. The whole business was a fucking front. Tell me the truth, AJ, who put you up to it? Who made you ruin my life?"

He shook his head. I needed him to say it. Needed to hear the fucking truth from his mouth even though I already knew everything. I'd figured it all out. It finally fell into place two months ago. That's why I was back. To end this once and for all.

"No one."

Meredith held out the phone, almost shoving it in AJ's face.

"No? Maybe this will remind you," she hissed.

It was a photo of him with another man's arm wrapped around him. They looked close.

"Or maybe this?"

She flicked to the next one, showing the same man only much younger holding a baby in his arms.

"Who is that, AJ?" I asked. "I mean, I don't strictly need you to tell me, but admitting the truth will make this go a whole lot easier on you."

AJ stared at the phone for a long moment.

"My father," he said, sounding almost resigned.

"His name, AJ, tell me his name."

"Demetri Turgenev."

And there we had it. The reason why AJ had tried to destroy me. It wasn't because he had a vendetta, but his father. The man who'd lied to me when he told me I had to go on the run. The man who'd ruined my fucking life. His son carried out his plan. And his son was going to die for it. I didn't care if that made me crazy. Life had got so fucked up. I was more like my parents than I wanted to admit. Ruthless and protective. I would fucking kill and die for those I loved.

"It took me a while to work it out, you know, since you took after your mother and not him. Magda has no idea who you are, does she?"

AJ shook his head. Demetri's wife had no idea what kind of man her husband really was.

"You did this out of loyalty to him. That's why you ruined my life. So, I'm going to ruin both of yours."

My eyes flicked up to Meredith. She had a grim expression on her face.

"Little queen, close your eyes and turn around. I don't want you to see this."

I'd made up my mind what I would do to AJ when I saw him again regardless of the fact it was his father who instigated this. AJ had terrorised me. He didn't fucking deserve mercy.

Meredith stared at me for a long moment as if she realised what I was about to do. Then she did as I asked, closing her eyes and turning around. She kept AJ's phone gripped in her hand. We'd need that to finish this shit for good.

"Have you got any last words?" I whispered in AJ's ear.

"Fuck. You."

"The only one who's fucked right now… is you."

I dragged the knife across his throat, not caring about the mess it would make. Not giving a single fuck about anything other than ending it. I could feel the sticky, hot blood flowing down from the wound and coating my hand, but I kept digging, making sure to cut deep.

I released AJ and stepped back. His body jerked a few times before it slumped in the chair and his head fell forward. Not stopping to look at the blood, I walked around him, grabbed a handful of his t-shirt, wiping the knife off. Then I cleaned my hand as best I could before ripping the other knife from his thigh, wiping that blade on his trousers. I slid both knives into my pocket and approached Meredith, putting a hand on her shoulder.

"It's over, little queen."

She didn't move so I walked around her. Meredith opened her eyes. They immediately fell on my hands.

"You…"

"I had to."

She nodded slowly.

"Can we get out of here?"

I reached out and took her hand, pulling her away towards the door. As we walked into the corridor I'd entered by, the man I'd knocked out was still on the floor, but this time I knew he was dead. There were four other bodies along the floor, all with bullet holes in the back of their heads. I put a hand over Meredith's eyes, not wanting her to see them. I took her out of the warehouse, dropping my hand when I saw two people leaning against the warehouse doors.

"You've been busy," I said with a smile.

"Those fuckers?" Xav said with a shrug. "Well, they didn't want to be quiet so we had to silence them. Besides, we couldn't let them identify you, now could we?"

I shook my head. He and Dad shoved off the wall and came over to us. Xav handed me a packet of wipes from the bag he was holding so I could clean my hands properly. No doubt they'd thought of everything. Once I'd got rid of the blood, I turned to Meredith who looked a little pale. It's not like I wanted to her to see this side of me, but she didn't want me to hide anything from her again. No more secrets. No more lies. Just the two of us forever.

"I need to get to the garage to finish this. Will you stay with them?"

She reached up, stroking my face with her fingertips.

"Don't get yourself killed, okay?" she whispered.

"Never."

She handed me AJ's phone.

"I removed the need for a fingerprint so you can unlock it easily. End this for us… please."

I leant down and kissed her.

"I promise. I'm going to give us our future."

She smiled when I pulled back.

"I love you."

"Love you too, little queen."

I spent a few minutes talking to Xav and Dad who I'd texted before I'd left Aurora's. They knew I wanted to deal with most of this alone, but we still needed to make sure I didn't get caught considering I'd just killed a man. Plus someone needed to take care of my girl. I wasn't sure how she felt about what I'd done, but we could discuss it later.

When I was done, I got on my Ducati and rode away.

It was time I dealt with Demetri and his double-crossing bullshit. Then I could finally say I had reached the end of the fucked up path I was on so Meredith and I could travel down a new one together.

CHAPTER FIFTY FOUR

Present time

emetri stared at me for a long time as if he didn't believe me. He should, considering he'd underestimated me before.

"Dead?"

"Yes. I mean, not strictly by my hand, but they're dead all the same," I shrugged. "It's how this world works, doesn't it? All those who were loyal to you are gone. Funny that. Your bosses didn't take too kindly to being double-crossed."

His eyes narrowed and his hand went to his side again.

"What did you do?"

I took a step away from him and dipped my head to my chest.

"Merely told the truth, something you've had trouble doing. Don't you know karma is a bitch? Especially when you've dug yourself too deep and you can't get out. This is justice for me."

I watched him out of the corner of his eye, his hand sliding under his coat and curling around the handle of a small pistol. I knew he wouldn't come here unarmed. I didn't do guns, but I wasn't scared he'd shoot me. Hell, he could fucking try. He'd be sorry if he did.

"Justice? Is that what you want?" he all but spat.

"Well, you and AJ did steal five years of my life, I think it's only fair."

He drew the pistol out and left it hanging by his side.

"You should be fucking grateful I didn't kill you."

I almost laughed. It wasn't funny, but honestly, if he really thought I'd be grateful, he was fucking stupid. Why would I ever feel that way about someone who'd forced me to leave the love of my life and my family behind?

You're a piece of shit, Demetri.

"Grateful? Ha, as if you didn't try to do so multiple times over the past five years. I'm not stupid. I know it was you who sent them after me. I know everything, so you can just drop the act now." I raised my head, meeting his eyes. "I know this is all about money and pride. My grandfather hurt your fucking pride, didn't he? He made you feel small and insignificant when you asked him for help after you knocked up a woman who wasn't your wife. He wouldn't give you the time of day after all the things you'd done for him and Gregor when he was alive. That's why you wanted to ruin him, but you couldn't. So you picked on me instead."

Demetri took a step back as if my words had actually wounded him.

"That's right, Demetri, the truth always has a habit of coming out. He was all too pleased to tell me what really happened when I asked him. That's how I found out who AJ is to you."

I dug AJ's phone out of his pocket and opened it up to the photos from before. Then I waved it at Demetri. His eyes widened.

"Your son blindly followed you out of loyalty. He did all of this because you asked him to. It's a crying fucking shame, you know, that none of it panned out the way you thought it would."

I threw the phone down on the desk and walked towards the door, stopping a few feet away. My head turned in time to see Demetri raise his weapon and point it at my back. I merely smiled at him.

"You knew he was running drugs out of here. You knew because you wanted more than the mafia was giving to you. So you sold under their noses. This was all a fucking front. And you thought it was fate when I landed on your doorstep, didn't you?"

I shook my head. None of this had really been about me. I was just a pawn in his games. He made a mistake when he picked on me. He had no idea what kind of boy my parents had raised me to be nor the man who'd come back after five years to destroy everything Demetri had built.

"Took your time to plan it. To work out how to use me against Viktor and it all fell into place when I turned eighteen.

I bet you were so fucking pleased with yourself for getting one up on him. For getting one up on everyone who left you in the dirt. Such a fucking pity it's all coming back to bite you, isn't it?"

"Shut up," he ground out, cocking the gun.

"The truth hurts, doesn't it? Well, it's going to hurt some more."

The door in front of me opened. I stepped out of the way as my grandfather walked in. He might be in his seventies, but he was still formidable, nevertheless. No one messed with Viktor Bykov and got away with it.

"Hello, Demetri," he said with unnerving calm.

"You," Demetri growled.

I walked towards the door, knowing this wasn't between me and Demetri any longer. I'd got my revenge already having taken out AJ. This was Viktor's fight. Putting my hand on the doorframe, I turned back slightly.

"Before I go, you might want to know something." I looked Demetri in the eyes. "I killed your son."

I walked away before he could say a word, shutting the door behind me. I could hear terse Russian which grew quieter as I made my way down the hallway towards the exit. I'd just reached the outside door when the sound of a gunshot rang out. My body tensed up at the noise. I'd never liked the way they sounded. It's why I never used them, preferring up close, hand to hand methods.

I walked out into the night air, turning my head up to the sky and breathed in. A sense of peace washed over me. It was done. Yes, we had a few loose ends to tie up with the mafia, but the threat against my life was dealt with. I no longer had to live in fear.

Five years of it had drained me. It was only when I'd seen my girl again, my world was filled with colour. I was brought back to fucking life. Meredith was the person I'd fought so hard for. She is why I stayed breathing this whole time. The possibility of coming home and claiming what I'd lost all those years ago drove me.

A minute later, the door behind me opened. I didn't turn around, just waited until the man came to stand next to me.

"It's over now."

I nodded, digging my hand into my pocket and pulling out what I'd taken from Demetri's drawer. I offered it to him. My grandfather took it, turning over the lighter in his hand and looking at the inscription.

Anthony Jason, one day this kingdom will belong to you, Demetri.

It was the last piece of evidence we needed to prove to the mafia who AJ was. I'd seen AJ with the lighter all those years ago, but I'd never read the full inscription until today. Only the last word. Demetri. I'd wondered why AJ had it. And now I knew.

"It's a pity it ended this way."

"Guess so," I replied, shrugging.

Viktor slid the lighter into his pocket.

"I must apologise. My decisions brought this on you. I suppose we never know the true repercussions until much later in our lives. You'll learn that one day."

I smiled and leant against his shoulder.

"I already did."

My grandfather wrapped an arm around me, giving me a squeeze. Then he looked up at me since I was taller than him.

"Did she say yes?"

I nodded.

"You're lucky, Cole, to find the right one so young. Life has brought me many challenges, but the biggest one of all was discovering I had a daughter. Your mother is my pride and joy, as are you children. Never forget where you came from even if it's brought you hardships."

I inclined my head again.

"I won't."

He gave me one last squeeze before he walked over to a car idling nearby with his man, André leaning up against it. I turned and walked over to my Ducati, sliding on my helmet and straddling it.

It was time I got back and talked to my wife-to-be. We were free, but it had come at a cost. I just hoped she wouldn't hate me for it in the end.

CHAPTER FIFTY FIVE

Meredith

Xav and Rory made me sit in the car whilst they cleaned up the scene at the warehouse. Not that I had objected. Having seen the blood on Cole's hands, I knew what he'd done. It's not as if he'd kept his intentions from me either when he told me the whole story.

Did it bother me the man I was going to marry had killed someone?

Honestly, I didn't know the answer to that question. It probably should, but I'd known since I was eighteen what kind of life Cole had come from. What his parents had done to survive. So really, it didn't come as a shock to the system when Cole told me what he wanted to do to AJ. How he wanted to take him out.

Cole explained to me how their world didn't work like the normal one. It wasn't cut and dry, or black and white. It would probably bother a lot of people, but not me. I loved Cole despite all his faults and flaws. Love didn't come with conditions. You loved someone for who they were or not at all. Besides, I'd made up my mind about Cole Carter a long time ago. He was the one who made my world go around. He'd loved me unconditionally since the moment he laid eyes on me. There was nothing he wouldn't do for me. I was going to do the same for him. I accepted his decision and wouldn't hold it against him. It had guaranteed our safety and future so what could I really say about it anyway.

"You okay there, Mer?" Xav asked me as he and Rory got in the car.

I shrugged, staring down at my hands. The ones I'd used to stab a man with. Strangely, it didn't affect me in the way I thought it might. AJ had destroyed Cole's life. I did it to protect Cole and make sure he could carry out his plan.

"I know what you just went through wasn't easy."

"No," I all but whispered. "It wasn't, but... I did it for him."

Xav hadn't set off yet. He turned in the driver's seat and leant back, putting a hand on my knee and giving it a squeeze.

"We all do fucked up shit for the people we love."

"Yeah, I guess we do. Just didn't think I would be stabbing guys in the leg."

Xav chuckled and shook his head.

"You did get involved with our crazy family, comes with the territory."

He let me go and turned back in his seat, starting up the engine and pulling away. Rory looked back at me with sympathy in his eyes. His eyes fell on my hands. I'd not taken off my engagement ring. It made me feel sick to part with it when it symbolised everything Cole and I had to fight for. It's then I remembered Rory was the one who'd got this for Cole.

His eyes raised back to mine and he smiled at me in a knowing way. We hadn't told Cole's parents about it yet, but considering nothing got by Cole's dad, him knowing before everyone else didn't bother me.

I covered the ring with my other hand, biting my lip as I tried not to smile too hard. It didn't seem right given what had just occurred. But how could I not be happy? Cole and I were going to get married. That was something to celebrate.

Xav and Rory spoke in low tones for the journey whilst I stared out of the window watching the streets of London go by. It almost didn't seem real. That this shit was over. That Cole and I could be free of all the fucking heartache and pain we'd gone through together. We'd never done anything to deliberately hurt each other. It'd never been about the way we loved. It was always the outside world trying to rip us apart. It hadn't succeeded. Perhaps at one point, it had when Cole had been stolen away from me, from the life we'd wanted to build five years ago. But even that hadn't stuck. Hadn't become permanent. He and I were fucking well permanently bound to each other. We couldn't be split up forever.

"So, we'll see you at lunch on Sunday then?" Xav asked as they pulled up outside my building.

"Yeah, I look forward to it," I replied with a smile. "Um, thank you for dropping me home."

"My pleasure. Just don't give our son too much of a hard time, hey? He's been through a lot."

It only made me smile wider.

"Trust me, I have no intention of giving him any shit. I love him too much."

Xav turned to Rory.

"Sometimes I wonder how we ever ended up with relatively normal kids."

Rory snorted.

"I don't think I'd call our kids normal, especially not Cole."

Xav looked thoughtful for a moment.

"No, you're right. They're all as fucked up as we are."

I shook my head and put my hand on the door handle.

"I happen to love your fucked up family," I told them as I opened the door. "So don't change a thing, hey?"

All I heard was Xav's laughter as I jumped out of the car and shut the door. I adored their family even if they were just about the most unorthodox family I'd ever met in my life. I waved at them as they pulled away. Then I turned and opened my front door before going up to the first floor and unlocking the door to my flat.

I slumped down on the sofa once I'd slid out of my coat, feeling the weight of everything sitting on my shoulders. Who knew when Cole would be done. He hadn't exactly said how long it would take for him and his grandfather to deal with Demetri and his men. It seemed so crazy that this guy would go to the lengths he did to get back at Viktor. Then again, his moral code was completely different to mine.

I glanced down at my hands again, finding a couple of spots of blood on them. It made me think about what Cole had done. I got up and went over to the kitchen sink, scrubbing away the evidence with soap after I'd placed my engagement ring on the side. It had thankfully not got anything on it. My hands trembled thinking about how easily the knife had pierced through AJ's thigh when I'd plunged it into him. It's not that I felt remorse for it, but I'd never imagined I'd have to stab a man.

You did this for Cole. You did it to protect both of you. Remember, AJ was going to kill you and Cole. You made sure that didn't happen.

The door to the flat opened. I turned at the noise finding Jonah bustling in looking around with wild eyes. When they landed on me, they softened immediately.

"You're okay."

I smiled, shutting off the tap and turning around to lean against the counter, sliding my engagement ring back on. My finger had felt bereft without it.

"Did you really think I wouldn't be?"

He closed the door and dumped his bag on the ground before walking over to me.

"Well, when you tell me you've hatched some reckless plan to get the mafia off your fiancé's back, what am I supposed to think?"

I'd told Jonah the morning after Cole proposed about everything. He'd known the proposal was coming so I'd been wrapped up in his arms and swung around the room. I'd already agreed to have him and Rhys as my men of honour instead of having bridesmaids, not that the latter knew about it yet.

"You're supposed to trust Cole, that's what."

"Hmm, yes, trust the reckless younger brother, that always goes well."

I grinned, putting a hand on Jonah's waist and pulling him in for a hug.

"You did give him your blessing to marry me."

"Maybe I should have revoked that."

"Jonah!"

He chuckled, nuzzling my hair.

"You know very well I'm happy you two are finally tying the knot. You've been in love with that boy for far too long for it not to happen."

I rolled my eyes.

"Yeah, well, what can I say? He's everything I never knew I needed. You know, he said that to me right before we kissed for the first time."

"Sounds like Cole."

I snorted. Cole was one of a kind. His cockiness had been tempered a little over the past five years, but he was still the same person I'd fallen in love with all those years ago. Still the one I wanted for life.

My phone started ringing. I pulled away from Jonah and tugged it out of my pocket, glancing down at the caller. He looked down too.

"You going to tell him?"

I shrugged and bit my lip.

"I should… it doesn't feel right to keep it from him."

Jonah reached up and squeezed my shoulder.

"He's changed, you know, since he met Aaron. He'll understand."

Then my brother ambled off towards his bedroom whilst I answered the video call to Rhys and Aaron. Their faces filled the screen making me smile wide because even though they hadn't been gone long, I missed both of them. Rhys might be my best friend, but I'd got to know Aaron over the months they'd been together. And I could say I loved him just as much.

"Well, hello boys, what the fuck is the time there?"

Rhys grinned.

"Like two in the morning."

"And why are you two still awake?"

They looked at each other for a moment, giving me a pretty good idea of why they were up.

"You don't want to know."

I made a face. These two really didn't need to keep making up for lost time, but apparently, there was no stopping them.

"How's the trip? Still all loved up?"

Aaron kissed Rhys cheek before moving away, leaving Rhys and me to talk.

"Amazing and yes, we are. This one has been spoiling me the whole time. I can't deal with him."

I laughed, shaking my head as I walked over to the sofa and sat down, still holding the phone up.

"Well, you did marry the guy."

"I did, didn't I?" He had a stupid smile on his face. "He is a little bit perfect."

"Ugh, you two make me want to hurl, but you also totally deserve it. I'm glad you're having a nice time."

"Aw, Mer, you going soft on me?"

I snorted and shook my head.

"Never."

He leant back against the headboard of the bed, cocking his head to the side.

"How are you? I miss you, by the way."

My heart got all tight.

"But you're on your honeymoon with the love of your life."

He shrugged.

"Yeah, but A isn't you… you're like your very own brand of crazy and I love you for that."

I looked away, aware I had things to say to Rhys which I wasn't sure he was going to like. It's not like I felt right about doing it over the phone either. But with him being away, I didn't have any other choice.

"I have to talk to you about something."

I didn't dare look at him.

"What is it? You sound serious, Mer."

I sighed and decided to just bite the bullet. Raising my left hand, I wiggled it in front of the phone. I peeked at him the next moment, finding Rhys had moved his phone closer and was staring at the screen intently.

"Is that… is that an engagement ring?"

"Maybe," I all but whispered.

"How… what… who the hell did you…" He blinked. "Meredith, I know I said I love your crazy, but this… please tell me you've not lost your mind."

I smiled at him. Perhaps I had. Love made you do stupid things sometimes, but there was nothing stupid about me and Cole. Nothing at all. We were meant to be.

"I haven't."

"Who is it? I mean I've not even been away for a week and suddenly you're getting married."

I shrugged and gave him a look.

"I think you know who it is, Rhys. There's only ever been one person I've loved, who I still love."

It took a moment, a long moment for him to realise what I was saying. What I meant. Then he looked away. I didn't know how to take his expression because it wasn't good but it wasn't bad either.

"What madness is Mer getting up to now?" came Aaron's voice from somewhere off-camera. "You look… pensive."

"She's getting married," Rhys said with a note of resignation in his voice.

Aaron appeared in the screen a moment later, blue-grey eyes wide as he sat down on the bed next to Rhys.

"Married? Wait, what?"

I showed him the engagement ring which he cooed over for a moment before he looked at Rhys. He rubbed Rhys' shoulder, frowning at him. I knew what Rhys was thinking. How I was an idiot for letting Cole back in my life and that I shouldn't marry him. How he couldn't believe I would allow this after everything Cole put me through. The nights I cried myself to sleep in his arms. The days I'd mope around when I didn't have uni because I didn't know who I was any longer. Because I couldn't stand the thought of living without the boy who'd made my world go around. Those dark days where nothing seemed to make me feel better.

But if Rhys thought about it, he'd know why I'd said yes to Cole despite all of that. The heartache. The pain. The agony. He'd know why.

Rhys let out a sigh and looked at the camera again.

"You know, I had a feeling one day he'd come back. I just wasn't sure how you'd feel when he did." Rhys looked at Aaron who was still frowning, but it was in confusion. "If this one hadn't come back into my life, maybe I'd feel differently. Maybe I would tell you this was wrong and that he'll only hurt you all over again." He reached out to his husband and took his hand, placing a kiss on it. "But I've learnt a few things from this guy about forgiveness and letting go of the past." He looked at the camera again. "The only thing I have to ask you is if you're happy… are you?"

I felt tears pricking at my eyes. Hearing him accept it on some level made my heart hurt in a good way.

"Yeah, Rhys, I'm happy. I love him. I always have."

"Then I'm happy… and when A and I get back, we're taking you to dinner to celebrate."

"We are?" Aaron said, looking at him. "I don't even know who this guy is she's marrying."

"Yeah, we are, and I'll tell you when we get off the phone. It's a long story, but for now, we're going to say congratulations to this one since she's all loved up and shit."

Aaron grinned and turned to the camera, winking at me.

"Congrats, Mer."

"Thank you, boys. Now, get some fucking sleep. Can't have you coming home saying you're exhausted from your honeymoon."

"Okay, bossy boots, we're going. Love you," Rhys said, grinning.

"Love you too, fuckface."

He rolled his eyes and then the screen went blank as he cut the call. My hand with the phone still clasped in it dropped on the sofa. I rested my head back, staring up at the ceiling. My best friend had sort of just given me his blessing. It meant the world to me.

Now I had to wait for the love of my life to finish securing our future. And hope everything had gone to plan.

CHAPTER FIFTY SIX

Meredith

I awoke to my arm being shaken gently. When I opened my eyes, I realised I'd fallen asleep on the sofa. The owner of the hand on my arm knelt on the floor in front of me. A beautiful man with dirty blonde hair and hazel eyes who stared at me with a softness in his expression that made my heart thump.

"Little queen," he murmured. "I'm here."

Jonah must have let him in the flat. Who knew how long I'd been asleep. I reached out and stroked Cole's face, giving him a smile. The love of my life was here and that meant everything was okay. He'd come back to me like he said he would.

"Hey."

"Tired?"

I nodded. Cole rose to his feet and reached down, picking me up off the sofa. I didn't have it in me to object as he carried me away into my bedroom. I found myself stripped out of my clothes, a t-shirt tugged over my head and I was soon tucked under the covers. Cole leant down, kissed my cheek and stroked my hair back from my face.

"I just need to take a shower, okay?"

"Mmm, okay."

I snuggled deep into the covers, listening to him walk away. Knowing he was there settled me and I drifted off again.

A damp body wrapped itself around me, dragging me back out of my dreamland. His breath hit the back of my neck, warming me from the inside out.

"Cole."

"I didn't mean to wake you," he whispered, kissing my neck as his hand drifted under my t-shirt.

I shifted deeper into his embrace, loving the way he fit around my body as he held me close. This was the man I would spend forever with. No one else had even matched up to Cole Carter in my eyes. It didn't matter how many dates I'd gone on or how many people I spent the night with, I still couldn't shake Cole from my mind or my memories. He seared himself onto my heart and the bond between us was unbreakable. No one else but him would do for me.

My soulmate.

"S'okay. Is it over?"

"Yeah, it is."

His voice sounded hesitant. I turned my head towards him.

"You don't sound so sure about that."

The room was dark so I couldn't see his expression.

"I'm nervous… about how you feel… about what I did."

His hand slid up my stomach to my ribcage, his fingertips stroking down my skin. I couldn't help the stirring it gave me despite the seriousness of his tone.

"I don't know how I feel… wait, no, that's a lie." I placed my hand over his. "I love you, Cole, that hasn't changed. I understand why. You needed closure and it's the only way either of us could ever be truly safe. I'm not going to say I like what you did, but my love for you doesn't come with conditions. I'm tired of the world trying to rip us apart and knock us off our intended path. This is just another one of those things and I won't let it get in the way of us. You are it for me."

Cole leant over and kissed my cheek.

"Thank you, little queen. I love you too."

I smiled. No matter what, I couldn't allow shit to get in the way of us. Did it go against what I thought of as right and wrong? A little bit but being without Cole had taught me a fair few things about life. I was tired of living in a world where he and I didn't exist together. Tired of acting like my morality hadn't changed or that we lived our lives always sticking to the straight and narrow. I'd been through enough already to see sometimes you just had to accept the way things turn out. You don't always get to decide other people's fates, but you can decide your own. And my decisions had led me back to Cole.

So what if he'd killed someone out of a sense of justice and revenge? I couldn't say a fucking thing when I knew Cole had gone through a whole load of shit just to survive the past five years. His morals might be skewed but he loved fiercely and protected those around him. That's the reason I would let this shit go. Deep down, Cole was a good person.

"Are you okay about it?"

He let out a sigh, raising his hand ever higher until he cupped my breast.

"I wouldn't say I enjoyed it or that it's something I'd ever do again. It's not easy for me knowing I'm responsible for taking someone's life. Maybe I have a twisted sense of justice, but I don't regret it."

"Considering who your parents are, I'd say having a twisted sense of justice is normal."

He snorted, his fingertips stroking my nipple and making me shift against him, wanting more.

"I wish it hadn't come to this, but if I hadn't ended it like that, he would have come after us again and again. That's just how it works with them. I don't want to live in their world any longer, little queen. I want to be in our one."

"And what does our world look like?"

His stroking grew more insistent, distracting the fuck out of me. No question about it, I wanted Cole inside me, but we needed to finish our conversation.

"You and me, married with our own home."

His hand left my breast and drifted down, tugging at my underwear. I shifted to allow him to take it off me, realising he hadn't got dressed after his shower when his hard cock pressed against my bare behind.

"What else?"

"Well, it's not as if I did nothing whilst I was away and being a qualified mechanic had its perks. I'll work something out. It's what I've always wanted to do."

"You'll find something in no time, I'm sure."

"Mmm, well, there's a garage which no longer has an owner and certain individuals may have agreed to sell it to me in exchange for dealing with their little problem."

I arched against him, letting out a little pant as he pressed himself between my legs, sinking his cock inside me.

"Is that so?"

"Mmm."

"Does it come with any conditions?"

"No, Grandpa made sure it didn't."

He pulled back and thrust inside me again. I moaned in response, clutching his arm as he wrapped it around me.

"Then that's fucking amazing."

"I hope it means we'll be set for life, little queen. I don't want to live off my parent's money, even though it's paying for the garage."

Cole had always wanted to do things off his own back. It's something I loved about him. It's not like he didn't know when to ask for help, but if he could do it himself, he would.

"I'm sure we'll be fine. I make enough so we'll survive. I need to speak to Jonah about you living with us while we decide what we want to do next."

Cole stilled.

"You'd want that?"

I turned my head.

"Of course, I want that. Do you think I want to be without the man I'm going to marry every night?"

"I wasn't going to assume."

He started to move again and I thrust back against him, wanting more. Wanting it all.

"Assume away, Cole Carter. I love you and I'm never letting you go again, that means you're staying even if my brother gets pissy about it."

He snorted and kissed my neck before trailing his tongue along it. I panted, clutching his arm harder.

"I think someone is a little desperate for a hard pounding," he whispered.

My only response was to moan. Cole shifted, tugging his arm back so he could grip my hip with his hand. He thrust harder, our skin slapping together as he gave it to me. I reached around with my arm, tangling my hand in his hair, pulling him closer. Cole's mouth latched onto my neck, kissing and sucking the skin. It drove me crazy.

"Cole, please, more, fuck… harder."

"Oh, you want more, little queen? So greedy."

He didn't let up, giving it to me as I bucked against him, desperate for a release. He wasn't going to give me it that easily. No, Cole wanted to drag this out. I could feel it in the way he fucked me. It wasn't erratic but measured.

"Please," I cried out as he hit just the right spot.

"Patience."

"I have none, you know that."

He chuckled, merely kissing my skin again as his hand tightened on my hip. My free hand below me bunched in the covers, desperately holding on whilst he continued to pound into me, making me feel alive all over again.

There was nothing like this. Me and him. Cole was my first, my last, my everything. And I was his too.

When his hand fell from my hip in between my legs and he stroked my clit, it took mere seconds for me to detonate on him. I cried out his name, drowning in the bliss he brought on. Drowning in him like I always had. And when he came, I revelled in the knowledge I gave him the same pleasure as he did me.

We lay in silence for a long time when we came down, both content in our post-coital haze. Cole kissed my shoulder, stroking his fingers along my stomach.

"You're my whole world," he whispered. "I can't wait to marry you."

I squirmed at his words.

"Me either."

"Should we run away and elope?"

"Can you imagine what Ash would say if we did that?"

He laughed.

"Yeah, she'd murder me… totally wouldn't be worth it."

"Don't make stupid suggestions then, besides, we can't overshadow your sister's wedding. Aurora would crucify us."

Cole laughed harder.

"I can see her face now. No, that's not happening. We'll do it in our own time, just like we've done everything else."

I snuggled into him.

"Yeah, we will. It's like you said, we don't work to anyone else's schedule."

He kissed my shoulder again.

"No, we live by our own rules. You and I are going to work together from now on, little queen, I promise. I love you."

I let out a soft sigh.

"Love you too."

I couldn't wait to become Cole's wife, but he was right, we'd do it in when we were ready. For now, I was content to have him right here and know he wasn't going anywhere. This time we were on the same path, heading towards our ride into the sunset. And that was all I needed.

Now and forever.

EPILOGUE

Cole

It's crazy to think when I was eleven years old, I met the love of my life. Well, I saw her anyway. I didn't realise back then how much shit I'd go through when it came to that girl. How much I'd have to fight tooth and nail for the both of us. The things I'd have to do just to survive. Nothing could prepare me for the heartache, pain and strife.

But all of it was worth it.

Every single moment no matter how difficult and treacherous our path became.

It was worth it as, thirteen years later, I had my arms around that girl and she was wearing white.

Meredith looked stunning in her dress. It was quirky like the girl herself. She'd settled on a knee-length number which flared out and had lace sleeves. She had her strawberry blonde hair up, secured with a silver and pearl clip and little white flowers threaded throughout.

I couldn't be happier. We were married and in the middle of our first dance whilst our guests looked on. It'd taken us a year to organise our wedding. In that time, I'd taken over the garage, hired a whole new team and it was thriving. My wife was still working in stage production and happier than ever. We had our own two-bed flat and we were content with our lot in life. We didn't need anything more.

Meredith smiled up at me, her green eyes bright with unshed tears.

"I can't believe we're here, you know, that you're my husband and I'm your wife."

"Your toyboy husband."

She slapped my shoulder.

"Shut up, you sound like Rhys."

"Clearly I've been spending too much time around him."

She laughed before resting her head on my shoulder. We saw a lot of Rhys and Aaron. Rhys and I had settled our differences finally and he'd accepted me into the fold. The two of them were looking into adoption. Meredith was rather excited to be an aunty. As if she wouldn't get to be one several times over with my siblings and their partners at some point. Mum kept dropping hints to Aurora, but my sister was adamant she and Logan weren't ready yet.

"I love that you're friends with my best friend, you know, not to mention my brother. Makes my life easier."

"They're not so bad."

"Hmm yeah, okay, I'll tell them that you only hang out with them because of me then, shall I?"

I stroked her back, twirling her around the floor.

"You know I like spending time with them and it has nothing to do with Rhys being your friend."

I kissed the top of her head, settling my cheek against it. The rest of the world faded away when it was just me and her together. This was our moment. Our time.

"I love you, little queen," I whispered. "Or should I call you Mrs Carter?"

Meredith wanted to take my name even though I had never asked her to do so.

"You should so call me that when you strip me off and fuck me later."

I laughed which only prompted her to do so as well.

"You're a bad girl thinking about that in a room full of our friends and family."

"I'm a bad girl for my bad boy."

Her hand in mine tightened.

"Hmm, I suppose I'll take that."

"You better. I mean, you've got a motorbike, what's more bad boy than that?"

I spun her around again, smiling as the two of us swayed together.

"And I love you too, Cole. We're going to ride off into the sunset together, you know, on the back of your bike."

"And Mum will hate every moment of it."

She laughed then, pulling back and staring up at me. Her green eyes were so full of adoration, making my heart hammer hard in my chest.

"You'll always be Ash's baby boy."

"Don't I know it," I muttered, rolling my eyes.

There would never be a time when my mum didn't think of me that way. I didn't mind it so much these days. She was just happy to have me back on home soil. Besides, my parents had done a lot for me and Meredith. My girl had managed to get over the whole parents paying out a ridiculous amount of money to save her thing. She understood now it was because they loved her and wanted us to be happy.

The music was wrapping up then so we came to a standstill, staring down at each other.

"So, husband, are we going to force your dads out on the floor like Aurora did at her wedding? Because I want to see how much Quinn and Rory grumble about it."

I smiled wide. Those two had never liked dancing.

"You fucking well bet we are."

She took my hand and pulled me towards where my parents had congregated. The moment my dad saw my face, he made his own one, but I wasn't going to let him get away with staying seated. Meredith pulled up her brother, Rhys and Aaron, along with the rest of my siblings. The band started playing a more upbeat song and soon the dance floor was filled with our guests and family. Meredith was dancing with Jonah whilst I held Mum, who gave me the softest smile.

"I'm so proud of you, baby boy," she all but whispered. "We all are, Rory especially."

I leant down and kissed her cheek.

"Thank you, Mum."

"You keep her happy this time because I'm not going through another breakup with the two of you."

I shook my head.

"Trust me, I will. I'm never going to let Meredith go again."

There was no way in hell. I couldn't imagine a world without my beautiful fiery queen in it.

The rest of the afternoon passed with the cutting of the cake, more dancing and alcohol flowing. Meredith and I didn't partake. We hadn't wanted our wedding to go on late into the night, though I imagined some of our guests would be partying until the small hours.

I stood with Dad by the doors of the hotel, my helmet in my hand. He put a hand on my shoulder, giving it a squeeze.

"You finally got your girl."

I shrugged.

"Guess I did. I always knew she was the one."

"I know your mum said it earlier, but I'm proud of the way you've grown up, Cole. You've never let anything hold you back."

"You kept telling me I shouldn't. I took it seriously."

A lot of things in my dad's life had held him back so he never wanted me to live that way.

"Can't say I've given you a lot of good advice."

I snorted.

"Yeah, you have… you're my hero, you know, Dad. I've always looked up to you, and don't tell me you're not a good role model because of what you've done and been through. It's about how you came out of it which inspires me the most."

He didn't say anything, merely looked at me with a smile and no small amount of appreciation in his eyes. I turned to him and gave him a hug. My dad had always championed me and taken care of me. There would never be a day which went by when I wasn't grateful for my family. For the way they loved me and my siblings. For everything they'd done for us.

My dad pulled away and patted me on the back.

"Go start your new life with your beautiful wife."

Meredith had exited the hotel and was wearing a leather jacket over her dress now with a helmet clutched in her hands. She'd taken the clip out of her hair so it fell loose. I gave my dad a smile before I walked over to her. She let me take her helmet and place it on her head, securing the strap before I put my own on. Then I took her hand and we walked over to my Ducati together, which Xav and Eric had taped on a sign which said 'just married' on the back. I shook my head when I saw it. The way the two of them were smiling told me it had to be them.

I got on the bike and Meredith climbed on the back, wrapping her arms around me whilst her dress bunched up in between us.

"Ready to ride into the sunset, little queen?"

She clutched me tighter.

"I've been ready forever, Cole Carter."

With our family and friends waving us off, I kicked the motorbike into gear and pulled away from the curb, knowing

Meredith and I were finally on the right path to the life we'd always wanted. And we were doing it… together.

ACKNOWLEDGEMENTS

Thank you so much for taking the time to read this book. I really appreciate all of my readers and hope this book gave you as much joy reading it as I did writing it.

To my savage partner in crime, Sab. You are irreplaceable to me. No one gets me like you do. No one sees me like you do. You are my soulmate. I don't know how I would have got this book written if you weren't by my side, fighting my corner and telling me everything's going to be okay. You know I went through it with this one. The ups and downs. The stops and starts. The I don't know if this book is good enough. The extreme self-doubt. It's been the hardest one I've had to push through and I couldn't have done that if it wasn't for you. You're my personal cheerleader, giving me strength and reassuring me that I'm doing okay.

I love you to death. You are the best person in my life other than my husband. It's like Cole said, I can't live in a world where you and I aren't in existence next to each other. Every day I am thankful to have you in my life. I count myself as the luckiest girl in the world to know you the way I do.

You better believe you're stuck with me for the rest of our lives. I ain't letting you go.

In the words of our Quinn – you're mine, little girl!

Love you, bruv xxx

ABOUT THE AUTHOR

Sarah writes dark, contemporary, erotic and paranormal romances. She adores all forms of steamy romance and can always be found with a book or ten on her Kindle. She loves anti-heroes, alpha males and flawed characters with a little bit of darkness lurking within. Her writing buddies nicknamed her 'The Queen of Steam' for her pulse racing sex scenes which will leave you a little hot under the collar.

Born and raised in Sussex, UK near the Ashdown Forest where she grew up climbing trees and building Lego towns with her younger brother. Sarah fell in love with novels when she was a teenager reading her aunt's historical regency romances. She has always loved the supernatural and exploring the darker side of romance and fantasy novels.

Sarah currently resides in the Scottish Highlands with her husband. Music is one of her biggest inspirations and she always has something on in the background whilst writing. She is an avid gamer and is often found hogging her husband's Xbox.

Printed in Great Britain
by Amazon